KING ARTHUR AND THE CONSCIOUSNESS GENE

HOW TRUTH USES DECEPTION AND ILLUSION MASQUERADES AS TRUTH

A NOVEL BY DON CARROLL

ISBN: 0989865010
ISBN-13: 978-0-9898650-1-2

THIS IS A WORK OF FICTION

DEDICATION

For those Celtic Christians whose hearts and souls never forgot that God's incarnation has always been here in creation and who honored this wonder by calling her Goddess.

And, for my Mother.

ACKNOWLEDGMENTS

I am indebted to Gail Spach for her kindness and her librarian skills, which put me on the trail of the only extant works about St Armel.

The parts of the novel located in Brittany would have been impossible to complete without the aid of one of my oldest friends, Louis L. Lesesne. Without his French-speaking ability and GPS we would not have been able to encounter firsthand the many images of St Armel that are still vivid and alive in Brittany. With Louis' aid we met Madame Gatel Léa to whom I am greatly indebted for her patience and time in taking us into the church at St Armel-des-Boschaux to see the jawbone relic of St Armel, his empty sarcophagus and the extraordinarily beautiful stained glass windows in the church illustrating events in his life.

I am grateful to Christine Evans, once a resident of Ynys Enlli and now a perennial summer visitor, for talking with me while she fed her chickens, inviting me into her home on the isle and giving me the benefit of her extensive knowledge about Ynys Enlli. Ms Evans, a poet, is author of a lyrically written and beautifully imaged book about Ynys Enlli, which goes by the isle's Viking-derived, English name, *Bardsey*. Although Ms Evans is not convinced of the Barber Pykitt thesis of the isle's role in the life of King Arthur, she would no doubt affirm the likelihood of the isle playing a significant role in the life of a Welsh prince, just as it did in the lives of Arthur's contemporaries St Cadfan and St Dyfrig. Ms Evans herself exemplifies the temperament of the Sisters, which this novel portrays bringing a religious community to the isle, with her awareness that the isle is a "thin place" offering a "timelessness that comes from floating immersed in the moment," as well as an "intimate particularity" with which the isle rivets the attention in exquisite details. Thanks, also, to her son Colin for getting us on and off the isle on a rather tight schedule.

I am indebted to Lisa Kline for her editorial assistance and genuine commitment to the vision for this novel as an adventure story of not just people, places and olden times, but also of ideas, and for her heart for the characters it seeks to bring to life. Buffy Holt has again provided her invaluable assistance in the delivery room of bringing this novel to life. I am deeply appreciative of her skills and especially her help in getting a translation of the hundred year old *Vie De Saint Armel.* Buffy, thanks for making the technological side of novelistic creativity almost fun. I am grateful to Charles Hedgepath for his keen eye in reviewing a draft of the novel and to Suzanne Leitner for her enthusiasm and suggestions on portions of the draft. Grateful appreciation to Allison Simpson for her help in final proofing.

A special thanks to my son, William Carroll, MD, for his assistance in helping me understand the physiology of a heart attack and for his loyalty in his own life to the spiritual adventure which this novel explores. My wife, Cristy, has indulged my passion for telling this story, even when it had me traipsing halfway around the world and writing in seclusion on ships at sea. Cristy, thank you. You are a grace and blessing in my life.

"Truth did not come into the world naked, but veiled with images and archetypes; otherwise it cannot be received."

The Gospel of Philip, p.69, line 67, trans. Jean-Yves Leloup

"Nature gives the world that individual species, the phoenix, but once in five hundred years…"

Thomas Tenison, Archbishop of Canterbury, 1679

"What is interesting and important happens mostly in secret, in places where there is no power. Nothing much of lasting value ever happens at the head table, held together by a familiar rhetoric. Those who already have power continue to glide along the familiar rut they have made for themselves."

The Cat's Table
Michael Ondaatje

"We become true deceivers when we understand the purpose of our deceptions, when we admit that the stories we tell carry their own meaning within them, even if there is no objective reality beyond them, no movie actually seen, no stone actually rolled away from the tomb."

Leaving Alexandria
Richard Holloway, Bishop of Edinburgh

Preface

Much of this novel occurs in the time of King Arthur. For the most part, the modern names for places and regions a reader would recognize are used in lieu of names used in the sixth century, so that readers familiar with a particular location are more readily able to see it in their mind's eye; e.g. the Roman city of Aquae Sulis is referred to as Bath, Armorica as Brittany, etc. There are two major exception to this. The isle of Ynys Enlli, which in English today is called Bardsey, and the home castle of King Arthur, which was most probably located on a Silurian hill-fort in Wales that is today called Llanmelin, just north of Caerwent. Because the isle is an important "character" in the novel, it is referred to by its proper Welsh name. Because the word Camelot is important in the mythology of Arthur, his castle is referred to as it probably was in his time as Caer Calemion, the fortress of Calemion.

This is a work of fiction and no character is modeled after any living person. Certain historic characters in this book are both fictional and, to the extent available research allows, described in as historically an accurate way as possible. The accounts of the battles and course of King Arthur's life are described with the greatest accuracy the newest historical evidence and analysis make possible. The description of King Arthur's battles and his general whereabouts rely heavily on the work of Chris Barber and David Pykitt, *Journey to Avalon; The Final Discovery of King Arthur,* and the demonstrable weight of evidence they assemble in favor of the historical version of King Arthur which is painted here.

The usage in Brittany is to refer to saints like St Samson and St Gildas without spelling the word saint or using a period in the abbreviation. I have followed the Breton usage for Welsh and Breton Saints (e.g. St) as it implies a way in which their sainthood is now a first name, who they have become. For Irish saints like St. Brigit, or other saints, the traditional usage of St. is followed.

Timeline

480   A group of Sisters following the teachings of St. Brigit founds a religious community on the isle of Ynys Enlli off the western coast of Wales.

482   Arthur is born in South Glamorgan, Wales.

497   Arthur is nominated as King of Britain by King Ambrosius. He is crowned leader of the Britons by St Dyfrig. He is fifteen and a regent is appointed while he is a minor.

510   Arthur leads Welsh warriors in Brittany to assist his kinsman Riwal Mawr, King of Armorica (Brittany), against an invasion of the Visigoths. The Visigoths are defeated by Arthur and Riwal Mawr at Vannes in Brittany.

512   The leader of the British forces, who is titled the Pendragon and who served as Regent while Arthur was a minor, is killed leading British forces against the Saxons. Arthur takes over as battle commander and becomes the Pendragon. He then, in the next five years, leads British forces in a series of twelve battles, in all of which he is victorious.

515   Lady Bridgette and her sister, daughters of an Irish chieftain, are pledged to Arthur's Court through his diplomacy in order to prevent Arthur retaliating against an Irish raid on the Welch coast.

516   Sister Bendithion becomes the Mother Superior of the Sisters on the isle of Ynys Enlli. The Sisters welcome St Cadfan, who comes from Brittany and founds a monastery on the isle.

516   Although only a young girl of twelve, Gwenynen, in

recognition of her skill at finding medicinal plants and caring for wounded knights, is apprenticed to Lady Geirwir, who, like Merlin, is a trusted advisor to King Arthur at Caer Calemion, the Court of King Arthur in Wales.

518   Lady Bridgette is sent to the isle of Ynys Enlli for safekeeping. She requests that Gwenynen be allowed to come attend her on Ynys Enlli.

518   The final of twelve battles is fought by King Arthur at Mount Badon outside of Bath. It is a decisive defeat of the Saxons and brings about a period of peace for the remainder of the time Arthur is king.

522   St Dyfrig resigns his see as Archbishop of Wales and retires to a hermitage on Ynys Enlli.

523   Gwenynen is escorted to the isle of Ynys Enlli by Sir Gaiwain.

530   Count Gwythyr, the father of Arthur's wife, Gwenhwyfar (Guinevere), dies and she inherits his estate in Brittany. Arthur and Riwal Mawr's son, Deroch, now rule a large territory together in Brittany.

533   The Visigoths again invade Brittany and King Riwal Mawr's son, King Deroch, asks Arthur for help. Arthur is away for nearly four years fighting the Visigoths in Brittany.

537   Lady Bridgette returns to Ireland. Soon after, the Irish launch more raids against Welsh coastal settlements. Arthur goes to Ireland to avenge these attacks. He successfully defeats the Irish and Llwch Llawinawg, who is also known as Lancelot of the Lake.

537   While Arthur is away, Medraut seizes his realm and his
       Queen. Arthur returns with the remnant of his army and
       lands at a little harbor called Cadlan on the Lleyn
       Peninsula in Wales, where the family of Medraut has
       territory. He meets Medraut's forces, and, during the
       ensuing battle of Camlan, Medraut is slain and Arthur is
       seriously wounded. He is taken to the nearby isle of Ynys
       Enlli where he is nursed back to health by Gwenynen and
       Sister Bendithion.

538   Arthur leaves Ynys Enlli and goes to Brittany. He makes
       his kinsman, Constantine, Regent in his absence from
       Britain. Gwenynen and Sir Gaiwain go with Arthur. He
       lands in Brittany at a harbor he names in honor of the holy
       man who was his first teacher, St Illtud. Arthur establishes
       a community and abbey nearby at Ploërmel.

542   Arthur abdicates the crown of Britain in favor of his
       cousin Constantine.

541-   The plague destroys over half the population of Britain.
544

545   Arthur establishes a new monastery and abbey church at
       Ploërmel.

546   St Dyfrig dies while at his hermitage on Ynys Enlli.

549   Marcus Conomorus, who left Wales and settled in
       Brittany, assassinates Jonas the son of Deroch. To obtain
       control of the territories belonging to Arthur and Jonas,
       Conomorus marries Jonas' widow and becomes Regent.
       Jonas' minor son, Judwal, the rightful heir, flees to the
       court of the Frankish King Childebert in Paris.

555   The combined forces of Arthur, his kinsman Samson and
       those of King Childebert meet the forces of Conomorus.

After a fierce three day battle, Judwal slays Conomorus. Judwal rewards Arthur by giving him land along the River Seiche, where Arthur founds another monastery and builds the abbey church of Armel-des-Boschaux.

556   The new abbey church at Armel-des-Boschaux is dedicated by King Childebert and Arthur is declared a Saint. Gwenynen's daughter Derwen has her eighteen birthday.

562   Arthur dies at his monastery at St Armel-des-Boschaux at the age of 80.

565   St Samson, Arthur's nephew, dies at his monastery at Dol-de-Bretagne.

570   St Gildas dies, at age 94 at his monastery at St Gildas du Rhuys.

PART I

Chapter 1

Little Tree looks out a tiny window. A wiggly red smudge sits atop the mountains to the east. He slides out of bed. Ooljee, his Grandfather's Plott Hound, stands. Ooljee, who slept beside his Grandfather's bed for years, now sleeps and wakes in the pattern of Little Tree's life. The dog, though in his elder years, is alert as ever.

Little Tree pulls on his clothes. From the corner he picks up the bow he and his Grandfather spent hours making just a year ago. Though he is only seven years old, Little Tree's right arm muscles are already sharply defined from his constant bow practice.

His Grandfather Manuelito and his Grandmother Blaine are up already, drinking coffee, sitting by the fire and talking in low undertones in their Navajo dwelling, which is called a hogan. The hogan's main room serves as kitchen, dining room, living room and library. Little Tree nods a *good morning* to them both, reaches into the bread warmer on the stove, and pushes a fistful of fry bread into a pouch tied to his waist. Little Tree opens the hogan's front door, which faces due east as tradition requires, and he and Ooljee slip out.

Ooljee leads the way as he and Little Tree walk in single file toward an arroyo about a quarter of a mile west of his grandparents' hogan. Little Tree reaches in the pouch and pulls out a piece of bread. He methodically chews as he walks. The red smudge to the east gradually spreads sideways and upward, and the dusty gray shroud of night is slowly shed. They both know the way by heart—the shape of each clump of vegetation growing along the trail, where there are thorns and where the sweet smells are, and, in the case of a certain flowering cactus, where there are both.

They move stealthily down into an arroyo and reach a small stream that traces a path along its bottom. There is thick green vegetation next to the stream and a profusion of stalked, purple flowers he knows by the name of elephant heads. Beside the stream-side vegetation is a well worn game path. Little Tree takes up his position about thirty feet from where a covey of western partridges usually roosts. He signals to Ooljee, one of the hand signals Little Tree learned from his Grandfather. Ooljee responds swiftly and silently and begins to circle in a wide arc to the right. Little Tree knows that in less than five minutes Ooljee will be directly across from him, about a hundred yards away, crouching on the ground awaiting a hand or whistle signal from Little Tree.

Little Tree notches an arrow in his bow and holds his bow by his side in a relaxed grip. Then he begins one of the energy practices that his Grandma Blaine has taught him. He cloaks his energy so that the energy of his life force barely radiates three inches from his body. Slowly his breathing becomes very shallow. With his eyes closed he begins to read the energy of the plants and animals around him. Yes, the partridges are still on their roost about twenty-five feet away. There is a nest of small mice in a rock crevice not far above his head.

Little Tree is not here to snare one of the fat partridges that are slowly beginning to get off the nest and stir around. This might come later. For now Little Tree, with his grandparents' assent, is seeking to use his deceptive skills as a hunter to protect them. He waits.

Most animals awake at dawn. Like his grandparents, with their early morning coffee, most critters immediately are about scrounging up their first meal. Little Tree does not have to wait long. He is aware of a dark energy moving down the arroyo. It is a hungry, predator energy. He tries but is unable to enter the animal's life force. So, as he has been taught, since he cannot enter either the thoughts or the life force of the animal, Little Tree seeks to access the energy field of the Great Spirit. Thanks to his Grandmother Blaine's skillful teaching and his practicing over and over countless times the techniques she has taught him, Little Tree is quickly able to enter the field of the Great Spirit, the field of primordial life force itself.

Quickly and prayerfully he asks the Great Spirit for permission to take the life of the four-legged creature that is moving furtively towards him and the covey of western partridges. His Grandmother has taught him that he is not to lightly seek to alter nature's balance between prey and predator. Little Tree does not know what answer he will receive. He waits. He asks for the lives of the partridges to be lengthened so that they might reproduce, bring forth more coveys and be more abundant, as they once were, on the rugged terrain of the Navajo reservation.

Little Tree smiles to himself. The answer comes at the last moment. Grandma Blaine has told him this is usually the case. The Great Spirit is not a fortune teller she would say, it only speaks to you in the present moment about what is happening in the present moment.

The moment is now. Little Tree gives a sharp whistle. The dark energy stops. Ooljee rises slowly off his haunches and noiselessly moves forward toward the dark energy.

The dark energy form is on high alert, but because of the permission given by the Great Spirit, Little Tree now enters the creature's thought field. Little Tree asks the creature to give up its life for the sake of greater life. There is no pull or push in response. In the great energy field of life, there is always death and birth. The law of conservation of energy applies. Nothing is ever lost. Everything belongs. There is no value judgment attached to living or dying. Everything is always moving toward death and its opportunity for renewal, or moving toward greater life and the death that comes after the sweetness of life's full bloom.

Without uncloaking his energy, Little Tree slowly moves toward the dark form. Ooljee moves forward directly opposite Little Tree. To Little Tree the energy of the creature glows in the dark behind his eyelids. Suddenly, Little Tree instinctively opens his eyes. There, not fifteen feet in front of him, is a scraggly coyote. About forty feet behind the coyote, Little Tree can see Ooljee moving soundlessly forward.

The coyote's expression is neither sentimental nor fearful. Just the expression of a young coyote who, by the looks of it, has had a hard life and wandered far afield from its birthplace in search of food.

Little Tree raises his bow. Ooljee stops less than fifteen feet behind the coyote. The coyote does not blink. The arrow flies. The shot is mercifully deadly. It pierces an artery deep in the coyote's neck just behind the hard shell of the coyote's skull. The coyote slumps to the ground.

Ooljee turns backwards and looks left and right. He is smarter than I am, thinks Little Tree. Ooljee knows these kinds of creatures usually hunt in packs and Ooljee is not so entranced by one surrendering its life, to be oblivious to the possibility of another couple of coyotes close by.

Ooljee looks at Little Tree and gives an almost imperceptible nod that all is clear. Little Tree signs. Ooljee is immediately at Little Tree's feet. Little Tree gives the dog a rub on the crown of his head.

Little Tree looks about and finds a long sapling crushed among some deadfall. He removes the branches with his pocket knife. He ties the coyote's forelegs together and the hind legs. Then he positions the long sapling pole beneath the coyote's bound limbs. He now has a way to take the coyote home without it dragging the ground. Little Tree is not sure what his Grandfather and Grandmother will have him do with this creature whose life has been given so other creatures may live. There will be some ritual; the coyote's body will be honored with proper ceremony. Something will be done to assure that what has been done plays its natural part in the great hoop of life.

He gathers a fistful of desert marigolds sprouting from the rocky slope along the trail. He wraps a small string around their delicate stems and places the bouquet in his quiver. He will give these to his Grandmother Blaine so she will know he remembers the importance of honoring beauty in death.

Little Tree puts one end of the loaded pole over his shoulder and he and Ooljee head for home.

Chapter 2

Aline "Red" Elred surveys the stack of files on the corner of his desk. He picks up the one on top, sits back in his office chair and begins to thumb through it page by page. It is a worn file. The old filename, *1776*, is barely visible beneath his handwritten words—*Mind Field Project.*

In his view, Elred was promoted to section chief just in time. His predecessor, Charles Redmon, had been too much of the old school, involved in the lives of the officers he was supervising and valuing the Company's loyalty to them as much as their loyalty to the Company. That perspective might've worked in the old days; however, the agency cannot, under the threats the United States currently faces, operate quickly enough with that outlook.

Redmon had an easy opportunity to apprehend Melissa Dowling, a.k.a. Sister Magdalen, whom the Company had been trying to pick up for over a year. Redmon bungled the mission. She'd slipped the net.

Sometimes your foes give you your greatest opportunity, muses Elred. Elred considered it a break when Melissa disappeared after her folksy procession from Assisi to Rome. There had been no hard evidence Melissa had the ability to control other people's thoughts. Even if she did have that ability, she was obviously antagonistic to the Company's goals of using her skills to prevent terrorism. In addition, she had become hugely popular and well-known. She was not the kind of target the CIA could use covert interrogation techniques on. When they had done so on even a moderately well-known person in the past, they usually got no helpful information and a public black eye that set the Company back five years in its ability to operate free of Congressional restraints.

Yes, Elred thinks, *this project is finally making progress on my watch.* When he took over from Redmon, Elred immediately changed the focus of the project. The agency would not worry about the missing Melissa. Rather, under Elred's direction, the Company was focusing its efforts on the clues she had left which reflected her abilities. She did not really matter. Her skills were what they wanted. She was secondary. Now the agency was focused on what was really important.

He reclines further back in his desk chair and runs his hand gently over the thinning hair on the back of his head, an unconscious habit when he is thinking, which he inherited from his father. His hair, which he combs straight back, is smooth and silky. And, of course, red. Not that kind of coarse, carrotish red, which he associates with the Irish background of James McGavin, one of his superiors. McGavin cuts his hair in an old-fashioned flat top. To Elred the top of his head looks like a landing strip painted red, though the strip is now mostly white. Like Elred, McGavin had gotten the nickname "Red."

Elred resents their identical nicknames. Elred knows that his finely textured, silky hair is a genetic gift from his Scandinavian ancestors. To him it is an outward symbol of the physical toughness and dedication he has inherited from his forbearers— the ability to move forward and attack, to be the predator and never the prey.

On the other hand, Red McGavin, the departmental boss, is a part of the same old-school that Elred disliked about Charles Redmon. Everyone admits McGavin is brilliant, and he has the typical coarse Irish sense of humor—always ready to have a good laugh at somebody else's expense—and beneath the lighthearted humor a dark meanness. At least, that's how Elred sees him. Who cares that, after a couple of drinks, his boss with his photographic memory can recite, and would recite, Yeats or some other crazy poet for hours. Certainly not Elred.

Elred takes professional pride in his belief that he does not allow his personal emotional feelings about someone to interfere with his clear analysis of a problem. Despite his disdain for McGavin, and his total lack of any feeling for the elusive Melissa, his close observation of both of them has gotten the *Mind Field Project* going in the right direction. Elred noticed that both of them had green eyes at about the same time he was reading a research article on a genetic study of the eye. He came up with the hypothesis that Melissa's green eye color might be a genetic marker for the consciousness gene. Because his Irish boss also has green eyes, it was a slam dunk getting McGavin to authorize significant expenditure of covert funds for research on this hypothesis and by extension the nature of the consciousness gene.

As the file reflects, the CIA's research grants were causing medical advances. Researchers were discovering, if not the truth of the old saw, that the eyes are the window to the soul, at least that they are the window to the body. By examining tiny blood vessels in the retina, researchers found that thickened blood vessel walls in the eye signal potential risk for stroke. Another group of researchers figured out that dark spots on the back of the eye are associated with certain forms of colon cancer.

Anyone with significant changes in their vision may be getting an important message of something negative happening in their body. Vision changes are providing clues to the onset of autoimmune diseases like rheumatoid arthritis and lupus. The research is confirming more about the long known affect of diabetes as an illness causing major problems in the eye.

Elred closes the file. All the good medical benefits of the research he initiated are, in his analysis, beside the point; but they are, he hopes, getting him closer to the project's goal of finding the consciousness gene, and perhaps it will be found in the structure of the eye. Admittedly, there is no hard research evidence supporting this yet; however, Elred is convinced he is on the right track. At least he is doing something positive and proactive, rather than waiting around for somebody like Melissa to stumble into their hands.

Elred turns to his computer and begins typing. He will get out a memo to the grant monitors asking them to re-double their efforts and speed up the research process. He is convinced that if he can continue to move this project forward diligently, before long he will have knowledge that will allow the thoughts of people around the world to be controlled in a proper way.

He gets up and walks in front of his desk and stands before a picture hanging on the wall. He adjusts his tie in the reflection of a framed portrait so his tie's presentation is just so. He notices the way his jacket hangs perfectly from his shoulders. *When he breaks open this* Mind Field Project, *he will finally start getting the appreciation he is due.* He smiles at his reflection.

Chapter 3

"Mother Mary, why in the world do you think I would be a good person to undertake this task of tracking in the quantum field, whatever in the world that means?" asks Blaine, sitting nervously on the front edge of her chair, her eyes darting back and forth between Mother Mary and Manuelito. "I know we talked about this a lot when you first came out to see us several years ago. I guess I was kind of hoping the idea had gone away."

Mother Mary, Blaine and Manuelito are all three sitting outside the hogan under the apple tree, the place all serious conversations seem to occur in Blaine and Manuelito's household. Just beyond their treasured fruit bearing tree are two native squaw apple trees, suffusing the outdoor living space with a delicate sweet smell. As she did several years before, Mother Mary suddenly shows up on their doorstep. The late afternoon desert air is beginning to cool. Soon the temperature will be in the fifties.

"No one ever feels worthy when called like this," says Mother Mary. Mother Mary is a short woman, no more than five feet. She is wearing pink sweat pants and a red sweat shirt. Manuelito thinks she looked like a fire hydrant. "Rest assured, Blaine, we have prayed about this long and hard and believe that you are the best person on earth to do this."

"Give me a break... Mother Mary, I mean no disrespect. I have none of the abilities which Melissa, I mean Sister Magdalen, had.

Nor have I ever had any of the life-changing mystical experiences which she passed through. How could you want me? Don't give me some nonsense about your namesake being called to be the mother of Christ and never once uttering a 'why me.'"

Mother Mary does not respond immediately. She looks closely at Blaine's dark penetrating eyes, which constantly take in everything around her. Mother Mary is only a few years older than Blaine. Both are small in stature, though each seems psychically to take up a much larger space. Blaine's hair, except for a few strands of gray, is dark and glossy. She wears it pulled up into a twist on top of her head. Mother Mary's hair is cut short and is as white as the long Swedish winters, where the Order's main Convent is.

Mother Mary takes a deep breath and exhales slowly. "Blaine, you are certainly correct. Your experiences have been entirely different than those which Sister Magdalen went through, but you have had the most extraordinary experiences of healing and spiritual growth of any human being I know. You have gone from someone whose life was a web of fear, to a person whose ability to access life force has made you a sensitive healer."

"Dammit, Mother Mary.... I apologize again. I am very agitated by what you are asking. Yes, I have many healing experiences, and, as you know, I needed them badly. I grew up without parents, without love, abused and abandoned, someone who cut themselves all over their body as a teenager, and then later covered the scars with tattoos. I had to find a a way to come out of that life, and did. That's all. I don't see how it connects to what you're asking. How could you want me, much less need me?"

"Spiritual experiences come in all varieties," says Mother Mary.

Manuelito chuckles to himself and mumbles under his breath *I wonder...stuck away in a Convent...can she possibly understand the variety of spiritual experiences nature provides?*

Mother Mary looks at Manuelito. "Excuse me?" she says.

"Nothing," says Manuelito. "I didn't mean to interrupt you."

Mother Mary directs her attention back to Blaine. "The healing, which you experienced with the sisters in our Order, is tantamount to the vision that Sister Magdalen had at St. Issa's pond and her near drowning experience. Your healing is a Grace just like Sister Magdalen's experiences, but, in addition, you work so hard to make yourself a vessel for that Grace. Not only has your healing significantly increased the kind of neural wiring you need to access the quantum field, you have the proven ability through your hard work to expand the neurological capacity required for spiritual work. This capacity is vital if we are going to discover the consciousness gene."

Blaine gets up from her chair and paces back and forth across the worn track between the apple tree and the front door of the hogan. Finally she speaks. "Okay, let's just assume I'm the right person. I'm not willing to agree with you on that, but let's just set that aside for the moment. Say I agree to help. Tell me what you want me to do and why you think it might have a ghost of a chance of working?"

"Absolutely fair question," says Mother Mary, reflecting a nickname some of the Sisters had given her at the Convent, 'Mother Fair.' "As you know from the studies you did with the Order, we believe that current quantum biology and field theory explain the biological basis for consciousness."

"Yes, I understand that," says Blaine.

"The greatest expression of human consciousness, or enlightenment if you prefer, occurred in the reality of Jesus—his level of consciousness reached a level we call divine.

Consciousness is not a biological structure *per se*, yet it has to have an underlying biological platform to arise out of or to connect from. All biology is created by the expression of some gene. So we have done much pondering about what causes the expression of a gene, which creates the neurological structure to be both in the human field and the unified field.

"After a long session of centering prayer one day, several Sisters in the chapel at our Convent in Sweden flashed on the same idea: we realized that Jesus's birth came approximately 500 years after the first expression of the consciousness gene seen in those awakened individuals around the start of recorded human history circa 500 B.C., especially in the Buddha, Plato and Pythagoras.

"We also happened, then, to be helping Swedish alcoholics in one of our local outreach ministries. In this work, we came across literature showing that the basic pattern of individual human change is repeating cycles. The cycles may evolve and progress, and in the case of untreated addiction progress quickly, but there is a cyclical pattern in all human change.

"Addiction scientists were eager to find out what causes the expression of several different genes which facilitate the onset of addiction. Much to their surprise, they found that there were different patterns for addiction with great differences among them. The common denominator was that all the patterns had a repeating cycle." She notices Blaine appearing to drift off. "Is it okay for me to explain a little of this addiction background further?"

Blaine nods *yes*. She is trying to take in everything Mother Mary is saying about the evolution of consciousness and the addictive patterns she has experienced in her own life.

'It is extraordinarily interesting. We know that most often, to have a problem with alcoholism, or other drug addictions, there is usually a genetic predisposition to the disease. Then certain things in the environment happen which cause specific genes to be expressed which facilitate the onset of the illness. Usually the trigger from the environment is a particular pattern of abuse—that is a pattern of excessive use of the alcohol or other substance—or use of alcohol at a young age before the brain has a chance to finish maturing. Once the trigger occurs, the genes are expressed and there is the onset of the disease. The most common pattern for an alcoholic is to be a daily drinker. However, the pattern can also be seen in someone who drinks only on the weekends, or someone who does binge drinking every month or every three months. The basic physiological expression of the disease is the same regardless of the pattern of the cycle. Once the specific genes are expressed, the onset of the illness rapidly follows.

"This understanding has given us a working hypothesis—the consciousness gene in humankind, at least initially, has a pattern of expression in a 500 year cycle. So we think that every 500 years given the right stimulus from the environment the consciousness gene will get expressed in one or more individuals."

"Mother Mary, I follow your thinking, and I still don't understand how I can be helpful to you."

"Thanks to the ingenuity of your hacker friend Rat, we have been able to get samples of Jesus' bloodstains on the shroud of Turin. Please don't ask me how Rat did this. I don't want to know and would be the last person to ask him. Nonetheless, we have had the DNA in the blood stains analyzed and identified a gene which, in the expressed state, we believe is the consciousness gene. In its unexpressed state the gene is one we all have and you might say in that state this is the gene of Jesus the man. In the expressed state it is the Christ gene, the access to Christ consciousness which is potentially in all of us."

Blaine looks upward and smiles. If anybody in the world could have managed to get into the Shroud of Turin Museum and extract a sample of the bloodstain from the shroud it would be Rat. What a crazy guy. She misses Rat. At one time, he was one of the most important people in her life. His caring for her, his uncontainable good humor and his wizardry with computers and the Internet literally saved her life. "So is Rat involved in helping you in this quest for the consciousness gene?"

"Yes, he certainly is," says Mother Mary.

Blaine smiles. Mother Mary could see Blaine relax a bit.

"Okay, go on. Your painting this bigger picture is helping me."

"As I was saying," continues Mother Mary. "We have Jesus' DNA sample thanks to Rat and we believe we have isolated the consciousness gene in its expressed form from this sample. To prove our hypothesis, we must analyze the genes of key people, who appear to have achieved great consciousness, occurring in this roughly 500 year cycle since the life of Jesus. Much to my surprise, when you look at our history, while there are significant figures throughout our history, often those with the most impact seem to arrive on the planet every 500 years."

Mother Mary lets this idea settle in. "So this is where you come in, Blaine. We want you to access the consciousness of a key individual occurring in the 500 year cycle and get a sample of their DNA for us to test for the consciousness gene."

Blaine frowns. Finally she speaks. "I understand how one can access thoughts and feelings outside the ordinary timeframe in the quantum field. However, my understanding is that a person cannot go materially into the quantum field except by death. You know, like we are assuming Sister Magdalen decided to do."

Mother Mary nods gravely. "You are right. At least that's the way we think reality works and I would not be asking you for your assistance if we in any way thought it might lead to your death." She stops. "Though I must be frank, Blaine, there are risks. But certainly, we don't want you to physically cross what we might call the consciousness blood-brain barrier into the quantum field."

"Well, I don't quite get it then. If I go back to a time and place 500 years after the life of Jesus through accessing those events in the quantum field, and stay in this time and place physically, how can I get a DNA sample for you?"

"It is an excellent question, and to be totally honest we are not sure. We think it is possible and we have Rat working on it full-time."

Blaine thinks *what a hopeless idea.* Then she brightens. If Rat is also working on this project that is the only thing that conceivably might allow her to make up her mind to help Mother Mary.

Manuelito has been quiet throughout the conversation between Blaine and Mother Mary. Even at mid-life, the coppery skin of his face is unlined. His black hair is combed straight back. He is not someone whose emotions are easily read.

He understands the art of letting a conversation unfold, and he is not quick to speak. Now he speaks. "Mother Mary, let me tell you what worries me. I am not worried about Blaine de-materializing. Her life force is too strong. She has too much warrior energy to let that happen to herself." He looks at Blaine and smiles, his love and respect for her palpable.

"What worries me is the experience of time. I know that when I was on a vision quest early in my life, I was in the place where the vision was occurring, which nowadays I think is what your white scientists would call the quantum field. I felt like I was there only for fifteen or twenty minutes; but when I returned to this cause-and-effect reality, I had been gone for four days."

"Man, you raise a good point, and I am afraid we don't have any way to control the experience of time. This is a risk, Blaine. You could be gone on this quest for just a few days, and it's possible when you returned from the trance-like state of accessing experience in the quantum field that several years might have passed. Or, the reverse could be true. You might be gone a few hours here and experience events over weeks or months there. Honestly, we don't know how to evaluate or minimize this risk yet. It seems to be inherent in the different way in which time works in the quantum field. Time is not linear there."

After a minute Mother Mary speaks again. "All I can tell you, Blaine is that we will have all the resources we possibly know to have, including your dear friend Rat, to try to assure that your time in the quantum field does not distort your time experience when you return to the Newtonian reality in which we live.

"Why are you being asked? Why take such risks? It is simply that the stakes are so high. We see that humankind is stuck. We are moving toward the maximum population the earth can support. There is political gridlock in most developing countries and in the United States, which once was a country with a vibrant democracy. Now, its political structure is defined by big money interests and corporate media control more than anything to do with self-government. The solution, if humankind is going to make it, has to be humanity's development of greater consciousness."

Chapter 4

Early in the morning Little Tree slips out of the hogan at sunrise. His faithful Plott Hound, Ooljee Two, follows him. Little Tree pulls the front door shut. It is a familiar ritual. Little Tree and Ooljee Two engaging in early morning tracking before Manuelito is up.

Little Tree believes that to have his bow and quiver over his shoulder is to feel the same way OoljeeTwo feels about having his sense of smell—connection with an intimate part of himself that makes his experience of life more natural and meaningful. Little Tree's favorite childhood white-man stories, read to him by his Grandfather, were obscure medieval adventures of Welsh longbow warriors. Though Manuelito assures LittleTree that it is a biased white perspective which ignores native bowmen, the book about the Welsh longbow men stated flatly that they are the most deadly accurate warriors with bows to have ever lived.

A half hour later Little Tree and Ooljee Two are back. Manuelito is whistling as he fixes his morning coffee. Little Tree bursts into the hogan and puts his bow and three new arrows that his Grandfather helped him make on the kitchen table. The arrows are each tipped with ancient arrowheads LittleTree found, which he and his Grandfather have re-sharpened.

"Grandfather, tell me how Grandma Blaine was asked to be a tracker in the quantum field!" pleads Little Tree.

"Ya'zhi, you are so curious," says his Grandfather, referring to Little Tree by the Navajo word for little. Ya'zhi, or Little Tree, is what everyone called the young Navajo from an early age. He received his name because of his slender build, his patience and his ability to be present. He looks intently at his Grandfather.

The day is beginning to warm, even though the night was cold, as is common this time of year at elevation in the New Mexico high desert. The smell of baking half-flatbread, or cross-cultural bread, as Little Tree's absent Grandma Blaine calls it, makes the day already seem warmer.

Manuelito shakes his head and looks at his grandson. Not the normal early morning question for a twelve-year-old. But, he muses to himself, no one has ever called Little Tree normal, nor the grandparents raising him.

Manuelito misses Blaine. She has only been gone a few months, but it already seems like a long time to him. He knows it is a long time for his grandson, Little Tree, who still experiences time as most young children do: as a vast extended perception. The other side of children's experience of time is that children are naturally more present in the moment than adults.

Thinking of his wife, Manuelito remembers how Blaine often teased him about becoming a taciturn old man, even though, like her, he is still very much in midlife. However, when it comes to telling stories to his grandson, she delighted in pointing out he was voluble as a young hen. He talks for hours with the youngster—in the wintertime by the kitchen stove and in the summertime under a faithfully watered apple tree, which serves as a ready-made brush arbor just outside the hogan.

When Little Tree was born, the tribal elders and Singers, who participated in the ceremony to welcome his spirit into the world, told Manuelito that Little Tree was a very ancient soul and should be treated as someone who possessed much wisdom.

When Manuelito answers Little Tree's questions, Manuelito tries to do so in much the same manner as he would in responding to an adult. A child needs to hear truth from an elder. Truth is usually complex and not something that can be tossed off in a few easy phrases. Truth takes time and curiosity. No wonder Blaine laughed at him about being so talkative with Little Tree and so silent with almost everyone else but her. Anyway, easy answers do not satisfy Little Tree. Manuelito has no patience with facile phrases either, and the vocabulary of the Navajo, the Diné, does not lend itself to them.

This does not mean that because there is much to be said you hurry an important conversation. Just the opposite.

"If you think you would be warm enough, I will get another cup of this supposed coffee, which I have been boiling to death on the stove, and we can go outside and talk a bit." Manuelito is wearing blue jeans and a red and blue check shirt he favors for any time of year in any weather. His hair is pulled back in a ponytail as is his grandson's.

"Well, certainly, we can," says Little Tree, the forty degree chill in the outside air completely beside the point as he warms enthusiastically to the idea of getting his Grandfather talking about his Grandma Blaine. It is a subject Little Tree knows—once his Grandfather gets started on—he could be talking for a long, long time.

Manuelito takes bread out of the oven and puts it in the warmer on top of the stove. It doesn't take but a few minutes for everybody to get settled under the apple tree: Manuelito with a cup of steaming black coffee, Little Tree wrapped in a hand-woven Navajo blanket, which his great-grandmother, whom he never knew, made, and, presiding over the whole affair, a Plott hound named Ooljee Two, or Two as he is called most of the time. Two is the offspring of the first Ooljee, Manuelito's much loved Plott hound that passed away a short time ago.

"I have to start a ways back, Ya'zhi," says Manuelito, shifting his weight in his chair and placing his feet up on a fire-pit rock so that his moccasins are bathed in the morning sunlight. He reaches out and pats Two's short glossy brindled coat, and Two returns the affection with a gaze of complete loyalty and strength. Once Two's non-verbal communication with Manuelito is complete he puts his long nose on his front paws and closes his hazel eyes. "It all started not long after the great procession on Rome. You remember? I told you about that."

"Yes, I remember," says Little Tree.

"Things had begun to quiet down. Your Grandmother and I had moved here away from the monastery, where we first settled when I traveled with your Grandmother Blaine back from Europe while Father O'Donnell was still alive. You were very young. We were beginning to make a life in this beautiful place in the way our people have always done. Like the lives most of our people have now, it is not an easy life. But, moment to moment, always, there is so much beauty." Manuelito nods his head toward a bed of orange, yellow and red flowers planted alongside the hogan. "Your Grandmother, planted those blanket flowers years ago and look how beautiful their blooms still are even with winter right around the corner."

Little Tree smiles but does not interrupt. He has heard his Grandfather's beauty talk before. Spotting a stray flower blooming, seeing a storm off in the distance—almost anything could trigger a talk about beauty. Often it is more like what his Grandmother called a lecture. Little Tree feels, like his Grandfather, that he can hardly look around at any point in his day and not feel awe from all the beauty around him. He loves how his Grandfather can go on and on about beauty; however, today he does not want him to get sidetracked down that path.

"We were surprised. It was totally out of the great blue yonder, when Mother Mary, the Mother Superior of the Sisters of the

Order of Mary of Magdala, showed up on our doorstep one day for her first visit. She had flown to Santa Fe from Stockholm." He chuckles. "In the traditional way we did not ask her why she had come, we simply made a place for her. She's a smart cookie. She seemed to settle right in and for the first week or two simply learned how to be helpful with our daily chores. We would give her a chore and she would go at it with a great burst of mojo." Manuelito laughs as the memory comes back with increasing vividness.

"Finally, I guess it was around week three of her visit, we had 'the talk.' I think she was reading the energy and knew it was the right time. Frankly, as much as we respect our guest tradition, the night before 'the talk' your Grandmother and I were discussing that we might have to ask her why she had come."

Manuelito stops and looks around, his eyebrows tilting upward. "Matter-of-fact, we were sitting right here under this apple tree, which I guess we learned a lot later probably was no coincidence, since after she went tracking, an apple tree was one of the important things that your Grandmother found. I'm getting a little off point. We were sitting here and Mother Mary tells us that despite the huge shift in consciousness, which was achieved by Sister Magdalen's bold procession to Rome, there is a fresh crisis.

"From her years of consciousness training, Mother Mary was not someone to reflect inner disturbance, but she was obviously upset." Manuelito pauses, waving his forefinger and pointing directly at Little Tree. "Right where you're sitting, Ya'zhi, I could see that she was getting increasingly perturbed by the minute."

Two erupts from what was a deep sleep. He is instantaneously on four paws and fully alert. Like his sire, Two is a powerful, muscular, medium-sized dog. Manuelito and Little Tree have trained the dog to respond quickly and assertively to deft hand signals. Though Manuelito's hand motion was for emphasis in his storytelling and not a command, Two does not take any chances.

"Good dog," says Manuelito. "Come, sit." Two positions himself a little closer to Manuelito's chair and his frame slides down smoothly unto the ground. Manuelito rubs behind his ears.

"For a time there was a sense of great relief among the Sisters of the Order of Mary of Magdala and all those involved in the procession. Sister Magdalen in one fell swoop flattened the hierarchy of the Roman church and turned it toward its mystical roots of direct inner experience. There was jubilation around the world. When she declined the papacy, or at least declined it in the materially manifested world, the CIA stopped the manhunt, which had been underway for years to capture her.

"Sister Magdalen had these very striking, beautiful green eyes. Don't know how the CIA could miss her." Manuelito lets out a long exhale.

Little Tree nods his head in anticipation of what his Grandfather will say next.

"Turns out the CIA intercepted a conversation Sister Magdalen had while she was on the walk from Assisi to Rome. In that conversation she referred to having the 'consciousness gene.' The agency shifted tactics at that point, abandoning their efforts to capture Sister Magdalen and turning instead in hot pursuit of this gene. They began pouring millions of dollars through the CIA's covert budget to several major university research departments to try to find this gene. The CIA believed then, and I guess they still do, that it was because of this gene that Sister Magdalen had the ability to penetrate other people's energy fields and thought fields. They believed if they could find the gene it would lead them to what they had been trying to capture Sister Magdalen for—the knowledge of how to control the thoughts of others.

"When Mother Mary told us all this we were nearly rolling on the ground laughing. All the energy that went into the procession on Rome to raise the consciousness level of humankind on planet Earth, and those, with enough consciousness to know, seeing a shift to greater consciousness occurring, and all the while the CIA completely missing the point—thinking there was an actual gene that could be exploited to achieve a capacity that takes years of spiritual discipline.

"After a couple of minutes of hooting and laughing, we looked around and Mother Mary was sitting there stony faced.

"I looked at your Grandmother Blaine and Blaine said to her, 'You mean there is?' Mother Mary nodded her head *yes*, and as she nodded her whole body moved backwards and forwards. You could have knocked your Grandmother and me over with a prick of a cactus.

"So you see that was what happened when Mother Mary came for her first visit—why she came to have 'the talk.' She wanted Blaine to go tracking to find this consciousness gene before the government found it. Mother Mary believes the consciousness gene is what contains the DNA structure that allows us to communicate with God, to send into and receive information from the unified field. She thinks that knowledge of the consciousness gene is not something that should fall into the hands of those who might use that knowledge to restrict access and limit an understanding of God. Rather, to her, access to expression of the consciousness gene is what the Gospel's 'good news' was all about from the start and that access needs to be shared with everyone. Her worse case scenario was that if the CIA got knowledge of how this gene is expressed, they would use that knowledge to practice controlling what they believed were the thoughts of would-be terrorists, and the CIA could inadvertently, or perhaps intentionally, block access to God."

"Did Grandma agree to go?" asks Little Tree. "Did she go

then?"

"One question at a time, Ya'zhi," says Manuelito, as he avoids the questions by rising to his feet. Manuelito at middle age retains the lean build he had as a young man and the ability to move fluidly with deceptive quickness.

"It is time to put something between that fresh amigo-gringo bread." Manuelito moves toward the kitchen as he continues to talk. "Your Grandmother did not go anywhere after the first visit by Mother Mary. However, Mother Mary came back again. She tends to see things in black and white, and once she sees a wrong in the works she doesn't give up easily. For that matter, she doesn't give up at all. I think it was about three or four years later when she returned." He turns and leads the way back into the hogan. Two follows directly at his heels, and Little Tree, his eyes bright with delight, just behind.

Chapter 5

Blaine has made hard decisions in her life. Breaking out of a mental institution when she was a teenager. Learning how to hack with a computer like a rogue wielding a knife in a street fight. However, deciding whether or not to go with Mother Mary to the Convent in Stockholm to be trained as a tracker in the quantum field was the hardest decision she ever made.

She faced the classic hero's journey dilemma: settle down with Manuelito, the man whose care for her had allowed her to find herself and to begin a new life, enjoy the big sky and rugged beauty of the American Southwest, and see her child's son, Little Tree, flourish as a young man; or follow this uncertain, fragile sense of destiny which Mother Mary urged upon her—one where Mother Mary argued Blaine's gifts were needed to save the world.

As Manuelito observed to Mother Mary, Blaine's spirit was bold. Ultimately in the face of Mother Mary's challenge, this spirit would not be denied. After thinking about the challenge daily for a long time, Blaine finally agreed to what, at the time of Mother Mary's second visit, she thought was a compromise with Mother Mary. Blaine's compromise was to travel to the Convent in Sweden and undergo deeper spiritual consciousness training to see if she did, in fact, have the gifts and skills which Mother Mary felt were needed to be a quantum field tracker. Looking back on it now, her decision-making process simply bought her more time to come to terms with her own destiny.

Once Blaine arrives at the Convent in Sweden, she realizes her decision to come was not simply a hard decision to make. It is a hard decision to live. She is only at the Convent for a few days when she experiences how deeply she misses Manuelito, Little Tree and the New Mexico landscape. On her third day, she goes for a walk and discovers a field of northern wolfsbane in a boggy area near the Convent. She is not familiar with the plant, but seeing the delicate blue and purple stalked flower make her homesick for the purple elephant heads growing along streams back home. She recalls the beauty of the white flower of the broad leaf yucca and the profusion of blanket flowers planted near her hogan.

She cares intensely for the Sisters who had helped her so much when she was a young woman; and though the training is challenging and rigorous, she is up to it. However, while being in Sweden to help Mother Mary is not a bad choice, it is not where her heart is. Every night when she lies down under the down comforter on her narrow single bed, her heart aches. Yet, the more she trains, the more she realizes her gifts, of being able to stay fully focused, mentally, emotionally and somatically for long periods of time, make it harder and harder for her to return home without undertaking Mother Mary's mission to save humanity.

After her third solo, sensory-deprivation, dark retreat, Mother Mary calls Blaine into her office.

"Blaine, you have been here now for well over a year. Though it may not seem like it on a day-to-day basis, from my perspective your progress over the past months is astonishing. I believe that you will be ready to start on a mission soon as a tracker in the quantum field. This mission will be presented to you in the next two weeks. Before you decide about the mission, I need, in all honesty, to be as candid with you as I can about the risks that we're now beginning to understand more fully, which are a part of what happens in a quantum field mission. We talked a bit about this when I visited you and Man back in New Mexico."

"Thank you, Mother Mary. I am very homesick to be back there with Manuelito and Little Tree. I need to know what the risks are." Blaine is thinking of a recent conversation on Skype with Man. He reminds her that the term quantum field tracker is simply a white man's science-sounding term for what native shamanic journeyers had been doing for centuries, traveling back in time through parallel realities. He mentions to her that there were many stories of how a shaman never made it back to present reality. Man had told her to be very careful in deciding if she is willing to do what Mother Mary is asking of her.

Mother Mary furrows her brow. "There is some risk, though we believe it small, that you might not be able to get back from the quantum field into our cause-and-effect reality. The bigger risk is that you may experience time differently."

"I remember Man brought this issue up before. Go through this again for me. Tell me what you mean," says Blaine. "How might I experience time differently?" Blaine thinks she understands this risk perhaps even better than Mother Mary does because Blaine has the benefit of Man's knowledge about the long tradition of shamanic journey traveling. Still, she wants to think it all through thoroughly and she feels, if she asks enough questions, what she ought to do will finally fall into place. She has learned that the antidote to living a fear-based life is to have a bigger, more complete picture of reality.

"As we discussed earlier, we don't know for sure what happens," says Mother Mary. "It is very possible that you could be in the quantum field for a time, which might seem like a day or two, and when you returned to this reality a year or more might have gone by."

"What can we do to prevent that from happening?"

Silence extends before Mother Mary speaks. "We don't know anything we can do. We don't understand how it happens exactly. We know generally that in the quantum field the thoughts and feelings of all past experiences and all future experiences exist simultaneously. The best science suggests that time simply is different in the quantum field. You could be gone for what might seem like two weeks and return much later. Or, you might be gone for a couple of days and have the experience of an entire lifetime in the quantum field. We hope that the latter would be your experience."

"You mean I could be on what seems like a two-week experiment with you here and come back and find that I had missed five years in the lives of Manuelito and Little Tree?"

"I am afraid so," says Mother Mary.

*   *   *

Years later, Blaine would recognize that she did not make the decision to become a tracker in the quantum field—who she was and what she had become made the decision. She would learn the field of consciousness is a huge ocean of awareness longing for conduits into it. In a sense, Blaine never had a choice. By her own journey overcoming childhood adversities, her own consciousness was raised. As she progressively put fear aside and came to live ever increasingly a life of faith in the life force of unfolding creation, she simply became a conduit that was inevitably drawn to the source.

Chapter 6

Navajo Nation
Southwestern United States
Spring 2012

"Let me tell you a story, Tree," says Manuelito to his grandson. Manuelito and his grandson are sitting outside their hogan under the apple tree, which is in full bloom. The air has the aroma of the white blossoms with their pink hearts sweetened by the fragrance of the squaw apples growing nearby. Last night it was very near freezing and the sun is warming them both up. Though Tree is fourteen years old now, he has never gotten weary of hearing his Grandfather talk.

In the latter part of his thirteenth year, Tree suddenly shot upward. Overnight he became a tall, slim young man. As if by conscious agreement, everyone stopped calling him Ya'zhi, and dropped the diminutive that had preceded his name since he was very young. Like his Grandfather, Tree's personality has a calming effect on others, because of his grounded equanimity. Nothing is little about the calm inner spaciousness he radiates.

Tree also gets very excited when something really engages him. He feels his excitement rising now in response to his Grandfather readying to tell a story. As usual, the important conversations occur outside their hogan under the dearly loved apple tree. The tree is a rarity for the climate and pampered by Manuelito during the arid days of summer. The spring weather is bracing, though neither Manuelito nor Tree minds the cool air. Two, situated as usual between the pair of humans to whom he is ever faithful, relishes the cool temperature and the warm company.

Over the past couple of years Manuelito's story telling, which was always important, has become a shared way for grandfather and grandson to experience not only their deep connection, but at the same time to experience together how much they both, in their different ways, miss Blaine. Under the apple tree, she has a silent presence with them.

Tree senses his Grandfather has something important to tell him. A question forms on Tree's face. Then he speaks.

"Grandfather, you told me that our people need to move beyond their stories. Why would you tell me a story?"

"You are right, Tree. It is my wish that we move beyond stories that create personal limitation around our experience—that we are poor or limited in some way. I want us to move back to when stories were not limitations on experience, but remembrances of the past that expanded the possibility of the present. If I had a story of limitation now I would not be telling it to you. Both the method and meaning of a story can be either a limitation or an expansion. The method for a story to be an expansion is for us to simply be present before the story and if you need to be told something the story will tell you. Then this would not be just a story. The narrative would have being. Or, as the ancestors of many tribes said in the old days, the listener's vitality would encounter the spiritual germ found in the aliveness of the story and the beingness of the story would be *waaken*.

"What I wish to tell you is part old story and part *waaken*. It is in part a story because there is some truth that I must give you while I'm here, which you may be too young to experience right now. I must, however, pass a few kernels on to you so that later, when it is the right time, you will remember and the truth will then come to live in your heart *waaken*."

Manuelito stretches out his lean body and puts his booted feet up on a fire-pit rock in front of him. Tree puts his feet, clad in new red sneakers, upon a rock on his side of the fire-pit.

Tree nods, and though his actions reflexively mimic his Grandfather's actions, he does not yet understand fully the meaning of what his grandfather is saying. More importantly, aside from listening to what his Grandfather is telling him, he is totally absorbed in the experience of his Grandfather—with that he is *waaken*.

"Let me tell you what kind of story this is not. It is not the kind of story which tries to tell people who they are. You know the story we stick with, till it sticks to us. This is not that. The white people have large bookstores for those stories. Bookstores do not carry words on pages which are *waaken*, not even pages with words alive before something becomes *waaken*.

"Let me explain. The white man's stories are not real in a *waaken* sense. You remember when you came home from school the other day, you asked me about a math problem?"

Tree nods.

"What is a math problem? Let's start with the word mathematics. It is a word that is an abstraction, whose definition is about the way numbers work. It is not actually any of the numbers themselves. A story as a pseudo-experience is similar. It is words that refer abstractly to events over a period of time, usually about one or two special characters. This kind of story has become the post-modern refuge of all disenchanted, alienated souls. A way for them to think perhaps there is some kind of meaning. The better the story sounds the more meaning seems to exist within the abstraction. But, the meaning of reading the story is soon lost because there is no direct experience of the story. White people read many stories, and their lives get emptier rather than fuller. As we have talked about before, they stay stuck in their thoughts and feelings and miss being present in their lives.

"So what I am about to tell you is not like a white man's story."

Tree nods his head enthusiastically as if he understands everything his Grandfather is telling him. And, Manuelito thinks maybe he does.

"I like what you told me about a story being clothing worn by a Mr. Frog," says Tree.

Tree's Grandfather smiles. His grandson uncannily remembers everything he tells him. "Yes, the white man's story is simply the tattered clothing worn by his Freudian ego to make it feel it is halfway presentable, so it does not seem so alone.

"What if you did not live principally through an ego? Then you would not have that kind of story. This is how our people used to live and what I have tried to lead our people back to. In the old days, they didn't need those kind of Frog stories as you call them; they were simply awake. They had many narratives which were called stories, which were *waaken* in their re-telling. However, what was most important was not the history in the narrative, but the experience of the narrative in the moment. In this way a narrative changes over time as the needs and vision of the people change. It is not just information strung together; it is our history and ancestors re-experienced again and again, changing as we change with the Earth.

"What I am trying to say is that I must tell you some narrative so that later on you will re-live, it and in that experience you will move closer to becoming a *waaken* being."

"I think I understand, Grandfather. Please, tell me this story that is not yet for me *waaken*."

"Yes, I will do that. First, it would be good to have something to drink. Run get me a glass of that cactus flower tea that you made yesterday using your grandmother's recipe. I think I put it in the refrigerator. Oh, and see if you can get a rawhide chew for Two." Tree jumps to his feet and runs into the kitchen, banging the screen door as he goes.

Two, the Plott Hound deeply loved by both Manuelito and Tree, gets up from one side of Manuelito and settles himself on the other. As he does, the dog looks at his master, Manuelito, squarely in the eye as if to say that he, like Tree, is excitedly anticipating a good story and it better be good.

Returning promptly, Tree hands the glass of tea to his Grandfather. Manuelito takes the glass from his grandson and gazes over the glass into Tree's startlingly blue eyes. Where did such eyes come from he wonders? He shakes his head and his eyes wander to admire the youngster's unblemished coppery skin.

"Way back in the middle of the last century a great war was fought. It was like no other war that had ever been fought. It involved almost all people of the world. Many of our people went, for we have a history of great warriors. It was not really our war. However, our leaders sensed the world was spiritually terribly out of balance and so they encouraged the young men to go. War is always fought by the young on the instruction of elders. When you are young, being brave with your arms and legs is all that matters. You have not yet grown to understand bravery in the heart.

"This was the second great war the white people fought after a period of history they called the Enlightenment." Manuelito begins to laugh from some place deep in his belly and soon his hand holding his glass is shaking and tea is sloshing on the ground.

"Grandfather, may I hold your glass?" entreats Tree, jumping up from his stool by his Grandfather's weathered, outdoor rocking chair.

"No. Actually, it is not funny. Laughter is one of the ways our people have always dealt with great sadness." Manuelito puts his glass down and wipes his eyes on his shirt-sleeve. It is not yet mid-morning and already the cool morning air is warming up on the Navajo reservation.

"Sit down, Grandson. Back to the story. For the first time in human history people of the Eastern world and people of the Western world were all fighting at the same time. In the early years of this war, it seemed like the totalitarian world of Hitler's Germany might succeed in completely conquering Europe. It was an extraordinarily dangerous time. Without a doubt the history of humankind hung in the balance. If the Nazis won the war, we would have entered a new dark age that would have lasted a long time.

"As happens in extraordinary times, extraordinary people arise. World War II was no exception. One of those extraordinary people was an Englishman named David Strangeways."

Tree interrupts. "Was that really his name?"

Manuelito chuckles. "Yes, truth *is* stranger than fiction. His name was Strangeways. The name was singularly appropriate." Manuelito takes another sip from his glass of tea and sets the glass down on a goat milking stool that serves as a small table next to his rocking chair.

"An appropriate name, because Strangeways was in charge of deception for the allies. Deception has always been important to our people, the Diné. It has been the way that our culture has survived over the past two hundred years in the face of the dominant and overwhelmingly powerful white man's culture. Deception is always important to those less powerful. In the case of the Allies fighting the Germans in World War II, except for the industrial might of the United States which came to bear late in the war, the Germans in 1941 were the most powerful nation in the world.

"To try to undermine Hitler's almost complete control of the European continent and to prevent Russia from falling to the Germans, the Allies had to find some way to advance against Hitler on the continent of Europe. Because any invading force is always at the time of invasion at a huge disadvantage, deception was crucial if the Allies were to be successful.

"After initially seeking to land a force on the European continent and failing, the Allies decided to open a second front in North Africa. Colonel David Strangeways was put in charge of deceiving the Germans about the Allies' intention. The Allied advance into North Africa was called Operation Torch. It was impossible to deceive the Germans in the buildup to the North African invasion because of the massing of landing craft at Gibraltar. The deception involved misleading the Germans as to when and where the invasion would occur."

Tree jumps up. "If we had been involved, I guess one of our Singers, who know how to communicate with the spirit world, would have given Hitler a dream. Is this what happened?"

Manuelito pauses. "In a way you're right. For deception to be most convincing the person being deceived must feel he has figured it out. In this case, what Strangeways did was go to Cairo and rent a hotel room. At the time Cairo was notorious for being filled with German intelligence agents. Strangeways took with him a novel by Dennis Wheatley, who happened to also be someone working in the London deception office. In the book Strangeways left a letter for an acquaintance. The letter for the most part sounded like a lighthearted exchange between two good friends and in passing mentioned that the landing craft being assembled at Gibraltar were going to be used to relieve besieged Malta.

"When he checked out, Strangeways left the book with the letter in it in his room. Apparently the book and letter made their way to German intelligence, and based upon this information the German military completely misjudged where the landing in North Africa would occur. The deception worked.

"Strangeways spent the next year of the war in the Middle East using radio nets to broadcast false information to the Germans. He also constructed decoy tanks and other vehicles, which were used to divert German forces away from areas where the Allies were seeking to advance. He once had the German commander Rommel mass an attack against a fictitious Allied force. Rommel squared off against a huge stretch of empty desert.

"In one of his most significant contributions to the war in North Africa, Strangeways was able to bluff his way into Tunis ahead of the invading Allied force and obtain secret military documentation and codes from a safe at the German headquarters before this information could be destroyed.

"Strangeways next was involved in a deception needed to enable the Allies to land in Sicily. Part of the ruse involved letting the body of a British officer wash ashore, who carried specific documents indicating that the Allied invasion would be in Sardinia or Greece. In response, the German army moved units to both of those areas, away from where the actual invasion occurred.

"In his chess game against the Germans, Strangeways was remarkably successful because he had the ability to have bold, out-of-the-box thinking, and he was also a meticulous planner who was able to execute a plan in careful detail. These two attributes are often not found in the same person—the lofty dreamer and the careful performer."

"Grandfather, don't you think I can do both?"

Manuelito smiles. "Most certainly, I do. That is part of the reason

I am telling you this story, because I believe you have a chance for it to be *waaken* in you." Two emits a low whine as if he also agrees.

Tree breaks into a huge grin. Always when he listens to one of his Grandfather's *waaken* stories or when he talks deeply with his Grandfather about anything, he ends up feeling lifted up in some way. This time is no different.

"When the British and the Americans got ready to begin to prepare for the invasion of Europe, Strangeways was brought back to London and put in charge of much of the plan to deceive the Germans. He had some very interesting help. Not only did he have a unit of engineers with special broadcasting gear, he had extraordinary human assets to deliver the deception to the Germans. Where before he had used a book in a letter and a dead body to deliver the deception, this time he had the most successful double agents who ever practiced that art."

Tree, who often watched old James Bond movies with his Grandfather, begins to hum the musical refrain from *Goldfinger*. Two growls, decidedly not in tune.

Manuelito laughs. "In fact, you are partially right. One of those double agents was a Serbian-born playboy named Dusko Popov, code-named Tricycle, after whom it is thought Ian Fleming modeled James Bond. But, the most important double agent was a man named Juan Pujol, code-named Garbo, a Spanish agent who worked directly for MI5 in London. As the war dragged on, the Germans became increasingly enthralled with the information that Garbo provided to them.

"The overall deception plan was called Operation Fortitude. Strangeways was in charge of Operation Quicksilver, a significant part of Operation Fortitude. Operation Quicksilver's mission was to create the deception that the Allied European invasion would take place at Pas-de-Calais rather than Normandy. Like the invasion of North Africa, it was impossible to shield from the Germans the build up of forces and landing vessels in preparation for an invasion of Europe. The best hope for deception was where and when that invasion would occur."

Manuelito stops. "I have been going on too long. Have you studied the history of World War II in school? Is this all boring you?"

Tree shakes his head vigorously *no* to each question. "What did our people do in this war?"

"Our people were involved in deception also. Like I say, it comes natural to those who are on the short-end of the power stick. Our people were Code Talkers. They passed messages in Navajo on the radio, knowing that the Germans had no way to understand our language, and no Navajos in Germany to turn to in order to figure it out. It was an important deception. The Germans never broke it."

He pauses. His voice becomes tinged with emotion. "My Grandfather, your Great-Great-Grandfather, was one of the Code Talkers. When I was young, my father took me to a museum where I saw a picture of my Grandfather and medals he received for his service to the United States as a Code Talker.

"I think it is time for us to stop for now. We will continue tomorrow."

Tree would've liked to have argued with his Grandfather. He would've loved for his Grandfather to continue to unwind the story, or *waaken*, whatever it was, he was telling. However, he was too respectful and patient to think about trying to change his Grandfather's mind. Of late, his Grandfather would take a mid-morning nap. He was just glad the story had begun. He knew his Grandfather would continue until it was completed. He always did.

Chapter 7

Navajo Nation
Southwestern United States
Summer 2012

"Grandfather, have you been trying to tell me that deception is good?"

Tree, Manuelito and Two again gather under the apple tree beside the hogan. The sun is up and it is already starting to get hot. In this semi-arid steppe climate it will get into the mid-eighties in the middle of summer. Nevertheless, Manuelito has a steaming mug of black coffee in hand. Tree hovers on the edge of his chair.

"Tree, you make your Grandfather happy with your probing mind." He pauses. "And, your love of the beauty of our country. Thank you for the bouquet of desert marigolds and apache plume you gathered for us. The bright yellow marigolds are accented beautifully by the delicate white apache plume."

Tree smiles. "I am glad you like them, Grandfather."

"As you will see as the story continues my hope is that the good power of deception may one day be *waaken* for you. In the abstract, deception is neither good nor bad. Rather like most things, what is right action in the moment depends upon all the circumstances and especially upon the heart connection of the person taking the action.

"There were many Jews during World War II, who became good Catholics in order to survive. There are many of our people, who adopted Anglo names to pass for white and get a job. There are many people who are gay who have suppressed expression of their gender preference in order to avoid being ostracized by the larger culture. We see deception in nature in how a butterfly might be colored to camouflage its presence and assure its survival. I am sure you can think of many examples of this from your wanderings on the high mesa."

Tree nods his head enthusiastically.

"On the other hand, there is the case of Karl-Erich Kühlenthal who was a half-blood Jew and one of the Nazi's most successful spymasters in World War II. Similarly, there are many stories of closeted gay men in power positions persecuting gays.

"Deception can allow people to do good and survive evil; and deception can allow powerful people to do tremendous evil. Usually deception by those in power leads to evil, deception by the powerless often to good. You have heard stories all your life of shamen who called upon the spirits in the other world to do good or evil. Deception can keep truth alive among the powerless, and deception can perpetuate the greatest evil when used by the powerful.

"There are several classic spy methods of deception. First is the bluff—an example would be telling an intriguingly detailed story that is untrue in order to elicit a response which is helpful to the teller. Second is the double bluff. This deception is only used by masters of the art. It involves giving details that are true in such a manner that the party to whom they are being given believes they are a false cover story. As you can tell, what is so important in either case is the masterfulness with which the deception is conveyed. Strangeways used both of these methods in deceiving the Germans. Perhaps we will explore other types of deceptions later. Enough about deception in World War II. I wanted to give you enough details of what happened then for you to realize that deception was what allowed the Allies to win. Goodness survived through deception. Often truth itself must be clothed in deception in order to survive.

"I have come to believe that the use of deception by the marginalized is the way in which transformation of consciousness will happen for the human species. Let me try to give you a few examples. First, go and see if there is another glass of cactus flower tea in the refrigerator."

Tree rushes back into the hogan, banging the screen door as is his wont. In a moment he emerges with a glass of tea for his Grandfather, a rawhide chew for Two and a small bowl filled to the brim with dark red cherries.

Manuelito pops one of the cherries into his mouth and savors the mixture of sweet and tartness. "Humm," he says. "With these we might be able to talk a long time."

Tree grabs for a cherry. A huge grin spreads over his face, arising from the delicious taste of the cherry and the prospect of being the center of his Grandfather's story-telling attention for the rest of the morning.

"Well, let's see where we were." Manuelito pauses thoughtfully. "Deception on behalf of others is what we might talk about for a few minutes. Deception as a way to perpetuate truth on behalf of the powerless, that is where we were. But, before exploring that, I want to talk to you about the meaning of your name."

The grandfather looks at his grandson wistfully, as if he is remembering in one moment all of his grandson's life. "You know, for people the world over, trees are experienced as sacred. We might ask ourselves—why is this? You will know, my grandson, from your own direct experience. Whenever we are in a canyon containing a stream lined with trees, we feel a warmth, an acceptance. One cannot walk among the tree people and feel judged. Trees embody patience. Trees teach us to listen, for they speak in the silence. Their speech is like the space between two notes in a melody. There would be no song without the richness of the emptiness between the notes.

"When we are among mature trees, not fifty or sixty year old adolescents, but trees which have grown into their own birthright—we find ourselves embraced in a subtle and profound way. We experience the tree's empathy for us and all reality around it. Empathy is the beginning of love. Empathy is what connects us within and between species. It is the trees which teach us unconditional acceptance and from this experience we learn to love. This is why trees have always been sacred and will always remain so.

"Like the mother caring for her newborn infant, the love and holding by trees is a subtle deception for those who do not understand the meaning of the trees' energy. You know this energy do you not?"

"Certainly, Grandfather. You know I do," says Tree, his eyes sparkling.

"Yes, I understand how much you do," says his Grandfather, murmuring slightly to himself.

"Because trees are sacred teachers, who teach in the invisible realm—to those stuck simply in the material world, their teaching is a deception. So my grandson even though you have never been taught how to move between the worlds, and even though you have much to learn about this, your namesake experience has already taken you back and forth, has it not?"

"Yes, Grandfather. Do you mean everyone does not do this?"

"Among the Diné, yes, many of us do and it seems, and is, quite natural. This is not true among the white consumer culture, where people are always chasing the future to escape their present. You will learn, once you understand moving between the worlds more deeply, why you are not impatient for the future—you will know how fervently time is on your side. The white people only see time as their enemy. Trees teach us that this is not true.

"Sometimes names in the larger culture allude to the deeper meaning of trees without even knowing it. The giant sequoia in California was named after a Cherokee chief and scholar, Sequoyah. It is a fitting name for these giant trees, which are remnants of an ancient race of trees which once flourished all over North America and today still remember the time when Christ walked on earth. Even the white people cannot walk among these trees without experiencing sacredness in the sentient personalities of these massive trees.

"Another tree long sacred to people of the First Nations is the wafer ash. Like the sequoia, the wafer ash is an ancient race of trees. In what was probably one of the first great deaths and resurrections on this planet, it deceived the Ice Age and survived, when logically it should not have. It is a remarkable medicinal tree. The chemical compounds within its bark and foliage, because they arise out of the margins of survival, do extraordinary things. These chemical compounds help change the metabolic rate of distressed organs and bring them back into health. One of these compounds called marmesin acts synergistically with other healing agents to increase the capacity for healing. Though the white man has now endangered the future of this tree, the sacred wafer ash tree has been used by tribal cultures for healing for thousands of years.

"White people are not entirely immune to the efficacious quality of trees in their history. It was under a large fig tree that the Buddha received his revelation. Most white people do not understand that it was the tree which taught the Buddha the meaning of non-attachment. Every autumn, deciduous trees, at the peak of their glorious color, teach us again what they first taught the Buddha. This peaceful and gentle religion was given to humans by this tree with its massive trunk and shiny green leaves. Jesus, the master teacher of transformation, was himself attached to a tree to glorify the process of emptiness and renewal which happens so beautifully to most trees every autumn, winter and spring. His teaching was that once consciousness is gained it deceives death."

Manuelito pauses and looks at his grandson to see if the things he is saying are being understood. Hmm, he thinks, like many trees, Tree's soul age is much older than his chronological age suggests. "Shall I go on, Grandson?"

Tree nods enthusiastically. He is not sure he understands everything his Grandfather is trying to tell him. However, he does not want the warm focus of his Grandfather's energy to be diverted elsewhere. Always he will remember these times, when he bathes so peacefully in the flowing and gentle energy of his Grandfather.

"Many native people have also learned from other tribal cultures. The ancient Celtic peoples who lived in Ireland, Wales and Scotland had spiritual rituals centered on the oak tree. This tree was sacred to the Druids. It was through the sacred oak tree that the Druids communicated with the other world. When we participate in a consumer culture, it is so easy to lose the sacred connection with the oak tree or the sequoia or the wafer ash. Sacred trees open up a moment in sacred time for the experience of everything, in eternity. This work by trees happens silently, in deception, to hold the world together.

"At one time, when the white Europeans first came to North America and were struggling against British rule, these white people, who mostly came to escape harsh conditions in Europe, were aligned against the forces of the British Empire and were marginalized people. They sensed that there was important energy in trees. It was an elm tree in Boston called the Liberty

Tree which was celebrated by Thomas Paine as the "temple" of the revolution. The flag, which was often run up by revolutionary schooners, depicted a pine tree with the inscription 'An Appeal to Heaven.' An illusion similar to the Druids communicating to Heaven through the oak."

Manuelito stops and looks intently at Tree. "These are interesting facts which make sense to us but without greater participation by us they are like white people's stories, not what is *waaken*. Do you understand?"

Tree smiles at his Grandfather and again nods. Manuelito muses to himself at his grandson's repeated gesture. Manuelito knows that a slight movement of the head affirming agreement is sweeter and more nuanced than speaking, while also allowing more space in the conversation. He is glad to see that his grandson intuitively understands this. Manuelito nods ever so slightly back to Tree in return.

"I do not know clearly what your life task will be, just that it will spring from this legacy for which you are named. So one day the stories I have been telling you about your tree ancestors and our people will be *waaken* for you.

"Years ago when I was at a place of unknowing in my life, I did a vision quest at Pipestone National monument, where I quarried for three weeks with an elderly Navajo woman who let me work with her on her claim. After the vision quest your Grandmother and the elderly woman helped me discover a chunk of pipestone that held the blood of my ancestors. From that point on I was freed from the burden of my father's un-lived life and his father's; however, the gifts of the Diné were not taken away from me, only the burden of my personal family history with its alcoholism and poverty—the same as most kids on the rez.

"Later I learned tribal people suffer greatly because of the burden of our community unconsciousness—the sufferings of the tribe weigh heavier on everyone than on those in more individualistic cultures. It is harder to escape this communal burden where we extoll our own suffering and stay stuck in a sort of woe-is-us mentality. However, it is not just native tribal cultures where you see this. It is also in the Irish tribal culture and Middle Eastern tribes.

"Humankind is at a crossroads where our continued evolutionary survival is dependent upon us living in a way that recognizes our mutual interdependence. The larger white culture is finally seeing the barrenness of the extreme competitive, striving-for-self-only approach to life. So while the larger white community must go forward to a greater understanding of community, our people must go forward to a greater freedom in community. We must free ourselves from the collective unconsciousness suffering of our people and white people must free themselves from their fear of not-enough that drives their individualistic greed and aggression.

"Tree, like I say, I do not know what the vision is for your life. My gut tells me it is about this new vision of community—where tribal people are freed of carrying the burden of their ancestors' hundreds of years of suffering and white culture is freed of its fear. You see that both of these limiting beliefs spring from a psychological structure, or emotional complex, a story if you will, which says who one is, and says that in a limiting way."

Manuelito looks at his grandson out of the corner of his eyes. "You think I am going off on another rant about how, as James Hillman says in his book by that title—*A Hundred Years of Psychotherapy and the World is Getting Worse.*"

Tree nods vigorously. "Certainly, you are, Grandfather."

"Humph." Manuelito looks about, as if searching for a sign from nature to tell him which course to take. "Maybe not this time. I will cut to the chase, a psychological solution is always an ego solution and the problem is precisely that—the ego. The limiting belief structure is the contour of the ego. The way out of an ego problem, as our people have always known, is a spiritual solution. When you are *waaken*, you are in the spiritual solution.

"Before I left Pipestone that time years ago, an elderly Lakota, who was also working a claim, gave me this medallion." Manuelito pulls an object from his shirt pocket which looks for all the world like a silver dollar, except it is bronze colored and about half again as big as a silver dollar. He squints at the writing on one side and reads: *"Perhaps you have noticed that even in the very lightest breeze you can hear the voice of the cottonwood tree; this we understand is its prayer to the Great Spirit, for not only men, but all things and all beings pray to Him continually in differing ways.* Black Elk"

"Black Elk was the great spiritual visionary of the Lakota who went back and forth between the two worlds. He suggests, like the Druids, that it is through the tree that prayer flows." Manuelito hands the medallion to his grandson. "You are well named, my son; the more you are tree the more you will know what you need to do in this world."

Tree eagerly takes the medallion from this Grandfather's hand. "Thank you, thank you, Grandfather."☐

"I think we have talked enough for now."

Manuelito chuckles, and, as if speaking to himself says aloud, "Maybe it is time for a nap for me." He reaches over and pats his grandson affectionately. "More will be revealed," he says, and with that he rises from his rocking chair and returns into the hogan.

Tree remains where he is sitting by his Grandfather's rocking chair. His dog stays at his feet. Tree turns the medallion over and over in his hands. There is a heft and weight to it which makes it seem a part of a grownup world he does not yet know. Yet, his having it in some way promises entry. He looks closely at the back side and sees what is written: *Twenty-five years of Sobriety. Thanks be to a Loving God.*

Maybe, thinks Tree, the man who gave the medallion to his Grandfather escaped from that tribal consciousness suffering-burden his Grandfather was describing. Tree knows intuitively that his Grandfather has escaped this burden; otherwise he would not be able to understand and speak about it. Maybe the medallion is being given to Tree by his Grandfather to symbolize that a tribal legacy can be a new way of knowing rather than a burden. And, that he, Tree, is a part of that legacy.

Tree speaks aloud. "What do you think of that idea, Two?" He does not need to describe his thoughts aloud because Two always understands his thoughts before he does. The dog raises his head from where it rests atop his crossed front paws. His eyes are alert. His moist nose quivers, taking in information from this world and the next. In a motion that reminds Tree of his Grandfather, the dog nods his head ever so slightly *yes*. Then he puts his long mouth and nose back on his crossed paws.

Tree grins to himself. Why, he wonders, does Two remind him so much of his Grandfather? He gets up and as he does Two stands also. "Okay, boy, let's go for a walk to explore and see what we can find. You know Grandfather always has something interesting to tell us when we bring him an odd animal bone or some special shiny rock."

The dog turns his head back slightly toward Tree and again almost imperceptibly seems to nod. In one smooth motion Tree reaches inside the hogan's front door and grabs his quiver and bow. The twosome then head for the sunlit high mesa, toward an arroyo off in the distance that shelters a stand of young cottonwood trees. There will be shade there from the hot sun.

Chapter 8

Navajo Nation
Southwestern United States
Spring 2013

"Tree, come and sit outside with me. I want to talk to you about how you track deception. It is something that I have been learning from your Grandmother. There are many ways to track deception. One is language."

The sun is hardly up. The air is cool. However, regardless of the weather, Tree is always ready to go sit outside under the apple tree and listen to his Grandfather. This is the highlight of any day.

"What do you mean you have been learning from Grandmother? She has been gone a long time and you have yet to tell me where she is and when she will be back."

"I can see that you are picking up on deception. It's time we talk about her travels. I believe your Grandmother thinks you are ready. Let me get another cup of that dark, bilious liquid that passes for coffee around here. Yes, it is time. But, tracking deception with language, let's start there."

Soon the two are settled in their respective customary chairs under the apple tree. Manuelito has a cup of hot black coffee and Tree is perched on the edge of his chair. Two is spread out as if he were a bridge between them.

"Lincoln. Have you studied Lincoln in school yet?"

"A bit I guess. We studied the Civil War in American History. There wasn't a big focus on Lincoln."

"Humm, too bad. Everyone should focus on Lincoln. A remarkable man. Truly a man who emerged at a crucial time in history and moved our history and civilization decisively forward. At seminal times in history, there is always this huge resistance before change can occur. The Civil War itself is an example of that resistance."

"I am not sure I understand, Grandfather. What do you mean by resistance?"

"Well, from the perspective of the great arc of history, clearly slavery was a doomed institution. Giving it up required Southerners to come to another world view. Any internal shift in perspective by a large number of people does not happen easily. Most people, even those who would in the abstract agree with such change, find that a part of themselves resists any kind of change, which requires them to increase their level of consciousness.

"One of the great psychic injuries of slavery was taking people's names. Our names connect us to our ancestors and help remind us of our lineage. They give us a sense of place in the world, grounded outside of what might be our immediate circumstances. By taking black people's names and giving them English names, the white people took something *waaken*. White people did something similar to native people, but in a reverse way. We were often given additional names by the white census takers. Many Navajos are called Begay. It is a corruption of the Navajo word 'biya' which means 'his son.' Or, the name common name Chee comes from the Navajo word 'Łichíí'' which means 'red.' As you know, we don't follow the surname practice found in the white culture. This is why you and I have only one name Tree. Both our names came to us from those who named us by seeing into our essence, into our past and future, and for that reason the names are *waaken*."

"Some of the kids at school have such weird names. Why is that?"

"Often that is a reaction to the white culture's stealing names or assigning to us non-*waaken* names. In trying to reclaim their naming, people can come up with some far out sounding names. Let me get back to Lincoln.

"To create the emotional impact needed for people to experience a shift in consciousness, Lincoln was a master in the use of deceptive language—that is, rather than telling people what they should do directly, he told them indirectly, deceptively, most often using the negative. The deceptive part is that he did not use the negative in a negative way; rather, he used it as a way the powerless always use deception—to increase the rhetorical truth of what is being said.

"Let me give you some examples. He didn't simply say slavery is wrong. He said, 'If slavery is not wrong, nothing is wrong.' Can you feel how that is more powerful?"

Tree nods.

"In his 1858 debate with Stephen Douglas he famously said, 'With public sentiment, nothing can fail; without it nothing can succeed.' Powerful stuff. Or, at the conclusion of his first inaugural, speaking to the South, 'You have no oath registered in Heaven to destroy the government, while I shall have the most solemn one to preserve, protect and defend it.'"

"Certainly, you better be memorizing the Gettysburg Address. I will have to talk to Ms Locklear if you are not."

Tree blushes at his Grandfather's mention of his teacher.

Manuelito's eyes go up to the clouds and he begins to recite as if pulling the words from the heavens: "'We cannot dedicate—we cannot consecrate—we cannot hallow—this ground.... The world will little note, nor long remember what we say here, but it can never forget what they did here.' Then as Lincoln goes on to reach the pinnacle of his speech, the most important idea is expressed in the negative, 'that government of the people, by the people, for the people, shall not perish from the earth.'

"The power of so much of Lincoln's great speeches comes from his use of the negative, because the ideas themselves if expressed straightforwardly would almost seem sentimental. I think it is safe to say that his deceptive use of the negative brought a force to his words that saved the Union.

"Tell that to your teacher. Maybe she will wish to argue with me." Manuelito smiles at Tree, as his grandson squirms at the delightful prospect of having to give Ms. Locklear a message from his Grandfather.

Chapter 9

Navajo Nation
Southwestern United States
Spring 2014

Growing up on the rez is schizophrenic. Never more so than during adolescence. During his teenage years Tree's friends fall into two camps: the traditionals, who disdain the white ways, and the white 'wanna-be's,' who also verbally criticize white culture, while at the same time seek to imitate it in every way possible.

The traditionals are like some of his friends who grew up in the church—they want to believe what the church teaches and outwardly they cling to it, but down deep, they really are not sure they are on the right side. The white wanna-be's are caught in the allure of the white culture—of wanting things in order to feel better from having them. The more miserable the teenager feels, the more escape from misery the white world seems to offer. Yet the more these teenagers pursue the trappings of the white world the more lost from themselves they become; and so, the harder they try. It is another version of the vicious addiction cycle that traps so many of the people.

Fortunately, his Grandfather prepares Tree. His Grandfather's own vision quest taught him that he was to walk between the two cultures—the culture of the people, the Diné, and that of the white man's world. Manuelito tells Tree that at times this is very difficult; however, the walk-in-two-worlds also has many gifts. The most important gift for Manuelito has been his wife Blaine, who is Tree's beloved Grandmother. Tree remembers that her white skin, sunburnt for so many years, looks as coppery as his

54   KING ARTHUR & THE CONSCIOUSNESS GENE

Grandfather's. When he was a young child, Tree was always wanting her to show him the dragon tattoo on her arm. She would let him push his fingers on her wrinkly skin so that the tired, saggy image became animated and he imagined what powerful medicine it was.

Tree never doubts for a moment Grandma Blaine's love for him, ever since he came to live with his grandparents as a young child on the rez, after both his parents were shot and killed on the mean, drug-dealings streets of Los Angeles. While he never doubts her love, he is aware that his Grandma is a bit weird. His Grandfather loves that about his wife, the way her differentness makes her special to him. Tree is aware that sometimes her strangeness bothers others and even makes him self-conscious at times when he is with her in public.

Tree remembers one time in a grocery store two young teenage boys were acting out. They were throwing large bags of potato chips over top of one aisle to the next aisle. They were diving on the floor trying to catch the bags, crushing the chips and generally interfering with other shoppers. His Grandmother focused her attention on the first boy she saw sprawled in the aisle. Later she told Tree when she entered the boy's energy field it was all black, red and pained. She used her energy to bring some warm green and yellow into the youngster's energy field. He began to feel less alienated and at the same time embarrassed by his misbehavior. The two boys looked at his Grandmother Blaine strangely. Without really understanding what had happened, the two boys suddenly stopped their commotion and left the store.

Tree knows that, because of incidents like this, among some of the people his Grandmother has a reputation of being a witch. It is easy to call someone a witch who is different and is from a different culture, but many people recognize in her different-ness her gifts and come to his Grandmother for healing. This is a source of tension also, because she is not a native Singer or traditional Navajo healer. However, those who seek her healing assistance never forget her kindness. Many years after her help, people drop off a few chickens or a turquoise bracelet for his Grandmother. Tree knows that somehow they have been restored to spiritual balance by something his Grandmother has done, and the gift is to recognize that balance and keep it in place.

Sometimes his Grandmother's language will also put people off. Growing up, Tree learned to speak Navajo from his Grandfather. His parents only spoke English and this was the tongue his grandparents spoke to each other. His Grandmother sometimes speaks a strange language, which he later learns is called German, which she speaks primarily because of her fondness for certain German expletives.

Tree's Grandfather told him that back when his Grandmother was a young woman she lived in Germany for a time and that her best friend there was someone named Rat. It was there she picked up the habit of watching European soccer matches. She would sometimes get these games on satellite TV on the rez with the game commentary broadcast in German or Spanish and, when the wrong side scored or made a big play, she was apt to let loose a string of German words.

Tree's Grandfather taught Tree the skill of bow and arrow making and how to be an exceptionally skillful marksman. Both Tree's Grandfather and Grandmother taught him to hunt and track game. Most Navajo dads taught their sons these techniques. For the most part a mother or grandmother never became involved in teaching a young man how to hunt. This was not true of Grandmother Blaine. She was even a better teacher than his Grandfather in some ways. She taught him the most subtle techniques of understanding the energy of the animal quarry, so that he could feel the instinctual response the rabbit or armadillo was experiencing. From her he learned how to read the animal's energy so he would know what the animal would do next or how to calm it down so it would not flee.

When he was young, Tree begged his Grandmother to show him where the tattoos on her arm went. She never would. He asked his Grandfather why she wouldn't. His Grandfather laughed and told him she had many tattoos and they were *waaken* and could only be experienced by others in a sacred way, never casually. Tree understood his Grandfather's explanation, but the exotic nature of her unseen tattoos added to the mystery which surrounded his Grandmother.

When he was young, Tree did not realize how much he was learning from his Grandma Blaine. He simply was following in her footsteps when he used his energy to disarm others or to walk past them without being seen. He learned her energy practices by watching her use them and then, in his most patient way, gradually experiencing how to make his energy match hers. Tree was intrigued by his Grandmother's talent and sought to learn as much as he could of her mysterious ways.

He found his ability to use his energy in certain ways worked almost everywhere, except he could not use his energy to trick his Grandfather or his teacher at the reservation one-room school house.

Like his Grandmother, the young woman, who taught him in school, seemed to understand everything he was about to do before he did it. She became his teacher when he was in the sixth grade. That was the first year she taught, having come straight to his school from a state teacher's college back east called Pembroke. Her name was Ms Locklear. She was only about five feet tall with long dark hair that hung all the way down her back, sometimes in a shower like a silky black waterfall and other times in a braid. She wore native jewelry, bright clothes and sneakers with a pink streak just above the sole. She always looked perfect to Tree.

Without him knowing it, she embodied for Tree the image of a person, like his Grandfather, who walked easily in two worlds. With her jewelry she seemed very traditional. She also knew everything about the white culture and other world cultures that she was teaching. She was not a Navajo but came from a tribe in North Carolina called Lumbee. She was sent to New Mexico by a program designed to bring bright young teachers to impoverished school districts. Unlike most teachers who came for only a year or two, Ms Locklear stayed.

Sometimes, in the sixth grade, Tree would allow himself to get caught playfully tickling the boy, who sat in the desk in front of him, or be discovered slyly drawing pictures of red-tailed hawks in his notebook, when he was supposed to be working on a lesson. He would have to stay after class for an hour and do chores for his teacher. The most thrilling part was when the class was dismissed and he would be called to her desk. Ms Locklear would look directly at Tree. He would gaze into her flashing green eyes. He had never seen anyone with eyes that color. He could feel her energy coming through her eyes and the pores of her flawless, melted-butter skin. She would tell him he must learn to behave better and he could see in her eyes that there was a mischievous side of her that was chuckling at his would-be-prankster efforts. Ms Locklear arrived in his life at a crucial time after his mother had died, and Grandmother Blaine was caught up in her own world of wrestling with the request that came out of Mother Mary's first visit, when she initially asked Blaine to come to Sweden.

In the seventh grade he became too self conscious to act out in order to have to stay after school. His schoolmates knew by then he had a crush on his teacher and would tease him mercilessly. By eighth grade, he didn't care and he would stay with two eighth grade girls to help Ms Locklear prepare lessons for the first and second graders for the next day. The three eighth graders would help teach the younger kids during breaks between their own lessons.

When it came time to catch the bus to ride eighteen miles each way to go to the ninth grade at the tribal high school, the worst part was not being able to see Ms Locklear each day. Still, he treasured the romantic notion she would not get married and that one day, when he was grown-up, he would return to the dilapidated rez school house and the trailer out behind it where the assigned teacher lived and sweep her away.

When he was in his last two years of high school, Tree often drove his Grandfather's pickup to school. This gave him the chance to go by and see his old teacher on his way home. Now that he was no longer her student, she treated him more as a friend telling him about her life.

Katrina Locklear grew up in an alcoholic family. She was born out of wedlock and her mother named her after a hurricane, because, as she frequently reminded Katrina, her birth had brought more chaos into her mother's life. Her mother eventually married her father and that was when the real chaos started. Her father when drunk, which happened almost every evening, was a rager. Katrina would rage back. She ran away from home at fifteen.

When she left home, she found a place to live with a sympathetic aunt and managed to finish high school. Her grades, initially, were not good because growing up in chaos she did not know how to focus and study; but despite these disadvantages, she was bound and determined to make her life different from the lives of her parents. She got a small scholarship to Pembroke and worked her way through college, each year getting better and better grades. After college she was accepted into Teach for America. When she was asked to choose where she wanted to go, she chose the place as far away from North Carolina as she could get. That is what brought her to New Mexico.

She did such a good job that the local school district found a way to fund her salary after her Teach for America contract expired.

She loved her work, but Tree could tell there was an emptiness in her life. Because she was so strikingly beautiful, many of the young men, who had finished high school, sought to date her. Her requirement of someone who did not drink severely limited the pool of possible suitors.

Like Tree, who had not grown up initially on the rez, who had lost his parents and had a strange grandmother, Katrina was an outsider. Most young Navajo men didn't hesitate to date white girls. It was a bit of a power play. Casually sleeping with a white girl was a form of cultural pay-back. You sure wouldn't want to marry one, but you didn't mind a bit of cultural revenge either. However, dating a native woman, who was not a Navajo, was moving in a cultural no-man's land.

Katrina confided to Tree that Navajo men simply didn't know how to relate to her. They couldn't put her in the pigeon-hole of white-girl-for-sex, nor take her seriously as a possible mate as they would a Navajo girl. Tree could read Katrina's energy and feel the bond of outsider-ness that they both shared. Because she was lonely, when Tree was in the eleventh grade, after his repeated invitations, she eventually agreed to go with Tree back to his home to have dinner with him and his Grandfather.

Manuelito and Katrina quickly developed a strong connection. Manuelito seemed delighted to have a woman around the house with an active and curious mind. He almost immediately adopted Katrina as a daughter to fill the hole he carried for his own daughter, Tree's mother, who had left home so very young, a few years before her untimely, youthful death. By the time Tree was a senior in high school, Katrina was like a member of the family. She would eat supper with them at least three times during the week and spend much of the time over weekends with her surrogate family.

Tree never went out with any girls in high school. This was partly because he was shy and introverted and partly because he never got over his childhood crush on Katrina. They would have serious conversations; and, much of the time, Tree's affection for Katrina would come out in his giving her a hard time or teasing her about something trivial. Even though Tree had become tall, slender and muscular, Tree always felt Katrina still saw him as an awkward twelve year old, who was her student in the sixth grade.

*   *   *

When it comes time for Tree to begin to work on his senior thesis his last year in high school, he goes first to Katrina to get her advice about what he should focus on.

One day after school, as the fall air is getting cooler and the sun is setting, Tree stops by his old primary school. Katrina is glad to have a visitor and they sit out behind Katrina's trailer under a brush arbor he made her.

"Tree, what are you most interested in? This senior thesis project that the high school requires now is a great opportunity for you to go beyond a school curriculum that is very rigid and delve into something that you really care about."

"I like the idea of it," replies Tree. "However, I don't quite know how to formulate my topic." He pauses. "What I am really interested in is learning about deception."

Katrina looks nonplussed. "Deception! Are you kidding me?"

"Of course, I'm kidding. You know I always kid you."

She doesn't take the bait. She can tell he is serious. "Tell me what you want to explore about deception? Why is this idea important to you?"

"Don't get mad at me. I'm not joking around now with you like I started doing. I'm interested for several reasons. Did you ever consider maybe your life is a deception? You live here and make a wonderful contribution to the kids on the rez, but somehow it is a deception, a way to avoid all the hardship you suffered when you grew up."

Katrina is amazed. However, she is used to being amazed by Tree and his insights, though it is a bit difficult hearing them when they cut to the bone of her own life.

"No, Tree, I don't think of my life as a deception." She pauses, trying to allow herself to get her mind fully around what he is saying. "Do you think your life is a deception?"

"I don't mean it in a negative way," says Tree. "In fact, I mean it in a very positive way. It is a deception that has allowed you to live and to flourish. Grandfather told me once, when I was much younger, that people who are marginalized and without power use deception as a primary coping skill. Although I don't know much about it, evidently my Grandmother Blaine was something of a master of deception when she was young in order to survive. Her being gone for the past few years is also a kind of deception I don't understand. My Grandfather, who will go to great lengths to describe anything to me, does not talk about where she went or where she is. I don't know why.

"While deception is a benefit that allows survival, it may also have a cost. The benefits and the costs, that is what I would like to explore. Grandfather has this strange idea that deception is the way Western civilization must advance now, that concentrated economic and political power is too inbred, too change-resistant to allow the next unfolding of consciousness and spiritual evolution that is necessary to save the earth, and the human species on the planet."

"Hmmm," says Katrina, taking in a long slow breath and trying to digest everything that Tree has said. "Well, if that is what you want to explore, then you should. I am sure there is research you could do on this topic. Maybe you can investigate how you think this is actually occurring right now in the lives of people you know." She pauses. "I will be here to help you in any way I can."

The sun is setting and it is getting cold. She stands up and comes toward him and he gives her his usual brotherly hug. As they release arms she looks up at him. He is now a foot taller than she is. He looks into her sparkling green eyes and feels this overwhelming desire to kiss her. Before he can even try, she turns her head. "Let's go over to your hogan. Your Grandfather will have supper on the table and be ticked if we aren't there soon."

"Thank you, Katrina, for offering to help me. Maybe this is a topic I need to live to find its truth, more than something I need to write about."

She looks directly at Tree. "That, my dear.... Oh, come on, let's go."

He realizes that she was unsure of whether to call him "dear boy" or "dear man." He turns and follows her, mesmerized simply by her movements, as he would be so often in the years to come.

Chapter 10

Blaine stands firm with Mother Mary on one point. Though her training has already taken much longer than anticipated, Blaine will not go tracking in the quantum field without being able to stay in communication with someone in linear reality.

No surprise to anyone, it is Rat who solves this problem. Voice recognition software has reached an elegant level. Rat starts with this software and adapts it to become brain neural network recognition software getting inputs from that part of the brain where language occurs. Rat's stroke of genius is to figure out a way that when Blaine is in a tracker's trance she can communicate with him through this software.

"Rat, I'm so delighted you have figured out how I can communicate with you, but two things worry me." Rat and Blaine are settled into the only comfortable chairs in the ante-room to the departure chamber where Blaine will be wired-up for her journey into the quantum field. She looks from Rat out the window to the snow falling on the meadow in front of the Swedish Convent of the Sacred Order of the Sisters of Magdala.

Rat has a way of keeping everyone's attention.

"Yes, Wonder Woman, what is it?" he says, and he wiggles his nose at her in his most rat-like imitation.

"Quit being a goof-ball. I am serious. What happens if I am on this trip and all of a sudden you decide to go for a coffee and I need some help? I mean they don't call you Dark Roast Rat in the hacking world for nothing. How will you be there 24/7 if I am gone for what seems like a week, and it is a year here?"

"Don't worry, my dear, the Rat will always be at your beck and call." Rat puts his hands under his chin and waves them up and down like two little paws.

"I'm serious, Rat. Knowing you love me almost as much as you love your newest Mac Book Pro is not an answer."

"Well, the answer is—I don't have an answer. Don't worry. Maybe you will be gone a day and it will just be a day. There are honestly so many potential problems. I don't think it would do any good to try to figure them out ahead of time. When real problems occur, you know, I am usually good at figuring out solutions."

This was absolutely true. Blaine first met Rat back in her old hacking days, which she had long since put behind her. Rat was truly a remarkably inventive hacker. She could not begin to even consider this mission if Rat—who had fallen in love with her many years earlier and then become her best friend, when she was living in Berlin—was not following her every footstep on the other end of reality. But, still...she must either go or not go. There was no way, as Rat was saying, to have completely solid answers to all the questions she had ahead of time. Or, maybe any answer.

She gazes at the bouquet of northern wolfsbane which she picked on her last walk. Somehow the delicate purple flowers from the buttercup family take her mind homeward. Suddenly, she realizes that being away from Man and Tree is making her feel a bit reckless. Part of her wants to jump in and give it a shot; that way she either gets what Mother Mary wants or not.

Regardless, she could do her bit and then get back to the Southwest where her heart wants to be—with her husband and grandson and that great blue bowl of wondrous sky.

"Okay, Ratie-pooh, let's go see Mother Mary and get this mission off the ground. She keeps telling me I am called in a way that is going to glorify God and I am sure that means all I will do is pee in my pants." She looks at Rat closely. He loves her and he loves the adventure of life, even if he prefers to have life mediated through a computer.

"You got it Princess Leah! Let's go see the Queen of Hearts."

"You better look after me better than the sorry way you mix literary allusions," she snaps, aware that her anticipatory tension is not wholly diminished by Rat's constant joking around.

"Oops, sorry about that," says Rat. "You're right. A bit over the top, referring to her Motherness as that dour monarch with a habit of lopping heads."

"Well, I should say so!" says Mother Mary, overhearing Rat's comment as she abruptly turns the corner and enters the small prep room where Blaine and Rat are talking. She quickly looks back and forth between the two. She knows Blaine's decision to go into the quantum field is almost completely dependent on her faith in Rat and his willingness to be there with Blaine no matter how long her travels might take. In leading the Order, Mother Mary has learned that faith in a divine touchstone never grows without a Sister first being able to have faith in a limited human being, whose skin she can touch and who can touch her.

Mother Mary's face breaks out in a huge smile. It is impossible for Rat to conceal any emotion he is experiencing behind his rodent facial features. He looks at Blaine with total wonder and love. If this fragile endeavor is ever to get going and have any chance of success, Mother Mary realizes it will be because, at its core, love is the glue holding it all together.

"Tomorrow morning come to my office at nine. We will do a final run down on all aspects of the mission. Then I will call the whole community together for prayer and fasting so we can all hold both of you in a good solid energetic field. Once I feel we have you securely tethered by our energy and our prayers, Blaine, then the next day the mission can begin."

Blaine looks at Mother Mary and back at Rat. Both have expressions of love and caring for her. "Okay, guys. I'm a go. I will call Man tonight."

Their eyes sparkle. Yes, they both love her. And, there is something else in that sparkle. Both have a longing for something that never can be quite named, an unquenchable thirst to be on the quest of grasping for the next rung of human consciousness. She smiles at them. *Maybe*, she thinks, *she does too.*

*   *   *

Mother Mary sits behind her sleek Danish modern desk. To Blaine it looks so un-nun like. Maybe it isn't.

"Good morning," says Mother Mary, looking at Blaine with the intense expression which always forms on her face when she is trying to ferret out exactly where another person's energy is. Mother Mary is wearing a warm, dark blue hand-knitted Norwegian sweater with random flecks of gold and white scattered across it.

Mary notes that Blaine is wearing a pale blue salwar kameez, which the Sisters had given her to celebrate her arrival at the Convent. Both she and the Sisters believe this traditional form of Punjab Indian dress would be the most comfortable clothing for Blaine's journey.

Blaine looks at Mother Mary. She is aware that there is a certain thread of anxiety in her voice. "I think I'm as ready as I will ever be," says Blaine. "I like your sweater; it is very pretty. Maybe the Swedish night sky in winter?"

Mother Mary nods. "First we must make decisions about something we have discussed a lot—where you will enter into the course of history. We discussed the possibilities of where to enter the field most when you first arrived to start your training, but with such intense focus on your energy work, we never made a decision about which historical entry point.

"I know you understand that it is our hypothesis that the consciousness gene finds expression approximately every 500 years. So in terms of recorded history, we know the starting point is with the Buddha and Pythagoras around 500 B.C. The next expression is Jesus Christ at the zero point in the way we record historical time." Mother Mary pauses. "Why is the zero point the zero point?" She refocuses. "We will save that for another time."

Blaine is impatient with Mother Mary. Her thought process habit of running interesting rabbits is not helpful to Blaine's anxiety at this point.

"The next stop in the cycle is around 500 A.D. The person in that time-frame whom we have discerned as someone who most probably experienced the expression of the consciousness gene is King Arthur.

"Next we get to the period around 1000 A.D. The person in this era who most obviously expressed the consciousness gene; well, who that person might have been is just not that obvious. This was the middle of the Dark Ages. We are still pondering which individual we should select then."

"I can understand the difficulty. Most historical threads are alternative during that era," says Blaine. Blaine had little formal education. However, because of her extensive hacking abilities she had once worked for a college professor as a research assistant. She was fond of telling others that this experience had given her a degree in alternative history. She did have a good grasp of Western history as told by the victors. However, like almost all hackers, her real interest was the alternative threads of history, which floated below the surface of the popular versions. The Internet had given new life to many alternative histories.

"The next era, around 1500 A.D., has many potential candidates, including Sir Francis Bacon and the Earl of Oxford."

"You know I never got much proper education, Mother Mary. I do know who Sir Francis Bacon was. Who was this Earl of Oxford?"

"I am sure you have heard of him by his pseudonym," says Mother Mary. "Most people know him by the name William Shakespeare."

"I have read articles discussing the fact that there is considerable controversy about who William Shakespeare was. I didn't know the controversy had been laid to rest."

"Well, it is not over for many people," says Mother Mary. "When you evaluate the possible candidates against the criteria we are using to discern expression of the consciousness gene—people who have reached levels ten or eleven on the Enneagram chart of consciousness development—then deciding William Shakespeare was the Earl of Oxford is a slam-dunk."

Blaine shrugs her shoulders. "You know I feel like I would need to read up on his plays before going back to Shakespeare's time. I mean the Earl of Oxford's. What I am most pulled to in this moment is the time of King Arthur and the time of Pythagoras. To one of these is where I would like to go to help you and the

Order in this mission to obtain evidence of the consciousness gene and what causes its expression."

Mother Mary breaks into a smile. Blaine is touched. The task of running the Order, and the stressful challenges before it, had molded the muscles around Mother Mary's mouth into a certain sternness. Blaine is glad to see that beneath her stern expression is playful animation. Blaine thinks, *it's probably going to take both— all of Mother Mary's strength and determination, as well as some playfulness, for me to make this journey and get back. I'm glad she has both.*

"You know Blaine, we had not thought about Pythagoras's time as being an option because it is so far, back and we have believed that the expressions of the consciousness gene might have more clarity after Jesus' magnificent expression of them." She pauses, then continues.

"Pythagoras is a most interesting choice. Interestingly, he is connected to the time of King Arthur. One of Arthur's great achievements was to hold both Christianity and the Celtic religion of Druidism in a non-dual way; that is, he did not use one to exclude some part of the other. The Druids were not so much an organized religion as they were an order of priestesses and priests who sought to facilitate an intimate connection to the land. The Druids orchestrated rituals that were important to participate in to celebrate the renewal and regeneration of the seasons.

"Pythagoras was a native of the Greek island of Samos. He later moved to Croton in southern Italy, where he started a mystery school, a school to help initiate people into higher consciousness."

"In some ways," Blaine interjects, "that would be like the school you and the other Sisters run here at this Convent in northern Sweden."

"Well, I guess you could say that," said Mother Mary. "Let me continue to unwind this connection a bit further."

"Pythagoras is known for his work in mathematics and for his belief in metempsychosis, the doctrine of the transmigration of souls. Tradition mentions the conversation of one Abaris the Hyperborean—that is the Briton, one living beyond Boreas, the home of the North Wind—with Pythagoras. The suggestion is that Abaris, a Druid scholar, brought to Greece and Italy by Phoenician sailors, studied at Pythagoras' mystery school. Hecateus, an historian, who was a contemporary of Pythagoras writes about that land inhabited by the Hyperboreans—the Britons—and refers to the 'remarkable temple, of a round form' referring to Stonehenge. He also mentions Abaris traveling to the Mediterranean and the Britons' awareness of the nineteen year cycle of the lunar calendar—the period of rotation required for the lunar and solar calendars to precisely align."

"Mother Mary, can you get to the bottom-line, here?" asks Blaine.

"Yes, this is so terribly interesting to me, though maybe not to everyone." She straightens in her chair as if to re-assert her focus over what she is trying to explain to Blaine.

"I guess the bottom-line is that Druidic ideas contain the same core as those taught by Pythagoras. Both believed in an idea of moral cause and effect, and that a person comes into life carrying the gifts and burdens accumulated by himself and those of his tribe before him. We have much the same idea in Christianity, that the sins of the father are visited on the sons for generations. At the time of Pythagoras and the Buddha this was a relatively new idea. It was also, at that time, an idea of the Druids.

"The second core idea for Pythagoras was that the entire universe is charged with number. He said, 'All things are assimilated in number.' The philosophical implications of this idea is that there is a truth which is ineffable and transcendental. Mathematics becomes the source of belief in eternal and exact truth, which can be conceived of as God's thoughts.

"Central to Druidic thought are these two core Pythagorean ideas: the doctrine of metempsychosis and the centrality of mathematics as seen in calendrical propriety. I recommend you go back to the time of King Arthur, and in doing so you are indirectly getting the opportunity to understand the Druid heritage which is connected to Pythagoras, and you would also be seeing an early Celtic Christian heritage expressed in Arthur. In other words, if Pythagoras represents part of the first expression of the consciousness gene and Jesus the second expression, then both these threads are current in Arthur, who we suspect represents the third manifestation of the five hundred year cycle of consciousness gene expression.

"Let's meet back here first thing in the morning and we can go over some of the known history about King Arthur. Rat may not have a great degree of accuracy as to exactly where we can insert your consciousness in the space time continuum. Rat compares this part of our effort to shooting a rocket up to land a payload on one of Mar's moons. In the great field of consciousness there are many moving parts. The only thing for sure is that there is nothing that is not in motion."

"Okay, then I will see you in the morning," says Blaine. She starts toward the door then turns back toward Mother Mary. "Phobos or Deimos?"

Mother Mary laughs. "Obviously, you have been spending too much time talking with Rat about all this. Leave it to him to be the one who knows the names of Mar's two moons."

Blaine does not laugh. "So I guess he also told you what the names of the two moons mean?"

Mother Mary shakes her head *no*.

Blaine opens her mouth to speak and words do not come out. She swallows. "Fear and Terror."

Mother Mary's upbeat expression dissolves into a kind of anguish.

"Yes, that is right. Fear and Terror." Blaine turns and strides down the hallway.

Chapter 11

Mother Mary's usually clean blonde slab of a desk is littered with books and images, of knights in glistening armor and green fields with rock wall fences. A wilted bouquet of bluish-purple northern wolfsbane, which Blaine picked and gave her several days ago, rests in a jam jar in the center of it all.

"Good morning, Blaine. I hope you rested well last night," says Mother Mary with a wisp of hopefulness in her voice. She had seen Blaine in the back of the chapel at morning prayers looking as if she had pulled an all-nighter. Blaine is still wearing the pale blue salwar kameez she had on the day before. It is very wrinkled.

"Like a cat chasing a restless moon. But thanks for asking."

Mother Mary picks up a note pad. She tucks a wisp of her gray hair behind her ear. She is not the kind of person to spend much time talking about how anyone else is feeling much less herself.

"Arthur is a fascinating figure. He lived three generations after the Romans, who ruled Britain for several hundred years, left in 410 AD. Like many of the people that we have studied for expressions of the consciousness gene, there are unusual stories about Arthur's parentage and birth. Arthur's father was Meurig, Prince of Morgannwg and Gwent in Wales. He was also head of the British forces under King Ambrosius. As head of the British forces, he bore the title Uthyr Pendragon, which means

Wonderful Dragon Head. Geoffrey of Monmouth, one of the early historians of Britain, describes accession to the throne of Britain of Arthur, the son of Uthyr Pendragon, as coinciding with the appearance of a comet:

There appeared a star of great magnitude and brilliance, with a single beam shining from it. At the end of this beam was a ball of fire, spread out in the shape of a dragon. From the dragon's mouth stretched forth rays of light, one of which seemed to extend its length beyond the latitude of Gaul, while the second turned towards the Irish Sea and split into seven smaller shafts of light.

This star appeared three times, and all who saw it were struck with fear and wonder.

"The appearance of this comet is recorded in the Anglo-Saxon Chronicle as taking place in A.D. 497. This is the year Arthur, age fifteen, was nominated by King Ambrosius to follow him as King of Britain. During his minority Arthur was aided in his reign by King Ambrosius brother, Uther.

"King Ambrosius' brother, Uther, displayed courage and bravery in opposing the Saxons who were, since the Romans left, continually pressuring and overrunning the native Britons. In 506, Uther was slain, along with 5000 of his men, in a battle with the Saxons on Dragon Hill near Uffington Camp in Berkshire.

"After the death of Uther, King Arthur began to rule in his own right. He also became head of all the British forces, becoming the Pendragon and adopting the dragon pennant as a battle flag. Purple dragons had adorned the standards of the Roman legions since the time of Augustus. Arthur would become the most courageous and victorious 'Wonderful Dragon Head.'"

"Arthur's name is interesting. In the Welsh language Arth Fawr means the 'Great Bear.' This name was associated with the two constellations called Ursa Major and Ursa Minor, and Arcturus is a star near the tail of the Great Bear."

Blaine shakes her head. "This is not exactly what I need to know, is it?"

Mother Mary pauses and looks directly at Blaine. "Unfortunately, Blaine, there is no amount of information we can give you that will be more than you need to know. The reason this historical overview is so important is that, once you are back there, some shred of this information I am giving you may assist you putting together clues. For now be assured that those naming Arthur, like all of those who understand perennial wisdom, would have named him in the context of a spiritual understanding that believed in 'as above so below.' The virtue of this view is that 'the above' gives us a picture not only of how the celestial universe works, but also a reflection of how life works at a subatomic level. The very level you are entering this story."

"Huh?" says Blaine. "You mean the reason it was important for the ancients to be watching the night sky is because it not only helped them understand the solar system, but it also gave them a template to understand how consciousness, or prayer, or anything that operates on the non-linear basis of subatomic reality works?"

"Bingo, you have got it," says Mother Mary. Her smile slowly disappears as she turns serious. "The reason we think you have a chance to enter an alternative reality not bound by linear time is because we and those who named Arthur, probably Merlin, have the same view of the universe that caused Arthur to be named after a star."

"Jesus," says Blaine, muttering under her breath. "Sorry, Mother."

"Arcturus got its name from its proximity to the Great Bear constellation and from being one of the brightest stars in the sky.

Literally it means Guardian of the Bear. The Great Bear constellation, Ursa Major, is also called the Big Dipper. This is the constellation which has from pre-history helped humankind know the direction of north and use the night sky as an instrument of navigation whether on land or sea.

"So King Arthur's name is linked to both celestial guidance and guardianship. What we know about his life supports the thesis his life was about those same qualities. Whether or not he was born under the sign of a star, being named after one may be even better."

"Okay, okay," says Blaine. "Where do you want me to get involved in all this?"

"Good question. We know he became King of Britain in 497, while still a minor. By the time he was ruling on his own in 506, he had his work cut out for him. His predecessors had been killed by the Saxons. Much of Arthur's reign would be spent leading the indigenous Britons in battle against the invading Saxons. There he proved that he was a great warrior-king. In Nennius's *Historia Brittonum*, Arthur is referred to as 'Arthur the Warrior.'"

"What makes you think that a man who was such a great warrior would also have a high level of consciousness? Seems like just the opposite might be true," interjects Blaine.

"Good question. Honestly, we don't know. One of the criteria for selecting someone to determine if their DNA reflects that they did express the consciousness gene is that he or she demonstrate the ability in their thinking to bring together both sides of the human brain." Mother Mary stops.

"Let me back up. Most historical world religions emerged after the first axial turning, which occurred around the time of the Buddha, Pythagoras and Plato. The first expression of the consciousness gene occurred when human beings began to conceptualize and think abstractly about themselves and religion. We had the emergence of the rational mind. Yet as human rationality broke on the scene, the Greeks kept all of their gods and mythic stories, which provided a web of meaning to everyday life. So what we have discovered is that the expression of the consciousness gene occurs in a person who is able to hold in a non-dual way the rational and the mythic, or a neuroscientist might say has an integration of the functions of the left and right sides of the brain.

"For spiritual awareness to blossom, which occurs when the consciousness gene is expressed, there must be anchoring in the mythic and the non-rational which opens a person into an intuitive sense of wholeness and at the same time critical rationality which keeps a person honest and humble about what he or she really knows. King Arthur seems to have integrated the mythic ideas of the Druids and also had the rational battle planning ability that is necessary for a great warrior to succeed. Beyond that, our prayers and, indeed, a vision of one of the Sisters strongly suggests that if the consciousness gene expressed itself around 500 A.D., then Arthur is our guy." She raises her hands in a gesture of uncertainty.

"A wing and a prayer, huh!" Blaine looks pensive. "Guess even what defines the meaning of the expression of the consciousness gene is another answer I am supposed to bring back," says Blaine, as much to herself as Mother Mary.

"Just because he was a famous warrior-king does not mean he was an uneducated man. As best as we can discern from historical fragments, Arthur was educated at St Illtyd's famous monastic college at Llanilltyd (Llantwit Major) in Wales. Later, he continued his education as a secular priest under an abbot named Carentmael at Bodmin, which lay within the principality of Gelliwig (Callington) in Cornwall. This area was under the jurisdiction of Count Gwythian where he must have met

Gwythian's sister, Gwenhwyfar, whom Arthur married. You know Arthur's wife by her anglicized name, Guinevere."

Blaine nods her head, *yes*.

"In his *History of the Britons*, Nennius records that Arthur fought twelve famous battles and won all of them. The first six battles were fought in the area that is currently Lincolnshire. Historians assume these battles were against the Angles of Lindsey. Arthur probably had his forces based at Lincoln where there was an abandoned Roman fort. During the time of the Romans, Lincoln was an important nexus for commerce. The Romans connected it to the sea via a system of canals, the longest of which was forty-eight kilometers and was built during the reign of Nero. Arthur would have gotten to Lincoln along a Roman road which later became known as the Ermine Way. The road most likely became known as the Ermine Way in memory of Arthur's sixth century expedition. Ermin being a variant of the name Ermel or Armel. Armel is the six century Breton version of the name Arthur.

"Arthur ruled Britain as a Celt and as one who followed in a long line of British Roman governors. Much of his success in battle was due to his use of fast-moving cavalry modeled after his Roman predecessors. The Romans, during their 400 year occupation of Britain, constructed more than 6000 miles of roads. Because the Roman road system was still largely intact during Arthur's reign, it was far easier for him and his forces to move about his kingdom than it would be centuries later during Norman times, or for that matter at any time during the eighteenth century. His next battles illustrate this. Battles seven and eight were fought north of Hadrian's Wall against the Picts. Nennius gives a more detailed description of one of these battles," says Mother Mary, picking up a book from the pile of them on her desk and starting to read:

Arthur carried the image of the holy Mary, the everlasting virgin, on his *shoulder (*meaning on his shield*) and the pagans were put to flight that day and there was a great slaughter upon them, through the power of our Lord Jesus and the power of the holy Mary, His mother.*

"Popular legend about Arthur emphasizes his Celtic roots and Druidic tutelage under Merlin. Perhaps there was uneasiness within him between Celtic Druidic practices and Christianity, but like his Roman predecessors the description of this battle suggests his clear Christian allegiance and lack of tension between being a Druidic Celt and a Christian."

"Hold on just a minute," says Blaine. "You don't expect me to remember the names and places of these battles do you? What would be the purpose of that?"

"You are right, Blaine," says Mother Mary. "What is important is for you to have some sense of the constant warfare which occupied his reign and most significantly his long running string of successes."

"Okay, I think I have the general idea," says Blaine. "So go ahead and do a wrap on the battles."

Mother Mary sighs. *I am just so sure this detail is important,* she thinks. *I really don't know why, and I understand Blaine's frustration.*

"Yes, I'm just getting ready to wrap up this history of Arthur's battles. His ninth battle was closer to home probably near Carelon in Wales. The tenth battle was also located near the River Severn. This battle is of particular importance to us because it suggested to others at the time that Arthur had supernatural powers, or what we would more simply define as access in a conscious way to the energetic field of the life force outside of himself.

"The tenth battle was a Moses-like crossing of the Red Sea experience. Arthur maneuvered the opposing force into a position on the battlefield and then blocked escape. A phenomena known as the Severn Tidal Bore then destroyed his enemy. Arthur, like a few who experience this gift in modern times, had a preternatural sense of when the tidal wave was coming and used this knowledge to defeat his enemy.

"Though he continued to be victorious, the fighting moved closer to home. The eleventh battle was probably at Catbrain Hill near Bristol in Avon. It was a warm-up for his last great victory for the kingdom of Britain, the battle of Badon. Gildas, a sixth-century historian, says that in this battle the Saxons suffered a crushing defeat such that there followed a fifty years period of peace. Nennius is explicit about the exploits of the warrior-king." Mother Mary turns the page of the book she has before her and reads:

The Twelfth battle was on Mons Badonis, where in one day nine hundred and sixty men were killed by one attack of Arthur and no one save himself laid them low.

"Here is Geoffrey of Monmouth's account," she says, picking up another book:

Then they (the Saxons) proceeded by a forced march to the neighborhood of Bath and besieged the town.... Arthur put on a leather jerkin worthy of so great a king. On his head he placed a golden helmet, with a crest carved in the shape of a dragon; and across his shoulders a circular shield called Pridwen, on which there was painted a likeness of the blessed Mary, Mother of God, which forced him to be thinking perpetually of her.

Arthur drew up his men in companies and then bravely attacked the Saxons, who as usual were arrayed in wedges. All that day they resisted the Britons bravely, although the latter launched attack upon attack.... When the greater part of the day had passed in this way, Arthur went berserk, for he realized that things were still going well for the enemy and that victory for his own side was not yet in sight. He drew his sword Caliburn, called upon the Blessed Virgin and rushed forward at full speed into the thickest ranks of the enemy. Every man whom he struck, calling upon God as he did so, he killed at a single blow. He did not slacken his onslaught until he had dispatched 470 with his sword Caliburn. When the Britons saw this they poured after him in close formation, dealing death on every side.

"You have to be kidding, or I mean whoever you are reading must be off the mark. Killed four hundred seventy people?" Blaine looks aghast.

"However many of the enemy Arthur dispatched personally, the twelfth battle, a short distance outside of Bath, was the pinnacle of his warrior-king career. Peace did follow in Britain for a time. However, peace was cut short by a thirteenth battle at a place known as Camlan.

"There is much historical dispute about where exactly Camlan was, though it is obviously somewhere along the River Camlan. Arthur's adversary was Mordred, and from accounts it appears that Mordred and his troops were in a fixed position and that perhaps Arthur walked into an ambush. Who Mordred was is also much debated. Legend has him as Arthur's son by his own sister. The best historical detective work suggests that he was Medraut the son of Cawrdaf ap Caradog Freichfras. Cawrdaf was King Arthur's chief adviser or prime minister. Cawrdaf's son Medraut was married to Gwenhwyfach, who was the sister to Gwenhwyfar. So probably Arthur's foe at this final battle was the son of his chief adviser, and also his brother-in-law—an intimate betrayal of Arthur.

"The clash was precipitated by a power vacuum when Arthur went to Ireland to deal with the Irish warlord, Llwch Wyddel, and left his government in the hands of his brother-in-law. Arthur took a large company of men to Ireland where his forces met Llwch's army. Many men were lost on both sides and Arthur killed Llwch. Evidently, when Medraut heard that Arthur's army was greatly diminished he took this opportunity to seize power. Arthur upon learning of this treason brought the remnant of his army back to Wales. He landed his forces on the far west coast of Wales where he met Medraut and his forces. Many brave warriors were killed on both sides. The battle came to an end when Arthur slew Medraut. Arthur himself was badly wounded. Arthur turned his reign over to a regent; then later he abdicated his throne."

Mother Mary stops her narrative. She looks at Blaine. Blaine seems to have been following her; however, she does not look fully present. The Welsh names were hard to understand, much less to remember.

"This is where, or rather when, we want you to intercede back into history. At this point, after Arthur has killed Medraut, or Mordred, as he is best known."

Blaine shakes her head, either in disagreement about something specifically or just to generally contest the notion that somehow she could, through access to the quantum field, go back into these events.

Mother Mary does not know what Blaine means. Mother Mary waits.

Blaine finally speaks, "Like Rat said, we might as well be trying to hit one of the Martian moons. But getting me there is your job, right?"

"It is all of our jobs," says Mother Mary. "However, you can't get there if you don't know where you are going."

"Sorry, Mother Mary, I am just tired and anxious and frankly all this early history of the Britons is a bit boring to me. What happens next to Arthur after he kills Mordred?"

"That is just it, Blaine. That is what we want you to find out. Legend has it that he went to the mystical isle of Avalon to recover. Avalon is the Celtic Druidic metaphor for going into the quantum field. If he could do this, he probably really is our guy, the man who in the first turning since Christ of the five hundred year cycle expressed the consciousness gene. Hopefully, you will be able to find out and tell us."

"You know what I can tell you is that I need to take a nap. Or, even better, a good night's sleep. Can we see where we are about getting this mission going in the morning?"

As forceful as Mother Mary is, she has no choice except to let Blaine call the shots. Blaine is, after all, putting her very life on the line.

"Okay, see you tomorrow after morning prayers."

Blaine gets up and walks down the corridor and makes her way to her room. She enters, closes the door and without taking off her salwar kameez tumbles into bed. She is exhausted. Despite feeling bone-weary, for the next hour she tosses and turns. Her mind keeps returning to Man and her grandson Tree. When she focuses on an image of them in her imagination, she feels they are trying to tell her something. Finally she sleeps.

*   *   *

Blaine yawns as she walks into the "departure room." Above the door is a hand-lettered sign *Avalon*.

"*Liebste, wie geht es dir?*" says the ever cheerful Rat.

"Not bad," says Blaine, having long ago gotten used to Rat's lapses into German and the meaning of his most common expressions, which revolve around telling her he adores her and asking her how she is.

"Wonderful," replies Mother Mary to no one in particular,

having never been asked how she is doing. She is not looking so wonderful. Her chin is sternly set.

"Wow, you guys have gotten me quite a setup here," says Blaine, glancing around the room and taking in the soft foam topper covering a hospital bed, a stand for a sterile drip and a virtual bird's nest of wires going to several computer consoles set up on a table right next to the bed.

"Once you are wired up," says Mother Mary, "Rat will induce a trance using the tape we played for you last week. Your induction should not take long. Then we…."

"I know," interrupts Blaine. "We have already been through all this before. Let's go. I got my salwar kameez laundered special for the occasion."

Indeed, Blaine looks better than she did the day before. Soon she is lying back comfortably in the bed, and there are wires running to all parts of her body. Rat is monitoring all her physical signs and particularly her brain waves. Around her forehead, above her prefrontal cortex, is a headdress of wires, which are the literal location of the nexus for Blaine to communicate with Rat about what she is experiencing. Rat is using this communication channel now to tease Blaine, as he always is doing verbally, through his direct connection into her brain.

"Quit pestering me," says Blaine aloud. "No, I will not have sex with anyone in the sixth century no matter what the circumstances."

Mother Mary, who is usually put off by Rat's constant joking around, is glad to see it having its usual effect of causing Blaine to relax. She reads the screen with the physical signs information. Blaine is quickly going into a state of deep relaxation.

"Looks like we are about ready for launch, Your Motherness," says Rat after a review of all the vital signs data and the flow of direct brain communication. "Shall we rock and roll?"

Mother Mary smiles in spite of herself. She nods her head *yes*.

Rat flips the switch to start the software program which will create in Blaine's mind an intention to go into the quantum field at the time just after King Arthur's battle with Mordred. He has no idea whether this has any chance to work. At least he feels sure that whatever happens he will be able to communicate with Blaine in the quantum field. He looks at Mother Mary. Her lips are moving. Well, prayer couldn't hurt, he thinks, since it was through studying how prayer works that he first developed an idea of how to access the quantum field.

A loud click startles Rat and Mother Mary. They look across the room where a printer has started up, then at each other. Neither expects Blaine to be anywhere near the sixth century this quick. Rat's brain/voice software is designed to turn her experience into a narrative that he can listen to and that will printout as the narrative unfolds.

Rat beats Mother Mary to the printer. He pulls the first sheet out of the bin. There is nothing except a row of nonsense characters across the page. He hands it to Mother Mary and quickly returns to his computer station and puts his headphones back on.

After a single printed page, nothing.

*   *   *

Six hours pass. Mother Mary goes out and comes back with cheese and crackers for Rat.

"What do you think is happening?" asks Mother Mary.

"I haven't a clue," says Rat. "All I know is that physically she is fine. She is probably more rested right now than when she first came in the room this morning. I don't know if the reason we are getting no communication is because she decided not to tell us anything, the brain/voice software communication is not working properly or she got there and decided to take a nap."

"Or, she is wandering around in some bardo?"

Rat nods his head in agreement. This was Mother Mary's biggest fear and so the thing she talked about least.

Rat has no qualms talking about anything. "Not like there are many sign posts out there in the quantum field. Go three miles ahead and the sixth century will be on your right. Look for an inn with a sign advertising bedbugs and hair lice."

"Maybe we ought to bring her back," says Mother Mary. "I am really worried."

"If it is not one thing, its a mother," mumbles Rat, under his breath and just loud enough for Mother Mary to hear him.

Mother Mary remains solemn.

"It's your call, your Motherness,"says Rat. "I assure you she is okay physically in our linear time. I don't know why we haven't had any communication from her."

"You know we were hoping that given the different time frames that she might be able to do this whole thing in a few hours. Let's bring her back."

"Will do," says Rat and he starts up the program he designed to bring her out of her trance.

Chapter 12

Navajo Nation
Southwestern United States
Fall 2014

Manuelito wakes with a start. The dream was powerful. Not since his Vision Quest as a young man has a dream experience shaken him in such a powerful way.

Even after acquiring the fundamentals to anchor himself in this world—fresh air and hot black coffee—he cannot get past his two strong emotional responses: *well of course* and *no way*.

He puts both feet up on the rock in front of him beside a small bouquet of bright yellow-faced desert marigolds gathered by Tree the day before, drains his coffee mug and lets his head rest on the back of his chair. The sky begins to lighten. High above wispy cirrus clouds become distinct. He chuckles. Another confirmation. As if to tell him the *no way* thought does not deserve consideration.

Tree sticks his head out of the hogan. With a blanket wrapped around himself to ward off the early morning chill, he walks over to where his Grandfather sits.

"What are you looking at?" asks Tree, his head arching back to follow his Grandfather's gaze.

"What do you see?" asks Manuelito.

"I don't see anything...well, yeah, it looks like, high in the sky, a cloud-horse and that it is going backwards."

Tree looks at his Grandfather. The usual twinkle is in his Grandfather's eyes and he also looks unusually serious. Most mornings being outside at dawn with a cup of coffee puts his Grandfather in a light-hearted mood.

"What do you see, Grandfather?" asks Tree.

A few long minutes went by. "I see that your Grandmother is up to no good." He grunts. "Maybe good. Who knows. She wants us to travel with her."

"Where does she want to go?" asks Tree, who since childhood has always especially relished any outing with his grandparents.

"That is the problem," says Manuelito. "You have been asking me, while your Grandmother has been gone, where she is and I have done my best to avoid answering. In the native tradition it would not be auspicious for me to talk out loud about someone traveling in the dreamtime. That cat is out of the bag now. She came in a dream to me last night and said that she wants you and me to join her on this dreamtime quest she is on."

Manuelito stops talking and gazes upwards again. Tree waits respectfully for his Grandfather to continue.

"I hardly get settled in my chair with a cup of coffee, and I happen to gaze upwards, and to my amazement there it is, as you described, an image of a horse going backwards. You and your friend Katrina probably learned about these horses in all those online courses you are always taking."

Tree feels his face starting to flush at the mention of Katrina's name. To avoid intensity of feelings about her he interjects a question. "I am not sure that we have. We have studied a little meteorology, so we know the names of the major cloud formations. Nothing about cloud horses," says Tree, looking puzzled.

"I am talking about prehistoric cave paintings. If you look at certain of them closely, you will see that the motion is of the horse going backwards. It is an image of the horse, our instinctual being, taking the spiritual warrior back into the dreamtime. You don't need a saddle." Manuelito looks inquisitively at Tree.

As usually happens with his instruction of Tree in spiritual matters and native perspective, Tree quickly comprehends the ideas Manuelito is teaching him.

"I understand, Grandfather. Are we going?" asks Tree.

"That is the startling question I am trying to get my arms around, young man. I don't mind undertaking such an adventure, if your Grandmother insists on it; however, I am frankly astounded that she thinks you should come, and she says to bring Two as well! We might as well take the whole rez. My first thought is that the idea is totally crazy, that she is into the Swedish communion wine."

"I didn't know that Navajo did dreamtime travel, Grandfather."

"Good point, Tree. We don't have a public tradition which talks about this. The truth of the matter is that all native people throughout the centuries have, from time to time, had shamen who were able to go into the dreamtime. Often this is done by following song-lines, which is akin to what some of our traditional Singers do. Not that shamans, like anyone else, can't get confused. This is confusing stuff. There was a Paiute Indian prophet named Wovoka, who, back around 1889, had a vision about the coming of the Kingdom for Indian people, and he urged them to do the Ghost Dance in preparation. Many thought the Ghost Dance would protect them from the white man's bullets. The result was disastrous. Yes, they were protected in the quantum field, as that is the nature of its non-materiality, where they went in their visions while Ghost Dancing. Their mistake was confusing their experience in the field with linear reality. Many were shot and killed.

"The Kingdom of God is here and now as Wovoka said. Again, however, it must be accessed by having a level of consciousness and capacity for being present that allows us to participate in the wisdom of the field. This is what the perspective of being born again means—giving up the old way of thinking, thinking that linear reality is all there is. Conversion of the old false self energy into a new higher level of consciousness is what leads to this new understanding of linear reality where, for the most part, we live. With the new perspective, we experience that our everyday linear experience is constantly underpinned by this other greater reality, the quantum field which supports it.

"We Navajo have always been a practical people. Our way of living and the stark natural beauty of the Southwest constantly remind us of the other reality beneath linear reality. What I am trying to say is that there is not a public Navajo tradition of accessing the dreamtime as a people. Like most tribes we often have spiritual guides, or shamans, who have a gift for this sort of travel in the quantum field.

"My experience with the dreamtime is limited. I have been in it before. It is not like I am a shaman who actively practices entering the dreamtime, as is often done by healers to find out how to help heal a patient. Your Grandmother Blaine simply thinks I can do anything." He smiles at Tree. Actually, I would much rather stalk a prairie rabbit than something in the quantum field."

"I am very excited, Grandfather. When do we leave?"

"Tree, I am not sure you are hearing me correctly. I said your Grandmother wants us to join her. I don't know if that is a good idea. Or whether we can. I will have to open up the prayer channel to get guidance, to see if this is a good idea, if this is *waaken* for us.

"Ironically, I will need to access the field to find out if we should go to the field."

Manuelito shakes his head wearily. "Moreover, we would have to get someone to look after us while we were in the dreamtime. Might have to ask our friend Katrina. What would you think of that?"

Tree blushes again before he can begin to speak.

Manuelito continues. "It is kind of intimate. As we have been discussing, the field does not run on linear time. Someone has to hold your arm and take you to the bathroom if you need to go. You need to have bodily functions without coming all the way out of the dreamtime state until whatever the encounter with the field is about is concluded. Does that give you second thoughts?"

"Certainly not. If you don't care, I don't either."

"Of course you care." Manuelito chuckles. "However, you wouldn't be enough in linear reality to be embarrassed, so there are some positives."

"I wouldn't mind, regardless," says Tree fiercely.

Manuelito smiles at his grandson. He has grown tall and he is strong with great endurance. "Let's get Katrina over to dinner tonight. We can see if she is going to be around enough to be available to help out. If she can't, we will have to figure out someone else. We will do this practical stuff and at the same time I will take a long hike today up our Brother Mountain." He gestures toward the Sangre de Cristo Mountains. I know about a peak where just being there takes you quickly to a dreamtime perspective. It is a good place for me to get answers."

Tree nods. He notes how quickly his Grandfather's perspective on making an important decision shifts from a personal reference to getting the participation of a larger reality. He looks at his Grandfather with awe.

"Well, get a move on. Take the pickup and go ask Katrina if she can come this evening. And figure out some decent food while you are out. I am getting tired of sardines and saltines. Regardless of whether she is able to help, we need to show our gratitude to her."

Tree knows that his Grandfather is giving permission for Tree to make something special for dinner. They will have corn cakes and cactus tea, and he will go over to the San Juan River and see if he can catch a couple of trout for dinner.

He is out the door and off in the pickup before his grandfather can give more instructions.

Chapter 13

Sacred Order of the Sisters of Mary of Magdala Convent
Northern Sweden
Fall 2014

Blaine has been back in linear reality for a few hours. Her pale blue salwar kameez is barely wrinkled. Mother Mary is in a huge stew over her request. It takes an hour for Mother Mary to realize that Blaine is not asking Mother Mary to bring Manuelito and Tree to Sweden and have them all wired up like she is as a traveler into the quantum field. Then it takes another hunk of time for it to sink in that Manuelito and Tree can go back on the space/time continuum in the quantum field on their own, as native shamans have done for centuries. Finally, Rat confronts Mother Mary with the reality that if Blaine wants Manuelito and Tree to accompany her and they can access on their own the place in the field Blaine would be, well there is nothing Mother Mary can do about it one way or the other, so she might as well consent to Blaine's request.

Daylight is already starting to seem markedly shorter and there is a foreboding dreariness in the air as Mother Mary looks out her office window where she, Rat and Blaine have been talking for well over an hour. "Okay, Blaine, I don't particularly like the idea. But, I guess I am on board," says Mother Mary.

"I always liked traveling on the family plan," says Rat, who, as far as anyone knows, has no family at all. He scrunches his nose and wiggles it at both of them.

Mother Mary looks at Rat and grimaces. Rat wiggles his nose some more.

"Thanks, I don't want to do this without Manuelito and Little Tree," says Blaine. "However, the biggest problem is not that I want my family along, which I do. The biggest problem is I can't understand the language. What they are thinking is usually coherent to me when their thoughts are without words, but most of the time what they think is in words and, of course, their speech is words. What they are saying is a foreign language to me."

Mother Mary is nonplussed. She is without any idea of how to deal with this language problem. In all her planning, this was something she had never anticipated. Now it is patently obvious.

"You did a good job on the insertion, Rat," says Blaine. "I really didn't know what to expect. I guess I was worried I might become this other person. I did not, but I was there in her reflective consciousness, that part of us which allows us to be conscious of what we experience. It seemed quite natural to be there since reflective consciousness is not experienced as local anyway.

"I seemed to have gotten there right after the battle with Mordred. One of King Arthur's warriors who had been wounded was being taken somewhere to be treated and was going on and on about *sard* this and *sard* that. I understood the meaning of what he was saying. Some things don't seem to have changed much over the last 1500 years, at least not when it comes to cursing."

Rats eyes brighten. "Yes, Mother Mary, this is a pretty sardy problem." He wiggles his nose side to side.

"See that is exactly what I mean about the difficulty of understanding what is being said," quips Blaine. "Not the *s* word, but the *f* word."

"Actually," says Rat, "in German, using this word not as a noun or adjective but as an interjection, it could be either one."

"Really," says Blaine. She did love Rat.

"Yes, you English speakers are so limited in your profanity. German is much more versatile. However, you are right, I guess. Sardy would be an adjective. But, I am not about to give up on helping you English speakers. We could call this whole problem a *diffuckculty*." Rat looks at Mother Mary. She glares back.

Rat is unfazed. "Mother Mary, the problem would not be all that difficult if we had a sixth century English language guide. In that case I could develop software that could do an instantaneous translation for Blaine. Medieval English like we find in the Canterbury Tales is late fourteenth century. It is possible with much guessing to work out what is meant when you read it. Listening to it spoken—impossible for a modern person to understand it. There is a 950 A.D. translation of the Lindisfarne Gospels, but that is worse. The reality is there are not any good examples of sixth century English."

"You are so amazing," says Blaine, "you were already on it."

"All this work, all the time we have devoted to this project and I never thought of this barrier. It seems impossible to overcome." Mother Mary sighs deeply. Tears well up in her eyes.

"Never fear, the Rat is on the job. I don't know what the answer is, and I will find one." He puffs out his chest and beams at Blaine. As usual he is dressed all in black, but he picks up a yellow magic marker from the desk in front of him and begins to etch a bolt of lightning across his chest.

"You have not changed one iota since we first met all those years ago," says Blaine. "I love your irreverent optimism. Mother Mary, if there is anyone who can figure out this problem, it is Rat. You know that."

Mother Mary nods, her eyes remain downcast.

"Maybe this is going to be a *black swan*," says Rat, almost to himself, referring to the idea that there are certain events which occur that are both unexpected and highly consequential.

"Here is the angle I started working on this morning. There are no good examples of sixth century British English. However, there is a good example of sixth century British Latin. There is a priest, who favored the monastic tradition, which was becoming more prevalent then, named Gildas. He wrote a history of Britain's kings. The history was in Latin not English. I am thinking that the language of King Arthur's Court would be Latin. These people were just a couple generations removed from the Roman occupation of Britain that went on for centuries. Arthur, you have indicated, was educated. Education must have been in Latin since that is the language in which almost all the books of the time were written. Were you able to penetrate King Arthur's thought field, Blaine?"

"No," says Blaine. "All I heard were the totally indecipherable comments of a common soldier."

Rat beams. "That is what I thought. As a well educated man, Arthur would probably even think in Latin. Anyway, I am working on an instantaneous voice translation software to convert classical Latin from that era into modern English."

"Oh, you are wonderful, Rat," says Blaine and she gets up from where she is sitting and comes over and gives him a hug.

Mother Mary looks up from her chair. Her face clears. "Rat, you are rather amazing, a divine blessing."

"I am not good at receiving so much adulation," says Rat, clearly basking in Blaine's affection and Mother Mary's grudging approval. "I will get back to work. And, Mother, if you wish to help out a bit, I could use a medium size hunk of gorgonzola and a few crackers. A Rat with a snack is a happy Rat, indeed."

He wrinkles his nose again at Mother Mary. This time she smiles. "Yes, anything else your Ratness wants?" she replies, mimicking him back.

"Careful your Nunness, I take humor theft very seriously. Things could get very *sardy* around here."

"As if they aren't already," says Mother Mary, rising from her chair and heading toward the door. She squeezes Blaine's hand on her way out and turns toward Rat. "Your cheese will be coming right up."

After Mother Mary leaves, Blaine motions for Rat to sit down again. Then she sits in front of him. She bends her head toward him.

"Rat, I am intrigued by the *black swan* notion in the context of what we are trying to do. Tell me more about what you mean by what you said. My brief experience of being in someone else's reflective consciousness gave me a lightning bolt awareness of how important it is for us all to experience our lives through the lens of our reflective consciousness and not simply through the patterned ways our ego filters our perceptions."

He nods, and, for Rat, rather remarkably refrains from trying to distract Blaine with his constant efforts to make everything something to laugh about. "As I said, a *black swan* is an event that is not anticipated, then in hindsight is extraordinarily significant, changes the course of history. You might say that the birth and life of Jesus was the biggest *black swan* of the last 2000 years. The launch of Sputnik or the rise of the Internet, these are a couple of twentieth century *black swans*."

"So how do we figure out if what we are doing is going to be a *black swan?"*

"Well, that is just it. We can't. If the culture sees it coming, it is not a *black swan*. So by definition, at the time something happens, we don't know it is a black swan; we only know it by hindsight."

"That is discouraging,"says Blaine, furrowing her brow. "So the most important things that happen in history, and this thing we are doing—to try to go back into the space/time continuum and find our something—we are helpless to know ahead of time if this is really going to be meaningful in human history?"

"If you did know ahead of time, you would live in Las Vegas, not on an Indian reservation. You wouldn't be a spiritual pilgrim willing to risk your life for the advancement of the spiritual consciousness of humankind. However, just because you can't know ahead of time if something is a *black swan* doesn't mean you can't be prepared for one. In fact, that is the whole point. How does humankind step forward in this adventure of life ready to respond to the next Jesus, or some rogue nation exploding a nuclear bomb, or your journey back into the space/time continuum where it is possible that not only will you get a bird's-eye view of what actually happened then, but—and here is the elephant in the room her Motherness avoids talking about—you could change what happens after it has already happened."

"Holy cow, you are right! The possibilities are huge," says Blaine.

"Yes, there are always a few people who do see the possibility of a *black swan* emerging before it does, but by definition the culture does not. And, more often than not, those individuals who think something will be a huge change are simply wrong."

Blaine sits for a moment taking it all in. "How do we prepare for a *black swan?"*

"The way for a culture to prepare for a *black swan* is the same way we have been preparing you individually for this trip.

"You have to have resiliency and build in back-up. We know that everything that occurs on the quantum level involves uncertainty. Things don't occur in a linear cause and effect way. Rather, they occur based on probability. Chaos is always a part of this larger system in which we live, even though at the linear level we live lives where we try to make life predictable. Understandably, we have this desire for certainty or predictability, which is ultimately impossible. In the long run, we have to be willing to learn to live in a universe far different from the Newtonian one we think we live in, and which, in our search for orderly meaning, we unconsciously seek to create.

"The civilization that built the pyramids in Egypt didn't survive because they did not change quickly enough to respond to a *black swan*. We don't know what it was—an outbreak of a disease or a breakthrough to greater consciousness—however, clearly some big idea or small virus, some *black swan*, came gliding unobserved down the Nile.

"You may come back from this trip with the answer that Mother Mary is so earnestly seeking, or with some other deeper understanding that alters the way we see each other as human beings." Rat wiggles his nose at Blaine. "Now that would be the mother of all *black swans*."

"I see what you mean," says Blaine. "Having had such a chaotic childhood, I have both sought stability in my adult life and I have also had the resiliency to deal with difficulties I never anticipated, like the death of my child.... Curious."

"More than curious, I think. The chaos in your life has given you the willingness and the resiliency to make this journey. What you find may change the whole way we look at the nature of the spiritual life. Very often spiritual seekers are after some sort of non-chaotic life, what they would describe as inner peace. Well, there are two possibilities here. One is that they are seeking a stable system. This will ultimately always elude them. It is not the nature of the universe, spiritually or otherwise. The other is that they are seeking a resiliency solution, how to live in a chaotic world. You and I, whether we like it or not, have had to put our bets on the latter. It is a trap, not the Buddha himself, but many Westerners who fancy themselves as Buddhist fall into. Be wary of those seeking a too peaceful God. I would much rather have a resilient one."

"Yes, you are right, Rat." She stops momentarily. "We almost never get to have a serious conversation because you are such a goofball, and then when we do I am amazed at your insight. As part of my preparation for this journey, Mother Mary has had me doing *lectio divina* on the 23rd Psalm. I would have never used these words before, but that process has been awakening my awareness that I have a resilient God."

"Good for her," says Rat. "Her Motherness is actually on to more of this than I would ever give her credit for to her face." Rat does his mouse face grin. "I wouldn't do anything to diminish my teasing leverage with her. I am all about trying to do my bit for building her resiliency."

"Rat, you never give a thought to building her resiliency. You just like to see her squirm when she gets annoyed with you and then is self critical for being annoyed. Go on, admit it."

"How is it you Americans say, 'I take the fifth.'"

"Rat, you are the best. When do you think you will be ready for us to give this another try with the software to instantaneously translate six century Latin?"

"Give me a couple more days. I have already got a couple of my best hacker buddies working on writing the software, and it will take a bit of time. So in the meantime, relax. Or go pester her Motherness. Nothing like being a pain in the arse to brighten a person's day." He wiggles his nose at Blaine.

She comes over and gives Rat a peck on the cheek as she heads for the door.

As she turns to walk down the hall, she looks back at Rat and smiles. "By the way, you look great with a bolt of lightning across your chest."

He nods his head at her. For the second time, his demeanor remains serious.

"You, liebste, are the swan."

Chapter 14

Dinner is going to be a treat. Tree caught a half dozen trout, cleaned and wrapped them each in foil with a hunk of butter. They will not take long to cook over the open fire outside of the hogan. He found a patch of desert marigolds still blooming in a rocky crevice along the stream when he was fishing. The profusion of little suns, which manage to bloom all summer and into the fall, provides a welcoming ambience for the table.

Katrina, as always, is delighted to come for dinner with Tree and his Grandfather. He told her they would eat outside if it was not too cool after the sun went down. As Tree prepares for dinner in the late afternoon, the humble hogan with its apple tree arbor seems to Tree to be the best place on the Earth to be living.

When Tree picks up Katrina from the trailer where she lives behind the school house, he is dazzled by how exceptionally beautiful she looks. Her long black hair, which is usually pulled back tight and wound up on her head or plaited in a long braid, cascades freely over her shoulders. She is wearing a green amethyst necklace that Tree and his Grandfather gave her for her birthday a few months back. The stone intensifies the sparkle in her eyes. She wears a brightly patterned native blouse that fits with an eye-enchanting tension across her breasts. The blouse is tucked in black slacks. Her feet are in sandals.

As they ride in the pickup back to Manuelito's hogan, Katrina is unusually quiet. Tree is used to her bubbling on about some project she is working on for her school kids. Tonight her mood is somber.

When they arrive at the hogan, Manuelito is not yet back from his hike.

"I sure hope Grandfather is going to make it back before too long. Are you really hungry?"

"I am in no hurry to eat," says Katrina, as she looks about preoccupied, her brow slightly furrowed.

"We both know him," says Tree. "He will find something interesting on the side of a rock, and he might be there for hours trying to figure out what some man was thinking when he was carving away 6000 years ago."

"Your Grandfather is an extraordinary man," says Katrina. "Wait, I think I hear him."

Sure enough, just then, out of the growing darkness, he appears.

"Come sit down, Grandfather, I have dinner all fixed. You look tired."

"I think I will," says Manuelito, plopping down in his outdoor chair and propping his feet up on a fire rock in a customary posture. "I am not getting any younger. Have made that trip so many times. Not sure why I am breathing so hard."

Katrina automatically goes inside to get him a glass of cactus tea. She is glad that she has been invited over tonight. For three days she has known she needs to come, and she has been putting it off. This is going to be hard.

"Here you are, Grandfather," she says, addressing him in a

reference, not of kinship, but honoring. "Can I get you anything else? You don't look too good. I mean you really look exhausted."

"Thank you, Katrina. I am sure I will be all right shortly." He begins to drink the tea she brought him.

"I am not sure I will be able to eat any of this wonderful dinner that you have fixed, Tree," says Manuelito. "For some unknown reason I have been nauseated since I started down from the summit of the mountain. It was a crazy message I got. What the message seemed to be was that I would not need to go in the consciousness of another with your Grandmother; however, you would, Tree. How you are going to be able to go by yourself I have no idea. Maybe I had my wires crossed."

"Where are you going, Tree?" asks Katrina. Her voice quivers a bit.

Both Manuelito and Tree look at her.

"Well, it seems we all have something to tell each other. I have been afraid to bring this up to tell you. I have the chance to go to the University of California and take this incredible course on teaching science in high school. I will even get to work on a research project about the Higgs boson.

"I have had such mixed feelings about it. This is a great opportunity and yet I have felt so down at the thought of not being near you. I would be gone for almost a year." As she says this she moves her hand to brush aside her hair, which began to obscure her eyes, and looks straight at Tree.

Tree looks directly back at Katrina, oblivious to his Grandfather watching the energy display between them.

"Humph," says Manuelito. "The Higgs boson, that would be

worth going for. Never been any big mystery to us that there is an invisible secret energy field running the universe. Glad they finally found Professor Higgs' little particle that seems to verify it all."

Katrina's and Tree's moods immediately shift. Again, they are amazed at the seemingly random knowledge Manuelito always seems to possess. At the same time they both are experiencing a mixture of emotions, including a rush of physical desire that anticipated separation brings. For a long moment they are off in their own shared fog.

Suddenly, Katrina looks at Manuelito and gives a little start. He is bent toward his left side and seems to be in pain.

"Grandfather, are you all right?"

"Sure, I am," says Manuelito, as he slides increasingly leftward. "I have just had this durn pain in my chest. It comes and goes so I don't think it is anything really. Hate to admit I am getting older."

Katrina notices that Manuelito is pale and there are beads of perspiration on his forehead. "Where is the pain?" she asks.

He looks at her as if this interrogation is entirely unnecessary. Then he relents. "My chest, a bit up to my jaw and down my left arm, I guess."

"Jesus," says Katrina, looking anxiously at Manuelito. "You could be having a heart attack. I think we need to get you to an emergency room. Tree, bring the pickup right up next to the door."

"Heck, no. I am fine," says Manuelito, just as he slowly slumps from his chair toward the ground.

Katrina nods at Tree with an expression that says *hurry up*. He is immediately up and out the door.

Soon they are in the pickup, speeding toward the nearest hospital. The trouble is it is thirty miles away.

Chapter 15

Mother Mary is frustrated with the delays that keep occurring: first the language problem, then glitches in the simultaneous translation software. *Lord knows what will be next!* She knows it will be something. She sighs. Blaine is already anxious about getting home and she hasn't even left on her mission.

Rat comes bursting into her office. As usual, it is covered with a mishmash of books and papers and a small cairn of stones that has been growing with each walk Blaine continues to take in the increasingly chilly fall air. For once he isn't twitching his nose and making a fool of himself.

"Mother Mary, I just received an email from Tree. I am sure he sent it to me because he knows I am always online. Manuelito is in the hospital. He had a heart attack. They do not know if he is going to make it. I thought you better come with me to tell Blaine."

She is up from her desk immediately and the two unlikely cohorts are racing down the corridor to Blaine's room. Her room is a mess. Despite the esteem in which Blaine holds Mother Mary and the Order, she cannot be cajoled into following the protocol required of the other Sisters, which involves making your bunk bed and keeping your room picked up. Blaine's room looks like she is still a teenager. Mother Mary cannot hold back a look of both disgust and disappointment. Blaine is nowhere to be seen.

Rat and Mother Mary both look at each other at the same time and nod in unison. They head for the kitchen.

Blaine, during her training, has been given permission not to keep the Convent schedule. If she sleeps late, as she was doing in the past few days because she was not able to sleep well, she can often be found in the Convent kitchen indulging in leftovers from breakfast or making a peanut butter and raspberry jam sandwich.

She is standing at the counter, a knife loaded with peanut butter poised in the air above a large chunk of the Convent's homemade bread. This time, the salwar kameez does look slept in. She turns.

"I can tell you two are up to no good," she says, sizing up their strained faces and heavy breathing.

"Blaine," says Mother Mary, "Man has had a heart attack!"

Blaine is speechless. Rat quickly reaches his arm out, holds her and gradually guides her to a chair.

"When did it happen?" she asks.

"A couple of hours ago. I just got an email from Tree," Rat says.

Blaine nods.

"How bad?"

"He is still unconscious," says Rat.

Blaine swallows hard. "Get me a ticket to go home Rat. I will go pack. I will need someone to take me to Stockholm to catch the next flight."

Mother Mary thinks about suggesting to Blaine that she could go into the field and see how Manuelito is; however, her better judgment is not to say something like that. She and Rat both nod.

Blaine starts to take a bite of her sandwich and then puts it down. She is no longer hungry. She gets up and starts for her room to pack. As she is about to leave the kitchen, she says over her shoulder, "Mother, can you give me a ride and, Rat, please come with me."

They both nod yes and all three quickly leave the room.

Chapter 16

The problem with being a CIA officer is not danger or risk, but boredom.

Red Elred cannot believe how slow the consciousness gene research is going.

His secretary knocks, then opens the door and comes in. She hands Red a piece of paper marked *Top Secret*. He reads quickly.

One of their identity search algorithms picked up a woman Blaine Astrid traveling to the United States from Stockholm. She is an American citizen and had been flagged because she had been a person connected to Melissa Dowling back before Melissa disappeared.

Red muses to himself. *Maybe this is the opportunity I need. It is time to stop waiting on the researchers and make something happen. I don't have a clue whether there is a meaningful connection between this Blaine person and Melissa; however, I have got to do something. How else can others recognize what a great job I am doing?*

Red straightens the knot of his tie until it's tight against his throat. He swivels in his desk chair and positions his hands automatically above his computer keyboard and begins typing. He will have Blaine shadowed and monitor her phone. See what she is up to. Then decide if it would be a good idea to pick her up. The report shows she is going to New Mexico. He will make sure there is someone on the ground to follow her when she gets there.

He finishes the memo and sits back in his chair. He smiles. He is feeling much better. He remembers the one thing he learned from the one humanities course he took in college: if you have an army, you will have war. He thinks—if you have a spy-machine, you will have people whose lives are secretly monitored. And people who go missing. His smile broadens. He wouldn't want it any other way.

Chapter 17

Navajo Nation
Southwestern United States
Late Fall 2014

Blaine arrives late. However, not too late. Manuelito has been brought to the Fort Defiance Indian Hospital located about eight miles from Window Rock, Arizona, the capital of the Navajo Nation. The hospital was built in 2002 and is the best care available to native people on tribal reservations in the United States. Manuelito is in intensive care, alive though still unconscious.

Blaine looks at Manuelito lying peacefully in the bed, his long black hair puddled on the pillow. She places her hand gently on his shoulder and immediately feels how much she loves this man.

Manuelito is hooked up to several machines monitoring his vital signs, although to her he looks like he could have been napping in the afternoon at home in their hogan. He has not broken into consciousness since he was first brought to the hospital.

Blaine is dead tired. She knew she would not be able to sleep. Not until she could at least have a chance to communicate with this man she loves so dearly. She looks around the room. Tree is dozing in a chair by the window. Two Brothers from Father McDonnell's monastery, who have been visiting almost around the clock, stand talking quietly by the door. She doesn't believe they would mind her request.

"Excuse me. I want to spend time with Manuelito alone. He seems to be stable right now. Would you mind taking Tree with you for something to eat?"

The Brothers nod assent. They rouse Tree. After Tree gives his Grandmother a big welcoming hug, the threesome head down the corridor. Blaine gets up and closes the door and returns to her chair. She puts her hand back on her husband's hand and moves it gently around his wrist until she can feel the quiet rhythm of his pulse.

There is a vase of store-bought, cut flowers on the nightstand by the bed. Many wildflowers bloom in New Mexico between February and April and a few like the desert marigold all summer long and into the fall. With no native flowers available the store-bought ones look like intruders, their colors slightly unnatural. A card is signed by the Brothers from Father O'Donnell's monastery. If Manuelito was awake she knows he would have these flowers given to another patient.

When you are used to bringing the natural world into the environment of your life like Manuelito does, all else rings false. Blaine realizes it is a symptom of how tired she is that her mind is so unfocused she is fretting about how Manuelito would view these well-intended store-bought flowers. She must change that. It is what her training has been all about.

Blaine sits back and begins to allow herself to slip into a deep meditative state. This is a lot better than being in Mother Mary's departure room. Here she relies on her own human wiring. In no time at all she feels an awareness of Manuelito's spirit, next to her. She cannot see him, or anything else, in reflective consciousness as she was able to do when she traveled to King Arthur's time. Instead, she experiences a strong feeling of Manuelito's energy presence with her and an awareness of a green emerald glow right behind her closed eyes.

She experiences a knowing from him that he is okay and that everything will be all right and how incredibly much he loves her.

Upon experiencing this reassurance, she immediately falls into a deep sleep.

Through the haze, Blaine becomes aware that someone is gently touching her shoulder. She opens her eyes.

"Grandmother, you have been asleep a long time," says Tree.

Blaine stirs. She looks at her grandson and then at Manuelito. His chest is gently rising and falling.

"I guess I have," says Blaine. "Has anything happened while I have been asleep?"

"I got something to eat while you were sleeping. Nothing seems to have changed with Grandfather. Now that you are here the two Brothers felt okay to go back to the monastery. They will return in the morning."

"I needed the sleep, I guess," says Blaine. "I am feeling somewhat refreshed. While you were away, I was hoping to go into the dreamtime and talk to your Grandfather. I guess I was too tired to stay very long. I would like to give it another shot. Are you okay with quietly hanging out here and if anyone comes by to check on your Grandfather just ask them to come back later?"

"Sure," says Tree. "I have you covered, Grandmother." He grins at her as if they did this every day.

*   *   *

"You are crying, Grandmother. Tell me what happened?"

"I'm not sure if these are tears of joy or sadness. Maybe they are both. I had a good talk with your Grandfather. I am sad because I do not think he is coming back. It is not that he feels his time is over. Whether he comes back or not, he wants to join me in the dreamtime exploration that I am committed to doing for Mother Mary. So I am happy about that. If I can go in the field and find King Arthur 1500 years ago, I certainly should be able to find your Grandfather and take him with me. I should say us. Manuelito wants me to take you with me and him, and also, if we can do it, take Two. He has some premonition that I may need you to keep me safe."

For Tree, the idea of such a journey with his grandparents and with the dog that was his dearest, best companion in all the world was a perfect scenario.

"Sounds wonderful to me," says Tree.

"There is one complication. Well, maybe there's more than one. This is what your Grandfather requested and I agreed to. I must return to Sweden to do this journey there, since I will need to have Rat helping me with the simultaneous translation software. He and I both agreed that you can come also, as long as you are physically here and being looked after by Katrina. We both believe that your...." She smiles, then starts again. "We both believe that your affection for Katrina and hers for you will keep you from staying in the dreamtime. Sometimes you need a strong anchor of longing to be able to come back to this world."

Tree blushes. He looks directly at his Grandmother and nods *yes*.

"There is one other difficulty that your Grandfather alerted me to, evidently from his wandering around in the dreamtime. It seems that the CIA is again monitoring my movements. After a couple of days I will say goodbye to your Grandfather here. He has told me that he prefers to be in this unconscious state right now so that he can more readily access my movements in the dreamtime. So I am not to wait around for him to die, or to get better. For reasons I expect you understand, he is in the ideal condition to travel with me."

Tree, with a serious expression looks directly at his Grandmother. "I understand."

Blaine returns the heart-to-heart look of her Grandson. "Tree, this would all be so terribly sad for me if the experience of being with Manuelito was not so intense in the dreamtime. Truthfully, he is totally on board to do this King Arthur adventure with me. Even though outwardly he seems to be dying, inwardly he is about as excited as I have experienced him in a long time. I feel totally distraught and delighted at the same time. A confusion of emotions.

"To follow his wish, the immediate problem is how do I get back to Sweden. Your Grandfather is not sure about that, but he has no doubt Rat will be able to come up with a solution.

"I will stay with your Grandfather tonight. When Katrina comes by for her visit with your Grandfather, go with her tonight back to the hogan. Contact Rat using secure, encrypted software. Ask him how I should travel back to Sweden and see what he suggests. Tomorrow, I will make arrangements with some of the Navajo Singers and the Brothers from the monastery for your Grandfather's transition should he decide to leave being anchored in his body while we are all off in the quantum field."

"Okay," says Tree. "I'll go downstairs and wait on Katrina to get here. After she arrives we will go back to the hogan and contact Rat." Tree is feeling a mixture of strong emotions. He is so excited that he is getting to go on this trip into the quantum field with his Grandfather and his Grandmother. He is also anxious that his Grandfather might not come back to being on the earthly plane. This thought causes him great sadness. Then there is the thought of leaving his body to be looked after by Katrina. This is scary and tantalizingly exciting.

He gets up from his chair and heads out the door of his

Grandfather's hospital room.

*   *   *

Katrina is sitting close to Tree. They are both peering at the computer screen and trying to read Rat's suggestions about the best way for Blaine to travel back to Sweden without being detained by the CIA. Tree can feel her left leg and shoulder touching his right leg and shoulder as she nudges up against him in order to be able to see the computer screen.

"Wow! Sounds like a wacky idea to me," says Katrina, turning so that she is looking at Tree.

For a moment Tree is totally distracted. He breathes her scent, which he experiences deeply because she is sitting so close. Her scent reminds him of being outdoors on a warm day—the scent of dry pine trees with the flavor of Southwest wildflowers and dust in the air.

Tree turns slightly. Katrina's face is inches from his. "Maybe the wackier it is, the better." Her eyes are so green. They sparkle even though she was up much of the night.

Tree picks up his cell phone. "I will text one of the Brothers about building a coffin. I will mention to him not to tell anyone what he is building. Except for a few people making a pilgrimage, they don't see many visitors anyway. The Brothers will assume that the coffin is for Manuelito. Furthermore, they are used to not talking."

The messaging complete, Tree puts down his cell phone. The intensity of their time together with his Grandfather has combined with the intensity of communicating with Rat about a secret way for Blaine to travel back to Sweden. His heart-dream since he was in her class in grade school was to kiss Katrina. She is so close. Without even thinking of what he is doing, he bends ever so slightly toward her and touches her nose with his. Then his mouth finds hers.

After a long, unrelenting kiss, she gets up and takes his hand. She walks over to his single bed in the corner of the hogan. She lies down and pulls him after her. They begin the slow process of exploration of two who make love for the first time. They savor each touch and moment. Each moment they desire to last forever. Each moment calls relentlessly for the next new moment. Finally, neither can stand the heightened tension of their arousal any longer. Katrina pulls Tree into her and begins to move her hips beneath him. The goddess of love with her terrible fury enters them both, storming with wonder until she finally throws them entangled upon the shore of sated sleep. They awake from the discomfort of the small bed. They make love again. It is a wondrously new experience, as it is again and again and again.

Pale white moonlight seeps in around the cracks of the doorframe of the hogan. As tradition requires, the hogan's front door faces due east. A full moon has risen. Tree watches the soft light play across Katrina's breasts as they rise and fall. He is amazed that after making love for hours, he still feels this painful longing for her at the base of his spine. Her breathing is light and steady. He rests his left hand on her right breast. Even though she is still asleep he senses her body responding and her legs moving slightly apart. *Jesus*, he thinks, *how can I ever go into the dreamtime and leave Katrina back in this world.* She opens her eyes by the smallest margin and smiles at him. He feels her legs moving farther apart and her hips begin to slowly move.

"I know what it feels like to cross the desert without water for a lifetime and then suddenly, miraculously finally get to a well," he says.

She pulls him back on top of her. "How deep is your well?" she asks, reaching for his erection, tucking it into herself and bringing the motion of her hips into sync with both of their breathings.

"I think it is bottomless." He gasps as she effortlessly brings them both once more to the plateau of intensity just below orgasm.

Soon they again are wild ponies galloping full speed across the prairie, each determined not to be the last, or first, to arrive.

*   *   *

Blaine looks up, from intensely gazing at Manuelito, to Tree and Katrina as they walk into Manuelito's hospital room.

"I was about to give up on you guys," Blaine says, looking down at her watch.

Before responding, Tree looks at Katrina. She has plaited her long black hair into a braid which curls around her neck and lies on her right breast. She borrowed one of Tree's T-shirts, since they had not had time to go back to her trailer, and it is haphazardly tucked into her bluejeans. Katrina returns Tree's gaze with a shy smile.

Blaine takes in her grandson's shirt on Katrina and their sidelong glances at each other.

"Oh, Jesus, as if we didn't already have enough going on." She stops and looks at both of them. "Maybe it's for the best. Katrina you have known that Tree has been in love with you all his life. Our family is honored that you should return his love. Did you guys completely forget to get in touch with Rat?"

"Thank you for your blessing, Grandmother," says Tree. "We did get in touch with Rat. He has come up with a scheme for you to get back to Sweden. It is a little bizarre. We will need to take you to Minnesota so you can leave from there. When would you like to go?"

"Go and get the pickup serviced and let's plan on starting in the morning. There is no reason for me to stay here now. Your Grandfather insists that he go from where he is with me on this journey into the field. My desire is to get on with it and do this adventure into the field for Mother Mary, meet your Grandfather there if he wishes, and then get back here and try to persuade your Grandfather not to leave this reality yet."

"Okay, I will go take care of the pickup right away. I'm not sure if the Brothers will have the coffin ready by tomorrow morning."

"Have the what ready?" asks Blaine.

"Don't look at me like that," says Tree with a big smile. "It is your good buddy, Rat, who has come up with this idea. I guess you will need to talk with him if you think it's too off the wall. Katrina can fill you in on it. I will go see about the pickup and send a text to the Brothers right now to get the coffin ready to be picked up immediately."

Tree reaches out and finds Katrina's hand. Gives a little squeeze. Turns and leaves. He is feeling the same confusion of emotions that his Grandmother had talked about from the possibility of losing his Grandfather in the linear world and the adventure of being with both his grandparents in the dreamtime. Plus, he is experiencing the intensity of the expression of his long-pent up love for Katrina and the thought of having to be gone from her for some unknown time period, if he is needed in the dreamtime by his grandparents. As he walks down the corridor he feels himself stepping deeper into the mystery of the unknown of his own life. He begins to whistle.

*   *   *

They are already in Colorado, gliding by the Rockies on their left-hand side. Tree is driving. Katrina is sitting in the center seat. She is asleep. Her head rests lightly on Tree's shoulder. Blaine sits next to the passenger door. Two takes up all the room there is at her feet. A newly made coffin covered by a tarp rests in the back of the pickup.

Blaine looks over at Tree. "I am beginning to like Rat's idea. I could use some quiet travel time."

"Rat says that is what you should have. Except when they load the coffin on the plane with a forklift, Rat believes that might be a bit unsettling. Other than that, smooth sailing. I do think it would be better if you let me and Katrina go with you to Sweden. What do you say?"

"I have thought about it a good bit," says Blaine. "The problem is someone needs to be close by to Manuelito. If your Grandfather decides to leave this reality, we can't all be stuck in Sweden."

"If we were all in Sweden with the Sisters to look after us, we could take Katrina into the field also." He looks at his grandmother. "Why not?"

"You would have terrible regrets if you were in Sweden and your Grandfather died and no one was nearby. In addition, unless you have been teaching her, even though Katrina is an extraordinary young woman, she has no experience in how to access the field."

Katrina begins to blink her eyes. She sits up straight.

"Katrina, I am sorry if our talking woke you up. We all need rest. It is also good for you to hear this conversation. The burden of Tree and me going on this journey into the quantum field really falls on you. I know that Tree is agonizing because he knows he will miss you terribly. My experience so far in journeying in the quantum field is that for those going into the field time gets all mixed up. This journey that we are about to undertake may be hardest on you, looking after Tree while he is in the field and also keeping track of how Manuelito is doing. Are you sure that you are up for this daughter?"

Katrina looks first at Tree, then at Blaine. "Tree has always been a little out of reach. First, he was too young for me to even conceive of him as a boyfriend. Then, because I was his teacher it was inappropriate for me to think of him as a boyfriend. Now because I want to go to California to do this science course, it has seemed impossible for me to think I could do what I desire to do for my career and have a relationship with Tree.

"Now that I know we both want to be together, what is a little more separation? There has always been some Catch-22."

Katrina looks back at Tree wistfully. "Right this minute everything under my feet somehow seems to have slid sideways. Yet, I feel happier than I have ever felt in my life." Very discreetly so that his Grandmother cannot observe, Katrina places her left hand on the inside of his right leg and slowly and gently massages his inner thigh.

Tree looks at Katrina and rolls his eyes in a how-could-you-possibly-be-doing-this-to-me-now expression. He feels himself hardening and extending down against his leg so that his erection soon reaches her hand. Very gently she moves her fingers up and down against him. He feels she has this all-encompassing connection with him. She seems to have complete control over his body. It is like his body belongs more to her than him. Maybe it is all the stored up years of longing for her that she is tapping into. Whatever it is, as painful as the tension in his pants is, he does not want it to stop. His Grandmother interrupts his thoughts.

"Daughter, if you need to go to California to start this course, while we are away in the dreamtime, our journey into the field need not hold you back. You can look after Tree there. The Brothers can look after Manuelito. If he should take a turn for the worse it would take you only a few hours to drive back. In that event, you could bring Tree back from the dreamtime."

Tree nods agreement.

Blaine continues, "Manuelito let me know that he wishes to be moved from the hospital out to the monastery anyway, while we're going on the dreamtime experience. From what he says there is so much interaction between the quantum field and linear reality at the hospital that it is not a good place for him to be to travel with me. He wants to be where there's not quite so much static on the line. The monastery is exactly the right place.

"So, if we are not back by the time your course starts, haul Tree out to California with you. He should be a great study buddy. I expect that being off in the quantum field is a bit like being zoned out in a grad school library."

Katrina takes her hand off of Tree. Fans herself with her palm. "Sounds like we have a plan. Works for me," she says.

"Guess I can't think of anyone else I would want to look after my body," says Tree, again rolling his eyes at Katrina. "I am on board, Grandmother."

"I am glad we have that settled," says Blaine. She wads up an extra jacket as a pillow, places it against the doorframe and rests her head upon it. In a moment she is asleep.

Katrina looks at Tree with a big grin and puts her hand back on his leg. He sighs.

Tree lasts for about ten more miles. He pulls over at a rest stop. Fortunately, there are only a few cars around. They leave Blaine dozing in the car. Katrina goes in to check out the stalls in the

Ladies. No one is around. She comes back to the foyer and winks at Tree, who stands leaning against the entrance to the Mens. They take the last stall nearest the back wall. She reaches under her skirt and pulls off a pair of pink panties. Katrina waves them in the air in front of him like a cheerleader encouraging her team with a pom-pom.

"You look like a magician who has just pulled a rabbit from the hat," Tree says, trying to hide his nervousness with humor. He unzips his pants and feels relief as his erection swings free in front of him.

"With a wand like that, I think you are the magician," says Katrina.

Before she can say anything more their lips meet. Tree easily picks up her lithe body and pulls her gently onto his erection. Her entire body quivers. Tree is flooded with relief just from the sensation of being in her. As she starts to slowly move her hips, Tree hears something. He puts his forefinger to his lips. Katrina stops. They both listen. Tree touches his finger to his third eye. She nods. He sends her a message, *I believe there is someone now in the next stall.*

Katrina nods. She moves her hips ever so slowly. *Do you think you can stand just a little motion.* She smiles at him.

Wait just a moment, let that first wave of delight subside a bit. He bites his lower lip.

I don't want anything to subside she says.

He grins. *Don't worry.*

Then the toilet in the next stall flushes. Their interlocked bodies begin to pivot around their point of deep connection. Suddenly, the sound of the toilet flushing stops.

Stop please, he says with his thoughts and pleading eyes.

She slows her motion. *I can't quite stop* she signals, true agonizing stretched across her face.

Just then one of those obnoxious noisy hand dryers cranks on.

Saved by clean hands, she says. Then the wild ponies are released again, thundering across the prairie.

On the way back out to the car, Tree stops by the shiny steel box on the wall. Pressed into the metal on the top of the hand blow dryer are the words—*Avalon Tor*. He points to the name and again speaks silently to Katrina: *Saved by the Tor*.

She smiles.

When they get back to the pickup, Tree asks Katrina to drive. He slips into the middle and immediately falls asleep beside his grandmother. Fifty miles later he awakes. His Grandmother is snoring lightly. Katrina's colorful Mexican skirt has slid up above her knees. He slides his hand up under her skirt and very gently massages her inner thigh. He notices that she either purposefully discarded her panties at the rest stop or they were forgotten in the blessed commotion of the hand dryer noise. He explores a little further. She is already wet again.

Katrina exhales a long slow sigh. She reaches down, her hand on top of her skirt, and finds his hand beneath her skirt. She looks at him and her eyes plead, *look for another rest stop? I need a Tor*.

Four miles later Katrina pulls off the road by a clump of trees. Neither has any idea where the next rest stop might be—neither of them can wait. Blaine stirs. "We will be right back," says Tree, as he and Katrina slip out of the car.

Blaine chuckles to herself as she remembers the time long ago when she and Manuelito made this same trip in the opposite direction engaged in similar *trip interruptus*. As she remembers her journey with Manuelito, having her young grandson caught up in the passion of love, when youth and passion make it impossible for one's body to become sated—well, having that memory made real is about as sweet a treat as a Grandmother can have.

She sighs and turns her head to find another comfortable position for sleep. *Not eager to get into that coffin anyway.*

Chapter 18

Aline Elred gets up from his desk chair and walks over to his office window, which provides a view of the interior courtyard of the CIA's Langley, Virginia, headquarters. There was an early snowfall and the courtyard has become instantly enchanting.

But not his work. He has just read the most recent field report on the monitoring of the activities of Blaine Astrid. She had arrived back in New Mexico from Stockholm. From there she has returned to her home on the Navajo reservation and is spending most of her time in Fort Defiance at the Indian hospital. Her husband is there in grave condition.

What caused the report to be written is that for two days she has not shown up at the hospital. Surveillance of her home shows she is not there. Elred is angry. While he ordered only a moderate level of surveillance, he believes it was more than adequate to keep some nobody Indian under surveillance. Now she has slipped away. To top it all off, she apparently does not have a cell phone. *Can you believe that. Someone in this day and time without a cell phone!*

Elred kicks at his desk chair. *I need to get out of this office before I go completely bananas.*

He picks up the telephone and calls his boss. Maybe he could go out to New Mexico for a few days and get the surveillance team back on track. Whether he is able to do that, or not, really doesn't matter. He just needs to get away from shuffling paper and typing memos.

The phone rings repeatedly; there is no answer. Finally he slams the receiver down. *Everybody except this woman Blaine Astrid has a phone, but no one answers their phone. My boss is probably off playing CIA golf—no one knows who they are playing with and each person keeps someone else's score. I think I will just go.*

*   *   *

By late that evening Aline Elred is in Window Rock, Arizona. It is the first time he had been on an Indian tribal reservation. A big sign, when he enters the reservation, welcomes everyone. Red feels like he is in a foreign country and very unwelcome. He has never felt more like a spy. Everywhere he goes he feels he stands out as an outsider and, regardless of what the sign said, not a particularly welcomed one at that.

The local CIA officer, who met him, has nothing new to report. They confirm that the husband, who is still hospitalized, has a vehicle registered in his name. It is a ten-year-old Dodge Ram. An alert has been sent out to all local law enforcement agencies with a description of the vehicle and the number on the license tag. No sighting of the vehicle had been reported until shortly after Elred arrived in New Mexico. A Colorado highway patrolman reports pulling up behind a vehicle that matched the description of the Dodge ram. The patrolman stopped to investigate the pickup because the vehicle was pulled over along an isolated stretch of road and he thought the motorist might be having mechanical trouble. When he walked up to the pickup truck, a young couple came bounding out of the shrub trees on the side of the road. Evidently, the couple stopped for a bathroom break. He checked the young man's license. He was a Navajo and the license was valid. That was all he remembers. The vehicle was traveling north.

Elred turns to his colleague. "Sure is not much to go on. Let's send out another alert for the vehicle to local law enforcement in those states directly north of Colorado. I think I'll just take a wild shot they are figuring to run to Canada or catch a flight from Minneapolis. I think I will head there. I need to get out of here. This place gives me the creeps."

"Maybe it is the wrong time of year for you. The country out here is absolutely beautiful. Even though the Indian reservation is situated on some of the poorest land in the West, there is a beauty which comes from the land's harsh ruggedness."

"Maybe I am too much of an Easterner," says Elred. "No trees, snakes, and people who don't seem all that friendly—not a winning combination for me. Thanks for all your help. Maybe I could get a lift from you to the airport."

Three hours later Elred is on a flight bound for Minneapolis.

*   *   *

As soon as the airplane he is traveling on skids to a stop, Elred has his cellphone powered up checking for an update. Much to his surprise and relief there is one. Not long before, local law enforcement installed cameras at all tollbooths on the few sections of interstate toll road in Minnesota. Recently installed software allows the authorities to check the license plate of every vehicle using the road. The Dodge Ram pickup from New Mexico went through a toll booth one day earlier.

There is no way of telling where the vehicle is now. However, given the trajectory of its travel from when it was first spotted in Colorado, his best guess is that the vehicle is probably in Canada by now. If it has crossed the boundary with Canada at a normal customs location, their person of interest should have been detained, and, at the least, a picture of the tag would have been taken. Since no positive identification of the suspect's vehicle has been reported at the border, maybe, just maybe, he will be able to find the woman he is searching for in Minnesota.

*   *   *

Elred spends the morning stomping around the Minneapolis branch headquarters of the CIA's section head's office. The weather is cold and getting worse with snow starting to fall. The coffee is terrible, the section chief's sense of humor even worse and no one in the CIA's back office, through monitoring phones or the local authorities surveillance on the road, has been able to spot the vehicle suspected of carrying Blaine Astrid.

A secretary opens the office door and pokes her head in. "I think we have the news you have been looking for." She grimaces. "Well, not exactly what you have been looking for. The vehicle has been located."

Elred brightens. "Give me the details."

"The car was pulled over by a highway patrolman in Colorado, this time going south. There were only two occupants. Both Indians. Heading to the Navajo reservation they said. They denied having any knowledge of an older woman named Blaine Astrid. The patrolman had no knowledge of any criminal violations to charge them with in order to hold them, so he let them go. Their route south is obvious and if you wanted them pulled again we could make that happen."

Elred curses under his breath. He has a raw, visceral feeling that he has been snookered by someone who is now laughing at him. He hates the feeling. It is akin to the feeling, which he often got when he was younger, that whatever he did was not good enough for his father.

"Okay, if there is someone around who can take me to the airport, I am going back to D.C."

As the force of acceleration pushes him back in his seat, and the aircraft bound for the nation's capital thunders down the runway, Elred resolves. *I will not be shamed by some group of amateurs. I will up the pressure. Whatever needs to be done to bring in this Blaine woman, I will make happen. Time to take off the gloves.*

KING ARTHUR & THE CONSCIOUSNESS GENE

Chapter 19

Snow is falling in Minneapolis, though the tangible arrival of winter does not suggest winter has settled yet into the bones of the aging. At least these are the quixotic thoughts rambling through Rat's head as he is scanning the obituaries in Minneapolis/St.Paul and across Minnesota on the Internet. He is looking for a deceased, first generation Swedish immigrant whose dying wish is to be buried back home. When he originally hatched his plan, his belief was that there would be at least one or two people a week coming from Minnesota's principal airport, heading homeward to Sweden. So far nothing.

The most recent encrypted email Rat receives from Tree estimates that he and Katrina will have Blaine in Minneapolis by tomorrow. The dearth of dead body travelers is worrying Rat. Plus, he needs a dead Catholic Swede. Those might be harder to find.

With Mother Mary's help, Rat is in touch with the Minnesota Convent of the Sacred Order of the Sisters of Magdala. It is a sister Convent of the Order where Blaine is headed in Sweden. The plan is for Tree to drive Blaine to the Minnesota Convent. The Sisters will then dress her as a nun and take her with them to visit the deceased at the funeral home after the local service and before the body is to leave to go to the airport for burial in Sweden. The Sisters will switch Blaine for the decedent's body, along with a supply of granola bars, water, iPod with headphones, and, in case the cargo area de-pressurizes, an oxygen tank. Mother Mary and several of the Sisters from the

Swedish Convent will go with the Swedish funeral director to meet the flight in Stockholm and at the appropriate moment retrieve Blaine.

At first Mother Mary is aghast at Rat's plan. He is thrilled by his own inspiration. He jumps up and down saying, "The internationally traveling dead are not required to go through customs." Finally she agrees. She does not have a better idea.

*   *   *

Rat turns to look at one of the five computer screens in front of him. He has moved back into his former haunt, a storage room above a video arcade in the heart of Berlin. An email message from one of the Sisters of the Sacred Order of the Sisters of Magdala in Minnesota summarizes what has transpired so far. Blaine has arrived. She was brought to Minnesota by Tree and Katrina, who evidently at some recent point have become engaged to be married. They were all tired and the Sisters put them straight to bed in the Convent's guest cottage. Evidently Blaine wanted to wait several days before leaving, as the Minnesota Sisters were organizing a big feast to celebrate Tree and Katrina's engagement.

For a moment Rat stops staring at the computer screens in front of him. He breaks into a huge grin and wiggles his nose at his own reflection. *I am not a chaos theory* aficionado *for nothing. Good to see everything working out, no dead Swedes wanting to get home, and Mother Mary's envoy into the dreamtime has to party first. Just wish I was there.*

*   *   *

Blaine is feeling so much better after getting a good night's sleep at the Convent. No matter how much she dozed in the car, there is nothing like sleeping in a real bed to restore the body and spirit. Plus, her car-dozing posture was cramped so as not to interfere with her grandson's and Katrina's entry into their new life of intimacy. Before they reached Minnesota, they were bubbling over with talk of marriage. Marriage is a sacred ritual for the Navajo. She assured them it was not something they should jump into hastily. Indeed, they would want to be back home, where there was real Indian maize for use in the marriage ceremony and they could be surrounded by the sacred mountains of the Navajo people when they got married. She mused, *maybe Manuelito would come back to see his grandson get married.* Marriage plans would take time.

An engagement party was another thing altogether. The Sisters at the Convent were always up for a good party, and that was a perfect way to celebrate the physical and spiritual deepening that was happening with Tree and Katrina. Blaine did not need or want to hear about the physical pleasures of what was happening between the two of them. The last couple hundred miles of the trip she'd had to roll her window down a crack to ameliorate the heavy scent of bodily fluids in the pickup truck cab. What she was more interested in was their spiritual connection. They had discovered that they could talk to each other without speaking. The two of them would make great candidates to help in this quantum field journey she was embarking on. If Tree went with her into the field, Tree might also be able to communicate to Katrina what was happening. This would mean that Blaine might not have to be the sole conduit of information back to Mother Mary.

Speaking of the twosome, she wonders where they have gotten to. Right after breakfast she overheard Katrina asking Tree if he wanted to go for an Avalon Tor. Whatever that is. Tree perked right up and off they trotted hand in hand.

*   *   *

Rat's plan comes off smooth as Rat himself. The Minneapolis Swedish funeral home director is totally enthralled talking to the Swedish Sisters about how important it is for a last dying wish of *burial back home* to be honored. Assuming, without asking, the Sisters are friends of the deceased, the funeral director is willing to have the coffin, which was just about to be taken to the airport, opened again in the back room of the mortuary so the Sisters can pay their last respects to the deceased.

Blaine is stowed away with food supplies, blankets, an oxygen bottle and an iPod with earplugs in less than five minutes. The Sisters slip the decedent's body back into the mortuary refrigeration room where other bodies are awaiting cremation. When a few minutes later the Sisters explain they are ready to leave and have closed the casket already, the funeral home director does his best to stall his visitors so they won't leave too quickly. His desire to continue chatting with the Sisters is assuaged by the fact that one very blonde and beautiful Sister volunteers, out of respect for the decedent as she puts it, to ride with him in the hearse to the airport.

Twelve hours later Mother Mary and two other Sisters are in Stockholm meeting with the funeral director to whom the body of the decedent has been shipped. He is quite enamored by the liveliness of the younger nuns and is quite taken by their request to go with him, out of respect for the decedent, to the airport to pick up the body.

The plane is on time and the cargo is unloaded within forty-five minutes. The coffin is the last thing taken off the plane and it is quickly loaded into the hearse for the drive back into downtown Stockholm.

As soon as the coffin is unloaded at the mortuary, Mother Mary asks the funeral director if the Sisters might spend a few quiet moments with the body. The decedent has only very distant relatives in Sweden and there will be no service or formal burial. The director's job is simply to implement the decedent's last wishes of burying the body in a Stockholm cemetery. The director has already secured a burial plot and the grave for interment has already been dug.

The director laments doing a burial when there is no family at all involved. He believes a ritual of some kind of good-bye to a body is important. He is delighted to give the Sisters more than a few minutes to be with the body when they arrive back at the funeral home from the airport and he readily acquiesces in their wishes that they open the coffin alone in the back room. He is used to family members of decedents often having bizarre requests. Upon hearing their request, his mind all too quickly recalls the recent plea of a young widow who insisted on taking her dead husband's body with her on a sailing outing before he was buried. The Sisters' request seems mild.

The Sisters explain that in their tradition it is best for them to lock the casket themselves after final prayers are said since there is going to be no burial service. They complete their prayers, close and lock the casket. The funeral director is genuinely appreciative of all the time they have spent with the decedent. So he does not protest when Mother Mary explains that having fulfilled their obligation to the decedent's family, they are obliged to be on their way back to their Convent in northern Sweden. The director fails to notice that as the Sisters get back into their van there is one more nun in their party than when they arrived. What he does notice is that, in spite of the death, how light in spirit, almost joyful, the Mother Superior and her troupe of Sisters are.

Chapter 20

Navajo Nation
Southwestern United States
Early Winter 2014

Tree and Katrina walk down the hospital corridor towards Manuelito's room.

"Did you see those two guys talking to the receptionist as we entered the hospital lobby?" asks Tree, loosening his jacket as he walks. It is already wintry cold outside but the hospital is warm.

"Now that you mention it, I remember seeing them. They didn't stick in my mind. What of it?" replies Katrina. She and Tree are both wearing jeans. Tree in a brown hoodie sweatshirt and Katrina in a dark blue sweater adorned with her green amethyst necklace.

"When I walked by them, the hair rose on the back of my neck. My sense is they are some brand of police or operatives of some kind, and we need to get Manuelito out of here as soon as possible."

They pick up their pace and turn the corner and are at Manuelito's room. Much to their surprise and delight he is awake and conscious.

Manuelito immediately senses the urgency in Tree's movements. "What is up, my son?" he asks.

"Here is what I think," says Tree. "They missed intercepting Blaine because of Rat's plan and now they want to come put the pressure on her through you. I believe, if we are not gone in five minutes, there will be a couple of suits in this room asking questions."

Oddly, Manuelito brightens at the prospect of a stressful encounter.

"I am ready to leave. Katrina, go scrounge up a wheelchair and we will hightail it. Tree, from the sounds I have heard through the wall, there is a duplex next door with one guy nearly free from the mortal coil. See if you can swap my bed for the almost defunct guy, while Katrina gets me down to the car."

Tree's eyes burn with delight at hearing the animation in his grandfather's voice. "I will meet you at the car in less than three minutes."

Katrina is already bringing a wheelchair into the room. Together Katrina and Tree help Manuelito pull on his pants and a jacket and lift him into the wheelchair. Katrina accelerates the wheelchair out of the room and down the corridor toward the elevator at the far end of the hall.

Tree looks into the next room. He is worried that the dying man might be hooked up to a number of monitors. He is; but the vital signs monitor has a very long lead on it. The switch will be easy to discover with all the wires on the floor running from one room to the other; however, all they need are a couple of extra minutes. Quickly he wheels the dying patient into his grandfather's room. He puts the man's identification on the door of his grandfather's room and rolls the bed his Grandfather occupied into the other room. His grandfather's room identification he drops in the laundry chute in the hall, as he heads down the corridor in the same direction Katrina went. As Tree gets to the end of the corridor, he glances back and sees the two suits arrive at the nurses' station.

When Tree exits the hospital at the far end of the building, he surveys the parking lot. Just a few rows over is the faithful old pickup. Katrina has already helped Manuelito into the front seat. She is pushing the wheelchair onto a parking lot isle covered with grass. Tree bounds for the front seat, driver's side.

The pickup cranks up with a jerk as it always does. Katrina slides into the passenger side against Manuelito. Tree maneuvers the pickup out of the lot and onto the highway. He takes a deep breath, looks at Katrina and grins. "That was close."

"Where should we take your Grandfather?" Katrina asks Tree. "You are more than welcome to bring him to my trailer."

"Thank you, Katrina," says Tree. "Let me think a minute. You know, I don't think they would get to your trailer immediately, though I expect they will be there in a day or two. I believe we ought to take my Grandfather to Father O'Donnell's monastery. That is the idea we discussed earlier with Grandma Blaine. Furthermore, the spooks will be a bit more cautious about nosing around there and the Brothers would be happy to look after Grandfather."

"You are talking about me like I am already gone. A bit of a nuisance, am I?" croaks Manuelito. "I think you are right, Tree; get me to the monastery. The Brothers can find a place where I can lay low for a while. You two then go back to the hogan and send Rat a message as to my status and then you better chuck any computer you have been using to communicate with Rat. They will be on your electronics like bees on a cactus flower.

"I must admit, with all this activity, I am feeling much better. When you email Rat, ask him to tell Blaine to go ahead and go without me. Tell her that it is too much fun in this reality now that I get to practice disappearing from these CIA boys. I will catch up soon. While I was under, I discerned that I could follow her better in dreamtime consciousness, rather than being unconscious from a heart attack. I am glad to be back, I wouldn't want to miss my grandson being engaged." With that he smiles broadly at them both.

"If I need anything at the monastery, or if I am getting really sick again I will have Brother Will leave a message for you at the Little Creek Trading Post. I have known Sierra, who runs the post, all her life. She is nosy as hell and totally discreet about who she shares all the gossip she accumulates. I will have Brother Will leave any messages for you in a Skoal box taped up under the T-shirt counter. Otherwise, I expect it is best we not to have any contact for a while, until we know the spooks are gone.

"Tree, you can expect the hogan to be searched and bugged. Probably your trailer too, Katrina. You might want to take a couple ponies and head to Canyon de Chelly, or somewhere else, to enjoy a little break together and then head on to California in time for Katrina's course." He stopped speaking to get his breath.

"Tree, you guys will be needles in a haystack in California."

"You are feeling better, aren't you, and with Grandmother Blaine gone you are filling in mightily for her, taking over planning what other people need to do," says Katrina with a grin.

"Sorry about that. Guess I was channeling her a bit," says Manuelito. "From what I am observing, you two need no advice whatsoever, when it comes to what to do to have a good time. I will miss you. It shouldn't be too long. These modern sleuths have the patience of a four year old. I expect you two, on the other hand, won't have any problem at all keeping a low profile and hanging out together for however long it takes. Tree, with all the discussions we have had about deception, what to do should come naturally."

Tree looks at Katrina. She is smiling and soothingly squeezing

Manuelito's hand. Only a day ago his hand trembled constantly. Now it is as steady as a good rain. "I am so glad you are recovering, Grandfather. After all, we want you to be around for our wedding, which we decided to have when Grandma Blaine returns," says Katrina.

"Well, I am planning on being there and seeing again how beautiful that green amethyst looks on you, Katrina. Thoughts of your marriage reminds me that despite this cold weather, spring is coming before too long. Maybe I will even need to stay for a great grandchild or two." He looks at them both with a radiant smile.

Chapter 21

CIA Headquarters
Langley, Virginia
Winter 2014

Elred kicks the corner of his desk. Not only have his men failed to pick up Blaine, they have not been able to find the husband to interrogate him.

After Blaine slipped the net in Minneapolis, Elred had immediately ordered that her husband be brought in. Evidently he was an Indian living on the reservation. These were the kind of marginal people that could be roughed up with impunity. Even if the press found out an old Indian was mistreated they would not even yawn. There would be zero interest in investigating.

His men had not been able to find the husband to interrogate him. *Some old Indian living on the reservation and they couldn't even bring him in!* Elred is furious. For once there is no one in his line of fire for him to gratuitously strike out at. He is, however, a man who is a miser with his anger. *Someday,* he thinks, *sooner or later, someone will pay.*

KING ARTHUR & THE CONSCIOUSNESS GENE

PART II

KING ARTHUR & THE CONSCIOUSNESS GENE

Chapter 1

Life is hard, Rat. I see now I didn't really know what to expect in going into the field, back so far in time. I believe I thought I would be able to hover like a disembodied spirit, check out everything that is going on and report to you. Either Mother Mary didn't know what the real deal was, or she told me, and it didn't register.

I am not experiencing life 1500 years ago as some kind of ghost. Although I see all events through the lens of reflective consciousness, it is almost like I am a real person. As scary as that is, I also have prescient knowledge and I know that the person in whose consciousness I exist is not just that person, that I am somehow more, something that is not time bounded.

Rat, let me give you an overview. This is a time of terrible transition. Everyone longs for the good old days when the Romans efficiently provided infrastructure for a peaceful growing country. There were powerful Celtic governors for the Romans. The Romans prevented the Celtic princes from quarreling, presided over the orderly administration of the country and kept the Saxon invaders from crossing the English channel into southern England and the Picts from invading from the North.

Then the Visigoths sacked Rome in 410. This did not immediately bring the end of the Roman peace; however, gradually things began to change. Hope flourished for much of the remainder of the century that the Roman empire would revive. A group of British fighters traveled to France in 470 to fight for Emperor Anthemius. Six years later, the last western Roman emperor was deposed.

However, the eastern part of the Roman empire remained together, ruled by Constantine, who made his capital in the city that would eventually bear his name. The continuation of an eastern empire was important in keeping hope alive for a revival of a Pax Romana in Britain, because, at least on the ecclesiastical side, the Celts with their strong Druidic heritage relate more easily to the eastern Orthodox version of Christianity than Roman Christianity. Centuries later it will be a harsh Roman church that wipes out almost all vestiges of Celtic Christianity, which thrived in the milieu of the Druid Goddess religion it first encountered. But, in the timeframe of my character, Rat, in the late 400s and early 500s, the Celts easily assimilate an Eastern Orthodox style of Christianity, not yet laden with dogma and authoritarian clerical structure.

The most telling detail of all about how Eastern Christianity meshed with the Druid Goddess culture is that in Ireland there were never any Christian martyrs. The version of Christianity that first came to Ireland, Wales, Scotland and southern Britain morphed into a homegrown variety of Christianity which was compatible with the older Druidic Goddess religion in the most essential ways. Ironically, after the time of King Arthur, as Christianity became increasingly Romanized, even though the secular Roman rulers were long gone, the only martyrs in Britain were not Christian, but Druidic/Goddess followers.

Rat, I am getting ahead of myself. It is one of the great difficulties in coming back into history like this. I am present in the moment in the consciousness of an actual person, and that includes suffering contemporary hardships, and yet, at the same time, I also have my consciousness from the twenty-first century and can see at least partially what is going to occur. I need to tell you this historical context to get my bearings. So let me tell you a little more of what I see from my prescient perspective.

Justinian was the most famous of all the rulers of the Eastern Byzantine empire and in the early part of the sixth century he sought to re-conquer the lost western territories. He had spectacular successes. He reclaimed North Africa and Italy. Trade once more flourished with Wales and with Somerset and Cornwall, which were huge exporters of tin and lead to the East. The extent and impact of trade on Britain during Roman times is reflected at

Fishborne, the mansion of an early Celtic governor for the Romans. The structure was roofed with over 100 tons of Italian tile. In exchange British lead mines were supplying the metal for the plumbing of wealthy Roman villas. It may be the impact of lead poisoning and the ensuing mental illnesses it causes which were the real reason for the decline and fall of the Roman Empire.

In addition, to the non-time-defined me being able to see the future, as my character I am a curious, self-educated person who knows the contemporary historical setting. By the time the Romans left, and for the next two hundred years, all the Celtic princes, whose forbears worked in the Roman administration of Britain, considered themselves in part Roman. The Romans were not seen as invaders of Britain, as they were subsequently portrayed, rather as the superpower which befriended an existing tribal country, which in turn willingly became a colony state. Along with Roman administration and trade came ideas and education. During the period of Roman control through the mid-500s most Celtic chieftains were educated in Latin and read and spoke it.

During the 500s the successes of Justinian on the continent gave hope to the pro-Roman factions among the Celtic chieftains. There was a continued longing for the Pax Romana *of the centuries before. These hopes intensified around the figure of King Arthur.*

All of this background is important, or at least I think it is to Mother Mary. This was a period much like when Jesus arrived in Roman-repressed Judea. There were then, and in Arthur's time, astronomical displays of great light. There was then, and is now, much hardship among all people. The country is ripe for a deliverer. So it is not surprising, like the description of the wise men coming from the East to see the baby Jesus, that in Geoffrey of Monmouth's History of the Kings of Britain, *that he introduces the life of Arthur through the prophecies of Merlin in an age of despair and darkness* when the very sky was falling down and when the wrath of the stars dried up the crops in the fields. *And then there is the appearance of a* star of great magnitude and brilliance, with a single beam shining from it. At the end of this beam was a ball of fire, spread out in the shape of a dragon. From the dragon's mouth stretched forth two rays of light—the second split up into seven smaller shafts of light. The star appeared three times, and all who saw it were struck with fear and wonder."

Rat, if you really do think that Arthur was the bearer of, and an expression of, the consciousness gene, looks like he was getting the same kind of celestial drum-roll as Jesus received. Based on a bright comet appearing in the sky, Merlin sees the death of Arthur's predecessor and prophesies the coming of a mighty warrior-king, a Pendragon, who would rule all of Britain.

Most important, Rat, you must also understand the meaning of Arthur's name. Mother Mary tried to tell me some of this, but I am only now getting a better understanding of the meaning of Arthur's name. Like Arthur's father, whose title Pendragon has come to be thought of as his last name, or like Jesus, whose last name has come to be thought of as Christ—Arthur's name is an anglicized version of a Celtic title. In the Welsh language Arth Fawr means the "Great Bear." In Druidic times, this was the name given to the polar god, which symbolized those forces that hold life together and come to us from the constellation called Ursa Major, the Great Bear. Arcturus is a star near the tail of the Great Bear. Arcturus is a Latin root name for Arthur that also relates back in pre-Roman history to the Celtic word Artorix meaning Bear King. On the literal level the title suggests a man who is strong and powerful like a bear. On the symbolic level it connects the man who holds the title to the Celtic bear deity. In even earlier times this same polar constellation was called Draco, the dragon serpent. So in a sense Arthur's name is a more up-dated version of the Druidic title given to his predecessors. Both represent this bright constellation in the heavenly firmament which rotates across the sky around the polar star. Because of this, many ancient cultures in the Northern Hemisphere revered this constellation and its seven stars.

Arthur's name and title, on a mythological level, symbolize the alignment of the world axis, a mythic Mount Meru. Alignment with, or being this mythic bear mountain, represents congruence with the celestial north, the birthplace of initial motion and the beginning of time. It is a Druidic celestial way to give Arthur divine ancestry, just as in Christianity and Hinduism, Jesus and Krishna, respectively, come from divine virgin births. And, just as in the

Gospel stories of Jesus' birth, it is important to describe his lineage.

From the Bear Constellation comes the sacred number seven, which is identified with the seven chakras, or the seven energy levels through which a bearer of this name must move in order to come to hold the name. In holding the name, its bearer is carrying out both a cycle of personal transformation and a cycle of renewal and regeneration for the land. So you must understand that there is a historical King Arthur and a mythological one. The mythological one has become shrouded in mystery and his mythological life given many alternative plot lines. None of this diverse faux history takes away from, rather indeed adds to, the power of the myth. I will stick with the historical Arthur, though just like the historical Jesus, it is impossible not to also be aware that Arthur also carries a mythological persona that over time continued to grow as the importance of his holding a mythological identity for the people of Britain has grown.

Arthur was born in 482 at the Roman station of Caput Bovium, which later became known as Boverton. He was the son of Meurig and Onbrawst. Both his parents were of noble stock. He was educated at the famous monastic college at Llanilltyd Fawr (Llantwit Major). One of his instructors was St Illtud, who was known for his learning. His classmates include two men who would both later become sainted, Samson, a cousin of Arthur's and Gilda's. Later, Arthur was also taught by a secular priest under an abbot named Carentmael at Bodium in Cornwall. As a young man he traveled to Armorica (Brittany), where he visited with his extended family and the family of the man who became his father-in-law, Gwythyr, Count of Leon. Arthur, by his hereditary lineage, was entitled to be King of the Silures in South Wales.

Arthur was crowned King of Britain in 497, the year that his predecessor, King Ambrosius, died. Ambrosius had his greatest victory over the Saxons in 493 at Bown Hill, overlooking the Severn Valley. Close by at Woodchester was where Arthur was crowned by St Dyfrig, who would become archbishop of all of Wales. Arthur was fifteen years old. He will be followed by other young monarchs to the British throne, Richard II at ten and Queen Victoria at eighteen.

Let me try to sketch out Arthur's lineage. His Grandfather Tewdrig was a good king who had fought the Saxons and established the school where Arthur was later educated. Toward the end of Tewdrig's life, the Saxons invaded Wales again crossing the Wye and entering Gwent. Tewdrig led an army against them and successfully repulsed the invaders, though in the process he was mortally wounded. His son, Arthur's father, Meurig, rescued his father, who died at a place which became known as St Tewdig's Well. Meurig became Prince of Morgannwg and Gwent. Of course, he was also later known by his military title, as the Pendragon, head of the British fighting forces. He married Onbrawst. They had four sons, including Arthur, and three daughters. All the daughters married sons of Emyr Llydaw, Emperor of Armorica, cementing an alliance between the two families and the cross-channel connection between princes of Brittany and Wales.

On his maternal side, Arthur's mother, Onbrawst, is the daughter of Gwrgant Mawr, the King of Erging. Gwrgant was kicked out of his kingdom by Vortigen. Later Gwrgant was reinstated by Ambrosius. One of the sons of Gwrgant is Caradog Freichfras, Arthur's cousin, who often takes over the reins of government when Arthur is away fighting battles.

I am currently in Arthur's court. Well, Rat, what I mean is the person I am in this place in the field is in Arthur's court. My name is Gwenynen. In English it means bee, which may be a reflection of how my personality is seen. Truthfully, I am always busy buzzing around doing things and often asking questions.

I am much, much younger here than I was when I left your time zone. Maybe twelve, I would guess. Incredibly, I have some of the tattoos that I got when I was eleven and twelve in your time, including a dragon wandering down my arm. I cannot believe that I have now the same tattoos that I got again 1500 years later. That is not the only parallel. Just as happened in your time, I grew up here without parents. My life in your time would have ended up with me cutting myself so severely I died, or from a drug overdose, had I not hacked myself out of the mental ward and been befriended by Professor Gallagher.

A similar fate would have occurred here with me dying from wretched poverty and perhaps prostitution. However, when I was young here, I spent much time with an old Druid priestess who taught me the knowledge of healing herbs. I am precocious and became very good at using this knowledge, and during a time of illness among many at Arthur's Court, I was taken by the Druid priestess to help minister to the sick at Court. After the wave of illness subsided, I was befriended by a lady in Arthur's Court who had been very ill, whom I tended constantly at her bedside. When she recovered, she asked me to stay on as one of her ladies-in-waiting. I jumped at the opportunity. There was never an alternative.

Arthur's Court is at Caer Calemion near Cernyw in southeast Wales between Chepstow and Cardiff. Later writers identify Cernyw as in Cornwall, but Cornwall did not become known as Cernyw until the tenth century and this mistake is the reason much of the story of King Arthur is later wrongly located in the West Country of England. As I mentioned, I am sticking with the facts, and I doubt my information will have any negative impact on the South England King Arthur tourist trade.

Have no doubt about it, I am stuck along the coast of Wales and the winter weather is unremittingly rainy and cold. As a lady-in-waiting for a member of the Court, I do not lack for food, although there is not that much variety, especially in winter. Much porridge and the occasional stag that gets roasted. Rat, I can't wait to get some fresh fruit and veggies when I get back. Caer Calemion is a far cry from the stories and movie sets of Camelot. Already I see how later in history the Camelot myth helps conceal the important spiritual aspects of Arthur's life that were transpiring, and, certainly, we all need a good Camelot myth.

My mistress is something of a Druid priestess herself. She is not an official priestess who has spent the required twenty years of training to become a Druid priestess, but she is very involved in keeping worship of the great Mother Goddess alive among many in the castle. King Arthur allows his Court to be a place of religious toleration. He is well aware of his Celtic heritage with its divine associations, and I don't think he would lightly give that up, though there is increasing pressure by the Roman priests he keeps at Court to conform to a more Roman form of worship and living.

I see how Roman Christianity is slowly being turned against the old Goddess ways. Life is so hard that many are willing to give up sovereignty over their own lives and accept guilt-motivated rule by priests in exchange for the promise of a kinder and gentler eternal life. It is the classic bait and switch. Even under Arthur, the rise in power of the Roman form of Christianity continues unabated.

For now there is a blend of Christianity and the old Goddess religion at his Court and among the Celts. This blend is called Celtic Christianity. Celtic Christianity focuses on original blessing, not original sin. The seasonal feasts to celebrate the gifts of the earth are incorporated into the church calendar. There is a focus on Mary Magdalene, the first apostle, as a feminine figure as important as Jesus. Her reputation will suffer greatly later at the hands of the Roman church, as the Celtic church is driven underground, because of her important role in holding the sacred feminine in the early Celtic church. In her place the Roman church will substitute the Virgin Mary. A person portrayed so pure she is less human than Jesus. In the Druid Goddess religion, women are the primary priests. Men cannot be because they do not possess the physical ability to bring children into the world; thus, women are most naturally closest to the process of rebirth and regeneration each year, so necessary for the new crops that come each spring and so essential to life.

Because of their traditional role as priestesses, most of the first Celtic Christian church leaders here were abbesses. This was true for example at the great cathedral at Wells in England. Over time the role of women is repressed. Women are not just being kept from being leaders of the church; they are being prevented from being priestesses. To the traditional Celtic people this is an effrontery which they believe invites divine retribution. There have been, and will be, portentous celestial events that to the Celts represent a rebuke by the Goddess because so many do not follow the old ways. To the Roman church these signs are evidence of the unfaithfulness of the many Celtic people, who do not yet follow Roman orthodoxy. Regardless of which side you are on, my prescience leads me to see a remarkable sequence of spectacular natural events and calamities occurring in this period. In 524, there will be two extended periods of comets being bright during day and night. In 530, Halley's Comet makes a dramatic appearance. Again in 533 and 535 sizable comets appear in the sky.

In modern times, tree-ring evidence will show extreme climatic disruption during this era. Ice core investigations will reveal the presence of a major dusting of the earth with sulfur apparently caused by volcanic eruption or the impact of a meteorite or part of a comet.

In the life time of the character I am here, Rat, I can assure you these climate disruptions cause bitterly cold winters, failed crops and much hunger. There are no relief organizations, nor any place that has food from which relief could come.

The role of men in the Goddess religious culture was to be sacrificed in order for the fertility of the earth to be maintained. Jesus fits exactly into this paradigm. In the Celtic view he died not for our sins, rather he died, as ancient kings like Osiris died, for the regeneration of life through the Earth Goddess. Death of the king, symbolically, or literally, was the sacrifice necessary for the rejuvenation of the earth. Needless to say, by the time of Arthur, Celtic chieftains were downplaying the literal part of this mythology; however, the capacity for this kind of sacrifice is still real and potent. It is seen in the willingness of the king to lead his warriors into battle and put his life on the line for the good of his people.

A Roman-educated Celtic king like Arthur is pulled in two directions. He has a historic and bodily sense of the rightness of the way in which the Druidic Goddess religion balanced feminine and masculine energy. He understands the great administrative advantages of the Roman system of organization. And, part of the Roman heritage includes the Roman church, which is increasingly taking all power from the feminine and reducing the feminine to a sterile Mary. As I said, women are being denied leadership at abbeys, and they are being stigmatized rather than being honored as priestesses. Eventually, only men will be allowed to be priests. It is as if, with the loss of masculine authority in the political realm after the Romans left, the Roman church seeks to pour itself into and expand the role of patriarchal power. The political chaos which will follow after Arthur is no longer King will lead to an even greater overweighting of masculine in the religious realm. The church will turn a yearning for order into a rule of rigidity.

Complementing this over-weighting of the masculine, as the church seeks to increase its material wealth, it will impose a requirement of celibacy on priests. This will be done purely for economic reasons. If the priests had families at their deaths, they would leave their lands and the goods they acquired to their families. Being in the priesthood is often a way to amass considerable wealth. For the priests are very active in civil economic matters and at the same time supported by tithes extracted from the populace. By requiring celibate priests the church prevents any of the wealth, which resourceful priests and abbots acquire, from slipping out of the hands of the church. Forgive me, Rat, I am getting way ahead of my life here.

For now, suffice it to say that Arthur himself and Arthur's leadership reflect these competing pressures, at times leaning more toward the old ways and at other times looking more like a Roman Christian.

*   *   *

Rat, I am not sure you or Mother Mary are interested. I needed to give you some of the background I have learned in my short time here and some of what my prescience tells me is about what will unfold. You may be even less interested in what the intrigues are at Court and generally what is going on there; however, let me tell you about that. It is the world in which my character lives.

Arthur is married to the daughter of Count Gwythyr from a region in Brittany later known as Leon. Gwythyr's name also can be spelled Uthyr and this is one reason that historians will mistakenly call Arthur's father Uthyr. Uthyr is the father-in-law of Arthur, not his father. Gwythyr's daughter is Gwenhwyfar. Her name is later anglicized in literature to Guinevere.

She is indeed a beautiful woman. She is small, only about four feet ten inches tall and has long black hair, which is always pulled back tightly. She does not appear to long for one of Arthur's knights. She grieves for the loss of their only son. Their son died because of treachery. Arthur himself deeply grieves, feeling he is responsible for having put his son in danger and is having a large monument erected in his son's honor. Losing a child is always a heavy burden on any relationship.

There are knights of the Round Table. I am not really sure how many there are. Some say originally twelve, I think now Arthur might be up to twenty-four. The number is perhaps not as important as that, again like Jesus, Arthur's fame and legacy are built on having a band of at least a dozen loyal followers. Here are the ones that I see most at Court.

First, there is Sir Tristram. He is the son of Marcus Conomorus, a Glamorgan prince, who held sway in Cornwall and Brittany. Because of the connection with Brittany he is often called Tristan of Lyonesse. He is a handsome man, with long dark hair and a bold energy. You always know when Tristan is at hand because his energy draws your attention.

Then, there is Sir Bedwyr ap Bedrawd, or Sir Bedivere. He is known as one of the most courageous of Arthur's knights. He is of diminutive stature, only about five feet tall. He keeps his hair cut short, which is not the fashion. He was one of only two knights that Arthur took with him to avenge the death of Lady Helena, a relative of Arthur's who lived in Brittany.

Sir Cei ap Cynyr Ceinfarfog, or Sir Kay, has fiery red hair reflecting his Irish ancestry. He is a fierce fighter and one of Arthur's principal lieutenants. He has been at Arthur's side in all the important battles Arthur has fought.

Sir Riwal Mawr, or Sir Howell, is one of Arthur's principal allies. He is married to Arthur's half-sister Gwyar and he will be a leader in the battle that pits Arthur against Llwch Wyddel, who is the famed Lancelot, Lord of the Lakes. The lakes are in Ireland, a land of many lakes, not England or Wales.

Sir Gwalchmai, Sir Gaiwain, or 'Hawk of May,' is also related to Arthur and is not only a great warrior, he is one of the most courteous and loyal knights here at Camelot.

Rat, you are saying that you want me to forgo the Welsh names. Okay, just one more. I guess what they tell us more than anything is that the true place of Arthur's Court and the Round Table was in Wales.

I cannot omit Sir Gwalchaved, Sir Galahad or 'Hawk of Summer.' He is an older knight, who is married to Lady Alienor. He founded the house of Leon in Brittany. He is deeply respected by all.

Now, needless to say, there are many more knights. These are the principal ones whose names have gone down through history. What is significant is that Arthur's knights are as deeply woven into the family and social connections of Brittany as Wales.

Arthur has his knights and their vassals in a constant state of mobilization and presence at his Court. Thus, there are numerous brave and handsome knights here, while there are only a few women at Arthur's court. The intrigues among the women for the attention of the men are ongoing. Even though I am barely twelve years of age, I am at times given attention by several knights. This, for once, is something that is not parallel to my own adolescence in your time, where I was never sought out by any man close to what you might call a knight, and was more often prey for those men who see women as objects to be used. The knights here do not seem to mind that my figure is wholly undeveloped. They like my lively wit, though when not in conversation I am often teased that my brow is furrowed in concentration, which most likely it is.

Arthur is a shrewd warrior-king. He has a natural open-heartedness and upbeat energy that makes men and women alike want to be around him. When not on the road in battle mode, he keeps his knights engaged in tournament jousts. This has the dual result of keeping them battle ready and practically winnowing the field of suitors for the available women in the Court to those who have achieved the most skill for warfare. A knight whose battle skills are not outstanding need not worry about pining after some lady in the Court.

There are three levels of knighthood. They are the white knight, the red knight and the black knight. They represent three levels of consciousness that Arthur wishes his knights to move through. For as much as Arthur's Round Table is a school for warriors, it is also a school for consciousness. The white knight is the young, innocent knight who charges out to do good. It is the first stage of knighthood. Arthur does not accept young knights in his

Court who do not initially feel this commitment. Ultimately the naive, white knight takes the part of someone who is not purely innocent. He suffers remorse at championing the wrong side. He then becomes the red knight. His passion is to separate those who do good from those who do evil. He becomes a zealot to right wrongs. Then he encounters a trial where he loses his temper and does evil himself. Then he moves into the black knight stage. The black knight is the knight who explores his own shadow. He becomes less attached to what he thinks his view of good and evil are and more attached to what he believes the Goddess is asking him to do in each moment to promote the best for the kingdom. Those who are black knights are Arthur's most trusted comrades, though younger knights by virtue of their youth are sometimes superior on the field of battle.

Who are the available women? That is a good question. Queen Guinevere seems above it all. Whether she ever had a romance with Lancelot, there is no evidence of it now and I think unlikely. Everyone knows that Lancelot is an enemy of the King, and he is off in his homeland of lakes in Ireland, so of little concern at this moment.

I personally attend Lady Geirwir and I like her a lot. She is tall, at least for these times. She is a willowy woman with long brown hair. Like all the ladies of the Court she has access to the King's library. She reads Latin and has read many of Arthur's books. Books are rare and expensive items and not something you would likely own yourself, though Lady Geirwir has a few volumes of her own.

Sir Bedivere is very attentive to Lady Geirwir. She is either playing her hand very cautiously or put off a bit by the fact that he is shorter than she. She gets the attention of many of the knights because her mind is so lively and she easily engages in repartee with them at dinners in the great hall. Often when some of these knights come to leave her messages, I will answer the door to her chambers, and while delivering their messages for Lady Geirwir, even though I am too young to even be thought of as a woman, they will flirt shamelessly with me. My character, I see in my prescience, will try to follow the general mores of the Court and not be seduced by easy attentions. In the older days, sex with your peers of the opposite sex was encouraged, especially on Beltane and other sacred days. Now with the growing influence of the

Roman church, getting laid for the fun of it can easily result in a young girl like me, who is not of noble birth, getting banished from Court.

Sometimes, in the future, when my character is ministering to wounded knights, they will fall in love with me in a very real way, especially some of those who are delirious and severely wounded. Often these do not recover; however, if they do, my presence with them when they were struggling to survive causes them to project some angelic qualities onto me. I have to admit that when these knights recover, I am sorely tempted to oblige the ones who gallantly and respectfully share their desire to take me to bed. Nothing quite so seductive to a girl, even one only twelve or thirteen, who is of the old Beltane school and not shamed by sex, than to be honestly desired and put on a pedestal at the same time. Sure never got a taste of that in my youth in your time zone, Rat.

I see that I am wandering. Who else in the Court would you like to know about? I don't have a clue who is important. There are twin sisters from Ireland, who are daughters of a chieftain there. They are here as a peace offering after an Irish raid. Arthur agreed not to retaliate if the two beautiful nieces of the Irish King were sent to be raised in his Court. One is Brigid and the other Bridgette. As you would expect they both have long red hair and green eyes and attract the attention of all the young knights. The rumor is that one is sleeping with Sir Tristram and one with Sir Kay. There will probably be a different rumor of who they are sleeping with next week. If I had to wager on it, I would bet on all the rumors being true. Both these young women are lusty adherents of St. Brigit of Kildare, who is a proponent of the true version of Celtic, Goddess Christianity.

Adherents of St. Brigit often keep the tradition of Beltane, the seasonal ritual in which the most beautiful woman waits for the young man who would show the greatest bravery and cunning in slaying a stag. He is brought fresh from his kill, the testosterone still raging, to her bedside. She does not meet him passively. She would have spent her day being bathed and massaged by priestesses in such a way that her libido is also in high gear. The two would meet in darkness, or with masks on, so that the sexual union was not personal, rather an act of worship so the great Mother Goddess would renew the land with spring. Meanwhile, men and women from the *local villages would be dancing around the fire half the night and at some point the dancing would lead to their somewhat arbitrarily pairing together and going to lie, two by two, off in the woods.*

To tell you the truth, Rat, Beltane reminds me of what used to happen at tent-meeting revivals in the South where I grew up in the United States. The teenage boys and teenage girls, wanting to experience sex for the first time, would go to the revival tent-meeting and sit on opposite sides of the center aisle. At some point in the service when people were getting "slain in the spirit" while dancing around in a pitch of emotional fever, the girls would slip off their panties. One girl would slip the handful of panties to one of the boys at the back of the tent. As the revival reached its pitch the girls would sneak outside and head for a wooded area nearby. There, each boy would have a girl's panties. Whoever had your panties, you went with him into the woods. The shy girls were emboldened by their control of the process. The really bashful boys got to have a manhood experience, as the girls were careful never to turn away a timid boy. However, a girl could always decide not to go with a boy who was a bully. He would be left literally holding the panties and he had absolutely no way to know whose they were. Well, Rat, Beltane is sort of like that.

Beltane should give you the flavor of the approach of the two Irish sisters. In a strange way their sleeping with different knights, and especially Brigdette's seeming desire to bed all the great knights, appears to elevate their status and they accept the attention and liaisons not in a flaunting way, but as simply their due. While such behavior by other women, and especially a non-noble woman like me, would bring quick condemnation by the priests who seek to influence the elders in the Court, for these two Irish women it seems to simply enhance their image.

King Arthur, I know, is hoping they will both marry and stop hopping from bed to bed. Good marriages to knights loyal to him would go a long way to help Arthur assure the security of the West coast of Wales. This would allow Arthur to focus his attention on the incursions of the Picts from the North and the Saxons from the East. The only rumors that fly more rapidly around the Court than who is seducing who, and who is sleeping with which Irish sister, are the rumors of Arthur's next campaign.

Chapter 2

Caer Calemion, Wales
Summer 518

There is a knock on the door. Gwenynen looks up. Her room serves as an anteroom for Lady Geirwir's chambers. Anyone looking for Lady Geirwir has to enter Gwenynen's room first. Lady Geirwir gives strict instructions that no one should come into her chambers without her permission. Part of Gwenynen's job is to serve as a buffer against those wishing to visit Lady Geirwir.

The knock repeats. It is not a loud or demanding knock. It is firm and solid. Gwenynen's brow furrows. She gets up and cracks open the door. Yes, she is right; it is Lady Bridgette.

"You look well and vibrant today," says Lady Bridgette. "It is good to see you, Gwenynen." She looks at Gwenynen with her piercing green eyes.

Gwenynen curtsies in reply as is the etiquette. Even though Brigid and Bridgette are in a sense hostages, they are entitled to be treated by all like ladies of the Court.

"I am in need of your lady's help. I need a love potion. I have yet to sleep with all of Arthur's men." She pauses. "And, for that matter Arthur himself."

"Lady Geirwir asked not to be bothered this morning. I shall give her a message that you came calling on her," says Gwenynen, sounding to herself rather formal as she seeks to assert herself in protection of her mistress.

"Maybe you can help me, Gwenynen. I understand you are quite knowledgeable about the herbs that Lady Geirwir uses." Bridgette's gaze hovers on Gwenynen expectantly.

"Thank you for the compliment, Lady Bridgette. I have some facility with the plants that I am being taught about by Lady Geirwir. However, I never make any potions except under her instruction. And actually, we are quite busy. I am afraid it signals that King Arthur is going to war again. I am spending much time at Lady Geirwir's direction preparing the compounds we use to treat wounded knights."

"That is discouraging," says Lady Bridgette with a frown. "I want to finish bedding all the knights at Court, and then I hope I will be able to return home. First and foremost, I believe it is the will of the Goddess that I allow all these Welshmen to experience the glory of the feminine." She gives Gwenynen a sly smile as if she is exchanging illicit contraband. "Especially the Irish feminine.

"I know you probably do not approve. You are young and you Welsh are so used to listening to those Roman priests. Sex is sacred and powerful. It is even more powerful when engaged in ritually to please the Goddess. As long as a woman like me mates with men for the pleasure of the Goddess and not simply for personal pleasure, the Goddess approves. Without it we would have no crops each year, and you know how bizarre and erratic our harvests have been. It is my hope to do my little part to get the cycle of regeneration back on track. I know most of the Court thinks I am promiscuous, even though I am only doing my sacred duty. I promise you I am causing more joy than those Roman priests lurking around Arthur's Court with their perpetually sour expressions. The only one whom I think truly understands me here is Merlin. Thank goodness for him and that he always has the King's ear."

Gwenynen looks at Lady Bridgette. She is strikingly beautiful. More than her physical beauty, there is an energy about her that immediately attracts. She is not an overly sexualized woman like distant cultures would promote later, and certainly not sexually anorexic, the other extreme resulting from that promotion. She completely embodies her sexuality. It is not a part of her that is different from the rest of who she is. She is full of vitality and life force which obviously comes from being totally at home with her sexuality and who she is. Her sexuality is not something separate from her. Gwenynen, who has always experienced men as predators to be avoided, can't help but be astonished at Lady Bridgette's completely different perspective. Most of all, Gwenynen likes the easy way conversation is with Lady Bridgette. Lady Bridgette treats Gwenynen as if they have a special bond of kinship merely by both being women. She makes Gwenynen feel quite comfortable.

"Lady Bridgette I would be glad to help you, if I may. Let me give your message to Lady Geirwir. I will tell her that if she cannot help you that I would be glad to try."

"Gwenynen, thank you so much. I hope you can help me. I must say I like the mysterious tattoo you have winding down your arm. I can only imagine that it must be tantalizing to young men, who wonder where it goes."

Gwenynen blushes. Her tattoos were from a Druid shaman who helped her escape from her dire situation when she was young without parents. The tattoos are powerful medicine to protect her. So far they have worked. Gwenynen has never thought they might be intriguing to men. She works her sleeve down her arm.

"Oh, do not bother," says Lady Bridgette. "I quite approve of your tattoo. I have several myself given to me by the Goddess. They are not where I can show them off to you easily." She smiles at Gwenynen knowingly.

Then Bridgette turns and walks toward the door. At the entranceway she looks back at Gwenynen and smiles again. It is a lovely comforting smile. "I will call back before long to see if Lady Geirwir will allow you to help me." She shuts the door and it is as if the sun has gone behind a cloud.

*   *   *

Lady Geirwir listens to Lady Bridgette's request, brought to her by Gwenynen as she motions for Gwneynen to sit down. They are in Lady Geirwir's work room, which is the center room of her chambers. Beautiful tapestries hang on the wall, which help keep the cold of winter at bay. The central feature of the room is a very large window that allows a great sheet of light to fall across a worktable placed in the center of the room. The table as usual is covered with plants being dried, potions being mixed and books on loan from King Arthur's library. After Gwenynen finishes speaking, Lady Geirwir looks out the window for a long moment before replying.

"Gwenynen, I believe I can talk to you directly, knowing you will be completely discreet in what I tell you."

Gwenynen nods *yes*.

"I was speaking with King Arthur and Merlin about Lady Bridgette. She is a beautiful, smart woman and a complicated problem. It was a stroke of brilliant diplomacy when Arthur got the two young women to come to his Court in lieu of his striking back at Ireland after the Irish Gewissei attacked western Wales. It has allowed Arthur to focus on the Picts in the North and the Angles and Saxons on the East in his efforts to reunite Britain as it was for so long under the Romans.

"The two young women are very different even though they are twins. Brigid is quite the serious student and has read much in the King's library. Bridgette, on the other hand, has made it her self-appointed spiritual mission to bed all the knights at Court, and it is causing increasing havoc.

"First, she has a tryst with Sir Tristram. Well, who could fault her for that. He is a handsome man, though he knows it all too well. Then many others followed. However, her sleeping with Sir Kay and now Sir Bedivere...." She frowns. She spits out Sir Bedivere's name like rancid food. "As I was saying, she has caused two of Arthur's closest lieutenants to be at odds. I think she has slept with every knight at Court, except Sir Gaiwain, Sir Galahad and the King.

"Gwenynen, as you might have inferred from our hectic efforts to make dressings and have compounds ready for wounded soldiers, Arthur is preparing to go to war again. He has reliable intelligence that there is a considerable threat massing not far off. He cannot defend the kingdom and have two of his most important knights not speaking to each other.

"Bridgette leaves a wake of broken hearts and knights more interested in reciting poetry than fighting. Arthur has to do something. That is why Merlin and I met with him last night. He has decided to send Bridgette to a Convent on a small isle off the coast of Wales called Ynys Enlli. At first we thought he might send her to an abbey in England. She would go berserk with the Roman version of Christianity practiced there. Arthur quite wisely wants to put her away from causing turmoil at Court, and not under such harsh conditions that she causes such a furor that her chieftain father, or the King in Ireland, might again strike Wales.

"The community on this Welsh isle is special. It is where St Dyfrig has declared he will retire. He will go there to live in a small hermitage after he retires in a few years as Archbishop of Wales. The isle itself is under the ecclesiastical control of a group of Sisters who are followers of St. Brigit of Kildare. Bridgette is a follower of St. Brigit, so this should soften the blow. Nonetheless, Bridgette will probably look at it as some kind of exile, though Arthur will present it to her as a chance to have a holiday of sorts and avoid the risk of being near the fighting that is about to commence.

"This is a long answer to your rather short question, Gwenynen. Before you could make a potion for Bridgette, she is going to be on her way, far away—kicking and screaming probably, both literally and figuratively. Merlin, who is quite fond of the two Irish women, agrees that this plan is necessary. Brigid will be given the option either to go with her sister or stay here for now.

"If you hear further from Bridgette, please avoid giving her an answer. She will be gone by this time tomorrow."

"I understand, Lady Geirwir," says Gwenynen. As she starts to leave she feels as if a voice in her head is requiring her to speak. Out of her mouth pops a question she could never have imagined that she would have asked. "I would like to better understand the difference between Celtic Christianity and Roman Christianity in Britain. What is the difference and what does the difference look like?"

Lady Geirwir is at once taken back by the temerity of the question and intrigued by the young woman's interest in such matters. As a councilor to the King herself, she immediately empathizes with Gwenynen's desire to understand the political-spiritual reality in which they live. Indeed, understanding such matters and using this knowledge wisely are keys to Arthur's successful rule, and, unlike non-Celtic rulers, Arthur relies on the sage advice of wise women councilors, who are Druidic in perspective, and the Druid Merlin, at his Court.

"This may take a bit of time," responds Lady Geirwir. "If you are really interested pull up that stool, and I will try to explain."

Without hesitation Gwenynen pulls up a small stool and sits down as Lady Geirwir settles into her favorite chair.

"You must first understand that before Celtic Christianity, there was Celtic Druidism. You have met Merlin at Court and you know that he is a Druid. He underwent the normal twenty years of training to become a Druid priest. Druids take a vow that they will never write down what they have learned. This is why their training is so long because there is so much to be remembered, and the Druids believe that by not writing down what they learn they retain what they learn as wisdom not just as information.

"Merlin is a contemporary expression of Druidism, as he represents an accommodation with Celtic Christianity because he seeks to serve King Arthur in Arthur's desire to be both a Celtic Christian King and a Celtic Goddess King. In the old days before the advent of Christianity all the spiritual needs of the people were looked after by Druid priestesses and priests. The Druids were responsible for leading the ritual celebrations of renewal and regeneration so important to the livelihood of agrarian, tribal people. The Druids were scholars and ambassadors between tribes. They were not chieftains; however, they were the most respected segment of early Celtic society in Britain. Because of their influence on the people, even though they had no armies, the Romans early in their occupation sought to eliminate the Druids as a potential political force.

"This effort by the Romans came to a terrible climatic end in 60 A.D. when the Roman general Suetonius Paulinus marched his forces to the extreme northwestern corner of Wales and assembled them opposite the island of Anglesey. For the Druids the land is the church. Rituals occur outside. A hill becomes an altar. A grove of oaks a tabernacle. It is the tradition of the Druids to create their centers on islands so that traveling to them by pilgrims involves going across the liminal space of the sea. The greatest of these centers was Anglesey. General Paulinus' troops crossed the Menai Strait and destroyed a vast encampment of Druids as well as many sacred ritual sites and thousands of artifacts.

"This was the end of an era. After the massacre of Druids at

Anglesey, the Druids went underground. They became masters at thriving among the Romans without being seen as a threat by the Romans. They were never a threat politically anyway. Their deception, necessary for their survival, allowed a strain of Druidic belief to persist that later became part of the warp and woof of Celtic Christianity.

"Christianity came to Britain with Joseph of Arimathea's journey here after the death of Christ. Joseph thrust his staff in the ground at Glastonbury and symbolically planted Christianity in Britain right at the beginning of the Christian era. So both Celtic Christians and Roman Christians look back to Joseph of Arimathea and claim that their tradition goes back to the first Christian in Britain—in other words, each version claims it is the purest, or most authentic.

"However, meaningful efforts to spread Christianity among the Britons did not come for a while. Remember that before Emperor Constantine's conversion, Christianity was illegal, and, for the most part, Christianity only existed in desert locations in Egypt, in caves in Cappadocia and in Palestine among small groups that met in individual homes. After Constantine's battlefield dream and conversion, Christianity was legalized in 313. Not long after, Christianity became the imperial religion of Rome. So Roman Christianity came to Britain over the next hundred years of Roman occupation. The form of it was the same form as the Roman governmental structure, a hierarchical top down model. This worked in those places in England that were thoroughly controlled and long occupied by the Romans. It did not work so well in the more tribal and rural areas of Wales. Such structures, religious or political, had no presence at all in Ireland, which was never occupied by Rome.

"In the fourth century, the first prominent Celtic theologian came on the scene, Pelagius. You will often hear the Roman clerics refer derogatorily to Pelagius, accusing him of heresy. The truth of the matter is those charges were largely trumped up.

Pelagius was home grown. He was the son of a distinguished Welsh bard. He was a large man with a jolly appearance embodying that natural sense of joy in creation, which is a part of the British Celtic character. He wore his hair in the pre-Christian Druidic style, long on top and shaved on the sides and back, as opposed to the style of the Roman cut, shaved at the crown of the head.

"In the 380s Pelagius traveled to Rome. His physical size and presence made him noticeable to others, and he was regarded as a man of personal sanctity and deep conviction. In Rome he lived as a lay monk and became known as a teacher and writer. He developed a substantial following.

"His writings reveal the themes that would characterize Celtic Christianity in Wales and Ireland and eventually in Scotland. He focused less on relying on the spiritual authority of the church and its class of priests and more on finding a soul friend, an *anamchara*."

Gwenynen sees Lady Geirwir stiffen as she refers to the priest class.

"Pelagius, in contrast to the Roman priests, who always harped on the sinfulness of everyone and the need for people to pay priests to pray to redeem them, focused on the goodness of creation and the many ways in which God is present in creation. He saw God present not only in people, but in trees and animals. His view of the goodness of creation and God's presence throughout it fit perfectly with the Druidic view of the Goddess present in all things.

"His emphasis was not on particular religious beliefs and church doctrine, rather on living a life of love toward all people and things. He also had a passionate belief in the need for Christians to demand justice for all, and even that wealth should be distributed more evenly.

"You can image how well his views on the redistribution of wealth went over with the Roman elite."

Gwenynen nods, totally entranced by the story of Celtic Christianity that Lady Geirwir is unfolding.

"That is not all. Pelagius also believed women should read scripture and he taught them how. This and his conviction that in the newborn child one could see the image of God—a part of his belief in the goodness of creation—was what finally got him excommunicated by Rome. His focus on the need for women to read scripture, just as well as men, fit entirely with the Druidic Celtic practices where women were the primary priests."

Lady Geirwir smiles. "Perhaps his excommunication was for the best, for it brought him back to his Celtic homeland.

"Here is how it actually happened. He wrote a letter, which became public, to a young woman named Demetrias, who was from a leading family in Palestine, responding to questions she asked. This made the Roman church mad from the start that he would be that concerned about the spiritual journey of a woman. However, the woman had sought his advice, and he responded advising her to seek her answer in the inner recesses of her soul where she would find the answer." She pauses in her story telling.

"Well, you grasp what I am saying, I believe."

"Yes," says Gwenynen. "I understand. I surmise one reason you do not condemn Lady Bridgette is that she takes a stand for the leadership and equality of women in spiritual matters."

Lady Geirwir looks at Gwenynen with renewed appreciation for her young apprentice. Lady Geirwir nods her head.

"Yes, while I do not necessarily approve of her bedding crusade,

I most certainly appreciate how she stands toe to toe with men in her knowledge, and her appreciation of the importance of the role of the feminine, and her embodiment of feminine power to show the living reality of the feminine as a source of strength—a different kind of strength, but a strength just as important as masculine energy.

"Anyway, enough about Lady Bridgette just now. Turns out that Lady Demetrias had also asked St. Augustine for advice. Lecher turned saint that he was, he did not like having Pelagius cast as his peer, and he most especially did not like Pelagius' advice—for her to find her answer from God deep within her inner most being.

"Augustine, based on his own experience, emphasized human depravity and so Pelagius was quite at odds with his emphasis. Under Augustine's view the only place to look for God was the Church. For Pelagius you could find God in many places, and most especially beyond the bounds of the Church.

"After Pelagius' letter was published, Augustine sent his friend Orosius to Jerusalem to try to get Pelagius convicted of heresy. Two attempts were made to have Pelagius convicted in 415 and twice he was acquitted by the Church. The next year Augustine and a couple of his bishop buddies convened two diocesan councils at which Pelagius and his Celtic friend Celestius were both condemned. The Pope was drawn in to the controversy the next year and convened a synod in Rome to consider the conflict. The synod found Pelagius' teachings entirely orthodox.

"Having failed in their efforts to have Pelagius declared a heretic by the Church, Augustine and his cronies turned to the state. Rome was disintegrating at this time, so it was easy in 418 to get an imperial edict banishing Pelagius from Rome. Building on the momentum of the banishment, Augustine was successful in having Pelagius excommunicated later that year.

"Pelagius then returned home to Wales very much the hero. Because Rome had an even a more tenuous connection to Ireland, he eventually went there for sanctuary. In Ireland, Pelagius teamed up with one of the other leading lights of Celtic spirituality, Ninian. Ninian trained in Rome also. Later he returned to the Isle of Whithorn just off the coast of southern Scotland, within view on a clear day of Ireland. Ninian modeled his monastic community there, not on the Roman hierarchical diocesan structure, but on the model of the Eastern Church. This model was less hierarchical and much more suited for the rural and tribal nature of the Celtic lands."

"So Ninian and Pelagius brought a version of the Gospel to the Celts that emphasized a non-hierarchal form of Christianity, where access to divine guidance was from one's inner knowing, and women and men were equal participants in stewarding the religion," says Gwenynen.

"You understand very well, my dear," replies Lady Geirwir. "You could say that if you have to look up to find the Divine through a hierarchical structure the word for the Divine becomes God. If you look down into creation for the Divine, without your gaze being mediated by a priestly power structure, then the word for the Divine becomes Goddess.

"Around approximately 430, when Ninian was already at the Isle of Whithorn, St Patrick, who received his training in the Ninianic tradition, began his mission to Ireland. Just like Pelagius, St Patrick emphasized that all created things are carried in the grace and goodness of God. His famous breastplate prayer has such wonderful lines."

Lady Geirwir began to chant in a quavering voice:

Christ be with me, Christ within me,
Christ behind me, Christ before me,
Christ beside me, Christ to win me,

Christ to comfort and restore me.
Christ beneath me, Christ above me,
Christ in quiet, Christ in danger,
Christ in hearts of all that love me,
Christ in mouth of friend and stranger.

A lovely silence extends after Lady Geirwir finishes. Gwenynen is totally entranced.

"That is Celtic Christianity. The very feel of it resonates with the way the Celts have worshipped the Goddess for years. St. Patrick and Pelagius effectively integrated Goddess worship into Celtic Christianity or Christianity into Goddess worship, you take your pick. A well that was once named for a Druid Goddess might now be named for St. Mary. However, the feel of the life-giving nature of the water coming from the Creator remains the same. So smoothly does the glove of this form of Christianity fit the soul of the Celtic psyche, that many believe that Christianity was present among the Druidic Celts before the coming of Jesus. That is also why many refer to Jesus as the son of the Goddess.

"One of the strongest advocates of Celtic Christianity is Lady Bridgette's heroine, St. Brigit, Abbess of Kildare. Kildare means 'church of the oaks' so we can surmise that it is a church built on a Druidic site; and, if Christianity had not come along with Patrick, Brigit would have presided there as a Druid priestess. St. Brigit is known to embody the power of a Celtic triple Goddess, that is she represents three aspects of a woman: the young virgin, the nurturing and loving mother, and the crone or wise woman. The triple Goddess energy is very fiery and she is known to protect those tirelessly who call upon her.

"From the start Kildare has been a religious community for both men and women, with Brigit at its head. If you believe in the natural goodness of creation you are not going to embark on weird practices like celibacy. Celtic Christianity as Lady Bridgette so well illustrates does not separate the sexes, or fear sexuality or think it is evil. Just the opposite: sexuality is something to be celebrated and made a part of the most important rituals of life and the church. Lady Bridgette in her taking-all-knights-to-bed campaign does get a bit far afield, for there is no tradition of promiscuity at Kildare, but certainly her approach to the goodness of sex is very basic to the notion of Celtic Christianity. If it were not for sex we would not be here, so to the Celtic mind it seems obvious that sex is sacred.

"St. Brigit has become revered as a saint, rivaled only by St. Patrick in the esteem with which she is held. She was my first teacher, Gwenynen, in the science of healing herbs. She was a great healer and knew how to heal both with love and herbs, and especially with both together, which is the most potent healing combination there is."

"I am even more honored to be your student," says Gwenynen. "I did not know that you were taught by the revered St. Brigit."

"Yes, I went to Kildare when I was very young and learned to read and write there. After the first few years, St. Brigit took a personal interest in me, and, like you, I seemed to have some facility for finding medicinal plants, curing them and making elixirs from medicinal herbs. I always celebrate her feast day, which is February the first. It was formerly celebrated as the Imbolc quarter day of the Druidic year. This day marks the beginning of the first phase of spring, lambing, and the beginning of lactation in cattle and sheep. St. Brigit was always so generous to the poor and performed amazing healings through her great caring. Her healings are often called miracles. They simply represented her keen knowledge of natural healing herbs and the great compassion of her heart.

"One of her projects at Kildare was the creation of several illuminated Bibles, which were completed at the Kildare scriptorium. King Arthur received one of these most sacred volumes when the twin sisters came here from Ireland. I have seen it and the letters seem to just jump off the page in the vivid wardrobe of their illuminations.

"So there you have it my child, a short history of the Celtic church in Wales and Ireland. I hope you can sense how very different it is from the Roman church. Part of King Arthur's greatness...."

She stops and looks out the window for a moment. "Perhaps part of his great weakness is that he is so solidly heir to the Celtic tradition from which he derives his name, and he is also so completely heir to the Roman culture which gives him his gifts of administration and his learning of Greek and Roman ways.

"I have gone on way too long talking. Off you go, girl. It is such a beautiful summer day outside. Take that large basket with you for gathering. We do need more cloves for antiseptics and pain killing. Don't forget lavender. I need to compound something for Arthur's headaches. Check the supply of myrrh gum. I know Arthur ordered a large lot that came on the last merchant ship arriving from North Africa. We need as much of it as possible ready for treating wounds."

"Yes, Lady Geirwir," says Gwenynen, picking up the large basket and heading for the door. "Thank you for telling me so much about Celtic Christianity. My understanding is much better."

Lady Geirwir gives a quick nod and closes the door as Gwenynen leaves.

*   *   *

The next morning Gwenynen is up early preparing for a scouting trip to look for more medicinal herbs. Winter and early spring were so cold and dreary the days of summer are a precious delight. It is barely sunrise and she is surprised to see people mounting horses. Then she sees Lady Bridgette. She is mounted on a horse. She holds a rein, and there are also leads going to soldiers mounted beside her.

With some effort Lady Bridgette stops her horse. She calls to Gwenynen.

"Gwenynen, please attend me for a moment."

Gwenynen walks over. The soldiers look at Sir Tristram, who is apparently in charge of the escort detail. He makes a motion of acquiescence and says, "Hold up a minute, this cannot possibly be of any harm."

Gwenynen walks right up beside Lady Bridgette's horse. Lady Bridgette leans down. "They are shipping me off to Ynys Enlli against my will. Arthur will rue the day he did this. Enough of that for now. What I want to ask you is would you like to come join me there? There are many medicinal herbs on the isle I understand. Some quite rare. There are priestesses there from whom we could both learn, not only about plants, but of the old ways. I would like you to come if you would like. Once I get there, I will write Arthur and ask to have you as a lady-in-waiting. If you would like to visit with me there, please come."

Gwenynen curtsies. "Thank you for asking me, Lady Bridgette. I know I cannot come right now because of the impending battle. After that, if Arthur consents, I would love to visit the isle and learn more of healing and the old ways." Even as she speaks Gwenynen has a curious inner knowing that the invitation to go to Ynys Enlli is not just from Lady Bridgette, but from Gwenynen's own destiny.

Lady Bridgette smiles one of her radiant smiles. Gwenynen, who never had a mother's love growing up, feels buoyed and full of joy.

"Wonderful," says Lady Bridgette. "I will hope to see you before too long."

With that, Sir Tristram signals his men to start up, and the horses are off with a start. Lady Bridgette pulls a hood from her cape over her head and does not look back.

Chapter 3

The trip to Ynys Enlli is difficult. The weather is poor. Most days it rains much of the day. Lady Bridgette is in such a state of pique for the first few days that, much to the amusement of Sir Tristram, she hardly speaks to him for the first part of the journey.

Her lively nature does not allow this to last for long. By the time they get to Pwllheli, she and Sir Tristram are sharing the same tent at night and in the evenings there is much singing and laughing among the escorted and the escort.

The final part of the journey out along the Llyn peninsula is more difficult, as their journey takes them away from the coastline. Finally, they are only about a day from the place to catch a boat to the isle. Lady Bridgette and Sir Tristram have spent a torrid night abed together. They are both tired and pleasantly sated. The morning sky clears, rain-washed blue.

"Sir Tristram, you have been most pleasing company on this trip. I have a proposition to make," says Lady Bridgette.

"Yes, what is it, my dearest? This is truly the most wonderful duty I have ever had to embark on for my King."

"Well, that does get to the heart of it. I would like us to continue on from the Llyn peninsula to Ireland. Once we reach the end of the peninsula, on a clear day, we will be able to see Ireland. It is not that far.

"Now, I know Arthur is not going to be immediately happy about this, but you will be able to convince him you did absolutely the right thing. For if you dump me on Ynys Enlli, I will be in touch with my father and he shall revenge my mistreatment, much to Arthur's regret. On the other hand, if you deliver me back to my home in Ireland, I will cause Arthur no trouble, my father will handsomely reward you and Arthur will still have my sister as a pawn in the politics of kingdom rivalry and war, which you men persist in playing."

She walks up to Sir Tristram and pulls his head down to her and kisses him fully on the lips.

"Lady Bridgette, I would be delighted to continue our trip regardless of the destination. Nowhere have I ever met such a fiercely beautiful woman as you. Yet, I have to consider my obligation to my King.

"I must tell you that when Arthur gave me this assignment he said for me to expect that you would make a proposition such as you have made. He asked me to decide before I left his Court what my decision would be. I swore an oath to him then that I would abide by his wishes to deliver you to this isle."

Sir Tristram looks at Bridgette. Her hair is tousled. She only has a shawl over her bare breasts since they have not yet started to dress for the day's ride. He feels a physical longing for her that is almost overwhelming, despite the fact they made love most of the night. He takes her hands and places them on his chest.

"My dear lady, if I did as you wish, you would be home, and I would be where I could never return home. I understand your desire to go home and it is my very understanding of the intensity of that desire which tells me I cannot fulfill your wish. I am sorry."

He continues to look into her eyes until she averts her gaze and pulls her hands away.

Finally she says, "There is home and there is home. I could make a home for you that would surpass the pleasure of any piece of geography." She touches him gently between the legs. "Something tells me you would find that reward enough."

"My lady, you have shot a true arrow of longing into my body. Having felt the hard edge of Arthur's sword on my shoulders, such longing has been ransomed to him. We will have to continue our trip as planned."

Lady Bridgette turns and goes back into the tent to get dressed.

*   *   *

Once they arrive at Porth Meudwy, it takes some days for them to convince Barinthus, the boatman, to make the trip to Ynys Enlli. While Ynys Enlli is only a short distance from the mainland, the stretch of water separating them is one of the most hazardous anywhere on the coast of Wales. Many stories are told of men attempting to row to Ynys Enlli, who end up being pushed far out to sea or into the sheer, rocky northeastern face of the isle.

After a time Barinthus is able to deliver them, without incident, to the small sandy beach on the west side of the isle, the only point at which it is possible for any craft to make land. Sir Tristram does not tarry. Barinthus insists they immediately turn around and head back across, while there is still a neutral tide.

Lady Bridgette finds herself relieved to be on the isle. She writes a letter to King Arthur in the last few days of their journey asking him to allow Gwenynen to come attend her on the isle and gives the letter to Sir Tristram to take back to Arthur. As soon as she steps off the boat, she feels an overwhelming sense of peace.

"Welcome to the isle, I am Sister Bendithion. I am glad you are here."

Lady Bridgette looks closely at Sister Bendithion. Sister Bendithion is not dressed in the disciplined clothing of a convent sister, but rather wears a gaily patterned wool jumper, a friendly smile and a purposeful expression. Lady Bridgette asks, "Did you know I was coming?"

"Well, not for certain. We do practice looking into the future and I saw clearly that someone special was coming to the isle. I think you will find it very pleasing to be here. St. Brigit sent a group of women here some years back. We are also expecting to have more men join us here in our religious community as is the practice with those who follow St. Brigit. St Cadfan has come with monks from Brittany recently and our prescience tells us that St Dyfrig may join us before too long.

"Enough of what might happen. Come, let me show you your quarters, get you something to eat and then I can give you a tour around the isle."

"Thank you, Sister Bendithion, you are quite generous. You know it is not my own wishes that bring me here. I am a pawn in the silly games King Arthur and my Father, a noble Irish chieftain, are playing. I am unhappy to be here, but I thank you for your warm welcome. If I end up staying very long, which I certainly hope will not be the case, perhaps I can improve my knowledge of healing plants."

The two women begin to walk from the small beach back to the Convent that is located at the base of the large stone massif that provides the isle its protection from north easterly winds. As they walk, Lady Bridgette is amazed at both how small the isle is and how productive it appears to be. There are shepherdesses out looking after sheep that are scattered about grazing everywhere, a few cows in a stone enclosed pasture and several large productive-looking garden plots.

"I see so many different birds here," says Lady Bridgette.

"Yes, this is a special place in so many ways, including being holy for birds as well as humans. Many birds come here from different places to nest because there are no predators for them here. I love to watch the fulmars soaring majestically above the waves. One Sister has seen over four hundred different species on the island."

"That is astounding," says Lady Bridgette. "I have never glimpsed so many birds that I have never seen before."

"Yes, we say on this holy isle—no prey, only praying," says Sister Bendithion with a grin.

Lady Bridgette can't help but return a smile.

"Birds always remind us of our spiritual nature because they are flying over us, enlarging the space above us. Yet here they are all nesting on the ground and calling to each other perched upon the gorse. They seem to move back and forth between heaven and earth seamlessly, and that is our desire in the life we lead here on Ynys Enlli."

"You must feel very fortunate to be here," says Lady Bridgette.

"Indeed, we are so fortunate in many ways, which you will soon discover. Listening all day to the birds chattering is just one of the things which I find adds a certain lightness of spirit to being here."

"As I told you, Sister Bendithion, I am not happy about being here, but I will try to adjust. I see you have some interesting looking buildings in your convent compound. Maybe I can explore them later, but for now if you can show me to where I shall have my lodgings, I need a bit of rest. Trying to introduce my escort to the ways of the Goddess on the trip over here was time consuming and a bit exhausting, if you know what I mean."

Lady Bridgette gives Sister Bendithion a knowing look. Sister Bendithion's response is a kind smile, which does not indicate one way or the other how much she infers from Lady Bridgette's comment and glance.

"Coming to an isle like Ynys Enlli is itself a pilgrimage, a call away from distractions. Maybe the reasons that got you here are not that important. The fact that all of us Sisters have flourished here is living proof of the Goddess' desire that we be here and have time for her. What an extraordinary blessing!" says Sister Bendithion.

"You are too," says Bridgette, warming a bit to Sister Bendithion's efforts to make her feel welcome. And well named, she thinks, remembering that Sister Bendithion's name in Welsh means blessing. "Perhaps tomorrow you can show me around the rest of the isle."

As they walk over to the Convent, Lady Bridgette feels a sense of peace and reluctant surrender and, at the same time, a wonder at the mystery of how her life has unfolded in such a way that she is here.

The sky has cleared and the air seems to tingle as the sun starts to set in the west. Lady Bridgette turns again to Sister Bendithion. "On the far horizon, what is that I see, the faint tent-like shapes arising out of the sea?"

Sister Bendithion cannot suppress a smile. "It is right that your attention should go there. Those are foothills you may remember. That is Ireland in the distance."

Lady Bridgette smiles to herself. Nods *thanks* to Sister Bendithion. She is still very upset at Arthur for sending her here against her will, and at the same time she recognizes that Ynys Enlli may be a place where she will have much to learn. Still, on clear days, she will have a constant visual reminder of her longing to go home.

Chapter 4

Two days after Gwenynen said good-bye to Lady Bridgette, she returns to Lady Geirwir's chambers with another basket overflowing from her foraging for herbs. She puts the basket on Lady Geirwir's workbench along with a small bouquet of purple bell heather she gathered during her foraging. She feels emboldened.

"Lady Geirwir, I have been worried about this, so I must ask you what I should do. Just before she left, I saw Lady Bridgette on her way out the courtyard. She stopped me and told me that she would ask King Arthur to have me sent to her to the island convent she was going to. Once this next battle is over and I am not so sorely needed, do you think I might go? Do you think it is a good idea for me to go?"

"Many questions, dear girl." Lady Geirwir pauses to consider them. She glances at the bell heather and smiles. "I think that you are learning much from me. Because you have real natural skills as a healer, if you would like to go—and I expect there is much knowledge about plants to be learned on that isle and Sisters there with much wisdom—then I believe, when you are a bit older, you should go."

Gwenynen nods in appreciation of the advice. She furrows her brow. "I know there are more immediate things we are facing now. Do you expect there to be many wounded knights to care for?"

"There is no way to have even a good guess. Some of Arthur's battles have resulted in many wounded, others seem to have resulted in fewer wounds than occur on the jousting grounds."

"I know nothing of King Arthur's battles and how things stand in his quest to defeat the foes of Britain. Can you tell me?" Gwenynen asks.

Lady Geirwir hesitates, but it is in her nature to help others and she wants to respond to the young woman's interest in learning what is happening around her. "Sit down my dear. If you are going to spend your days making compresses and mixing healing herbs, you might as well know something about what the warriors you are ministering to are fighting for."

Gwenynen sits on the same small stool she had listened to Lady Geirwir from earlier and pulls it close to Lady Geirwir, who sits down in her favorite chair beneath the large window.

"Arthur is a great warrior-king and leads at the front of his army. He always has loyal knights close to him. However, if on the field of battle, the leaders of the two forces meet, it is the practice that the protective knights on both sides will fall away so that the leaders themselves can battle it out. This has happened to Arthur more than once.

"His first five battles were against the Angles in Lincolnshire where Arthur completely conquered the Angle Kingdom of Lindsey. Arthur then fought a battle to defend a kinsman and Druid shrine, and then battles in lowland Scotland just north of Hadrian's wall against the Picts. These different battles pick up the two bold threads of Arthur's spiritual life: his commitment to the Goddess religion of the Druids and the Christian religion of the Romans. In the battle near the town of Lichfield, the battle was fought by Arthur to help his friend and because the Angles were desecrating a sacred Druid grove nearby. Within a dense copse of oaks was a temple to the Celtic Goddess Brigit. The same Goddess who at the great Roman temple at Bath was Romanized into Minerva. This shows the degree to which Arthur is willing to use the force of arms to protect the older Celtic religion just as he has done to protect the Roman. In an interesting twist to the intertwining of the two religions, just recently the great grandson of Cunedda Wledig became bishop to King Arthur. You will have seen him in the great hall giving blessings. He is now known as St David.

"Arthur's next two battles were fought in lowland Scotland, just on the north side of Hadrian's wall. In the first of these, battle seven, Arthur fought against the Picts and a British nobleman who had defected to their side. After the battle the British nobleman was beheaded by Arthur. The second battle in Scotland was something of a symbolic turning point. For the first time, at the urging of Guinevere, Arthur carried an image of Mary on his shield. Arthur attributed much of the success of the battle and slaughter of the enemy to this spiritual imagery."

Gwenynen, caught up in the story, forgets herself and interrupts: "You think differently, Lady Geirwir?"

"My dear, I do not know. What I do know is that Arthur has managed to do a remarkable job of keeping intact his Celtic heritage and its connection to the old ways, while allowing the new Roman church to continue to expand throughout Britain. On the one hand, it would not be that strange for a great warrior-king to carry an image of a woman on his shield into battle. On the other, the image of the Virgin Mary is seen by most Celtic women as an image of a woman deprived of feminine life force.

"His next battle, the ninth one, was against the Irish Gewissei much closer to home along the River Usk. His tenth battle was a continuation of this earlier one. Arthur pursued the enemy across Gwent to the Severn estuary. The defeat of the Gewissei here was what led to the handing over of the Irish twins in exchange for Arthur not attacking Ireland. His victory at the Severn had all the makings of a miracle, like the crossing of the Red Sea.

"Arthur knew that in certain phases of the moon there is a massive wave that comes from the sea up the Severn estuary. It is known as the Severn bore. Brilliant tactician that he is, Arthur managed to entice the Gewissei warriors out on the flat plain of the estuary and hold them there at bay until the tidal bore came upon them. The bore moves faster than a man in armor can run and those who didn't drown were thrown right against Arthur's troops who were in a protected raised position."

"That is amazing," says Gwenynen. "Can I go see the tidal current come in sometimes?"

"Yes, perhaps you shall be able to do that," says Lady Geirwir.

"His eleventh battle is one where you were previously involved in providing medical assistance to his knights who fought there. This battle was in Somerset, not really that far away. As you know, even though Arthur won and the Saxons gave ground, the battle did not put an end to the current Saxon threat. That is the reason that Arthur will go back into the field again shortly. He will leave in the direction of the great Roman city of Bath in the next few days. In the meantime we have much work to do."

Lady Geirwir stops abruptly. "I have gone on quite long enough."

"Thank you so much for helping me understand Arthur's battles. I hear the bards singing about them at Court. Honestly, I have not had a clue how they have unfolded and the relation between them and the various threats to Britain."

Lady Geirwir inclines her head toward Gwenynen and Gwenynen knows she is being dismissed. She curtsies, turns and leaves the room.

Back in her ante chamber room, Gwenynen marvels with delight that Lady Geirwir has shared so much with her. She knows that King Arthur trusts Lady Geirwir's opinion. She is known among the Court as Lady Truth. Gwenynen is gradually learning that, next to Merlin, she is the King's closest advisor.

She can feel a kind of racing buzz in the back of her head. War is gory and terrible, and it always brings excitement and new routines. She sits for a moment to quiet her mind. She knows from all that Lady Geirwir shared with her that she will be given even more responsibility in the preparation of medical supplies in the days ahead. She best get to work. She picks up her large basket for gathering herbs and heads out the door.

Chapter 5

"This battle will be one that is sung about centuries from now. All the signs suggest it will never be lost in the mist of history. Surely, we will remember the year 518, the year of this battle, for the rest of our lives. Hopefully, it will bring fifty years of peace to Britain," says Lady Geirwir.

Lady Geirwir and Gwenynen are taking a break. They make some hibiscus tea and sit back to relax. They have been up for 48 hours straight tending to the line of wounded warriors being returned to Arthur's castle from Badon.

"I have only gotten snippets of what happened from various knights able and wanting to talk about the battle," says Gwenynen.

"Well, I am not sure that I have the complete picture," says Lady Geirwir. "As best as I can put the pieces together, it seems the battle centered near Bath. Even though the city was abandoned after the Romans left, it irked Arthur that his enemies gathered there and took up residence in what was once such a great Roman city. As much as Arthur considers himself a Celt, he also is a Roman.

"Arthur besieged the enemy at a hill fort just outside of Bath. As you have learned from earlier battles, these battles are for the most part usually over in a day or two. War for King Arthur and his knights is essentially hand-to-hand combat. Even the strongest man cannot go on hacking and failing away with an axe or sword for more than a dozen hours without giving out in complete exhaustion.

"Arthur's opponents at Badon were a coalition of his enemies. The Gewissei, under the leadership of the Irish chieftain whose daughters Arthur has, joined forces with their Jutish and South Saxon allies and the invading Saxons from the Upper Thames Valley. I met with Arthur and his senior leaders before the battle and we were all convinced the future course of British history hung in the balance. If Arthur did not stop the coalition, who knows what language or religion our grandchildren would experience.

"It is interesting, Gwenynen, these men dress up for these battles in several ways, not only with armor to protect themselves, but also to meet their maker. Around Arthur's neck was a golden torque, a symbol of a Celtic chieftain for hundreds of years. On his head Arthur wore a helmet burnished in gold with a crest carved in the shape of a dragon. He carried his circular shield which has served him so well in the past, Pridwen, which has painted on it the likeness of Mary."

"He was taking both Druid and Christian likenesses into battle for protection, wasn't he?" asks Gwenynen.

"Quite right you are, my dear. At a battle like this, indeed at any battle, he has never forsaken any of his heritage," says Lady Geirwir. "Of course, he also had at his side his famous Druidic sword, Caliburn.

"Arthur drew up his men and attacked the enemy which arrayed themselves in wedges as the Saxons are wont to do in battle. All the first day the enemy were able to resist Arthur's onslaught despite his repeated attacks. At nightfall with a contingent that vastly outnumbered Arthur, the enemy managed to secure the high ground on a neighboring hill.

"At dawn, King Arthur attacked straight up the hill. It was a costly attack and many of the knights we are nursing now were seriously wounded in it. The enemy was at a great advantage being able to hurl itself down the hill at Arthur's forces. Nonetheless, Arthur successfully managed to reach the summit, though without his calvary. There his warriors engaged the Saxons in close quarter combat and the Saxons stood shoulder to shoulder and did their most to resist.

"When the greater part of the day had gone by and Arthur's forces were still unable to subdue the enemy, Arthur sensed that victory was slipping from his grasp. At this realization Arthur went on a one-man rampage going straight into the thickest ranks of the enemy himself. He cut such a swath that one warrior I treated said he had heard reliably that Arthur killed four hundred and seventy men himself with his sword, Caliburn. When Arthur's men saw what a single-handed blow he was inflicting on the enemy, they rallied and came behind him in close formation dealing death at every step. Thousands of the enemy were slain.

"This is by far the greatest victory Arthur has ever achieved."

"It is the most wounded men I have ever seen," says Gwenynen. "I understand now why you were so insistent about me foraging for as many medicinal herbs as possible."

"Unfortunately, the greatest victory usually comes at the greatest cost. I do not know what the cost of this triumph is yet. For sure there will be one. Mark my word," says Lady Geirwir.

Gwenynen looks at Lady Geirwir and studies her poised but unreadable expression. She always seems to understand more than simply what is apparent on the surface of events. Gwenynen has the sense if Lady Geirwir had been King, a way other than this great slaughter would have been found.

The celebration of victory, which followed the battle, is colored with grief over those who lost their lives or were seriously wounded. Lady Geirwir understands deeply the pain that is a part of victory on the battlefield.

"It is time for us to get back to tending the wounded," says Lady Geirwir. "We have much to do."

Gwenynen rises and starts back to work. She is aware of an annoying feeling in her head which seems to be saying—*this is fine helping with the wounded but you really need to talk to King Arthur.* What an absurd notion for a young girl of her station she thinks. I am lucky to be able to have the conversations I do with Lady Geirwir. As she turns and enters the large room where most of the wounded lie their need for immediate attention quickly drives such an errant thought away. The room she enters is enclosed within its own world—the stench of infection, the gloom of death and the sparkle of light from those who, against all odds, will live.

*   *   *

It takes more than a year after the battle of Badon for King Arthur's Court to begin to regain a sense of normalcy. Arthur has re-opened the Court's function as it is aptly named: a court, an institution for the dispensation of justice, and sometimes mercy, among his subjects. The Court as tribunal is open for business every Thursday afternoon from 1:00 PM until justice has been adequately dispensed for the week. Petitions against another person have to be registered with the clerk a week ahead of time so notice can be given to the other party. Petitions brought by the King against a subject can be issued at any time without notice.

Gwenynen has spent all this Thursday morning, just as she has every morning for the past year at the infirmary with Lady Geirwir tending to injured knights. Her duties are gradually diminishing. Those knights with very serious injuries have, for the most part, died, and for them her time had been spent administering potions to diminish their pain and ease their transition. Those with lesser wounds are on the mend and require less care. Many knights have been lost. Still the battle is being proclaimed as the greatest victory ever for Arthur. So sweeping is the victory that everyone is convinced there will be no threat from the Saxons for years to come.

Just as Gwenynen is about to open the door leading to her quarters in Lady Geirwir's anteroom, she hears someone approaching from down the opposite corridor. Soon Sir Gaiwain comes into view. She has seen him often at meals in the great hall. He has never spoken to her, or she to him. She awaits his approach.

"Miss Gwenynen, good morning to you," he says, addressing her as a knight might address a lady of noble birth. Gwenynen curtsies in return. "The King has summoned thee to the session of court being convened this afternoon."

Gwenynen is shocked. Terror crosses her face.

"I would not worry, Miss. This is not a suit being brought against you by the King or anyone else. I do not know the reason for the summons. I should not think it is something to worry about."

Gwenynen is still flustered. She does not know what to say.

Sir Gaiwain sees her discomfort. "Since I brought the summons, I would be glad to come for you and escort you to Court, that way I can be beside you and be moral support. Would that be helpful?"

"You are too kind, Sir Gaiwain. That would be absolutely wonderful." She curtsies again and looking at Sir Gaiwain's friendly smile, her fear begins to recede.

Sir Gaiwain catches the impact of his reassurance in her eyes. "So be it. I will see you anon." He turns, walks back down the corridor and disappears around the corner.

Gwenynen opens the antechamber door and goes inside.

What in the world have I done, she thinks. Her mind begins to race. Then she remembers Gaiwain's reassuring smile. She smiles inwardly. Perhaps this is not as bad as it looks. Maybe she will have a chance to talk to Lady Geirwir before 1:00 PM comes around.

*   *   *

A bell is struck ten minutes before any important event at Court. When the bell tolls Gwenynen is ready. She has washed herself and changed into her nicest outfit, a finely seamed hand-me-down from Lady Geirwir. At thirteen she is just beginning to fill out the contours of the dress. Soon Sir Gaiwain is knocking on her door.

She opens the door and curtsies to him. He in return bows his head to her. "Thank you again, for coming to fetch me," she says.

"You look like a lady, Miss. I am sure you will be warmly received by the King at Court."

"You are very kind, Sir Gaiwain." Gwenynen is glad she has changed and pleased that Lady Geirwir had given her one of her old dresses. She is dressed above her station, but there are no rules against that and the realization from Sir Gaiwain's comment that she looks nice helps steady the anxiety she is feeling at being summoned to Court.

There is a long docket. Many of the petitions are from wives of fallen knights seeking some compensation from Arthur for the loss of her husband. These families have lost their primary breadwinner. Arthur takes time to ascertain how many family members there are, their ages and what other means of support they might have. For each he takes a genuine interest and for each he provides some additional means of support. Although he is known as a man of action, in his Court he presides with patient deliberation. His chin often resting on one of his large hands with his elbow on a knee as he physically leans into the problems of his petitioners. After he listens attentively he has a habit of shaking his head, his mane of dark hair scattering about on his shoulders, as if he were clearing his mind so that the truth he would need to speak arises afresh from within.

Finally Gwneynen's name is called out. She rises. Sir Gaiwain stands with her. He whispers, "Walk to the front of the room before the King and curtsey. Then wait for the King to speak to you. I will be right behind you."

She nods, takes a deep breath to quell the nervous energy she feels running down her fingers and allows herself to find the solid grounding at her center. Then she does as Sir Gaiwain directed.

King Arthur looks at a letter in his hands, then up at Gwenynen. He smiles. "My dear, a request has been made of the King that you should attend Lady Bridgette on the isle of Ynys Enlli. Do you know of this request and are you disposed to accept it?"

Gwneynen nervously curtsies again. She sees kindness sparkle in King Arthur's eyes. They are hazel gray with bright specks of green and gold in them. She begins to relax. "Sire, I know of the request by Lady Bridgette. She asked me if I might be willing to join her for a time at Ynys Enlli just before she left. I believe it might be salutary for me to join her for a spell, that I might be able to advance my knowledge of healing herbs so that in time I might be of more service to you and the Kingdom, your Grace."

"You are well-spoken, indeed, my dear." He turns then as he always does to Merlin, who is on one side of him, and then to Lady Geirwir, who sits on the other and then addressing them both, "Your thoughts?"

Merlin, as he always does, goes first. He pulls on his long, white Druidic beard. "Sire, I do not believe that Lady Bridgette was too enthralled with her chance to visit the sacred isle of Ynys Enlli. I would think that anything that could be done with small outlay of resources that might engender favor would indeed serve the long term interests of this Kingdom."

King Arthur then turns to Lady Geirwir. "Gwenynen has been attending me for some time. She is a good and able student of the art of healing herbs. She has a curious and thoughtful mind. Although she is beginning to blossom into a young woman, she is young and there is still much she can learn from me. I agree with Merlin that the Kingdom might be best served by her increasing her knowledge of healing herbs and also learning more of her Druidic and Christian heritage from the Sisters who keep sanctuary on Ynys Enlli. However, I believe she should remain in Court here until she is past the age of eighteen."

The King is about to speak and Merlin interjects. "Sire, I have one other thing to add. I am not able to see clearly how in the future this will unfold, but by allowing this young women to go you will start a chain of events unfolding," Merlin pauses. "Great Goddess! Well, this is clearly what I see in the future. You will start a chain of events unfolding that will allow Gwenynen to provide you wise counsel, my King, when I am not there to advise you."

"Indeed, are you sure, Merlin? I mean that you will not be with me? That does not seem possible."

"Nothing is sure that is seen with the eye of prescience, my King. As always, I only tell, as truthfully as I can, what I see."

"Then it shall be done," says King Arthur. He realizes for the first time that Sir Gaiwain is standing right behind Gwneynen. "Sir Gaiwain, when Miss Gwenynen is eighteen, will you do your King the pleasure of escorting this young woman to the isle of Ynys Enlli?"

"Your wish is my command," says Sir Gaiwain, as he bows his head to his King.

Before more can be said, the clerk calls the next matter. Gwneynen curtsies again toward the King and quickly follows Sir Gaiwain to the side of the room.

"Miss Gwenynen, will you be eighteen soon?" asks Sir Gaiwain, like most men not often in the company of young women, at a total loss to comprehend what age a young woman might be.

"Oh, no. I am afraid that will be awhile." She looks at the tender expression of Sir Gaiwain and senses, even as a young thirteen-year-old girl, the Goddess stirring within her, as she receives the attentions of a handsome young man.

"But, it will not be that long. Thank you for being willing to take me." She unconsciously puts her hand on his arm. "Thank you so much for your assistance to me. I was quite ruffled having to appear before the King, and your presence steadied me. I am very grateful." With that she curtsies, turns and heads back to her quarters.

*   *   *

Rat, what do you mean you want me to hang out close to King Arthur and not go traipsing off to some woebegone island with my character. I may get to make subliminal suggestions; however, I can't control what my character does. Sometimes I get her to ask the questions you want. That is about the best I can do. I can't determine where she goes and what all she does. You and Mother Mary put me in this character, so tell Mother Mary to quit complaining.

I will try to speed up my experiencing of time here so I just spend time with my character during the important events in her life. My prescience tells me she will not leave King Arthur's court to go to Ynys Enlli until she is nineteen. I will fast forward my experience of her life until then. I would like to re-enter her life at a better time. The trip to Ynys Enlli across mountains and then along the Welsh coast in this miserable weather will be rather appalling. The only positive thing going is that my character finds being thrown into an adventuresome journey with Sir Gaiwain...well, let's put it like this—for her, a young girl who grew up on the very margins of society, which I can relate to, the company could not be finer. She is beside herself, and so I am glad to be along for the ride.

Chapter 6

In the years after arriving on Ynys Elli, Lady Bridgette writes King Arthur twice more asking if Gwenynen might be allowed to come attend her. King Arthur does not respond.

In 522, St. Brigit of Kildare dies. Lady Geirwir grieves the loss of her spiritual and healing mentor. For a time, she takes little interest in her life, even in tutoring Gwenynen, who has now become a young woman. In early 523, a bright comet appears in the sky. The appearance of the comet is like someone tapped Lady Geirwir on the forehead and said "wake up." She immediately goes to see King Arthur.

She finds King Arthur in his private room, behind the large chamber where he holds Court.

"King Arthur, have you seen the bright light in the sky?" Lady Geirwir blurts out as soon as she enters his room.

He looks up from a design he is working on for a shield with a large curve in it to better deflect an opponent's blows. "I have, but you must be seeing more in this celestial omen than I."

Although Arthur does not expect any court formality from Merlin or Lady Geirwir, the stiffness in his response makes her realize her own abruptness. She curtsies. "Sire, I am sorry to barge in so rudely."

He notices that in her agitation she is winding and unwinding a string of beads around her wrist.

"Lady Geirwir, it is quite all right. Please sit down and get your breath."

Lady Geirwir takes a tentative seat on the edge of a chair. "Thank you, Arthur. I am agitated, I guess. This is what is on my mind." She pauses. Arthur gets up from the table and sits down in a large, comfortable chair covered with blankets and furs. He gives Lady Geirwir his full attention.

"I realize I have been in a dour mood. I apologize for it. I have been grieving the death of St. Brigit. Her death has led me to feel the burden of my prescient knowledge about the future of both the Goddess religion and Celtic Christianity.

"When I first saw this bright light in the sky, it as much as said to me 'stop moping around, you have things to do for the Goddess.' It made me recall the request Lady Bridgette made some years ago, when you first sent her to the isle of Ynys Enlli. She requested that she be permitted to have a young girl, who is in my care, attend her. At the time, both Merlin and I advised you that this was a worthy suggestion, but I felt it best to wait until the girl was grown.

"The light in the sky reminds me that the time has come. Gwenynen is now nineteen. You will also remember Merlin's startling prophesy that one day this young woman would be of great aid and counsel to you. The strong sense I have from the Goddess and this light in the sky is that this prophesy must not be interfered with. I think it is best if you send Gwenynen on to Ynys Enlli, as Lady Bridgette asked. I believe the Goddess desires this also for your own well being."

"A bright light in the sky surely can stir things up," says Arthur with a smile.

Lady Geirwir's furrowed forehead eases. "Yes, it can. Shall I convey your wishes to one of your knights that he take Gwenynen to Ynys Enlli for you? I have noticed over the past couple of years as she has grown into a woman, that many of your knights have begun to notice Gwenynen. When she came before you a few years ago, I believe you suggested then that Sir Gaiwain escort her to Ynys Enlli. It would be good to send her with your most honorable knight. Sir Gaiwain is a good choice."

"Let it be so," Arthur replies. "I wish all my decisions were so blessedly straightforward. Thank you, Lady Geirwir, for recalling this request of Lady Bridgette. It is hard not to love the fair isle of Ynys Enlli, but I expect she is getting a bit tired of biding her time there. Perhaps if this young woman Gwenynen is with her, it will be a pleasant distraction for her. The last thing we want to happen is for her to return to her father in Ireland. I sent the other sister back recently as a gesture of goodwill, but we need to keep some leverage with those Irish marauders if at all possible."

"I am quite in agreement with you on that score, Arthur," says Lady Geirwir. "If you will excuse me, I will be off to let Sir Gaiwain know of your wishes."

The King returns to the drawings at his table and Lady Geirwir quietly leaves the room.

*　　　　　　*　　　　　　*

Gwneynen, accompanied by Sir Gaiwain, is soon off on the trip to western Wales.

The first day, Sir Gaiwain precedes Gwenynen by several horse lengths. Then behind her come their attendants on horseback bearing tents and supplies. However, Sir Gaiwain is a talkative sort and by the second day he is riding beside her. He often identifies birdsongs and signs of animals for her. She identifies plants for him. First, she points out the beautifully delicate Welsh poppy.

"Gaiwain, this flower is like the Welsh people. This small yellow flower is so hardy it will sometimes bloom all winter, if the winter is not too severe."

"Gwenynen, you are right about the ruggedness of the Welsh," replies Gaiwain, "although I cannot vouch always for their beauty."

Gwenynen looks at Gaiwain with a slight frown. " I mean," he stammers, "present company excepted." Gaiwain looks away in embarrassment.

Gwenynen eases his awkward moment by pointing out an abundance of flowering bell heather that puts a purple glaze on a passing fields. "Gaiwain, perhaps we will also come upon white bell heather. It is quite a good omen to see white bell heather."

"I shall keep a sharp lookout for white bell heather. I must say that where the bell heather and the Welsh poppy—the purple and yellow—are mixed together is a colorful treat for the eye."

Gwenynen nods her agreement. They both make an inner commitment to look for the auspicious white bell heather.

As evening comes on each day, Sir Gaiwain scouts about and finds their camping spot. At first, she can tell that he is choosing places that are more protected from the dangers of any possible criminal elements, which might be at large in the countryside. As the trip progresses, she believes he is choosing spots more for their natural beauty. She even allows herself to consider that the choices might actually be more romantic in nature, though this is not a thought she considers for long.

Their trip soon takes on a routine. After camp is pitched and dinner served—adequate though usually nothing special—she and Sir Gaiwain sit by the campfire and talk. She usually has found rose-hips or some other herb from which a good strong, hot drink can be made to complete the evening meal. Sir Gaiwain knows all of Arthur's battles and he enjoys telling her tales of his many adventures with Arthur. He loves telling a good story and often laughs so much at his own recounting that frequently Gwenynen loses track of the thread of the story as she gets caught in her own laughter, and at the end of the story has to ask him to tell her again. That usually brings more laughter.

Gwenynen shares much of the knowledge she has learned from Lady Geirwir about Druids and Celtic Christianity. She shares with Sir Gaiwain that she has been taught to read in Latin and Lady Geirwir has let her read several books, including one by Pythagoras and also a history of the Celts. Sir Gaiwain is a keen follower of Celtic Christianity, including a common view of God as more feminine than male. He also honors all the Druid festival days and considers them holy for him as a Christian. He mentions that Beltane, the traditional Goddess rite of renewal each Spring, will occur sometime while they are on their journey. He is surprised when Gwenynen tells him that the Celts settled in Britain about a thousand years ago at the same time they migrated into Galatia. Paul's letter to the Galatians could have also been called Paul's letter to the Celts. Gaiwain is delighted and amazed that Gwenynen, from her time of studying with Lady Geirwir, has such broad and interesting knowledge.

After their conversations by the fire in the evening, Sir Gaiwain is scrupulous in escorting Gwenynen to her tent at night. He is attentive to her, but never drops the least hint of romantic overture. Gwneynen, on the other hand, feels completely stuck. She cannot lower herself in Sir Gaiwain's eyes by doing anything that might be construed as an advance toward him. However, not only is she a young peasant woman alone on a journey with one of Arthur's most celebrated knights. She is totally infatuated by the courteous and fun-loving Gaiwain.

By the time their journey takes them to the coast of Wales and they are making their way toward the Llyn peninsula, neither Gwenynen nor Sir Gaiwain is sure they want their journey to end. They begin halting their day's journey earlier, setting up camp on the beach and then going off together.

Sir Gaiwain hunts for a boar or deer to add to their dinner. He marvels at Gwneynen's ability to move along beside him stealthily through the forest without a sound. He watches her keen eye pick out a sought-after plant from horseback.

Gwenynen notes with approval how at home Sir Gaiwain is in the natural world, how he experiences himself a part of it and how skillfully he prays for a young buck to stop and surrender its life for their benefit before he lets a sure arrow fly.

Their side trips bring them greater appreciation of each other's gifts and greatly increase the quality of their nightly meals. After they have been gone from King Arthur's Court about ten days, as they are sitting around their campfire on the beach after dinner, Gwenynen speaks. "Can you tell by the moon, Sir Gaiwain, are we close upon Beltane?"

"If we were at Court, Merlin would be keeping track of this. I have been trying to keep count since we left Arthur's Court. I do believe tomorrow will be Beltane." He counts on his fingers. "Yes, that must be correct."

"That is what I was thinking," says Gwenynen. "What should we do to honor the Goddess? Some say that the appearance recently of a bright light in the sky is an admonition from the Goddess that the Beltane festival should not be neglected this year."

"I have heard similar comments about the celestial omen." He ponders her question. "I am not sure what we should do."

Gwenynen cannot decipher the expression on Sir Gaiwain's face in the flickering firelight. "We should do something, I guess," says Gwenynen. "We have been having unusually harsh weather and many old people believe that it has been caused by our failure to properly honor the Goddess."

Her comment hangs in the air.

"What would you suggest?" asks Sir Gaiwain.

Gwneynen does not know what to say. She fears any suggestion by her that they enter into the Beltane ritual would condemn her in Sir Gaiwain's eyes as being too forward. "What is important is that we invoke ritual that does not involve our personal desires, but is of service to the Goddess."

"Yes, yes, of course, that is exactly right," says Sir Gaiwain, responding enthusiastically as if Gwneynen had struck a chord that freed him from his own uncertainty. "I suggest we stay here an extra day. Tomorrow we fast during the day in her honor. At dusk we each shall go our own way to honor the Goddess and be led by her."

Gwneynen nods her assent. "We should be masked as Beltane requires. If the Goddess wants us to meet, we meet not as ourselves but as surrogates for the male and female principles of regeneration of Spring."

Sir Gaiwain looks relieved. "Yes, I expect we will not meet. If we do, so be it. If not, so be it."

"Well, we will have a long day of honoring the creative source of all life tomorrow. I believe I shall turn in now. Good night, Sir Gaiwain."

*   *   *

At sunset the next day, Gwneynen sets out a potion for Sir

Gaiwain and herself with the small meal that has been prepared to break their fast. It is not a potion she has made often. She hopes it will have the desired effect. They both down their glasses and eat sparingly, as sometimes happens when you break a fast. Or perhaps their lack of appetite is the unspoken excitement of anticipation. Another meal will be celebrated later around midnight after the ritual of Beltane has been consummated.

Following their brief meal, Gwneynen and Sir Gaiwain set off in opposite directions down the beach. Gwneynen does not go far. She has bathed and is attired in her best dress. She wears a mask that is shaped and colored to look like the face of her namesake, the bee. When she gets to a place where a second row of dunes starts, she leaves a thread from her shawl in the high grass, where she turns off. After a short way, she finds a spot where the sand is shaped into a rounded bowl between two dunes. She lays down her blanket and sits to rest. To wait.

Sir Gaiwain heads off up the beach. He has some worry at the idea of the Beltane celebration, but now walking up the beach he feels free of anxiety. If the truth be known, and it wasn't, Sir Gaiwain's' gallantry toward women is in large part the legacy of his fear of them. Some of this fear comes out indirectly in his faithful homage to the Goddess. However, he is most at home in the company of men. He loved his mother deeply, but she died when he was still quite young. He knows the negative power of women from the rages of the aunt who reared him after his mother died. That power scares him. He was quite happy to escape that household and begin his training as a knight at a young age.

Sir Gaiwain walks for about half an hour, until he feels this intuitive tug to return back down the beach. It comes as a visceral feeling that he is being guided. As he always does, when he feels there is divine guidance, he obeys.

Before too long he is back where he started, and then, walking not too far beyond, he sees the thread from Gwenynen's shawl trailing off to the side. Unlike himself, he does not hesitate, but follows it unthinking. When he comes around a set of dunes, there sits Gwenynen. She looks so beautiful in the moonlight he is startled. He struggles to regain his composure. He is glad that both of them are masked.

Sir Gaiwain realizes that Gwenynen sees him. According to the ritual, he has no choice except to proceed up to her. Wordlessly, he kneels before her. He quietly whispers a prayer to the mother Goddess. Gwenynen reaches her hand to him. He grasps her hand. A jolt of current goes through his body. He feels heat rising up his spine. He feels as if she is truly possessed by the Goddess. Despite his fears and his inexperience with women, it is all the permission he needs. He pulls her to him.

Gwenynen cannot believe he has come. She remembers the prayer told to her by Lady Geirwir, which St. Brigit gave to Lady Geirwir and all the young Sisters at Kildare:

Bless this body, that is your vessel of creation
Bless this body, that is tender and strong
Bless this body, that it may be fecund for You
Bless this body, that in You is love.

She keeps repeating the prayer over and over, and it gives her courage. Yet she, in her inexperience, feels suddenly shy. Just as she feels herself withdrawing, she feels this sudden jolt in her system, as if the potion she had drunk has finally kicked in, or perhaps the Goddess herself has answered her prayer and, as Beltane requires, entered her body and her spirit. She puts her arms around Gaiwain's neck and pulls him to her. They kiss long and fiercely.

Almost together they begin to take off the clothing of the other. When they are both bare-breasted, another surge of current strikes them both at the same time. They kiss the rest of their clothing away. Gwenynen senses Gaiwain's inexperience and as he gently lowers himself on her she allows the Goddess within her to guide his erection inside her. As quickly as she feels the pain, it dissipates into pleasure. Both of them sense that they are possessed by a power much greater than themselves, something so much more powerful that it could make seeds sprout and new crops grow in the spring.

Gwenynen is surprised at how quickly the Goddess' power peaks in their bodies. Just as surprising is the warm glowing feeling afterward as Gaiwain lies at her side, his breath coming in long slow gasps. Then, the Goddess is there again in both of them. Now less afraid of the unknown, they allow the Goddess' passion to completely consume them, and it does again and again and again.

Towards midnight they make their way, hand in hand, down the beach back to the campfire. They are starved.

That night and every night thereafter Gaiwain spends the night in Gwenynen's tent. When on the second night Gaiwain looks concerned, Gwenynen says, " Look what I found today while you were out hunting for meat for our dinner—white bell heather." Gwenynen points to a bouquet on the table. "It is the auspicious omen we have been looking for the entire trip. I believe the Goddess spoke through us at Beltane and is pleased with us. I don't understand why; she simply seems to want our pleasure for her to continue."

"I was beginning to worry that it was just me wanting you," says Gaiwain. "But I think you are right. I do believe I am powerless not to follow Her will in this way and I cannot imagine not being with you every night, beautiful Gwenynen."

Sir Gaiwain's worry lifts. They are doubly happy in the daytime riding and exploring together. At night their happiness knows no bounds. The pace of their journey slows to a crawl. Finally one day, midmorning, they arrive at a small harbor. Barinthus, the boatman, is preparing for a crossing. Because he is anxious to hit the tides just right, their farewell is abrupt. Sir Gaiwain assures her that after he returns to advise King Arthur that he has done his duty and accomplished the mission he was given, then, when he can get Arthur's permission, he will return for her.

"What if when you return I am a Druid Christian priestess?" asks Gwneynen.

"Well, in that case you would be a fit match for a knight like me, that is if you would have me, dear Gwenynen."

"Come back for me, Sir Gaiwain, I love you dearly," says Gwenynen.

"I love you, dearest Gwenynen. I shall return."

With that, the boatman interrupts their lovers' goodbye and hastily casts off.

*   *   *

When the boat carrying Gwenynen approaches the narrow beach landing on Ynys Enlli, both Lady Bridgette and Sister Bendithion are on the shore to meet Gwenynen. Lady Bridgette has told Sister Bendithion that she had invited Gwenynen to come to the holy isle. Still, Lady Bridgette had about given up hope that her young friend would ever be sent to her. Two days earlier Sister Bendithion intuited Gwenynen was on her way and soon to arrive.

"Welcome to our fair isle," says Sister Bendithion.

Welcome, indeed," says Lady Bridgette. She eyes Gwenynen closely. "Oh my Goddess, I left you a maiden and you have come here now a woman. We do, indeed, have much to talk about."

Gwenynen grins shyly at Lady Bridgette.

"Do not be shy, you have made my day, my dear young friend. I am sure the Goddess is smiling as I big as I am."

*   *   *

Rat, tell Man that my character's romantic adventures have got me missing him really bad and we will need to have some make-up sack time when I get back.

What do you mean Mother Mary says don't enjoy my character too much? She put me in the character and all I can do is enjoy the adventure. Tell her I know what my mission is and I will try to skip forward to the big events in Gwenynen's life.

Chapter 7

Ynys Enlli is not what Gwenynen expected. But then, she did not know what she expected. The isle is different from any place she could have imagined.

Sister Bendithion first takes her on a tour of the isle. They walk along the western shore where, except for the small sand beach, the ocean washes in between huge slabs of rock, which look as if a giant hand had stacked them diagonally along the shore. They pause when they get to the foot of the massive grass-covered, rock headland which makes up the northeast end of the isle. Many birds of different species dart about over the gorse and heather.

"This is so beautiful," says Gwenynen. "However, I think I would like to rest a bit now and complete the tour of the isle later."

"That sounds like a good idea," says Sister Bendithion. "We are near our lodgings. I will show you where your quarters will be."

As they are getting ready to enter the long, low building which serves as lodging space for most of the Sisters, Gwenynen notices a peculiar-looking round building nearby. Her eye is drawn to the building by the dazzling reflections which come from a row of circular forms that have the appearance of windows.

"What is that building there?" asks Gwenynen.

Sister Bendithion smiles. "You are quite right to notice it. It is a very different kind of structure and it is the reason we are able to live here so well supplied all year round. We call it our solarium. It was built pursuant to instructions from the Mother Goddess so we can have fresh things to eat all year round."

"Can I go see it now?" asks Gwenynen.

"Certainly, let's put your baggage down and we will go right over."

Gwenynen walks into the solarium with Sister Bendithion. Gwenynen's mouth drops. She is astounded. Particles of sunlight seem to burst like sparks in the air. She puts her arm out to touch the wall and steadies herself.

The solarium has an ordinary wooden door, but that is the only thing ordinary about it. Gwenynen feels muggy heat. She does not know its source but surmises it has something to do with a huge many-faceted crystal that hangs in the center of the room and reflects and refracts light in all directions. The large center crystal receives light rays from round windows. Embedded in the center of each window is a large crystal that focuses the light from the outside onto the central crystal. All around the main crystal in each window are a myriad of smaller crystals also magnifying and reflecting light into and about the solarium.

As her eyes adjust to the unusual light in the room, she can see that there are rows of plants in earthen containers all over the room. Many appear to be bearing fruit, although it is far too early in the spring season for that to be occurring ordinarily.

"What in the world have you done?" asks Gwenynen her mouth agape.

"You perhaps know," says Sister Bendithion, "that it is the tradition among those governed by the Druidic calendar for all fires to be extinguished at the dark time of the year just before St. Brigit's feast day. Then, on that day, fires are all lit anew from a new fire source that the head priestess brings to the various villages.

"Many years ago priestesses were taught by the Mother Goddess that within the earth there are certain crystal stones that when they are turned in the right direction and capture the rays of the sun, they magnify those rays so much that if they are held steady for a minute or two and focused on a flammable material, fire will start from the rays' heat.

"When women priests first came to build a retreat here, to be away from the ordinary distractions of life so that they might more completely feel the presence of the Goddess, they brought a number of these crystals with them. The priestess who was the leader at the time had a dream in which she was given a vision of how to build this solarium. The design concentrates the rays of the sun on the central prism which disperses the light so plants can grow. The dispersal of the light also allows the room to stay warm, so it never freezes in here and plants grow and thrive all year around.

"Look, in the corner there is an apple tree which bears apples now, even though we have barely put mid-winter behind. We have a fondness for apples all year round and that is the reason the isle is sometimes referred to as the 'Island of Apples where all things are produced without toil.'"

"This is absolutely amazing," says Gwenynen. "Do others know you are able to do this?"

"No, not even King Arthur. St. Brigit felt it was best to hold this as a secret among the women of her Order. Crystals large enough to do the job are rare. She was afraid that if men became aware of their power and how to use these crystals that this would undermine the equal balance of feminine and masculine power."

"I cannot imagine why you would want to keep anything from the King," says Gwenynen.

"I can understand why you might say that," says Sister Bendithion. "As you may know we practice prescience on this isle. We are aware that the Goddess is in danger in the future."

"You mean Mother Earth literally?" interjects Gwenynen.

"Maybe so, certainly an understanding and resonance with the Goddess so that all life on the Earth can thrive. Yes, we are perhaps being a little deceptive in keeping the solarium secret from the King. However, the Goddess has informed us that is what we must do for now."

"I see," says Gwenynen. "I have been brought up to believe that one must try to be honest in all things. So I am not sure I understand completely."

"It is something we shall teach you in the advanced stages of your training here. If you reach the third level of our teachings you will learn when deception is necessary to preserve a larger truth."

Gwenynen shakes her head. "It has been a long day for me. I have taken leave of someone I love very much. I find myself in a place with strange and wonderful things." She looks directly at Sister Bendithion. "And strange ideas. I think I really do need to rest now. I look forward to talking with you more tomorrow."

"Yes, my dear," says Sister Bendithion. "I understand. Let us get food and give you the opportunity for a good night's sleep. I am sure you will sleep well on the isle. No one has ever said that they did not sleep well here."

*   *   *

The next day is one of those beautiful days that so often happens on the fair isle of Ynys Enlli. Gwenynen's breakfast is delicious. She is amazed that they have strawberries to eat and the grip of winter has not yet relaxed.

Gwenynen awakes bursting with curiosity and she is glad when Sister Bendithion searches her out before she leaves the refectory and pulls her aside to a table at one end, where they can talk and enjoy more of a hot morning beverage which Gwenynen finds out is brewed from the roots of a flowering plant.

"Sister Bendithion, tell me about the isle," asks Gwenynen.

"The isle traditionally was called Ynys Afallach. In doing my prescience practice, I realize some will mistakenly later shorten the name to Avalon. The isle has long been in my family and named for my father, Afallach, who was a prince on the Llyn peninsula. I was once married to Urien of Gorre and lived on the mainland. I was known then as Modron. I came to Ynys Afallach some years back with nine other Sisters, at the urging of the Goddess to create a sacred sanctuary here for a purpose that was not revealed to me at that time, with the promise that the purpose would be revealed later.

"After St Dyfrig retired and moved here in 522, I thought that purpose was perhaps to maintain a place for him. He keeps to himself in his hermitage up on the hill and the Goddess' message to me is that my purpose in being here is still to be revealed. After I entered our Order, my name became Sister Bendithion." She looks at Gwenynen to ascertain if her curiosity is satisfied. There is kindness in Sister Bendithion's dark brown eyes carved by her willingness to step ever more deeply into the mystery of her own life.

"Thank you for what you have told me." Gwenynen stops as if momentarily checking herself. "I do have another question, Sister Bendithion. Can you tell me about the beliefs of the women here on the isle in your religious community?"

Sister Bendithion directs her piercing gaze onto Gwenynen. "First, let me ask you if you are interested in joining our community?"

"Yes, I think I might be, and I must confess to you, as Lady Bridgette has already pried out of me, I am very much in love with a knight at King Arthur's Court and I do not wish to forego that relation, although I very much wish to learn from everyone here and be a part of your community."

Sister Bendithion nods her understanding. Gwenynen senses how carefully Sister Bendithion listens to everything she says. Her presence is palpable to Gwenynen in such a way that the thought flits through her mind: *I want more of what Sister Bendithion has.*

Sister Bendithion begins. "That is good. We would love for you to be a part of our community. We believe that the strong instinct which women and men have to procreate is what will ultimately save the world. Why? Because giving birth to a child takes both men and women out of their little self-contained lives. Our prescience has shown us that years from now women will be denied roles in church leadership and men will become celibate priests in order to increase the church's wealth. This will turn priests into misogynists. Their repressed fear and preoccupation with sex will make the church an enforcer of shame and guilt rather than a creative force of love.

"It is, perhaps, an overly long answer to your question. We value the idea of pilgrimage and time alone in spiritual seeking for both men and women, but this part of the spiritual life is not something to be done at the expense of a meaningful relation with a special person to whom the Goddess opens your heart. For it is in the crucible of such a love relation that our consciousness has the greatest chance to grow. Remember, as I told you, I was once married.

"Because of what our prescience tells us about the changes in the Roman church in the coming centuries, we are using our retreat on this sacred isle as a place to keep alive the true message of the Goddess and Christ, and frankly to strengthen our spiritual resiliency for what is to come."

Gwenynen interjects, "I am not quite sure I understand completely."

Sister Bendithion gives one of her extravagant smiles, which makes Gwenynen want to curl up in her lap. "You think you don't get it. Unfortunately, the not-getting-it is what we are working to counter. Judaism is a patriarchal religion that arose, like similar religions, in opposition to the fact the prevailing Goddess religion was keeping people unconscious. It sought to counter-balance an over-weighting of the feminine, which was keeping the thinking mind from finding its full potential. Judaism thrived because its timing in the history of the world was right. But soon it over-balanced the masculine—it developed a purity code of hundreds of rules that must be followed to be a loyal follower of Judaism. And as was true of all religions when it arose, and as its race name implies, it is a tribal religion.

"Jesus came to restore the correct male-female balance and to bring a non-tribal, spiritually inclusive vision. His most important apostle was Mary Magdalene. Unlike all teachers of the time, he treated men and women who sought his help equally. His life followed the classic trajectory of the Goddess myth of the king being put to death in order to reassure the regeneration of the kingdom. His message, when it is boiled down, is one of selfless, inclusive love. Women are the ones who as child-bearers have learned to the greatest degree the art of selfless love. He acknowledged that women stand on the fringe of patriarchal society and there he took a stand on the margin with them.

"Because we see Jesus as the restorer of female-male balance, being a Goddess Christian is not only easy, it reconciles all of our experiences as women and the experiences of generations of women who have come before us."

"I think I understand," says Gwenynen. "What do I need to know about what it would mean for me to join your community?"

Just then the door swings open and in marches Lady Bridgette. She looks quickly at Sister Bendithion and Gwenynen. "So is the Sister trying to enlist you in her spiritual bootcamp?"

Sister Bendithion rolls her eyes. "I am not trying to recruit Gwenynen into anything. I am trying to let her know the opportunity that lies before her. We all like to have options."

"Yes, it is an opportunity," says Lady Bridgette, "and it does take some stamina and perseverance. I will not speak badly of it. Only the truth, that her training of the women here to raise their level of consciousness is rigorous."

Gwenynen jumps in. "I have never minded hard work. That is all I have ever really known." She looks closely at Lady Bridgette. "Is there something you feel I should be concerned about?"

"No, not at all. I only had to walk into the solarium after I got here and I knew these women were doing something special. Myself, I am feeling a bit frustrated about the lack of more men around. St Cadfan's followers are too taken with being hermits for me. I want to do my part to keep the earth bountiful."

Sister Bendithion and Gwenynen exchange knowing looks.

"As wonderful a place as this is, I am getting more and more frustrated that I have been exiled here."

"I have heard, Lady Bridgette," says Sister Bendithion, "that you are in communication with your father in Ireland. Will you perhaps be leaving us soon?"

"This place is tight as new wool. You can't breathe the air in on one side of the isle without someone exhaling it on the other." She stops to consider her answer. "If I had my wishes, my father would have come and gotten me already. I have not given up all hope."

Rather than have to answer an even more penetrating question from Sister Bendithion, Lady Bridgette looks off in the distance, then nods a farewell to the two women and walks away.

"Gwenynen this is not a prison, though it has become to feel that way to Lady Bridgette. You can leave at any time you like. And we would also like you to make a commitment as the other women here have done, Lady Bridgette excepted, to faithfully strive as a woman to step deeper into the experience of being human and more conscious."

"I was around Lady Bridgette for a good while at King Arthur's Court. I know how she is. I do not think her remarks in any way undermine what I think you are trying to do here, Sister Bendithion. Far from it, I am more than interested. I am very excited about the opportunity to try to raise my consciousness, even though I confess I am not sure what exactly that means. Lady Geirwir helped me in certain ways in consciousness training, and I know I am a rank beginner."

"It is something that I am going to talk about tomorrow in the morning lecture," says Sister Bendithion. "Your timing is exactly right."

"Good morning, everyone," says Sister Bendithion. "Welcome to our class this morning. A special welcome to Gwenynen. We're so glad that she has joined us to enliven her own spiritual journey and ours." The Sisters all gather in the refectory as the breakfast meal is being cleared away. The Romans had brought the art of glass making to Britain. It would die out a few centuries after the Romans left, but for now the Sisters continue to maintain access to window glass. A long row of refectory windows faces due south and lets in streams of sunlight, which warm the room's stone walls and sunny the dispositions of all who come through.

"Our class this morning is something that Gwneynen and I were talking about recently—what is consciousness? What does it mean to be a religious community seeking to raise its level of consciousness? And why do we see Jesus as a teacher of transformation of consciousness?

"Today, I will try to start to answer those questions. Plus any other ones you may have.

"First, let's start by looking at what consciousness is not. To do this we must understand the developmental process we all go through as children to become adults. How many of you have had children?" A scattering of hands are raised among the older women.

"Those of you who have had children know, and all of us who have watched children grow up know that for the first year and a half the child has not yet learned that it is separate from the mother. The child exists in a state of symbiosis. It has been described as a state in which the child rests inside the architecture of the mother's brain. Then something happens. The child is left alone for a while and experiences the loss of connection to his mother. This jolt can happen in a number of ways; however, the result is the same. The child experiences this underlying anxiety from the loss of connection. He or she senses that something is wrong, that the world is not safe.

"In response the child then develops a persona to help decrease the anxiety from the separation, to buffer the possible jarring that can come unexpectedly from reality. We know from the teachings of St. Brigit, who learned them from Ponticus Evagrius, one of the great Desert Fathers, and from Pythagoras, who was in the lineage of Evagrius' teachers, that the child develops one of nine types of personality. My own belief is that the particular type which the child develops depends upon the gifts and burdens the child receives from his parents and ancestors.

"The persona that the child develops is a defense against missing his symbiotic relationship with mother. Put more succinctly, we could say that our personality is a defense against reality."

"So our persona is a bad thing?" asks one of the young Sisters.

"No, not at all," replies Sister Bendithion. "Our persona is quite necessary developmentally. We could not make it into adulthood without it. The problem that arises is one of shedding the persona, after we become adults and no longer need it. We are like the terrapin that needs to shed its shell periodically in order to grow. The process of this growth is the transformation, or evolution, of consciousness.

"Our goal here in this school is to shed the film over our eyes, which our persona gives us, so that we can encounter reality directly, not through the filter of our prior experiences, which is how our persona was shaped."

"I do not believe that I am afraid of reality," interjects one of the Sisters sitting on the front row.

Sister Bendithion smiles. "We all start from that place. Believing that we do not try to buffer ourselves from a real experience of reality tells us that we are at the beginning point to evolve our consciousness. Tell me, Sister, what was your work activity this morning?"

"I was in the kitchen cleanup."

"How did you feel when you started washing all those pans used in preparation of breakfast?" asks Sister Bendithion.

"To tell you the truth, I thought I have to do cleanup way more than my share. I could not wait to finish."

"Thank you for the great example," says Sister Bendithion. "We all have experiences which give a lens that colors how we experience any task. The bias of that lens is what prevents us from experiencing reality directly."

"How in the world can we get rid of the impact of all our old experiences on new experiences?" asks another Sister. "This seems an overwhelming task."

"You are right," replies Sister Bendithion. "It is a tall order, though not an impossible one. We have examples of those who have done this: Pythagoras, Ponticus Evagrius, Jesus, St. Brigit, etc. This is the goal of our community—to evolve our consciousness together."

"Is that the reason we spend an hour each morning and evening in silent contemplation?" asks another questioner.

"Precisely," says Sister Bendithion.

"And the reason we do those inquiry questions each night?"

"Right again.

"Yesterday morning, another Sister and I did a look into the waters of our most holy well. The Goddess foretold that difficulties are imminent. For that reason, we will be increasing our spiritual practices. Ultimately, it is only our level of consciousness which will give us a chance to prevail against those who do war on Britain. War is the lowest form of pre-consciousness among humans. It is the ego persona's base survival instinct taking over and running amok.

"So I stress to all of you, and especially to you, Gwenynen, as our newest arrival, that I am not encouraging the deepening of our spiritual practices out of any desire to be severe, but rather to prepare us for calamities, which I fear we will all face before too long.

"I am talking too long. Let's take a break. I will see you all over in the chapel for our midmorning service." Sister Bendithion turns and prepares to leave the class. The room is immediately abuzz with chatter and laughter. On her way out she comes over to Gwenynen. "Tomorrow, we will talk again and see where you are in your journey of consciousness and if our sisterhood is a good fit for you."

"Thank you," replies Gwenynen. Sister Bendithion leaves the room and Gwenynen turns toward the crowd of Sisters around her.

A young Sister comes over and introduces herself to Gwenynen as Sister Derwen. Gwenynen immediately notices that though she is younger than most, what a solid, reliable kind of person Derwen appears to be. "Your timing of arriving here just as we are increasing our spiritual practices is either your great good luck or your great misfortune. I hope that it is not the latter. I do not mind increased spiritual practice time, and I am not anxious to be facing new calamities."

"Where do you come from?" asks Gwenynen. "And who is that

with you?" Gwenynen notices that at Derwen's heels is a dog. Gwenynen reaches to give the dog a friendly pat and the dog licks her hand as if they are old friends. It looks to her like an Irish wolfhound.

"From the northern part of Wales. This is my dog Ci. He goes with me everywhere. When I first came, Sister Bendithion was going to make me leave him on the mainland. She did not want any predator animals on the isle, since it is such a bird sanctuary. I had to convince her Ci would never leave my side. He does not." She pauses, recalling what she was asked.

"In recent years the attacks from the Irish have increased near my home. My father sent me here, thinking that if I was here at least one member of the family would be safe and that I would gain valuable instruction from the Sisters here."

"How long have you and Ci lived on this beautiful isle?" asks Gwenynen.

"For about a year now. I love being here. I like that the climate is milder than the interior and almost every day I can get a good workout outside. I love walking over the isle with Ci, tracking the small game that is on the isle. Do not worry; we just track and observe. I never let him kill anything. Except occasionally Sister Bendithion asks me for Ci's help in harvesting for the kitchen one of the overly plentiful rabbits on the isle."

"I recently turned fourteen. I will remain on the isle until I am at least nineteen. Some time after that I will return home, for then it will be time for me to learn the ways of being with men." She smiles shyly.

Gwenynen returns the smile with a huge grin. "I have just turned nineteen myself. I just had my introduction into being a woman with a man. I had no idea how the Goddess could possess me and what a beautiful celebration connection with a man might be. My prayers to the Goddess will go with you."

"Thank you, Sister Gwenynen, if I may call you that. I am glad that you are here. I hope we can spend time together roaming around the isle."

Later Gwenynen realizes she is beginning to feel connected with the Sisters here, especially Derwen, even though they just met. Derwen reminds her of a younger brother she has never had.

Like Derwen, Gwenynen fell in love with the isle as soon as she stepped ashore. At night when she goes to bed, she longs for her knight. At the same time, deep within her soul she knows that this is where she needs to be.

*   *   *

Weeks later, Gwenynen awakes with a start. She looks over at Derwen, who is sleeping soundly, as is Ci beneath her bed. At first Gwenynen thinks what she was hearing was in her dream. But again comes a sound like some deranged human cry. She can't stand it. She puts her hand on Derwen's shoulder and shakes her.

"Huh, what is it?" asks Derwen sleepily.

"Don't you hear it? Listen."

"There it is again." They listen to an inhuman sound that seems to be made by a human—a strangled war-whoop abruptly cut off by an uncoordinated chorus of cackles just above their heads.

"Yes, it really does sound quite awful, doesn't it?" says Derwen. "Don't worry it is just birds."

"Great Goddess, it is horrible," says Gwenynen. "What kind of bird could make such ghastly sounds?"

Derwen sits up in her bed and leans down to pat Ci, who is awake as soon as Gwenynen rouses Derwen.

"Well, it depends on who you believe," says Derwen. "Roman Christian monks call it the devil bird and believe it comes here each year to fight off the influence of the devil from reaching this holy isle and that is what all the noise is about. On the other hand, the Celtic Christians call it the Christ bird because when you see it floating in the sky above you—and I am sure you will tomorrow since apparently many of them are arriving tonight—it is a beautiful white cross. The Celtic Christians believe it is a bird bearing Christ's spirit that comes from a far distant land where the Goddess is. It comes to Ynys Enlli to nest because this isle is holy. The cries you are hearing are the cries of the suffering of Christ. Because all suffering is carried by the Christ birds, the isle remains an especially holy and thin place."

"Doesn't matter whose theory you buy, the noise sure is awful," says Gwenynen.

"Once the nesting season starts, you get used to it quick. We will go out along the western edge of the isle tomorrow and I will show you some of their nests. They nest in little burrows they make in the ground. Each pair look after one egg and raise one chick together. They will be here all summer."

"I am not sure I want to go see anything sounding like what we are hearing now," says Gwenynen.

"Don't worry they don't make all this noise in the daytime. Because there are such large numbers of them that come here to nest, their night sounds do make an infernal racket."

"Why do so many come to this small isle?" asks Gwenynen.

"Because they raise their young in the ground," replies Derwen. "As a holy isle, Ynys Enlli has been given three gifts by the

Goddess. People here only die in natural succession, that is the oldest first, and there are no snakes or rats on the isle. Without ground predators the isle is a wonderful breeding place for the Christ bird."

"Thank you for telling me all this, Derwen. I might even be able to get back to sleep." Gwneynen gets up from her bed and leans over and gives Derwen a kiss on the cheek. Derwen slides down in her bed and is fast asleep in minutes. Gwenynen pulls her pillow up over her head and tucks it in under her ears. The cacophony muted, she is soon asleep.

*   *   *

The next day Gwenynen is summoned to Sister Bendithion's office.

"Come in and sit down," says Sister Bendithion. "I thought we should talk about your taking a vow to be here as a committed Sister in consciousness training. I want to answer any questions you have and also to ascertain for both of us where you are on your spiritual journey."

"Thank you, Sister Bendithion, I am a little sleepy from all the bird noise last night, but I am very excited to learn."

Sister Bendithion smiles. "Yes, the Christ birds are arriving. I am sure you will get used to these holy birds making such unholy noise.

"Let me start by asking you a few questions. In your instruction with Lady Geirwir, did you focus on the way of emptiness or the way of single-pointed attention?" She pauses. "The technical terms are apophatic and kataphatic?"

"Not sure about those last words. She was instructing me in the way of emptiness," says Gwenynen.

"Wonderful, that is the place we like to start. It is more the way of the Eastern Orthodox Church than the Roman Church. We believe it is more suited to the Celtic disposition. Can you experience emptiness in all three domains—mental, emotional and somatic?"

"Mentally best, and somewhat in the other two," says Gwenynen.

"Good, good. The mental is usually the hardest. We have such chattering minds. Now tell me what you are thinking right now."

Gwenynen laughs. "I am wondering what in the world you are going to ask me next. I had no idea the geography of consciousness might raise so many questions."

Sister Bendithion nods. "When you reported your thoughts just now to me, were you aware who reported them? That is, are you aware you can have thoughts and that you can observe yourself having thoughts at the same time?

"Yes, certainly."

"Are you aware you can have feelings and be aware of the feelings and observe them at the same time, and, similarly, that you can have sensations and be aware of them?

"I am aware of it theoretically," replies Gwenynen, "but not often do I hold both the feeling or sensation and awareness of the feeling or sensation."

"I see," says Sister Bendithion, quickly adopting the language of Gwenynen's dominant domain. "Are you aware that the part of you, which we call witnessing consciousness, or Goddess consciousness, or the lucid observer, is that part of you that observes the thinking, feeling or sensing?"

"I am aware of that, yes. But, do I live there most of the time?

Definitely no." Gwenynen frowns. "Does that mean I am too far behind to qualify for the consciousness school here?"

"Oh no, absolutely not. You are starting with more training and understanding than most. Just a couple more questions," says Sister Bendithion. "Have you begun any single pointed attention exercises?"

"No, not yet."

"Fine, no problem. We like to make sure that the path of emptiness is well developed in our brain before practicing the path of single-pointed awareness. Both are aimed at the same goal, to strengthen your lucid observer or Goddess consciousness. This capacity has many names, and Goddess or Christ consciousness is the result of this awareness capacity."

"Do you know why strengthening the capacity for inner observation is necessary?"

Gwenynen shakes her head *no.*

"Do not worry, it takes awhile for most students to get this. This is the part of you that can experience reality directly, like you first did as a little child. It is what Jesus meant when he said we enter the Kingdom of Heaven like little children. We only enter when we are living from witnessing consciousness, or Goddess consciousness, because only from that place can we see reality clearly and not through the smudged lens of our own ego stories."

"Why do you call it Goddess consciousness?" asks Gwenynen.

"Gwenynen, you are very astute. Good question. It is called Goddess consciousness because when we are there we have access to this energy of the Goddess. We are not limited by our own mental and emotional energy. We are able to participate in a field which is life-giving. Our lucid observer is a conduit to that field. The Goddess exists in the field, or maybe better said is the field, and is longing for conduits to appear so the life force she is can energize and vitalize more of reality."

Gwenynen hesitates, then she speaks. "For some of those Roman Christians, Goddess is a loaded word they associate with black magic and other pagan practices. Is there another word besides Goddess that works just as well? I am thinking about explaining this to Sir Gaiwain and not sure what language to use. He is a wonderful Celtic Christian."

"You could call it Christ consciousness or the consciousness of beingness and I am sure there are other apt names," says Sister Bendithion. "The most important part is that there is energy there, there is wisdom there, there is beauty there. None of this energy, wisdom and beauty can be accessed from your ordinary state of conditioned mind. It is like we are dolphins swimming in a huge sea above which is this air-energy of being. Our practices are to teach us how to continually rise above the surface of our conditioned trance so we can breathe this vitalizing air."

"I get it," says Gwenynen. "The different ways of languaging are helpful. Let me get you to take me through an example, just to be real practical. Say I have a problem and I am considering it not from the point of view of being attached to a particular solution or having an attachment or an aversion to a particular outcome—but the point of view of witnessing consciousness, Goddess consciousness or Christ consciousness—then what happens?"

"Then from that perspective, you get an outcome that has more energy for you, has beauty and more wisdom than you could ever imagine. Your outcome is not the result of your little ego self, but is supported by this infinite field of being.

"Amazing. That sounds incredible."

"In fact, it is." Sister Bendithion smiles a huge smile. "You have a wonderfully curious mind, Gwenynen. That is an awesome characteristic for someone on a spiritual journey. We need much curiosity to question our small-self persona view of the world. This may sound strange, but sometimes curiosity is what leads to conversion."

"How so?" asks Gwenynen.

"When we are curious, we have a natural openness. It is this openness that leads us to question the traps that our conditioned personality causes us to fall into repeatedly. Our contemplative practices then allow us to see the conditioned patterns and use their energy, literally convert their energy into being present, so we are in a state that is not reactive because of our past experience. That in a nutshell is the process of conversion. As we grow spiritually, we convert that old energy into our new way of being over and over again at deeper and deeper levels."

"Who does not long for that experience?" asks Gwenynen.

"Our view precisely. So, I take it you are committed to training in the consciousness school while you are here. I understand, at some point, you will want to leave to be with your beloved Gaiwain. Not only is that appropriate; we would encourage it. It is in committed relations where we are forced to look at our entire false self. A committed relationship is the most powerful mirror to reflect to you where you get most stuck.

"It is also in committed relations where we are most loved and, therefore, most willing to let down our persona and be in our authentic essence. Committed relations are the ultimate crucible in which to forge consciousness and the greatest opportunity to get stuck. It is easy to get stuck in them because it is so easy to project our issues on our mate, that is why we believe that a period of doing consciousness work, like you are beginning to embark on, is so important before marriage, not later.

"Thank you Gwenynen, for spending all this time with me. Welcome aboard; each individual journey here strengthens all of us. We are so glad you are willing to be a part of our sisterhood."

"Thank you for having me," says Gwenynen.

"Oh, one other question?" asks Gwenynen. "When you get where you are aware of your lucid observer, observing your thinking, feeling and sensing, are you at this place of transformation?"

Sister Bendithion smiles. "That gets you to level three. Above that are energy practices where you learn how to use your own energy, how it can be used to affect others, how to use it to heal and many other things. First, you have to get the energy, that is access to Goddess consciousness or Christ consciousness or the greater energy field of consciousness, whichever term you prefer. Once you learn you are not the story, which you tell yourself that you think you are, you have opened access into the field. When you know you are more than yourself, you get access to this abundant energy source with which to be creative on behalf of the Goddess."

"I had no idea," says Gwenynen, flushed with excitement, "that there is so much more to our being."

"Stay curious, I have to meet with some other Sisters now. Obviously, we still have much to talk about. Bless you my child." With that Sister Bendithion rises and heads out her office and across the courtyard.

*   *   *

Rat, what do you mean Mother Mary doesn't want me to overly encourage Gwenynen to push harder in her spiritual exercises so she can become more conscious? Tell her I am just doing my job and that I am not trying to change history. Well, not yet. Furthermore, no one ever told me I would have to put up with listening night after night to thousands of Manx shearwaters. Tell her to give me a break.

Chapter 8

Her first few years on the isle fly by more quickly than Gwenynen could have ever imagined. That is—the days go by quickly with all the teaching sessions on consciousness, practices to do and the chores that keep the community functioning. At night, it is a different story. Until she falls asleep, the minutes get longer and longer, as all she can think about is Sir Gaiwain.

Once, she received a written message from Sir Gaiwain. Even though years have gone by since they were together, he promises that he will return. Sadly, his return will be later rather than sooner. In 533, the Visigoths again invade Brittany and Arthur gathers his knights, Sir Gaiwain included, and goes to Brittany to help his kin repel the invaders.

Over the years Gwenynen progresses through stage three of her consciousness work. Sister Derwen becomes her closest friend. They are so different, but there is a bond there, which after awhile they both take for granted. Although Gwenynen is a few years older than Derwen, they are both eager to learn all they can, and they both love walking all over as much of the isle as they can each day. Derwen is not as good as Gwenynen at making tinctures and compounds from medicinal plants. She is better than Gwenynen at finding a particular plant, once it is identified for her. Gwenynen and Derwen delight in spending most of their days together, sharing their plant knowledge. Gwenynen finds an abundance of hazel and willow on the isle to use for medicines, and she is sure the beautiful purple foxgloves they have found must have an important medical use.

Gwenynen is experimenting with using crystals in the solarium to make special tinctures. She uses the magnified rays of the sun to heat different elements so that they fuse together. She then experiments with the particular properties that come from this fusion. She is amazed at how different the fused properties might be from the properties of either of the single elements. Her work is allowing her to greatly expand the repertoire of herbal medicines she has at her disposal with which to heal.

Derwen does not like spending hours in the solarium. She leaves Gwenynen to her experiments and instead spends hours running up the steep headland with Ci and practicing with her bow. She is a deadly shot. She reminds Gwenynen of the old stories of famous Celtic female warrior chieftains.

Derwen is now anxious to return home. She is past the initial age when, as a young woman, she might with the Goddess' help learn the ways of being with men. Yet her father has not sent for her and she worries for the well-being of her family.

Just a year earlier, Lady Bridgette steals away back to Ireland. Derwen is upset about not getting passage back to her home in Wales when the Irish ship, oared by twenty lusty Irishman, comes calling at the behest of Lady Bridgette's father to pickup Lady Bridgette. Lady Bridgette would not take Derwen with her without Sister Bendithion's consent, and Sister Bendithion practically locks all the Sisters in the Sister house until the Irish vessel leaves. Lady Bridgette leaves the isle in fine style, preceded by an all night party on the beach in which Sister Bendithion and all the Sisters take part in much Irish dancing and singing to everyone's delight.

Sister Bendithion counsels Derwen that even though Lady Bridgette commands the oarsmen, this is not appropriate transportation for a young woman back to the mainland. Besides,

Sister Bendithion is sure the boat will be headed straight back to Ireland and fears Derwen would become a hostage of some petty Irish warlord.

Derwen dismisses her concerns. She believes she is a match for any man. She feels she has been away from home far too long. However, Sister Bendithion prevails in keeping Derwen on the isle, when she also shares with Derwen that Sister Bendithion believes that the Order may need Derwen's special skills in the days just ahead. Still, time is dragging by for Derwen and she is restless.

"Derwen, I must tell you," says Gwenynen. "The talk about calamities coming, well I am afraid that I know what the calamity is and that it will be upon us soon." The pair are warming themselves by the fire in the refectory before the mealtime bell rings. Ci is at Derwen's feet.

"What in the Goddess' name is it?" asks Derwen.

"Yesterday, Sister Bendithion asked me to lead a group of Sisters to start making bandages and the preparations for dressing wounds. If you had lived at Arthur's Court, you would know what that means." She pauses. "War!"

Derwen, who has skin so fair it almost seems transparent, flushes with excitement. "How can that be? A war here? On this holy isle?"

"I do not know how it could be. I have seen the kind of preparation we are doing many times before and it has always meant war. If the war comes here, all the work we have been doing to transform our consciousness, may be too little, too late; and may not be to much effect to protect us. Do you think we should be armed and fight as the men do, like the Goddess inspired our women to do before the Romans came?"

"So you really think there will be war?" asks Derwen. She flexes her right arm, with which she pulls back her bow. "Yes, I am ready to go to war like the Goddess prepared women to do before and after the Romans came, like our Celtic Queen Boudicca did against the Romans, when the Roman General Suetonius Paulinus was massacring the Druids on Anglesey."

"Derwen, I am so thankful you have such a strong feminine warrior spirit." She stops and reflects a moment. "Though I am not as prescient as Sister Bendithion is, I feel in my bones war coming."

*   *   *

"Wake up, wake up," whispers Sister Bendithion.

Gwenynen rolls over. "What do you mean wake up? It must be the middle of the night."

"Yes, it is. Quickly, we must go. We do not have much time. Please wake Sister Derwen also. Tell her to wear her toughest leather jerkin and bring her bow and quiver. Please pack a large supply of bandages and compounds for dressing wounds. We will meet at the beach landing in thirty minutes."

Sister Bendithion starts to move away. Gwenynen reaches out and grabs her arm. "Is war coming to the isle?" asks Gwenynen.

"I certainly hope not," says Sister Bendithion. "For now, we're going to it. I will tell you more later. What is important now is that we move quickly."

*   *   *

Rat, my character is very worried about this upcoming battle. Could you ask Tree to be sure he stays in reflective consciousness with his character? We may need his character to have the skill and agility of a young brave for my character to survive.

Don't argue with me. Just tell Tree to pay attention to being here. After all the deception to keep truth alive he has learned from his Grandfather, Tree should be pleased to be riding shotgun in the consciousness of a woman. And, yes, of course, he should bring Two.

Chapter 9

Caer Calemion
Wales
537

King Arthur meets with Merlin and Lady Geirwir all afternoon. They are in his private room that is just behind the great room of the castle where Arthur holds Court. In contrast to the formality of the ceremonial room where all guests and petitioners are received, this inner room is warm and intimate. There is a fireplace in the corner with glowing coals and bread and cheese spread on a board upon a narrow table against the back wall. There are several leather bound books scattered about as well as many stacked in a bookcase, each worth more than most of Arthur's subjects will earn in a lifetime. On two walls are three large maps—a map of Britain, a map of Brittany and a map of the known world. This is the place Arthur wrestles with decisions about what is best for his people and his kingdom.

Arthur will not proceed without the assent of Merlin and Lady Geirwir. He learned early as a young warrior-king never to make the decision to go to war without his most trusted counselors being in agreement. Now he and they seem to be at loggerheads.

King Arthur has received word that Lady Bridgette has returned to Ireland and that after talking with her father and the Irish King, the Irish King has sent one of his chieftains, the Irish warlord Llwch Wyddel, one of Bridgette's many lovers, with several ships of Irish warriors and attacked the western Welsh coast. Arthur knows the Irish chieftains relish any excuse to attack. The erratic weather has produced several years of famine in Ireland and incursions into Wales to plunder are the quickest way for the Irish King and his knights, like Llwch Wyddel, to assuage discontent and replenish their stores. Now the Irish have savaged and plundered several Welsh villages. The writing on the wall is clear to Arthur—he must take men to Ireland and exact retribution.

Lady Geirwir is silent after hearing Arthur state his case for making immediate war. As always, when she is attending the King to counsel him, she is dressed finely, as if for Court. She wears a gown made of several layers with gold thread stitched in bands around her neck and wrists. Around her neck hangs a delicately made triple Goddess Celtic silver knot. The outer layer of her gown is diaphanous, which with her genial mien gives her an ethereal countenance. Finally, she speaks. "Sire, I understand all the reasons why you feel that the Irish must be attacked. I do not have a good argument to use to tell you not to go. However, I have this uncertain feeling that this is not a good time for you to leave the administration of the Kingdom to others and be abroad. I do not know why, I just have an uneasy feeling."

"What do you say, Merlin?" asks King Arthur. "What about the climatic disruption we are experiencing. Isn't that a sign I should take action? Or, is it not?"

Merlin, as he is wont to do, pulls at his long, white beard. He is dressed somewhat carelessly, but the weight of who he is gives a dignity to his appearance regardless of what he wears. "Arthur, what to do is a conundrum. You are right; the weather is a portent. My prescience tells me that a Byzantine historian Procopius will write about this past year *that for the whole of 536, the sun gave forth its light without brightness like the moon.* Michael the Syrian will write of this year that each day the sun shines only *for about four hours, and still this light was only a feeble shadow.*"

Merlin and Lady Geirwir are the only ones at Court who address Arthur by his first name. "I see us between the classic rock and a hard place, which we have read about in Greek stories. You cannot be seen by your people to waver in their defense when they are attacked. So part of me knows that you must go to Ireland. You must teach the Irish warlords the lesson that they have been begging you to teach them. On the other hand, like Lady Geirwir, I too am worried that this is not a time to leave the administration of the Kingdom to others."

"I have often left the administration of the Kingdom to my relatives, when I have been forced to go to war. This has not been a problem. Is there any alternative?"

"My King," says Merlin. "I have tried to see into the future about this decision. I must tell you that whichever route you take the future does not bode well."

"Merlin, you know my whole life, whenever there has been a challenge, I have responded with action. This has always been the best way. At least it has been my way. Do you counsel me to change now?"

"No, Arthur, you have my assent, though I am deeply fearful. Here is the picture I see. In 530, some seven years ago, when your father-in-law, Count Gwythyr, died, you, through Lady Guinevere, took by inheritance the principality of Leon in Brittany. This land, together with the land which you already hold hereditary title to in Brittany, gives you a vast kingdom there. In addition, there is the Kingdom of Britain. When your relative King Deroch, with whom you have jointly ruled your kingdom in Brittany, asked you for help four years ago to repel an invasion of the Visigoths, you, as you feel now, felt you had to respond. You and most of your best knights were gone from this Court for nearly four years. The administration of your Kingdom in Britain is always in something of a vacuum when you are gone. Your further absence from the realm, coming on the heels of the Brittany campaign, is what bothers me about your decision to go to war now...."

King Arthur looks at Merlin and nods. "I understand well your concerns, Merlin." Then he looks at Lady Geirwir.

"Sire, I share all of Merlin's concern, yet I too know of no reason to ask you to defer from a path of action. I have explained to you the uneasiness in my heart. However, I have no clear alternative course to suggest. I give my assent."

"Thank you both for wrestling for me with what we should do. I will go in the name of the Goddess and Christ, and pray that the Divine will favor our actions and that Her will shall be done."

"Arthur, though I have not always accompanied you to war, my intuition tells me that this path is fraught with difficulties and that this time I should go with you," says Merlin.

"Merlin, because you and Lady Geirwir are distressed about this campaign I am embarking on, which as you have emphasized will again take me from my kingdom, I feel perhaps you should stay here and keep your eyes on the home fires."

Merlin ponders the matter. He is slow, as always, to respond. "Yes, Arthur, I believe that it is, indeed, best for me to stay here. Though in some ways it seems I shall be on this trip with you."

Arthur turns his back to Merlin briefly, as he paces back and forth across the room in a determined gait, his jaw set. "What was the last thing you said, Merlin? I could not quite hear you."

"Not to worry, my Lord, I was musing to myself."

*   *   *

Arthur knows how to go into action. He immediately calls together his finest knights from across his Kingdom, and in a few weeks they set out across Wales, cross the Irish Sea and stride across Ireland to avenge his people, who have suffered at the hands of the Irish warlord, Llwch Wyddel, who is also known as Llwch Llawinawg, Lord of the Lakes. The two forces meet beyond the mountain of Mynneu and many knights are slain on both sides. Finally, Arthur encounters Llwch and, as is the custom, the knights on both sides surrounding their leaders pull back, so that the two can meet in personal battle.

Lady Geirwir anxiously reads the dispatch she receives from Arthur.

Llwch is as tough an enemy as I have ever faced. Our brave knights fought his men for more than a day. Finally he emerged before me on the battle field. We engaged each other and he fought fiercely and gallantly. By my sword, Caliburn, I was able to slay him. When their leader fell the Irish warriors retreated. We pursued far enough to give them demand for repayment for the loss of life and property we have suffered. This they agreed to. Because of so many grievously wounded, it will be some days before I manage to return home. Please let all those at Court know of this victory and of the bravery of our knights.

In the Spring Season of the Goddess, in the year of our Lord, 537.
Arthur, King of the Britons

Lady Geirwir puts the dispatch down. She must immediately let Medraut know of this good news. Arthur chose Medraut, as Regent, to rule his Kingdom while he is away. Medraut's father, Cawrdaf, has been, next to Merlin and Lady Geirwir, the King's chief advisor as well as prime minister. Medraut's Grandfather was Caradog Freichfras, who was Arthur's chief elder and advisor when he was a minor and first became King.

Cawrdaf is not only an able political advisor, he is a leading light in the Welsh church, establishing a religious house for three hundred monks in Mid Glamorgan and providing patronage to the Welsh church on the Llyn peninsula. It is only natural that Arthur should now appoint his son, Medraut, the scion of a powerful Gwent and Llyn family and ally, to rule in his absence.

Indeed, Gwenhwyfach, the sister of Guinevere, is the wife of Medraut.

Medraut is delighted when Lady Geirwir gives him the news of King Arthur's victory. However, Lady Geirwir is surprised by the expression on his wife Gwenhwyfach's face. Upon hearing the news, her expression is not delight and relief, but one of cunning.

As she walks back to her chambers, Lady Geirwir realizes she feels a connection between Lady Gwenhwyfach's "look" and her uneasiness about Arthur leaving the Kingdom in the first place. Before she reaches her rooms, she turns and goes off in search of Merlin.

"Merlin, I gave Medraut the news of the King's victory, which I gave to you first, and when I did, I noticed an expression on the face of Lady Gwenhwyfach, who was standing nearby. I do not know exactly how to describe it."

"Would you say, maybe, evil?" asks Merlin. "I have never liked the woman and always been perplexed by the antipathy she has toward her sister, Lady Guinevere."

"Yes," says Lady Geirwir, "I think it was the fighting between the two sisters that led to the hurt feelings between Arthur and Medraut awhile back, which they papered over shortly thereafter, when Arthur led all the knights of Britain, including Cawrdaf's forces, against the Saxons."

"We should be on the alert about this, I agree," says Merlin.

*   *   *

Lady Geirwir knocks on Merlin's door. It is late at night and she wants to avoid being seen going to Merlin's quarters. She, like everyone else, knows he is usually up half the night.

"Come in."

She opens the door. Several candles are sputtering on a table spread with paper, carved figures and hunks of stone. Merlin raises his head from his work at the table.

"Merlin, I am heart-brokenly distressed. I now have conclusive proof that Medraut is gathering his men from Gwent. I believe that he is going to challenge Arthur!"

"Are you sure, my dear?" asks Merlin.

"Yes, I am. Arthur left none of his warriors here. Daily the courtyard is filled with more knights sharpening their swords and battle axes, and all of these knights are from Gwen and Llyn with clan and land loyalty to the family of Medraut.

"To top it all off, I have learned that Medraut has had Guinevere confined to a small castle about ten miles from here out in the country, where she is being kept under guard. Her sister, Lady Gwenhwyfach, has moved into the Queen's chambers."

"Gwenhwyfach in her sister's chambers, that does say it all."

"Merlin, I believe you must go and tell Arthur what is happening. Medraut knows that many of Arthur's knights were slain in the Irish war and that his men are only now beginning to cross the Irish Sea, returning to northern Wales in small groups. I believe that Medraut will lay in wait for Arthur, when Arthur returns with his men dispersed. You are the only person who can go safely to Arthur. If Medraut's men accost you on the way, they will be afraid to detain the Arch-Druid of Britain."

"My dear, I am too old to be out galloping across the countryside in the middle of the night. Sorrowfully, I have become accustomed to a few creature comforts." He stands and paces about the room. "Unfortunately, you may be right. Let me think about what to do. You best be getting at least a little sleep tonight."

Lady Geirwir rises and gets ready to take her leave. Wordlessly, she turns to him and kisses the old Druid on the cheek.

Silently, he nods farewell to her as she leaves.

The next morning Lady Geirwir again goes in search of Merlin. She wants to find out from him what he has decided to do. In her search she meets Lady Gwenhwyfach coming down the hall.

"Dear, Lady Geirwir, what are you up to, scurrying about so early in the morning?" asks Lady Gwenhwyfach in an acid tone.

"Lady Gwenhwyfach, I am in search of Merlin. Have you seen him?"

Lady Gwenhwyfach smirks. "No, not at all, but one of my informants in the night guard has advised me that he left early this morning. I let my husband know immediately. He will have some of our men go after Merlin. He should not have left Court without Medraut's approval. The old windbag thinks he can just blow about as he wants.

"So, why did you want to see him, Lady Geirwir?"

Lady Geirwir stiffens, though her tone remains steady. "We have been working on some new medicinal compounds. I have one for him to try for his arthritis."

"He should be brought back shortly. He may need more than something for joint pain, when he gets back." Lady Gwenhwyfach gives a smile that is dark as the approach of a thunderstorm.

Lady Geirwir, without more, turns and leaves. As she walks

down the hall towards her chamber, she thinks. *That old rascal. He knew he was going to leave last night and he did not tell me so I could authentically deny knowledge of his plans. His little deception worked out exactly as he planned. I just pray he gets away to warn Arthur.*

*   *   *

I am way too old to be shape-shifting thinks Merlin as he pulls his horse into a grove of oaks and takes on the form of the trees around him. Minutes later Medraut's men ride by. Merlin chuckles. A whole band of impatient young men is no match for a patient old man.

Merlin's slow pace soon outwits his pursuers, and in several days he is well beyond where Medraut's men are searching for him. In another ten days he crosses the Irish Sea. Upon landing in Ireland he finds Arthur and a few of his men making their way home.

"Sire, I have bad news for you," says Merlin, as he dismounts and walks with a stiff-legged gait up to King Arthur standing outside his tent beside a dying fire.

Arthur brightens at seeing his most trusted political and spiritual advisor. "And I have some bad news for you. You look like a tired, old man who has been ahorse way too long."

Merlin smiles. Arthur will need all his good humor.

"My King, I am afraid that Medraut has summoned all his men from Ghent and Llyn and is marching against you. He knows from your own dispatches that you lost many good knights in the battle with the Irish. He hopes to catch you trying to land back in Wales with your remaining men dispersed."

Before he even replies to Merlin, Arthur summons two men-at-arms and sends them with messages to quickly gather all that remain of his dispersed army.

"You are indeed, the bearer of bad news, Merlin. How did you get here and how much time do we have?"

"I am not sure how long we have. They know that I left Court, presumably to warn you. Medraut sent men after me to detain me. Eluding them was no problem, though it lengthened my journey. I should think that the sooner you can get your army safely ashore in Wales the better position you will be in."

"I am, indeed, battle weary. However, there is nothing quite like the idea of getting home to stir the imaginations and flagging energies of the war weary. Merlin, get yourself something to eat quickly. Obviously, we will be breaking camp soon."

Chapter 10

Camlan, Wales
537

The crossing from Ynys Enlli back to the mainland is so rough that there is no opportunity for Gwenynen to talk further with Sister Bendithion. Even getting the boatman, Barinthus, to take them across was difficult. Sister Bendithion has a way to summon him by a fire on top of the headlands at night, or by using a large mirror to reflect a beam of light across the water to the mainland during the day. The boatman has come. He requires considerable persuasion by Sister Bendithion to ferry them across before daybreak.

Once safely on the Llyn peninsula they mount horses and immediately start out. It is still dark. Gwenynen can smell it on the air and feel it in her gut. It is the smell of war. Before long she can also feel the anxiety and agitation of war, of men about to engage in life and death struggles with each other. Gwenynen looks at Sister Bendithion and Derwen. Sister Bendithion's face is masked in consternation. Derwen is looking straight ahead. She rides so smoothly on her horse, it is as if she and the horse are formed from the same musculature.

Directly, they surmount a large hill and stop. They dismount and walk to the top of a rock ledge. Before them is the scene of a great battle. It must have started the day before. There are bodies of downed warriors everywhere. The two sides apparently each withdrew to opposite ends of the plain below as the preceding night had fallen. Now dawn is coming and the battle is about to commence again.

Gwenynen asks Sister Bendithion, "What place is this?"

"It is Camlan, Gwenynen, and history will rue the meeting that is occurring here." Sister Bendithion turns her intense gaze back on the scene unfolding before her.

Gwenynen speaks to Derwen at her side. "See the knight on the huge horse with the dragon helmet and the image of a woman on his shield? That is King Arthur."

Derwen has her bow in her hand. "Do you know whom he faces?"

"No, I don't. Perhaps Sister Bendithion does. They look like Welsh warriors on both sides to me."

Their conversation stops as they watch in enthralled horror as the two sides press forward into the center of the field and the whole world rings with the cries of men dying or exalting in victory. Gwenynen and Derwen continue to keep their eyes glued on King Arthur. He leads his men directly into the fight and the two women can tell that several knights stay right on his flanks, protecting him from sudden attack from the sides.

The slaughter is horrific and yet by midday neither side has given ground. Then as if each great body of warriors were drawing a breath, the tide of soldiers parts and King Arthur is there facing the leader against him. They spur their horses and charge into mortal combat. After awhile both men are fighting, sword to sword, on foot, each having unseated the other from his horse.

Suddenly, both men are lying on the ground.

Sister Bendithion jumps up. "Let's go."

Quickly, they are on their horses riding onto the battlefield. Gwenynen notices that even though they are galloping full out,

Derwen smoothly pulls an arrow from her quiver and notches it in her bow. Gwenynen suddenly sees the danger out of the corner of her eye. Derwen smoothly lets her arrow fly at the warrior, who has ridden out of nowhere coming headlong toward them, waving a bloody sword above his head. Derwen's arrow strikes the approaching warrior square in the center of the forehead, and, as he collapses, his horse rears and turns aside.

Only when they are near the center of the conflict, do they slow down. Gwenynen can see several knights are staked out around the downed King Arthur. His opponent is lying nearby, a sword piercing straight through his body. At the sight of their slain leader his warriors begin to retreat.

"I am glad you are here," says a familiar voice to Gwenynen. As much as she tries, she sees no one familiar. Then it dawns on her the knight standing next to King Arthur sword at the ready, with blood flowing down the side of his face, is Sir Gaiwain.

She steps toward him. "Oh, Gaiwain, is it really you? Are you all right?" she asks in anguish.

"Yes, dear Gwenynen, it is truly me, and these are only surface wounds, please see to the King."

Both Sister Bendithion and Gwenynen bend over Arthur. He has been grievously wounded. The first task is to stop the blood flow.

"Gaiwain, help me remove his armor and see if a litter can be brought up quickly," entreats Gwenynen.

Yes," says Sir Gaiwain and he bends to assist her and Sister Bendithion in the task of removing King Arthur's armor. All the time Sister Derwen is standing right beside Gwenynen, her bow partially drawn, her eyes scanning in all directions.

When the armor is off, Arthur's blood-soaked shirt is stripped away. Gwenynen immediately applies some myrrh dressings to his side and leg to stop the bleeding. Without knowing why, she gives the bloodied shirt to Derwen and asks her to put it somewhere safe. Derwen takes the bloodied shirt and wraps it in a clean leather pouch. Carefully she stows it in Gwenynen's saddlebag.

Suddenly an elderly man with a long white beard appears out of nowhere. "Sir Gaiwain, please assure Arthur's men that he is okay and tell them they should finish this battle for him to avenge their King against those who followed the traitor Medraut."

"Yes, Merlin, I will see to it," says Sir Gaiwain.

By now a litter has arrived. Gwenynen manages to stop the bleeding and, at least for the moment, Arthur's vital signs are beginning to stabilize. Carefully he is shifted onto the litter and just as carefully his men begin carrying him from the battlefield.

"Return with us, Sir Gaiwain, to see to the care of King Arthur," says Sister Bendithion, much to the relief of Gwenynen.

Gwenynen bends over Arthur to hear what he is whispering. Finally she understands. "His sword. He wants someone to bring it," she says. "He says he left it in Medraut's chest."

Sir Gaiwain signals to Gwenynen that he understands and that he will retrieve the sword and catch up with them shortly.

What was such a quick trip from the landing on the beach at Porth Meudwy to the battlefield takes forever transporting King Arthur by litter.

The small group carrying Arthur has traveled several hours and is passing through a thickly wooded area when Ci stops, the short hair on his back bristling. Ci gives a low growl. There is no misunderstanding its meaning.

"Sir Gaiwain," cries Derwen, "there is danger ahead."

Gaiwain and the other knights on horseback pull in close to the cart carrying King Arthur, and at Gaiwain's order they all pull their swords to the ready.

Ci's forewarning is barely soon enough. Several of Medraut's warriors come charging on horseback from up ahead on both sides of the narrow road. Gaiwain and his knights charge forward to meet them.

Derwen quickly observes that they are well outnumbered. Deception will be necessary if they are to get King Arthur out of there alive. Hurriedly, she urges the driver to steer the cart into a thicket. There she and Gwenynen and Sister Bendithion take the unconscious body of Arthur from the cart. Just as quickly a log is placed in the cart and the royal dragon banner is placed over it. Derwen instructs the cart driver that he is to drive a short distance down the road to where the road passes through an open field. As soon as the cart is in the middle of the field, he should abandon it and run for safety in the surrounding trees.

When Arthur is unloaded and the cart is being driven toward the open field, Ci and Derwen are off gliding through the forest beside the road. The cart driver manages to get the cart to the middle of the field before Medraut's warriors are upon him. They are increasingly tightening a circle around Gaiwain and two loyal knights fighting side by side with him. All three have had their horses slain beneath them. There are shouts of triumph and cries of unimaginable pain. The hand-to-hand combat is horrific.

Upon seeing the cart with the dragon banner draped over a form riding in its center, Medraut's warriors release the ever-tightening circle around Gaiwain and his knights and gallop toward the cart.

By then Ci and Derwen are well positioned behind a screen of trees near the cart. The lead warrior arrives at the cart and immediately lets fly a battle axe that strikes with a thud in the center of the dragon banner. In his exuberance he jumps from his horse and pulls off his battle helmet. Just before he steps upon the cart, Derwen's arrow tears through the socket of his left eye. The arrow's force carries its tip into his brain. He collapses against the cart.

Medraut's warriors are uncertain where the arrow came from. Derwen quickly sends another arrow toward the warrior closest to her. Her target window is very narrow, a small space where the neck is exposed beneath the helmet and above the metalwork worn on the chest. The arrow deflects off the helmet. The warrior instantly turns in her direction.

Derwen gives a quick hand-signal to Ci. He immediately circles to the left so he can come at her foes from behind.

Derwen quickly notches another arrow, takes a deep breath, prays that the Goddess will let her arrow fly true and releases. By then the warrior bearing down on her is barely twenty feet away. This time the arrow strikes just below the helmet and pierces straight through her assailant's neck. He slumps over the saddle and his horse veers off to the side.

Her arrows have taken down the leaders of the ambush band. After two spears are sent through the battle-axed form in the cart, Medraut's remaining warriors turn back to re-engage the fight with Gaiwain and the two loyal knights fighting with him. Derwen, at a quick trot, moves toward them. Ci, at her command, has circled ahead on the other side of the road. Soon she is on one side of the fray and Ci is on the other.

Medraut's warriors have managed to separate Gaiwain and his two knights. Such separation is often the beginning of the end. Gaiwain and each of his knights need her help simultaneously.

She must use all her weapons, not just her bow. With deft concentration she focuses on the warrior closest to Gaiwain. She enters his energy field and then his thought field—it is all red and black. From his thought field she initiates a wave of emotion that causes the warrior to stop in his tracks. It is just the opening Gaiwain needs and he regains the upper-hand. At the same time, she is entering the thought field of that warrior, with a deft hand signal she sends Ci attacking the warrior fighting Gaiwain's knight on her left. When Ci sinks his inch-long incisors into the calf of the warrior, the warrior reacts by turning backwards. It is the opportunity the knight needs and he quickly manages a fatal blow.

Simultaneously with Ci attacking another warrior, Derwen pulls an arrow from her quiver and notches it in her bow. She lets this arrow fly at one of the other two warriors attacking Gaiwain. It thuds into the metal mesh on his chest. The shot is not fatal, but for the moment it takes him out of the fight.

Again Derwen signals Ci and again Ci attacks the unguarded leg of a foe. This time it is a warrior battling Gawain's knight on her right. When the warrior turns, it gives Derwen an open shot at his unarmored back and neck. Her arrow hits with a solid thump and the warrior collapses. Twice more Derwen and Ci deal their deadly choreography. Then the few remaining members of the ambush band, who are able to flee, head for the woods. The price of fleeing is exposure of their vulnerable backsides. Derwen's arrows fly after them with deadly consequence.

Once all the enemy are scattered or dead, Gaiwain heads for the cart which was carrying King Arthur. Derwen rushes to Gaiwain. "Do not worry, Gaiwain. It is not what you think. Arthur is safe."

However, arriving back at the cart and seeing the battle axe and spears thrust through the form beneath the dragon banner is for Gaiwain a horribly unsettling sight.

"Take me to my King," he says.

Derwen leads him back down the road and off into the woods. There they find Gwneynen and Sister Bendithion ministering gently to Arthur.

Sister Bendithion speaks. "I think a little rest off that awful, bone-shaking cart may have helped Arthur. He has mumbled a few indecipherable words, and he is resting a bit easier I believe."

Gaiwain puts his arm around Gwenynen. She nods toward him and their eyes both exchange messages of gratefulness that they are each unharmed.

"I am glad you have had a pleasant bit of rest," says Gaiwain, suddenly regaining his easy-going sense of humor upon seeing that Gwenynen and his King are unhurt by the attack. "However, there could be more of Medraut's warriors about. Let's get the cart back up here and Arthur loaded. We need to make it to the beach at Porth Meudwy as soon as we can."

By the time they get to the beach Arthur has lapsed into unconsciousness, though Gwenynen feels he is remaining stable. Merlin has by then caught up with them and she can feel this energy of healing pouring out of him toward Arthur. Sir Gaiwain goes to find the boatman.

The boatman is reluctant to sail. For good reason. Finally he agrees. The crossing is rough, the tidal current fierce. Halfway across, Sister Bendithion starts a chant asking the Goddess to calm the waters. Gwenynen and Derwen join in. Whether it was with Her help, or not, they finally make it to the narrow, sandy-beach landing on Ynys Enlli.

"Where shall we take him?" asks Gwenynen.

"I am not sure, maybe to the chapel," says Sister Bendithion.

"No," says Gwenynen after reflecting a moment. "I believe it would be best to take him to the solarium. He will stay warmer there and I think we will be able to use some of the crystals in his healing."

"A wonderful idea. Yes, that is exactly where we should take him."

A knot of Sisters is clustered around with a litter ready to take Arthur as Sister Bendithion directs. She points to the solarium and slowly the procession moves up the path.

Gwenynen falls behind. She grasps Gaiwain's hand. "Come with me so I can dress that wound you have. It is still oozing. I will also make a cot in the solarium where you can stay with Arthur. I will need to stay there also." She looks up at Gaiwain. He gives her a weak smile. She can tell he is totally exhausted.

Chapter 11

The next twenty-four hours are touch-and-go. Arthur is running a high fever. Although Gwenynen washes it well the first night the wound is still festering. Medraut's sword has cut a deep gash in Arthur's side and thigh. Gwenynen knows she will need to get all the infection out before she can attempt to sew him up. Fortunately, it does not appear that any vital organs are penetrated.

"We have put our strongest distilled spirits on the wound," says Gwenynen, "and the inflammation is still raging. I am not sure what we should do."

"All I know is for us to continue our 24-hour around-the-clock prayers," says Sister Bendithion.

"Prayer is good. And something dramatic is going to need to happen soon, if we are going to save Arthur's life." She glances over in the corner where St Dyfrig, who years earlier crowned Arthur King of Britain, sits. St Dyfrig has been summoned down from his hermitage and is in continuous prayer for Arthur, as is St Cadfan.

"I wish I knew what else to do," says Sister Bendithion. "You have remarkable skills, Gwenynen. I will pray for your wisdom in using those skills."

"I think I have an idea," says Gwenynen. "What if we took the large crystal that is suspended in the center of the room and used it to burn away the ragged, inflamed skin and muscle around the wound?"

"I do not know if that would work," says Sister Bendithion.

"Well, we are going to need to try something, the fever is getting worse and he is slipping deeper and deeper into unconsciousness."

"You are right. I do not believe we have much time. We should try something," says Sister Bendithion.

"Okay, let's give it a try," says Gwenynen. "See if you can get someone to help move that table of pea plants that are just beginning to bloom. I want to bring Arthur to the very center of the room, so I can maximize the concentration of sunlight from the large crystal."

Gaiwain re-enters the room and quickly accommodates Gwenynen's request to rearrange the furniture. Arthur is soon lying directly in the center of the room. His bed, carved of cherry wood, now bathes in the light from all the crystals and gives off a golden glow.

Gwenynen begins to focus the sun rays through the prism of a large crystal on to the edges of the wounded area. It takes her a few moments to find the right focal distance to maximize the concentration of energy from the sun's rays. When she has it, the edges of the wound begin to sear. Arthur, still deeply unconscious, begins to moan as if from both relief and pain.

"This smells horrible," says Sister Bendithion. "Are you sure this is what we should be doing?"

"I am not sure at all," says Gwenynen. "I am just trying to do everything I can to save the life of the King."

Sister Bendithion nods her assent.

Gwenynen motions with her head for Gaiwain to step up beside her. Her hand is beginning to shake from the tension of holding the crystal steady in exactly the right focal length. She gives the crystal to Gaiwain, who holds it steady, while she guides his hand.

Slowly, but surely, the edges of the wound are cauterized. When that is done, Gwenynen again liberally washes the wound in distilled spirits. Then she begins to sew up the interior muscle tear. After that is sewn, she sews the next layer. Finally, after about an hour and a half, she sews up the last layer of skin.

"I do not know if this will work. I sure hope so," says Gwenynen. "Gaiwain, I am tired, can you watch the King with Sister Bendithion for awhile? I want to take a nap on that cot in the far corner."

As Gwenynen starts toward the far corner of the solarium, she begins to fall from her exhaustion. Luckily, Gaiwain is right behind her and scoops her up with one arm, and the natural motion of saving her from falling brings her right up against him. She smiles.

Gaiwain sets her gently down on the cot. "I slept like an ancient oak last night, dear Gwenynen. Now you are as battle-weary as I was, though fighting for Arthur's life is a different kind of battle. I admire your skill and bravery."

"I can't wait to sleep with you again," she whispers, and she pulls him to her and kisses him gently on the lips. Gaiwain puts her carefully down on the cot and pulls a blanket around her.

Gaiwain stands back up. He turns toward Sister Bendithion, "Gwenynen was asleep before her head came to rest on the pillow. I think everything that can be done has been done for the

King now, Sister Bendithion. Please go and take some rest, I will stay with him."

Sister Bendithion nods. "Thank you, Sir Gaiwain, I will. Call me if anything changes significantly."

Sister Bendithion leaves the solarium. Gaiwain goes and stands by Arthur. He seems to be resting well, though he continues to be deeply lost in unconsciousness. Gaiwain opens the outside door. The room still smells strongly of burning flesh.

As he opens the door in comes Derwen followed, as always, by Ci. She has brought a bundle of lavender she has gathered.

"Sir Gaiwain, I did as you requested. I spent most of the morning up at the top of the headland. There is no sign of anyone following us. I also have some Sisters working on flammable wrappings to make flame-arrows should we need them as a possible defense against an attack. There are not really many resources here to defend with, other than spiritual ones. I brought this fresh lavender. I thought it might help."

"Wonderful," says Gaiwain, taking the lavender from her. "Thank you, Derwen, you and Ci have been most helpful to us all. I think we should keep the watch intensely for another week or so. After that we can re-consider,s depending on how Arthur is doing."

"I understand, Sir Gaiwain. I have a couple of Sisters who can also help watch. The water is so treacherous, it is unlikely anyone will try to cross at night, though I know Sister Bendithion has done that."

"Yes, I believe the Llyn boatman, Barinthus, is loyal to Sister Bendithion and sees the isle as a sacred, holy place. He would never bring an enemy across at night, and only during the day if his life were threatened. We should be able to relax a bit before long."

*   *   *

Arthur's recuperation is long and difficult. For weeks he lies unconscious. Finally, one day, he rouses himself. He looks at Gwenynen, not knowing who she is.

"Young woman, ask Merlin to attend me," is the first thing Arthur says.

"Yes, Sire, I shall fetch him right away," says Gwenynen. This is the moment she had been hoping for—Arthur finally regaining consciousness. It has been a sunny morning and the light is dazzling in the solarium.

Soon, Gwenynen returns with Merlin. He is elated that Arthur has regained consciousness.

"This is wonderful, my King," says Merlin. "I am so delighted to see you awake. How are you feeling?"

Arthur looks around. "Where in the world am I? When I awoke earlier and saw all the sparkles of light around me, I was sure I was in heaven. Then I felt this terrible pain in my side and decided maybe I had not yet arrived at that final resting place. How long have I been unconscious?"

"Arthur, it has been one and a half moon cycles. I have dispatched messages back to your Court to Lady Geirwir letting her know that you are alive. I have gotten a message back from her. I am afraid things are very much in disarray there. I have been thinking, if you believe it is best, that I should return to Court to be a steadying influence. However, I did not want to return until it was clear that you were recovering.

"Merlin, you are wise as always." He pauses. "I need water.

Could you get me a drink?"

Gwenynen brings a cup of water and holds it to the King's lips.

"Merlin, I am going to have to rest. But, yes, return to Court, and let everyone know that I am recovering. Then come back to me and report on the situation there." He pauses again to catch his breath. "When I awoke just now, to these lights of heaven, I awoke from a dream. The portent of the dream, I believe, is that I should not return to Britain. Instead, I am called to go to Brittany, the land of my relatives and Guinevere's people and where two of my sisters live."

"Arthur, that is enough for now. You need to rest. I will do as you say and return to your Court."

"Merlin, yes, I must rest. First, though, let me tell you of my dream. In the dream, I appeared before the Goddess. Her skin was very dark. She was beautiful. I knelt at her feet as if a young knight and asked her what she required of me. She said I was to give up the power of the throne for the power of prayer and selflessness, so I could discover where true power really lies. Her explanation was that I would not be able to do that in this Kingdom where I have served all my adult life as King. I must go where I am not a warrior-king, where I can practice the self disciplines of spiritual growth. She knows that it will be very hard for me to leave Britain, so she will send a great light in the sky to convince me that what my dream tells me is real. She says that by going to Brittany I will be near to the place where she retreated after the Goddess' son, Jesus, was killed."

Arthur closes his eyes. Merlin, Gaiwain, Sister Bendithion and Gwenynen all look at each other. It is such an incredible dream and its message is so unexpected. No one knows what to say.

Finally, Gwenynen speaks, "Obviously, the King needs to rest now. Whether or not his dream is a true commandment to him from the Goddess, he still has a long recovery ahead of him." She smiles at Gaiwain.

Gaiwain returns the smile. "Dream, or no dream. Arthur's awakening calls for a celebration. Wherever he is going to be later, right now Arthur is alive. Wherever he is, I will be there also." Then he looks at Gwenynen.

"I mean I will be there with him, if you can be there with me, too, Gwenynen," Gaiwain says. He reaches over and grabs her hand.

Gwenynen smiles. She does not respond. *I must do as Arthur has done*, she thinks—*find out the Goddess' will for me. I only hope it means that I will be with Gaiwain.*

"I will celebrate with you tonight," says Merlin. "As soon as possible, I must be on my way back to Court. I am deeply worried about what will happen to Britain, if King Arthur does not return!"

Unbeknownst to everyone, at some point, Derwen enters the room. "Sister Bendithion and Gwenynen, if it is all right with you, I believe I should return with Merlin to the mainland. It is time for me to go back to my home. I am of the age now where, I believe, the Goddess wills this for me."

Gwenynen turns and hugs her dear friend. "I will be so sad if you leave, Derwen. As hard as it is for me to think of you going, I agree. I can feel the Goddess calling you home."

"Derwen," says Sister Bendithion, "you have been a diligent student in your consciousness studies, and I affirm your wish. It is more than past time for you to return. We will all miss you deeply. You will go with our prayers and love."

*   *   *

Rat, what do you mean you want me to return? I don't care if you think my character has done her job. I understand Tree needs to come back, now that he has done his job of helping protect us on the battlefield. That does not mean I automatically need to do the same thing. My character is not out of the woods yet, and I am not about to abandon her.

Just tell Mother Mary to get over it. I think I'm going to France.

Chapter 12

Once Arthur regains consciousness, his recuperation continues slowly and steadily. Gwenynen begins spending less and less time with him in the solarium, and Sister Bendithion is spending more. At first, it is hard for Gwenynen to watch Sister Bendithion's growing infatuation with Arthur, while she is separated from her own beloved Gaiwain, who is continually off inspecting the isle's security.

However, Gwenynen soon sees that with Sister Bendithion hovering increasingly over the King, she can easily take more time to be with Gaiwain exploring the isle.

The tranquility of the isle seeps into everyone's bones. This peace, and the increased attention and ministrations he is receiving from Sister Bendithion, are certainly helpful to Arthur's recovery; and this tranquility also delays him deciding exactly what he should do next.

Three separate events bring things to a decision point. First, St Cadfan had arrived at Ynys Enlli shortly before Arthur. St Cadfan grew up in Brittany and was driven from his home to Wales some years earlier. Arthur is delighted to see St Cadfan, who is a distant cousin. St Cadfan becomes a constant visitor to King Arthur, severely curtailing the alone-time Arthur is spending with Sister Bendithion, much to the latter's disappointment.

St Cadfan, who was invited to the isle by St Dyfrig, is fond of extolling the virtues of the land from which he is exiled. He brought a dozen companions with him to Wales, who already have helped him found many churches on the Llyn peninsula. Many of these monks followed St Cadfan to Ynys Enlli. This influx of monks has overnight resulted in the expansion of the small monastery that has looked after St Dyfrig and is a joy to the women's religious community on the isle. Little do the women anticipate that the growing number of men on the isle will ultimately diminish their settlement and finally cause all Sisters to leave.

Second, after having been gone several months, Merlin arrives back on Ynys Enlli. He reports immediately to the King that there is much disarray back in his Court and he hopes that the King is well enough now to return.

The day that Merlin arrives back on the isle, the third event occurs, less human and more celestial than the other two.

Gaiwain and Gwenynen are the first to spot it. They are out late in the evening as has become their custom, walking around the isle, observing the many species of birds and watching the mesmerizing flow of the tides. The yellow flowers of the gorse brighten in the long rays of evening sunlight. One of the constant reminders of the holiness of the isle comes from the play of light. The light can be fierce and relentless or soothing as warm honey. The light in its many variations always carries with it an expectancy of an unseen presence close at hand.

On this particular evening, as often happens, they lie down on Gaiwain's cape and escape into their own passionate world. Gaiwain is above Gwenynen as they pleasure each other in their lovemaking, when Gwenynen exclaims, "Oh my, what is that?"

"The only 'that' I am aware of is you and how deeply I am connected in and to you, dearest," says Gaiwain.

"I am serious, Gaiwain, there is something preternaturally bright that has emerged in the sky above us."

"I feel this brightness up and down my spine and you, my dear, are the one who has birthed a million brilliant stars within me."

Gwenynen focuses back on Gaiwain's face inches from hers. "Okay, let's take care of your stars!" She slowly begins to move beneath him. Soon, they are both consumed with their own celestial fireworks.

Gaiwain rolls on his back beside Gwenynen.

"See what I mean," says Gwenynen, pointing up to the sky.

Sure enough, as Gaiwain's vision focuses on the late evening sky, he sees a huge light in the corner of the heavens he never saw before.

"Merlin has just arrived. He will know about this light. We can ask him tomorrow," says Gaiwain, and he moves back over Gwenynen blocking her view.

Later, when they awake in the early dawn, the light in the corner of the sky is gone.

*   *   *

"Merlin, I tell you it is the sign that was foretold in my dream," says Arthur. "I will go, as my dream has instructed, and St Cadfan has encouraged, to Brittany."

"Sire, you are certainly right. It is a powerful sign," says Merlin. "I cannot counsel you to disobey such a clear message from the Goddess. Last night I saw in a vision that Zacharias of Mithylene will chronicle that in 538, *a great and terrible comet appeared in the sky at evening time for one hundred days*. This light-show will persist approximately the amount of time needed to have a vessel sent from Brittany to carry you to the shores of your kin, if that is what you desire. What shall I do, my King?"

"Merlin, I know you just arrived, but go and bring to me Constantine, the son of my kinsman, Cadwy. I will transfer authority of the throne of Britain to him before St Dyfrig and St Cadfan, so that they can crown him Regent of Britain. Then I shall retire to Brittany to fulfill the destiny the Goddess and Christ have called me there for."

Merlin's face is drawn tightly. "As you command, Sire," he says, and he turns, his shoulders drooping, and leaves the solarium.

Outside, Merlin meets Sir Gaiwain. "What is it, Merlin, you look quite shaken?" says Gaiwain.

"Me shaken, I tell you, Gaiwain, Britain shall be shaking. It is a sad day. I see so clearly that the confederacy of kingdoms that King Arthur has brought together to make the Kingdom of Britain, which has been so effective at keeping the Saxon invaders at bay, will soon be falling apart. My heart grieves like it will break." Without looking up at Sir Gaiwain he continues on his way.

Gaiwain immediately goes and finds Gwneynen. She too has just heard the news.

"What will you do, Gaiwain?" asks Gwenynen. "Will you go with King Arthur to Brittany?"

"He is my King," says Gaiwain. "If he commands, I must follow."

Gwenynen turns her back. More than whether he would go or not go, she wants Gaiwain to tell her that what she wants Gaiwain to do will come first. She isn't trying to put Gaiwain to some test. She realizes life, as it often does, is imposing a test. A test on both of them.

She turns back around. "Let me know what you decide, whether you will go with Arthur or stay with me?" Then she turns around again. She cannot bear to face him. Particularly, now that she is feeling a stirring within herself as she begins to harbor the suspicion that she might be with child.

Gaiwain is stunned. He feels emotions of deep desolation and raging anger as Gwenynen walks away. He is desperate to speak to Gwenynen, but when he opens his mouth no words come. He finally turns in silence, slumps to the ground and sobs.

*   *   *

Sister Bendithion paces back and forth across the room. Her heart is in an uproar. Although her mind has known from his first arrival on the isle that one day Arthur would have to leave, her heart has held that reality at bay. She is in no mood to consider Gwenynen's request.

"You wish to leave our Order, Gwenynen?"

Gwenynen nods *yes*.

"You are making such great progress. I would be foolish not to counsel you to stay and complete the next stage of your consciousness training."

"I understand," says Gwenynen, her eyes downcast to avoid meeting Sister Bendithion's gaze.

"I am not blind, Gwenynen. I know you are deeply in love with Sir Gaiwain." She stops and looks closely at the young woman before her. "You know that our Order encourages intimate relations between men and women and marriage and children, it is the way of the Goddess. The Roman Church, which increasingly wants men and women to be celibate, is trying to bend the river of life upstream. It will never work.

"That said, timing is everything. You have the opportunity here to complete the fourth and fifth stages of consciousness training. If you do that, then a marriage to Gaiwain, or really anything you would try to do, has a much greater chance of flowering abundantly. I caution you not to leave too early."

"I have thought long and hard about this, Sister Bendithion. I know the timing is not good. I would love to stay and complete the next stage of my spiritual growth, but I am afraid neither Gaiwain nor I have any choice. The King is going to leave. Our destinies, if we are to be together, are tied to the King."

"Yes, the King is going to leave," Sister Bendithion says emphatically. For a moment, Gwenynen thinks this most assured and composed nun will cry.

Sister Bendithion turns on a point from sadness to seriousness. "Tell me how you did, Gwenynen, on level One?"

"I did well, I learned to clear my mind completely to a place of interior emptiness, where thoughts and feelings settled and did not run helter-skelter about between my ears."

"Level Two?"

"I learned to concentrate on a sacred stone or candle. I could do so for over an hour without my imagination pulling me away to how hungry I was, or any of the myriad of things it is prone to do in a moment."

"Level Three?" asks Sister Bendithion, her expression clear and focused.

"I learned to experience my 'lucid observer' not only in silent contemplation but as I am going about during the day walking across the isle or doing chores in the kitchen. I lose it over and over again. But more and more, I am experiencing that steady, calm part of me that is not pulled off course by the mind jumping from one object of attention to the next."

"Dear, yes, you have done well. You are on track. I do believe you will be able to continue your spiritual growth without being in this hothouse of growth possibilities.

"As much as I hate to say it, because it confirms that Arthur should leave, I believe Arthur is entering a new phase in his spiritual growth, where those around him will indeed be blessed and that your presence will also bless him. To some extent we all progress in tandem." She waits a moment, then continues. "Yes, my dear, you have my blessing to go. Has Gaiwain asked you to go with him?"

"No, not yet, Sister Bendithion. I pray he will, but you know how men are when it comes to things of the heart, they can freeze up and go totally blank."

Sister Bendithion smiles wistfully. "Yes, I am afraid I do."

She continues. "Remember, you must bring the Goddess into your relationship with Gaiwain. Two people by themselves in a relationship soon find that it is all about her needs or his needs, and they find their souls shrinking. You must keep the Trinity in everything. Do you understand?"

Gwenynen nods vigorously. "Yes, yes I do," she says.

"Well, enough of this advice. The next stage is about not needing advice—to receive it or give it. You don't need advice because you don't need to know ahead of time to plan or figure out, or all the hundred and one things the mind does to try to ease our anxiety. You simply show up with clear mind and open heart to experience what the intelligence of the moment has to offer."

Sister Bendithion looks at Gwenynen. "Like what I have been trying to do with you, Gwneynen, right now."

Gwenynen smiles. "Yes, I know, Sister Bendithion. And I know it is hard for you to have King Arthur leaving. I see how close you have gotten helping him recover."

Sister Bendithion immediately is on the verge of tears. "Gwenynen, thank you for the kindness of your words. I have always known the King was married. I thought our relation could always stay on the spiritual level, that I could easily keep my emotional options open. Despite my best efforts, I have not prevailed in that respect. He has won my heart, which is right that a king should have. But he has won, not just allegiance, but a place that has allowed me to understand there was an emptiness there I had not allowed myself to recognize. I have prayed to the Goddess about this and she has told me that my longing for him will be something that will shape the whole rest of my life."

She pauses. "What a comeuppance. Me, who has made a virtue of not allowing myself to feel anything too deeply has been given a deep heart-longing to carry the rest of my life. The Goddess assures me that it will bring a great gift to me and those Sisters, like you, I try to mentor. She has let me know that Arthur's true bride is always, and forever will be, the people he strives to serve, and in that sense we are similarly mated. However, right now my heart simply hurts profoundly."

Gwenynen realizes Sister Bendithion's vulnerable sharing is a way of telling Gwenynen that she has graduated. Sister Bendithion's is acknowledging Gwenynen as a spiritual peer. Gwenynen is deeply touched. She reaches out and presses lightly on Sister Bendithion's shoulder just as Sister Bendithion starts to turn away.

Sister Bendithion turns back and feels the warmth of Gwenynen's smile. The two break into a kind of quick laughter, which releases their pent-up nervous energy. They hug in a deep embrace.

"I guess we should get back to our chores," says Sister Bendithion. She hesitates. "I believe the Goddess will bring you Gaiwain."

Gwenynen wipes away a tear. She nods and leaves.

*   *   *

The day had come. There is much commotion. The comet is still visible in the corner of the evening sky. It is very low to the horizon, about where it first appeared. The ship that Arthur requested from his relatives in Brittany has arrived. It is anchored in the lee of the isle.

The assortment of things, which Arthur has gradually had brought to the isle, are taken by skiff to the waiting ship. The needed ritual to transfer authority has occurred. Constantine has been declared Regent of Britain and returned to Britain to take up his rule. Merlin, for the time being has decided to go with Arthur to Brittany, hoping that perhaps he can eventually persuade his King to return to Britain.

It is down to the matter of farewells. Arthur, though no longer seized with the authority to act as the King of Britain, still behaves like a King. He presides over an informal ceremony where he personally says good-bye to each Sister and Brother on the isle. There is a leave taking of Sister Bendithion, which is not shared publicly. Now she is present with the throng of those accompanying Arthur on the beach awaiting the return of the skiff. A scarf is wrapped around her head. Her hand is clasped to her throat, as if there is something trapped there she wishes to say.

Once the throng quiets on the beach, before Arthur boards the skiff, Sir Gaiwain calls out.

"Sire, I have followed you loyally through many hard-fought battles. I know that I am sworn to go with you now. Alas, my heart is with yonder woman." With his head he nods toward Gwenynen.

"I would ask that I be relieved of service to you, so that I might remain with Gwenynen, Sire."

Arthur surveys the two of them. "Sir Gaiwain, you have ever been a valiant and loyal knight. I am afraid I will need you in my journey in Brittany, though I know the battles there will be more inside the soul than out in the world." He pauses.

Sir Gaiwain's face betrays the agony he is feeling inside.

"Sir Gaiwain, I will not hold you to your vow. I release you from it this moment. Still, I wish you to follow me. You are free to choose. Which way shall you go?"

Sir Gaiwain looks at his King. Then he looks at Gwenynen. She is in her best dress. Her long hair is in a braid, the thick lower curl of which rests right above her heart. Her head is held high. Both she and the King look directly at Gaiwain. Only the sea breathes.

Gaiwain's mind tumbles over itself like waves rolling up the beach. Gaiwain starts to say to the King what a hard decision it is for him to make. Rationalizations go through his mind like a shower of arrows in the middle of a battle. He speaks none of this. Finally, after being quiet a minute or so, which seems forever to Gwenynen, he says, "I shall stay with Gwenynen."

Gwenynen sucks in a huge gulp of air. She walks over to Sir Gaiwain and whispers in his ear.

Gaiwain raises his head with a big smile on his face. "Sire, if you will take me as a married knight, my wife-to-be, Gwenynen, and I would like to go with you and serve you in Brittany."

King Arthur pounds his fist in glee on the side of the skiff. "You two, get in the boat. It is time we were off."

Sir Gaiwain helps Gwenynen into the skiff. One of the Sisters hands her a bag. Gaiwain seems quite oblivious to the fact that she is already packed. Then Sister Bendithion hurries forward and reaches out an apple toward Gwneynen.

"Gwenynen," says Sister Bendithion. "I know how you so love the apples grown on our isle. Take this one with you for the seeds, so you can grow some of the special apples of Ynys Enlli wherever you are." Sister Bendithion hands Gwenynen a beautiful golden red apple. The eyes of the two women meet and a sense of deep gratitude and connection passes between them. Gwenynen somehow knew that a part of Ynys Enlli would always be with her. Sister Bendithion, her friend, mentor and now spiritual confidante, has given a gift which makes that truth real.

Gwenynen puts the apple in a pocket of her cape. As she settles into her seat, she looks at King Arthur. *Yes,* she thinks, *the King did what he is always doing, forcing his knights to choose. Building their awareness so they don't really need an outer king. Making them learn to lead their lives from the wisdom inside their hearts and souls that connects them with Christ and the Goddess.*

Gaiwain is soon aboard the skiff. The crowd wades into the icy water, pushing the small craft out to sea. Gaiwain muses, as he looks at Gwenynen. *I wonder if the King put Gwenynen up to this. Was it his test or hers? Either way, I have learned again from her and the King to put the sovereign feminine, to put the Goddess, first. After all it was a woman who gave birth to God; men had nothing to do with it.*

Chapter 13

If not for the long fuse of his anger, Elred would have forgotten the Mind Field Project file a year ago. Just picking up the old file now makes his face flush bright pink. He is glad there is no one who can see him. As a young redheaded boy, when the pink color of a blush rose to clash with his hair, he was teased unmercifully.

Every time he spends a Saturday in the office, as he is doing now, and picks up this file his stomach knots. Even though the wet Potomac air was in the twenties, when he parked his car just minutes earlier, beads of sweat break out on his forehead.

He opens the file. He still can't believe it. No trace has ever been found of Blaine, the target, or her husband Manuelito. Because of the scope of the Company's data mining, this couple either has to be dead or somehow be managing to live without a cellphone or an email address for more than a year. He expects the first is much more likely.

Two years after he obtained the initial funding to seed the Mind Field research projects, his boss pulled the funding back. More money is needed for drones, and available technology always wins over hard research. He is deeply disappointed. He turns the file over and over in his hands. The dead-end that had been reached is as dead as ever. He would love to have a new idea. He doesn't.

He looks back at his field notes. After Blaine Astrid evaded their efforts to detain her in Minnesota, Elred's men found Manuelito's home. It was a simple dwelling. Elred had his men search it and install a listening device. The monitor never picked up anything except the noise of an ever increasing invasion of rodents and bugs.

Elred scratches his head. *The old Indian probably died, when he was too drunk to move, out in some arroyo that flash flooded.* Then he kicks his trash can. *I would rather deal with the Russians any day than some old Indian. At least the Russians are greedy, power seeking and too obsessed with the need for the broader culture in the West to reflect back to them their own self-importance than to disappear from civilization.*

When Elred was a young CIA officer, he was driven by the idea that the role of the Company was vital to maintaining an American democracy. Ever an idealizing patriot, he was having to admit, after the Supreme Court gave corporations the green light to buy elections, that this illusion was shattered. He has heard his boss say ruefully, 'The Supreme Court by disallowing any limits on corporate spending for elections made bribery legal.' Now a moneyed elite can buy control with what are essentially pre-election bribes and it is all above the law. Elred stops his rumination and gazes around his office at all the trophies of patriotism he has on display.

His mind keeps returning to the feeling of hopelessness about his country. There is no more democracy in the United States than in Russia these days. Every emerging power is modeling itself on China. Let the economic elite rule by using their financial muscle to manipulate through technology and its newest offspring, Internet media. After all, the whole premise of democracy is being shown to be invalid. Ordinary people really can't, as Jefferson believed, be trusted. Every time an Arab country has a new revolution, the people demanding democracy who gain power create more turmoil, less governmental transparency and fewer democratic institutions.

KING ARTHUR & THE CONSCIOUSNESS GENE

Then a strange thought occurs to Elred. Even though he knows he is fighting for a cause that no longer exists, he can't quit fighting. If anything, he is fighting harder than ever. *Best not to think about it too much,* he realizes. *I am going to find out how humans can control the thoughts of others, before some group of lunatics beats me to the punch.*

He puts the Mind Field file back on his desk and makes a note to diary it for review again in a few months. He will not close it. He will not give up.

Chapter 14

Katrina and Tree both deeply miss Tree's grandparents. Yet their lives together are good.

They followed Manuelito's advice and escaped to Canyon de Chelly for what they would realize later was their honeymoon for a marriage whose ceremony would be long delayed until Grandmother Blaine returned. The couple then made their way to Berkeley, California. Katrina enrolled in a graduate program for gifted high school science teachers. The program was hard, stimulating and everything she had ever hoped for.

When they get the message from Rat, for Tree and Two to join Blaine in the field, Katrina does not have difficulty arranging her schedule so that she can be with the pair at key times during the day. While they are in a deep theta brain wave state, she does her school work on the computer. After the first couple of weeks, she begins to worry about how long Tree is going to be gone. She faithfully keeps an IV drip going for both him and Two and makes sure all their bodily functions, though slowed to a snail's pace, keep functioning. Their brain wave activity is greater when they are asleep, and at those times the process of getting rid of bodily waste occurs, though there is not much to be eliminated.

Before Tree left, he told Katrina he didn't really expect to be gone more than a couple of hours or a day or two at most. Tree's theory is that an hour here might translate to a month there. The time magnification of going back into the past isn't as great as he figured. He is gone for weeks and Grandmother Blaine has now been gone much longer than anyone would have ever guessed.

When he is finally back, Tree is weak. He spends the first few weeks driving east of Berkeley and finding places to go on increasingly long hikes. He is a little embarrassed at first, that when he went into the field to where his Grandmother was, that he was back there in the reflective consciousness of a woman. It doesn't take him too long to tell Katrina the entire story of what he observed. She is amazed at his account and how startlingly clear his memory is of the battle scene where King Arthur is wounded and the wonders of the isle he is taken to. Every night over the dinner table, Tree recounts stories about what happened traveling with his Grandmother in the quantum field.

One evening Katrina interrupts Tree in mid-story. "Tree, don't you think it would be okay for us to go back to the monastery to see your Grandfather now? I will finish up my course in a couple of weeks and get my advanced science teacher's certification. Once I complete, let's go back and see Man and then I'd like to find a job on the rez teaching for the next year. This city life of coffee shops, weird white people and great learning opportunities is fun for awhile, but we've been here long enough. Part of me yearns to be among Native people and to have my soul enriched by the beautiful, desolate landscape of the Navajo reservation."

Tree gazes into Katrina's mysterious-for-a-native-girl green eyes. He is always so amazed and deeply grateful that he is sharing his life with his first and only sweetheart.

"You're right. Despite all the adventure of traveling in the quantum field with Grandmother, since I have been back here my soul has been yearning for the wide-open spaces of my people, and I can't wait to talk to Grandfather and get his observations about what I experienced when I was in the field."

He stands up and pulls Katrina to standing in front of him. He holds her close. They look into each other's eyes and both taste the moment of their minds coming together the same way their bodies and hearts do.

"We will go back. Just to be cautious, I will email Rat to check to see if he thinks we are in the clear. Whoever those people are who would seek to do harm to my Grandfather, it is almost worse to have them deny us access to him. I am sure he is missing Grandmother terribly and would like our company. I know he delights whenever you are around."

Even though it is two weeks before Katrina's graduation, the next day Tree starts packing.

*   *   *

Tree and Katrina make the drive back to the Navajo reservation a leisurely trip. As they leave California and the miles unfold, they both feel a weight slipping from their shoulders. Their journey becomes a joyous jaunt.

"Remember the old days, after you finally began to really notice me?" says Katrina. "We would never drive this far without stopping for an Avalon Tor."

"We were not that much younger then," says Tree. "In addition, I have been noticing you all my life, at least all of it I can remember very well."

Katrina smiles. "You are still younger than I was then and now!" She pushes Two off the middle seat of the pickup, slips over close to Tree and begins to run her hand gently up his inner thigh.

"For someone so smart and beautiful, you are just a bit on the trashy side," says Tree, a Grand Canyon smile on his face.

"You have been hanging out in the white culture too long, or maybe on one of those monastic islands. In my native tradition no one ever thinks of the life force as trashy."

"Hey, you're the one who has been studying all the time. Now you're accusing me of being too serious.... I am looking for a place to pull off. I can tell the quicker the better."

By now Katrina's hand has reached pay-dirt. "I hope we never get rid of this old pickup," she says. "I don't think they make them so comfortable for two people belly-to-belly in the driver's seat any more."

Tree guides the pickup off the highway onto a dirt side road. He drives until trees envelope them on each side. He pulls off to the right far enough that another vehicle can get by if one comes along.

The first period of their lovemaking was torrid and relentless. Now they are in a new phase where they are both aware of their emotional and spiritual energy converging, as well as their physical. It is a converging over which neither of them has control—like someone outside of them is conducting a four-piece jazz ensemble and each one of them is playing one instrument and somehow something else is playing them also. Their surrender to their experience adds a sweetness, a sense of intimacy, newness and discovery each time they make love.

Today, they are going home. Today, the beautiful spring weather is an invocation to make love. Today, their surrender is to torrid.

*   *   *

Their first stop on the rez is the Little Creek Trading post. The proprietress, Sierra, looks to Tree exactly like she did the first time he saw her when he was a young boy years ago.

Although they have been gone over a year, Sierra greets them both as if she had seen them yesterday. She greets them the way she greets everyone, with a nod of her head and a chew down on the wad of tobacco that is her mouth's constant companion.

"How are you, Auntie?" asks Tree respectfully.

"Can't say I have anyone to blame for anything," says Sierra. "What can I get you folks?"

"We will pick up a few items," says Tree. "By the way, any news these days?"

"None I know of," replies Sierra, as if the question was the strangest she has ever heard.

Once Sierra turns her back, Tree swiftly moves his hands under one of the counters in the middle of the store displaying T-shirts emblazoned with an image taken in the late 1800s of several armed Indians and the slogan "Homeland Security: Fighting the Invasion Since 1492."

He finds a Skoal can. Pulls it free of the duct tape holding it in place and sticks it in his pocket. Katrina brings the groceries she has gathered to the counter for payment. Sierra checks them out.

When they are back in the pickup, Tree opens the tobacco tin. He reads a message written on a small piece of paper inside. *Doing fine. Come whenever you can.* It is dated six months earlier. He reads it again aloud to Katrina.

The message jars them both. While it sounds like good news that Grandfather Manuelito is doing well, the fact that he asked them to come six months ago and that they are only now getting the message comes with the shock of one of those freak thunder storms, which rolls across the semi-arid plains and opens up like a water hose.

"Let's go straight to the monastery," says Tree. Katrina nods. Tree cranks the old pickup and leaves the parking lot with gravel flying.

In less than forty-five minutes they are pulling into the monastery. They both jump from the vehicle and run to the front door. Tree knocks.

Brother Will opens the door. He smiles and pauses. Brother Will says, "I think seeing you warrants breaking silence. Though, if he were alive, I am not sure Father O'Donnell would approve. What a welcome surprise. Come on in."

Tree and Katrina, as well as Two, follow Brother Will into the room that serves as the communal living room—the former living room/dining room of the old farmhouse.

Before they can sit down, Tree blurts out, "How is my Grandfather?"

"He is fine, I think," says Brother Will.

Tree frowns and looks at Katrina and sees consternation on her face.

"What do you mean, you think?" asks Tree, trying hard not to make his question sound too critical.

"Well, I haven't seen him for a few weeks."

"What, where is he?" asks Tree.

"Oh, I don't mean to make you worry," says Brother Will, looking more closely at their anxious faces. "He is up the mountain. About six months ago he seemed to have fully recovered from his heart attack. He was taking long walks every day, getting his strength back. Then one day he decided he is called to go to Father O'Donnell's hermitage up on the mountainside. So we all went up. The place had not been used since Father O'Donnell passed away years ago. We spent a few hours cleaning up the place and making it habitable as a primitive dwelling.

"Which reminds me, while we were cleaning up, I found a book in Father O'Donnell's handwriting called *The Book of Truth: Hints on Living in a Dualistic World With Unitive Consciousness,* which none of us here had ever seen before. There was a note attached to the book which said, 'Please give this to Manuelito's grandson, for his guidance in bringing truth from the margins.' Not sure I quite get the title or the meaning of the note. I have the book locked up. I am sorry to digress, but recounting cleaning up the cabin reminds me to give you the book before you leave. Anyway, your Grandfather has been up in Father O'Donnell's hermitage ever since we cleaned it up."

"Wow, I am surprised to hear about Father O'Donnell's book. I look forward to reading it," says Tree. "Getting back to my Grandfather. We got a message, which he left at the trading post. We only got it today," says Tree.

"Yes, I left that for you at his instructions a little over six months ago, back before he decided to go up to the retreat. We take him supplies every few weeks. He seems to be doing well, sort of. It is strange. When we get there he is always sitting under the shelter of the overhanging ledge looking out across the valley. It's like his gaze is directed inside, not at what he is looking at so intently. I do worry about him a bit, being up there zoned out by himself all the time."

Tree relaxes. He understands immediately that his Grandfather has found the ideal place from which to access and watch over his wife, Blaine, on her journeys in the quantum world.

"I know you are eager to see him. It is really too late to go today.

Let's go to the kitchen and get you guys something to eat. Then I will show you where you can sleep and we will head up at first light in the morning."

"That sounds great," says Tree. Katrina nods her assent. She realizes the monk keeps bringing a halting gaze back to her. She wonders if this Order is like the old ones that practiced celibacy or like Mother Mary's Order, which encourages partnership relations. As frequently as he gazes at her, she guesses the answer to her question is obvious. Then she remembers, she surely must smell of sex.

Katrina speaks for the first time. "Brother Will, if you could show us where we might be staying, I would like to get a shower first and clean up, then join you for something to eat."

"Certainly," says Brother Will. "Come right this way." He walks her outside to a small trailer that looks as if it has seen better days. "I am afraid our guest lodging opportunities are rather limited. However, you may like this because it is where your grandparents-in-law stayed when they first came to the monastery years ago. There is a solar shower out back."

"Thank you," says Katrina. She smiles to herself. What a waste she thinks. This middle-aged man who has been practicing spiritually for years and he is as nervous around me as an introverted sixteen year old boy on a first date. When will some of these Christian groups ever get it—the instincts and Spirit are supposed to be brought together. Creation did not place matter and Spirit into opposition of each other, but inescapably twists them together as creation impels matter forward to finer and finer levels of being. The universe is expanding not contracting. She shakes her head and walks into the old trailer. She is sure glad she was able to take the new science teacher training, confirming much that native mythology has always taught.

She looks around the trailer. It is musty, but it will do. She hopes they will not be here too long. She steps to the door going out the back of the trailer, opens it and spots the solar shower right outside. Quickly she pulls her clothes off and walks to the shower. She grabs a bar of soap from the crook of a tree, and, as she looks down at her legs, she can see tracks of semen gleaming in the late afternoon sunlight. She almost hates to wash them off.

Later that evening, after they have eaten, Tree and Katrina decide to go to bed early. The bed is spongy and uncomfortable. However, they are used to making the best of what is.

"How did that shower work?" asks Tree, "I am going to need one tomorrow."

"It was great. I hit it just right, the sun was warming the water all day."

"Okay, I'll try tomorrow after we get back. I hope we can bring Grandfather down with us. But I am not certain where he should be if he comes with us. We can't raise too high a profile, that is for sure."

"I can tell you what you can do next," says Katrina. She loved to tease Tree. Maybe because of how precocious he had been all his life, he tended to be on the serious side. She could tell he was already anxious about seeing his Grandfather and that made him pensive.

In his seriousness, he fell for it. "What can I do?" he asks innocently.

"I washed off the tracks of semen you left that had drooled down my legs, so as not to smell like a tramp and offend Brother Will, and I am wishing I hadn't."

He immediately catches her come-on. Soon, the squeaky old bed sways valiantly, as for that matter so does the rickety trailer. Two, as he always does, when his beloved humans are engaged in their lovingmaking, walks away from his usual spot by Tree's side of the bed and lies down facing away. Then all is quiet.

*　　　　　*　　　　　*

Tree is up early. It is still good dark. He has been away from his Grandfather for too long. Soon Katrina is up also. They dress, sit in silent meditation together as is their wont and then make their way toward the old farmhouse. As they approach they hear the soft peal of a bell, first the original ring and then an echo off the mountain rising behind the monastery.

"That bell is so alluring, should we go?" asks Katrina. Brother Will had mentioned to them that morning prayers would precede breakfast and they were welcome to come.

"My church is more out here," says Tree, gesturing across the plains and mountains. "But sure. Let's give it a try."

The chapel is already ahum with the sound of a chant by the small group of gathered brothers. Neither Tree nor Katrina recognizes what is being chanted; however, they experience the way the chant seems to lift their spirits. Then they all sit together in silent prayer. Because Tree and Katrina have already done a round of meditation, they immediately sink into deep places.

From that place, Katrina can see Brother Will's thoughts. Maybe she is drawn to them because he is thinking of her. Evidently, he had been standing in the shadows behind a tree while she was showering. The poor dear, she thinks and then lets go of what he is thinking as well as her own thoughts, just as she has been taught by Manuelito.

Maybe it is because Tree has recently spent so much time with his Grandmother in the dreamtime or maybe it is the anticipation of seeing his Grandfather and worrying about what is next.

Regardless, in his state of deep relaxation, he immediately enters the thoughts of his Grandfather. Yes, it is appropriate that he should since his Grandfather would be out at first sunrise also doing his contemplative meditation practices. Now after being apart for months, they are just a short distance of time and space apart.

Tree hears his Grandfather tell him he is eager to see them, and that he has known for some time they were coming. They are welcome to take as much time to spend together here with him as Tree and Katrina want. Still Manuelito is committed to being an observer in the dreamtime with his wife Blaine, until she gets back.

Manuelito was very frustrated that Blaine was away so long, until he came to realize his role right now was simply to be with her in the field. He can read all the thoughts that she is passing on directly to Rat, and it is a joy to him to be a part of her journey in this way. He hopes that Tree and Katrina will understand and not try to get him off the mountain right now.

Tree realizes the thoughts he is having of his Grandfather's thoughts are not the thoughts that come and go in ordinary meditation practice; rather, these are thoughts that come from the quantum field beyond the great emptiness. He then is aware that this realization has pulled him up out of the field. He chuckles to himself; obviously his Grandfather is giving him a heads-up so that he and Katrina will not be too disappointed, when he refuses to come down from the mountain hermitage. Tree lets go of his own temporal thoughts to see if he can slide back down into his Grandfather's thoughts beyond the great emptiness.

*   *   *

Breakfast with the Brothers is in silence. Brother Will's decision the day before that their arrival was something so out of the usual pattern it merited the breaking of silence has obviously come to an end. The meal of oatmeal and fruit is simple and hearty.

Though it is light, the sun is still below the mountains and the air is cool as they begin their hike up the mountainside. Brother Will, who has a long stride, is in the lead. He has a large pack of supplies for Manuelito on his back.

By the time they are halfway up the side of the canyon, the sun is on their backs and all three of them are sweating. They stop to rest a moment. Two's tongue lolls out of his mouth. Tree gives Two some water to drink, which Katrina pours from a canteen into his cupped hands. Two barely lets a drop escape.

Tree looks out over the plains from the side of the steep canyon trail. Way out across the plains are the makings of a late afternoon thunder shower. As they have hiked upward, they have passed bright patches of desert marigolds and clumps of mountain dandelions. The beauty and sense of dignity of the place is exhilarating to Tree. He drinks it in even more thirstily than the water from the shared canteen. He looks at Katrina. She is preoccupied. He touches her on the shoulder and nods toward the vast expanse unfolding before them. She smiles back at Tree.

Katrina is the one who usually instigates their sexual intimacy. Maybe this occurs because of the greater out-flowing energy of her extroversion, in contrast to Tree's introversion. Maybe because she is a few years older. However, whenever Tree sees something stunningly beautiful, like this scene of the vast expanse of his homeland embroidered with wildflowers, he feels, as he does now, a deep pang of sexual longing for Katrina.

Brother Will is struggling to get the pack back on his shoulders to begin the last leg of their journey. Tree leans down to Katrina and speaks softly. "That bed was a bit lumpy. Let's find a place outside as soon as we get a chance—all this beauty around me makes me want you."

Katrina stretches up on her tiptoes as far as she can to touch her lips to Tree's cheek. Two, as if feeling he has to assert parental caution, puts his nose between the couple, causing Katrina to momentarily lose her balance. Tree automatically reaches an arm out and grabs her. It is at least a thousand feet straight down from where they are on the trail. He pulls her close.

"Loving you is always like being on the edge of a precipice," she says. "All beauty and danger."

"We can always handle the danger of nature," says Tree. "She will tell you how to be with her so everything is all right. It is the danger that is man-made that worries me. I was hoping that we could talk Grandfather into coming down the mountain. He spoke to me in the dreamtime at chapel this morning. He is going to be unwilling to do that. He is having too much fun time traveling with Grandma Blaine. Also, I expect he has something else up his sleeve."

Katrina recovers her sense of balance immediately, and just as quickly her sense of humor, which directed toward Tree seems simply a piece of the larger fabric of being deeply in love. "I am not worried about what he has up his sleeve, it is what you have up your pant's leg that has me excited."

Just then, Brother Will turns back to look toward them. He is trying to ascertain why they aren't keeping up, especially since they were so eager to see their Grandfather. However, he doesn't know that Tree has already been talking to him.

"We will be right along," shouts Tree. Brother Will nods and turns back toward the trail and begins again his ascent.

Tree leads Katrina a short distance further up the path to where they come to a switch-back around a large boulder that shelters them from sight above. They both slip off their hiking shorts. Two stands for a moment looking at them and then turns his head, as if to say oh-not-this-again, and begins his way up the trail. Katrina motions that she wants Tree on the ground. He smoothes the ground and lies back on their two pairs of shorts. As she pulls her top over her head, his erection rises to meet her. She slips gently onto Tree. Her face and beautiful green eyes are framed in blue above her head. She begins a circular motion of her hips ever so slowly. Sighs of pure pleasure waft on the cool breeze.

After several minutes of sensuously languid motion, Tree pleads. "Please, beautiful, don't Tor-ment me any more."

"I wasn't named Katrina for nothing," she says, moving with practiced precision to their most sensitive shared sensations. In no time at all, they are the breeze, the warm sun, and the air they are both loudly breathing.

*   *   *

Tree pulls himself the last few feet onto the ledge, where his Grandfather is living in Father O'Donnell's old hermitage. The hermitage has been built in an opening in the cliff face high above the plain below. The small cabin is constructed in the back right corner of the cliff opening—two sides are the inside walls of the cliff recess, the other two are made of wooden planks that were arduously brought up from the canyon floor below. Mostly the cabin is for sleeping and storing supplies. The living room of the hermitage is sitting on the open ledge beside the cabin with its view of an endless horizon.

Tree drops his daypack and runs into his Grandfather's arms. Right behind him is Katrina. Manuelito opens his arms wide and embraces them both. Two runs in a circle around the threesome until finally a gap appears and he jumps in to be given a pat and an affectionate ear pull by Manuelito.

"I have sure missed both of you," Manuelito says, his eyes sparkling. "All of you, I mean," he says, reaching down to pat Two again.

"We have missed you," says Tree. Katrina stands beside him nodding.

"I was starting to fix tea for all of us," says Manuelito. "Come sit down. The kettle is just about to boil and I will get us a cup." He goes to the gas stove and pours the water from a boiling kettle into a teapot. He brings the teapot and cups over to the seating area around an old fire-pit. Manuelito pours tea for them all. Brother Will goes into the small cabin to unpack the provisions he has brought and gather up any refuse, giving the family members time to catch up.

"Tell me all about grad school at Berkeley," says Manuelito.

"She graduated in the top of her class," interjects Tree proudly.

"I didn't even know you were paying that much attention to how I was doing," says Katrina, looking at Tree. "Grandfather, it was a great curriculum, very challenging and I learned so much."

"Wonderful, wonderful," says Manuelito. "Do you know what you will do now?"

Before she could answer, Tree interrupts again. "Grandfather, we want to talk to you about what you will be doing first. We want to know your plans."

Manuelito looks gently at his grandson. "You know already, my son. Thank you for wanting to hear them aloud. Right now, I want to hear about you."

Tree bows his head. His Grandfather was always so gentle with Tree, but it was tough being scolded, however gently, especially about a conversation which occurred in the quantum field. But as Tree already knows in his young life—the field is the most important reality, not the linear appearing one, where humans think they manage cause and effect.

Katrina continues. "It was a great time at Berkeley and the truth is I don't know where I will be next. I would like to teach on the rez somewhere. I know they need science teachers. One thing is absolutely for sure, I want to be wherever Tree is. We are living together now and will get married when Grandma Blaine returns."

"The sooner the better," says Manuelito. "I mean, the sooner Grandma Blaine returns the better. I can see that your spirits are already joined. Marriage is an important ritual. I am glad you are timing the ceremony to occur when your Grandmother will be here. She would not want to miss such a happy celebration."

As if reading Tree's thoughts, Manuelito continues. "I will be staying here in the hermitage until your Grandmother Blaine returns. I do hope that wherever you will be that you will be close enough to visit me often."

There is a silence. Not an empty one, rather one of awareness as Tree realizes for the second time that his Grandfather has made his decision and it will not do to try to dissuade him now.

"I hope we will be close also," says Tree. "I am not sure where we ought to go. I did get in touch with Rat and I have not even had time to tell Katrina about our conversation.

"Rat advised me that if we went back to the old hogan, he was sure we would be detected and then we would lead the Company to you. He said that from what he can tell from hacking into some surveillance satellite, our hogan was bugged some time ago. He thinks we ought to go to Sweden to the Convent. That way, when Grandma gets back from her travels in the quantum field, we will be there to greet her and welcome her back. Rat thinks it would be very beneficial for us to travel with Grandma when she comes back to the States. What do you think?"

Manuelito takes a minute of quiet reflection. Katrina frowns and looks off in the distance. Finally Manuelito speaks, "I like the idea. I will very much miss your being close by and as you know...." Manuelito pauses and looks directly at his grandson. "As you know, I am spending time with her now anyway, so you might as well be there as the return welcoming party. I am feeling so much better, and there is no way I could travel to Sweden, and your chances of making that trip without getting detained are much better than mine."

"What about me?" interjects Katrina. Nervously she gets up from the rock she is sitting on and begins to pace about. "I assume Rat is talking about me going with you to Sweden, Tree?" Tree nods *yes*.

She continues. "I want to be with you, Tree. And I also want to be teaching science to these young kids on the rez. I want them to see how the quantum, scientific understanding of reality is so very similar to the creation myths of the Diné. I want them to become excited about science so that they can escape the cycle of despair and addiction so prevalent on the rez. I can't follow you, Tree, traipsing halfway around the world and do what I have been trained to do and my heart tells me is important." She turns from looking at Tree to Manuelito.

"What should I do, Grandfather?"

Manuelito ponders. "I don't think the Company will bother you, Katrina. In fact, it would probably be good for you to re-establish a life on the rez with Tree gone. If you both arrive back together that is liable to attract some attention. Everyone is used to a new teacher showing up for the school year. So, I think you guys being split up is very helpful right now to the overall mission of what your Grandmother is doing and us not being detected by the spymasters.

"Katrina, while you wish to raise the scientific understanding of young native kids, Blaine is trying to find a way to preserve the opportunity for the consciousness of everyone to be lifted. Your two missions are not unrelated. In addition, if you are away from Tree, it might give you more time to slip over to the monastery and visit with me from time to time. Not an ideal solution, I know, for a young couple in love, but it is not an ideal world either."

Katrina and Tree look at each other. Their glances are not casual, or, for that matter, really of this world. They look first into the place where they were physically just a short time ago behind the large boulder. They look past that into the quantum field where their lives have been tangled together. They look far enough to see that way into the distance their lives are a dance into and out of each other's energy fields, and into and out of the linear world and the other world. They experience in a moment that the only thing for sure is the dance and that Grandfather Manuelito's suggestion is simply another step in a great dance of their lives meeting and separating that spans many generations.

Katrina and Tree turn from looking at each other to Manuelito and nod. A red-tailed hawk swings above them along the canyon rim, gliding on an air current. It lets out its screeching *kee-eeeee-arr*, two-to-three seconds-long call. There is a pause, then another two-to-three seconds-long call again, another pause and the final *kee-eeeee-arr*. Manuelito remembers Father O'Donnell said the red tail hawk's call is nature's most solemn *amen*.

Finally, Tree speaks. "Grandfather, this is not the first time you have turned the tables on me. I thought we were coming here to persuade you to come out of your eyrie. Turns out we came here so we could better understand the great flow of life and see life from the perspective of that flow, not from our little ego perspectives. Thank you, Grandfather. Was this little deception something you had planned all along?"

"No, of course not," says Manuelito with a wry grin. "Deception is the way the marginalized preserve truth; and seeing through our own deception is the way we find truth. We native people are always both deceivers and being deceived."

Brother Will walks back over from the cabin to the threesome. "I think I have all the trash to go back down the mountain. I left the supplies sorted out that you requested," he says looking at Manuelito. "Probably best for me to head on back, unless I can be of further assistance to you."

"Brother Will, no one could ask to be better looked after than the care you provide me. I hope I am not too much of a burden. I am so grateful for all your assistance."

"No problem at all. In our Order, we are used to supporting people in hermitage. It is our belief that the crystal clear prayers that can be achieved from long periods of solitude are what holds the world together. It is deeply meaningful to me that I can be of service to you in this way." Brother Will bows deeply to Manuelito.

"Bless you, my son," says Manuelito.

Brother Will bows his head again toward Manuelito and then looks at Tree. "I will leave Father O'Donnell's book out for you on your bed in the trailer so you will not forget it when you leave."

"Thank you," replies Tree. With that Brother Will shoulders his pack, picks up an empty tank of cooking gas and heads back down the mountain trail.

Katrina says, "Grandfather, I am going to the cabin to see what good stuff Brother Will brought you. Maybe I can throw together a little feast. We need to celebrate being together again and your good health. We can probably stay the rest of the day until an hour before dark, can't we, Tree?"

"Sounds awesome. I am sure we can get down the mountain in an hour. I believe we have a three-quarters waxing moon tonight, so even if we leave late we should have plenty of light for walking."

"Right on the moon, and certainly on the need to celebrate," says Manuelito. "I cannot tell you what a joy it is to see the two of you and feel the love between you. While you are rustling up the celebration menu, Katrina, Tree and I can talk about the possibilities he might pursue going forward."

"That would be great," says Tree. "If Katrina goes back to teaching on the rez, after I help her get settled, I am not sure what my next move should be."

"Here is what I am thinking," says Manuelito. "I believe that Blaine is getting near the end of her travels in the quantum field. The way I read things, she is in a bit of a tug-of-war with Rat, which means Mother Mary, about what to do next. Mother Mary wants her to come on back. Blaine has the evidence. All she needs to do is put it some place it can be found fifteen hundred years later, so Rat can go retrieve it and get the DNA testing done. However, Blaine is evidently convinced that she needs to stay with her character. Her character has gone from Wales to Brittany. It is all new territory for her character and Blaine wants to be with her."

"What do you think Grandma should do?" asks Tree.

"I don't know. I am not so anxious about her being gone, now that I have learned to access the field where she is. Sort of like I tune in each day to a prime time Dark Ages sitcom. I want her back physically badly. Still, I know your Grandmother. She is going to do what she thinks needs to be done and she is loyal to a fault. She will listen to what Rat conveys from Mother Mary, but that will not persuade her not to do what she thinks best."

"Well, is the story unfolding far enough that you think, after getting Katrina settled, that I should head to Sweden to meet Grandma, to be there when she gets back from time traveling?"

Manuelito mulls over the question. "It is hard to say for sure. I think so. If you hang around here long, it will bring out the snoops. Who knows, Blaine could decide to come back tomorrow.

"I know one thing. She will be overjoyed that you are there to greet her when she returns from the quantum field. It will be a huge comfort to her for you to help her make the covert trip back to the States in whatever way Rat devises. I know, from what she has had to say, she will not want to come back in a coffin.

"Sit with these ideas for a few days. If they are right, you will feel a sense of peace about them, despite the conflictual feelings of leaving Katrina. If they are not right, then there will be dis-ease and you will know that the Great Spirit has other plans for you now."

"Thank you, Grandfather," says Tree. "I will do as you suggest. Katrina knows her life purpose and once she finds out where on the rez she might be teaching, I will get her settled. Then I will be back." He never ceases to admire his Grandfather's wisdom. Manuelito is always eager to talk anything through with Tree, and his Grandfather always leaves it up to Tree to get in touch with his inner knowing, and the other world it accesses, to make his own decisions.

They turn simultaneously. Katrina is bringing platters of food from the cabin and setting them on the camp table.

She smiles at them both. "Let the celebration begin!"

Far above, the red-tailed hawk again lets out its long, soul-piercing screech.

Chapter 15

Langley, Virginia
CIA Headquarters
Spring 2015

Elred grins. Persistence always pays off. He puts down the memo from the Southwest field office. Activity is finally detected in the old Indian's hogan.

He gives orders to his field office to immediately detain anyone using the hogan. It might not be Blaine Astrid's husband, but whoever it is, the Company has ways to find out things from people and he would not hesitate to use them. All they need is someone to give them some small clue.

With a smile, he picks up the confidential interoffice mail envelope and pulls out his mail. There is a 8 x10 manila envelope from his boss. Rarely does he get anything good from his boss, particularly not anything by interoffice mail. Usually what he gets is a summons to appear in his boss's office and a lecture on how things were done so much better in the "old days," which means how much better they were done by someone other than Elred. From Elred's perspective there is no love lost between the two.

Unusually, there is a handwritten note from James McGavin, *Aline, this is important! Read it and see if you understand it. Then let's talk. James*

His boss used his first name. The last time he remembers anyone addressing him that way is his mother when he was a teenager and his father was off drunk, She had no way to vent her anger on his father. Aline was the only target around. She would pronounce his given name with a long *a*. That first syllable would hang in the air like an expletive.

His boss never addressed him by the nickname they both shared, he usually used his surname. Elred is glad about that. The use of his first name this time piques his interest. He examines the document below the note. It is marked with the very highest secrecy classification. It appears to be one of the many research papers that are circulated from time to time among administrative officers at his level across the agency.

He reads the title: *Why the CIA is destined to fail in its mission— Understanding the Law of Three.*

Below the title, he sees that it was prepared by an outside consulting group. To get out-of-the-box thinking, the agency often contracts for analytical reports from the outside to avoid the inherent dangers of "group think." He doesn't recognize the group which prepared this one. Still the title takes him aback. He has never heard of anything called the Law of Three. Furthermore, normally some paper provided by an outside vendor would not be classified this highly. Though it looks like many of the papers that are generally circulated, as far as he can tell the paper was sent by his boss specifically to him.

He slides back into his chair, sits and lets the chair swivel backwards. He puts his feet up on his desk and begins to read.

Five minutes later he throws the paper down on his desk. Who the hell is some guy named Gurdjieff? Sounds for sure like a Russian agent. P. D. Ouspensky—he has never heard of him either, and he sounds like a Communist. Other names like Maurice Nicoll are not so ominous, but he cannot remember ever reading anything by or about any of the individuals mentioned. The last name referred to was a woman, and on top of that a priest. What the hell could she know that could possibly be useful to the Company?

He grew up going to Catholic school, and that experience was enough to turn him off from religion for the rest of his life.

He picks the paper up and reads it again. Why is McGavin sending it to him? Even after a second read, he has no idea what the Law of Three is. Surely, it is not relevant to any of the work he is supervising.

Then it dawns on him. It could only be because of the Mind Field Project. What is the paper suggesting he do? Was it telling him why this project would fail? No, the paper seemed to be directed toward the agency's failure. *I am sure lost on this one,* he thinks.

He goes back to his computer. Whenever his mind is overloaded and he needs an automatic task, email is always the answer.

Not only the paper from McGavin, an email as well! He opens the email and breaks into a huge grin. His funding for the Mind Field Project is being restored. He reads on. *Oh, no.* Who is going to administer the program is being reviewed. It will all depend on who can design a way in which the Law of Three can be applied to the project.

Elred looks up and out the window into the interior courtyard. *Holy Shit!* he thinks, *I have not got a clue.*

Just then his secretary, Melinda, pokes her head around the door frame. "James McGavin would like to see you right away in his office," she says.

Elred throws up his hands in exasperation. "Damn," he mutters, not really to his secretary, who stops and continues to stand in the doorway.

He continues, "Things can go for months around here moving at the pace of a snail with arthritis and then somebody's wants something yesterday. Do you know what this is about?"

"Sure don't," she says. "Will there be anything else?"

He scowls at her. *Bitch!* he mutters to himself.

She is new. The fourth secretary in less than a year. He will get points off his evaluation if he fires another one so soon, and he sure feels like it. She is more attractive than most clerical assistants these days and wears skirts with slits that slide revealingly open when she sits. She knows she has beautiful legs and isn't afraid to show them off. Elred's response is a Pavlovian stare.

Elred continues to consider his secretary. Usually the higher the security clearance a woman receives, the more unattractive she is. Melinda is an exception in that respect. Maybe that is the problem. Not only is she good looking, she is way too self-confident to get sucked into his whining and complaining. He is, in fact, angry all the time. Maybe outraged. The country is going to hell. Somebody needs to be pissed enough to do something. If people around him feel the bite of his edge, well, so be it. It cannot be helped.

He stops his reverie. *Better not keep the boss waiting.*

He grabs his id badge, which he will need to get the elevator to stop on the next floor up and heads down the hall.

Elred gets off the elevator and enters the hallway. He puts his forehead against a curved bar to get the iris of his right eye scanned. At the time he was being processed through security, when he first came to work, he was given the choice of which eye he wanted to use for identification. He would never have thought about using his left. Maybe that was one reason he didn't like or trust his boss. He noticed when they entered the office together, his boss used his left eye. *If I was running this place,* he thought with a grin, *everyone with left eye iris scans would be automatically eliminated.*

He opens the suite door to James McGavin's office. His secretary looks up. *She must have a very high security clearance,* he thinks smugly to himself.

"Please go right on in," she says in a flat atonal inflection that Elred associates with agents who have spent so many years interrogating suspects their voices never indicate the slightest quiver of approval or disapproval of what a suspect is saying. "The General is waiting on you."

No one, except McGavin's secretary, called McGavin "General." She was with him years earlier, when he was appointed interim Inspector General of the agency during a time the agency was under grave political scrutiny by Congress for some illegal covert operation.

McGavin had volunteered for the job, which meant being the one who testified in closed door sessions. It was almost a foregone conclusion that he would be the fall guy for the illegal ops. The title of Inspector General was simply something hung on him to give him credibility. Elred had to hand it to McGavin, he evidently turned things around before the Congressional committee. The matter was dropped by the committee and never came to public light.

For a few weeks McGavin was the hero of the agency. The man who was willing to step forward and fall on his sword for the good of the Company.

Elred steps inside James McGavin's office. His boss has his back turned to him, working over a pile of papers on a credenza behind his desk. Without even turning, he speaks. "Aline, thanks for coming, have a seat."

There are two facing, red leather armchairs in front of the desk. Elred sits in the one on the right. McGavin's once carrot red-hair is now almost completely white. *The same cut he must have had since he was six years old*, thinks Elred as he studies the back of his boss's crew-cut flat-top.

McGavin turns in his chair. As always he is direct and to the point.

"How is the Mind Field project going?" he asks.

"We finally got a break," replies Elred. "Monitors in the old Indian's house picked up activity. Things are being checked out as we speak."

"And the research?"

"Well, as you know," says Elred, "the money spigot just got turned back on. So nothing new to report yet."

"So what is your approach going forward?" asks McGavin. He is totally focused on Elred, reading his body language as much as listening to his responses.

"Keep pushing. Stay persistent. Just hang in there till we get a break."

"And," McGavin pauses, "based on the article I sent you, how might what it has to say affect your plan going forward?"

"Same thing, Chief. Keep pushing. Investigate any lead and hope for a break."

"I see," says McGavin. "Anything you would do different based on the article?"

Elred is puzzled. "No, not that I can think of."

"Okay," says McGavin, sitting back from his desk, as if pulling back from all the data sensory inputs of his attentiveness to Elred.

There is silence.

"Is there anything else, sir?" asks Elred.

"I guess not," says McGavin. "You are reassigned as of right now away from the Mind Field project. You will report to our field office in Jackson, Mississippi, for your next assignment." McGavin begins to turn back toward his credenza, signaling the conversation is over.

"But sir, might I ask why? I don't know how I could push any harder."

"Did you understand the article on the Law of Three?"

"Well, not really," says Elred.

"I didn't think so," says McGavin. "Now if you will excuse me, I have some rather urgent matters to handle this morning. You just had a little Law of Three quiz, and I am afraid you flunked. Good day."

With that, McGavin turns back toward his credenza. Elred stands up and starts to walk toward the office door. He hesitates and then begins to speak to his boss's back, "Sir, I think I am entitled to a little more of an explanation. This is totally arbitrary."

James McGavin turns back around to face his subordinate. "You are correct. The decision is from your point of view absolutely arbitrary. Lest you forget, you work for an organization which owes allegiance to being arbitrary for what it sees as a higher good. I admit it often misses the higher good mark. However, this agency operates on the principle of being arbitrary. Didn't you learn that at The Farm?"

"Yes, sir, I did. But...."

"No *buts*, thank you. The decision has been made. For you to understand why, you would have to understand The Law of Three for starters. Let me see if I can translate just a bit. The agency is in this race to learn the mystery of consciousness before some rogue state or lunatic fringe organization does and sets back civilization a thousand years. We are trying to prevent a nuclear detonation of consciousness, which sets the world back to the survival mentality of centuries ago. Are you with me?"

"Yes, Sir, certainly. I was and am two hundred percent committed to the mission. I don't know why you should be removing me from heading up the project, which is our most likely prospect to garner a leg up in this fight."

"Because you can't lead what you don't understand." McGavin pushes back from his desk. "Your consciousness is stuck in the old binary—what they are for, I am against—dualistic consciousness."

Elred does not have a clue what his boss is talking about. He can feel his frustration fueling his anger.

"I wish you the best, Aline. There is always room in the agency for officers with many different talents. Yours are just not suited for this project."

"Well, who the hell has the right talents?" explodes Elred.

"That, my friend, is an exquisitely good question, which we should have asked months ago. I am not sure I know. It has to be people who are deep spiritual seekers." He pauses. "Did you grow up going to Catholic school by any chance?"

"Unfortunately, yes," says Elred. "What does that have to do with the price of milk in China?"

"If you were asking questions like that earlier, I dare say you would be staying."

"What do you mean? Sure I had a Catholic schooling and I guess the Catholic hierarchy figured that by schooling kids they could brainwash them at the start and bring up a bunch of zombies who would mimic back whatever the church wanted. Well, that sure as hell backfired. All the kids that I know who went to Catholic schools had such a hellish experience that they, including me, never darken the doorway of a church. The church by its educational mission accomplished exactly what it did not want."

"Precisely, Aline. This agency often does the same thing. By our use of force, persistence and all those things you mentioned you would do going forward, we keep ourselves caught in an uncreative downdraft. We end up producing what we don't want. It is the exact definition of dualistic thinking. That is why, at the highest level of the agency, we are trying to catch up and learn about non-dual thinking. I was hoping that from all that parochial school training you might have learned something about the Trinity."

Elred interrupts. "Sure, I learned about the damn Trinity. Three persons in one, what the hell has that got to do with the agency?"

McGavin smiles. "Aline, all you are doing is making an airtight case to uphold my decision you should not be administering this project. The Trinity is more than just personhood; it explains the dynamics of how things change. The secular term is the Law of Three. We need someone running this project who understands how to think in those terms. A person who understands the Law of Three is able to experience the portion of truth in two things that seem opposed and hold the tension of the apparent opposition long enough for a third reconciling force to emerge. For a spiritual person who lives a Trinitarian life that third force is called the Holy Spirit."

Elred shakes his head and looks at the floor. "Thanks for explaining, Chief. I guess you are making the right decision, because I don't understand what you are talking about and how you would want me to think differently." Elred raises his hands in a gesture of frustration. "Where are you going to find such a person in this agency? I don't think I know anyone who might fit the description of what you want."

"I am not sure we can," says James McGavin. "As I said, the most likely candidate is someone who is on a serious spiritual journey. While that will rule out most priests, there is a chance these guys might have been exposed to some of what I am talking about. At least a few may have some idea of the terrain ahead for the growth of human consciousness. That in itself requires a kind of free thinking that is not usually found in this office. I know you have done the best you could, Aline. There will be much more in the agency you are well suited to do. Good day."

McGavin turns back to the pile of material on his credenza. Elred hesitates, then pivots and walks toward the office door.

Outside the door McGavin's secretary looks toward him and speaks in her flat tone, "Good-bye, Mr. Elred."

Elred walks into the hallway. *Good-bye, bitch,* he thinks. To him her tone crawled with sarcasm.

He punches the button for the elevator. He has a fleeting thought. *Did the way he understands McGavin's secretary's 'Good-bye' have anything to do with him being stuck in a dualistic way of perceiving the world?*

Chapter 16

Navajo Nation
Southwestern United States
Spring 2015

Tree is communicating with Rat on how to safely travel to Sweden, when he gets a priority text from Rat telling him his Grandfather's hogan has been compromised.

Tree realizes the electronic invasion of the hogan is like the loss of a faithful member of the family. He decides to act on Rat's information on that basis. Tree follows the Navajo custom when a person dies, which requires knocking a hole in the wall to remove the body through, since it would be inappropriate for the body to be taken out through the door. Then for good measure, after knocking a hole in the wall of the hogan, Tree decides to set the structure on fire. The beloved apple tree is just starting to bloom, the apple blossom scent delicately on the air. Tree sprays the apple tree with water before he ignites the hogan. The wood framing inside the hogan is quickly consumed.

Happily the wind is blowing away from the apple tree. The tree will likely survive the hogan's cremation. Any Navajo who gets asked about what has happened at Manuelito's hogan will surmise there was a death in the family and pass that on. In a way, Tree reflects, there has been.

Fortunately for Katrina, an opening for a science teacher is available in an Indian reservation school. She applies quickly and is immediately accepted. There is good news, bad news. The

314   KING ARTHUR & THE CONSIOUSNESS GENE

good news is that the school is near the western border of the reservation in Arizona, a long way from the school house mobile home where she was living before she went to California. If the Company is still trying to find her to get to Blaine, the good news is that they will not discover Katrina around where Blaine and Manuelito have lived. The bad news is that she is a long way from the monastery where Manuelito is now secretly living.

Both Katrina and Tree begin experiencing a new sense of meaning about the strength of the commitment they each have to their relationship. They slowly begin accepting a new notion of being committed to the idea of their longterm being together while being apart and not fighting the different immediate directions their individual lives are heading. Admittedly, their new perspective is bittersweet, because they will be apart for some unknown period of time.

Though unmarried, Katrina considers herself wedded and she begins looking for a new place to live on the western part of the rez with a sense of domestic excitement she has never felt before. Tree is equally excited about her finding what will be their first house together. After Katrina has her job secured, she discovers she is qualified for a house loan, which will allow them to acquire a double-wide. The house itself is not so much the focus of their excitement—the choices are not that great between this double-wide or that double-wide—as the place they would locate it. They want something which will not be that far from the school where Katrina will be teaching, and also off the beaten track, where they will feel their nearest neighbor is the natural world around them.

After driving miles and miles on reservation dirt roads, they find just the site on the Black Mesa in Arizona. They are two miles from a paved county road. The turnoff onto their dirt track is in the middle of a curve, where most of the traffic heads in the other direction. Anyone hoping to find their drive, and not already knowing where they are going, will miss it.

They are able to place the double-wide between two huge boulders and still have its front door face due east. With the boulders—each one of which is larger than the doublewide—on each side book-ending their new home, the setting could not be more natural.

Water is a problem, as it often is on the rez. There is a spring about a mile away in an arroyo where it flows into a lovely pool. There is no natural source of water near the house. They could always drill for a well, but there is not money to do that. For now, they will have to rely on bottled water and the regular routine of the Navajo water truck. They fit the double-wide with gutters and install a cistern. This is as much of a water supply as many native families on the res have.

Once Tree helps get Katrina settled into their new home, and with school starting soon, they agree Tree will leave the next morning. He plans to go visit with his Grandfather, then make his way to Sweden in whatever manner Rat suggests. Katrina and Tree will stay in touch through a chat room which Rat sets up for them. In an abundance of caution, they decide not to have internet service at home. She will do all her communicating through the school's internet system using the address of a fictitious student. They have done all they could to follow Manuelito's direction to keep a low profile and Rat's instructions on how to do that.

Still, they are not about to rely just on technology for communication. All night before Tree is to leave, they sit up practicing how to meet each other in the quantum field. It is very hard at first for Katrina. It all seems so much like make-believe to her. She has to use her intention to have access, and then she starts to believe everything she is experiencing is her projection. How can she really know she is communicating with Tree? That is the rub. She can't. She has to learn to trust—herself and the field.

Tree is confident in his ability to communicate to and from the field after his quantum field trip with Grandma Blaine. However, in a way, it is harder for two people in the same time continuum to communicate with each other, than for someone in this time-frame to communicate with an older field, particularly a field, that had been around awhile, where many people continue to have a field-energizing emotional stake.

Tree explains that the interest in participating in a certain field actually raises the energy level of the field. King Arthur's field is certainly a favorite field to be in. Somehow a post-modern culture longs, without knowing why, for everything Arthurian.

Tree and Katrina are helped in their ability to communicate with each other in the field because their deep emotional connection is so enlivened by their rich experiences of frequent and lengthy sexual celebration of their love. Because they practice bonding at an emotional and spiritual level in their sexual lives, they are able to recognize the part of the other existing in each other's energy field.

As the night wears on they celebrate each meeting of their energies in the quantum field with a fresh round of sexual intimacy. Katrina is delighted they have found such a lovely way to reinforce the experience of how to meet each other in the quantum field. She can remember the feelings in her body to know later that her communication with Tree is true. Tree is not as externally emotionally expressive as Katrina, so she loves how by accessing his interior lucid observer in the field she is able to experience the richness of his emotions, especially how their lovemaking creates in him pure delight.

*   *   *

Tree arrives back at the monastery the next afternoon. Brother Will greets him in silence, affirming that Tree's being there is now a natural part of the routine. Tree eats the evening meal, which comes early at around 5:00, of soup and bread with the Brothers. This schedule suits Tree fine. He has had no uninterrupted sleep in any of the last few nights with Katrina. He goes to bed immediately after dinner. He plans on being up before dawn to start the trek up the mountain.

The first hour before sunrise is always magical. There are the pre-dawn birds that start trilling, and the sounds of animals shifting out of sleep and silently slipping out into the world to find breakfast. Tree has slept like he was in a coma; however, once he begins to hear the subtle stirrings of the morning, he is glad to be awake early. This is also a favorite time for Two. Like most dogs, he is an early morning dog.

Brother Will asks Tree to carry the large pack, already stuffed with supplies for Manuelito, up the mountain. Tree is glad to oblige and Brother Will is relieved for once not to have to make the trek with a heavy burden.

Tree has been working on regaining physical stamina and by the time the sun's rays get halfway down the wall of the canyon, he is pouring sweat. He feels great. His workouts have been productive. His lungs expand and take in huge quantities of cool morning air.

After a brief rest and water at the halfway point, for himself and Two, Tree is off again. About an hour later, he is at the top.

As he pulls himself up onto the ledge, where Manuelito's cabin is, he hears the banging of a kettle as it is put down on an iron grate above a gas burner.

Manuelito turns and looks at his grandson. He is so glad to see him and to see he is looking as fit as ever. *Tree may need that fitness*, Manuelito thinks, *to help bring Blaine back to me.*

They each walk quickly to the other and lose themselves in the exuberance of a hug that holds nothing back.

"So great to see you," says Manuelito. He holds his grandson at arm's length, a hand on each shoulder. "Yes, your mother would be very proud of what a brave and handsome young man you have become. Welcome, welcome. Tea is ready. Come sit and have a cup."

They do, and Tree goes over all that has transpired since his last visit with his Grandfather, particularly the details about leaving a hole in the wall of the old hogan, then burning it, and about Katrina finding a job and acquiring a new home in the Arizona part of the rez. Tree had clipped a bouquet of apple blossoms from the apple tree before firing the hogan. He places them on the large rock beside his Grandfather's chair.

Manuelito looks at the bouquet and nods in appreciation. He listens with eagerness to the new developments in his grandson's life. Eventually, the conversation comes to a lengthy pause. It is the kind of pause that often makes white people uneasy and is loved as punctuation in a conversation by native peoples—the place where something else that is unsaid can enter the conversation.

Eventually, Tree speaks. "Grandfather, while Katrina was in school in Berkeley, I had several part-time jobs. Mostly one at a coffee house. I am a little perplexed by some of the things that you have taught me. All these white people seem so caught up in things—their new MacBook Airs, their five dollar coffees. I am not sure how to reconcile all that with the way we live here on the rez. I know you have told me that my path will be like yours in both worlds. Walking in two worlds is jarring at times."

Manuelito pours another cup. "Yes, it is confusing. I don't want to make it more confusing. I have taught you that deception is often necessary for the marginalized to survive and that it is on the margins where truth is held. If you are too secure in your ego self you do not have access to the other world, which is entered from the margins." He stops and looks out across the rolling plains below.

"We must not confuse deception as a way to preserve a path to greater consciousness with illusion. There are three great illusions in white culture. I say white culture as a handy generalization. Sure it contains many native peoples and does not contain all white people. You know what I mean."

Tree nods his head.

"A deception occurs when we intentionally deceive in order to survive, to keep intact truth, beauty and goodness. An illusion occurs when a structure is created that people buy into in order not to see truth, beauty and goodness.

"All three illusions arise from a distortion of one of our three primary instinctual drives. There is the instinctual drive for self preservation—the need to have power so that we can find food to eat and have shelter. The next instinctual drive is to reproduce the species—the need for the two sexes to produce offspring. The third instinctual drive is to be part of the tribe—in white man's language part of a social group.

"The first great illusion of white culture is the pornography of power. This arises when the need for food and shelter becomes a power drive to have more means than is needed for adequate food and shelter. This is the principle of a consumer culture, what the American economy is built on. The illusion gets its energy from the instinctive drive, which we all have and which is necessary. The illusion itself is the idea that having more than you need is good. We worship this illusion. It is false. It creates all kinds of systemic evils."

"Grandfather, I understand what you are saying, but being able to have adequate material well-being in the white culture, which we are inevitably a part of, seems so necessary. Existence, otherwise, seems so precarious."

"Yes, you are right. In order to reinforce the power illusion, the white culture sends the message that not to have more than enough risks you being thrown under the crush of poverty at any second. The culture also creates institutions that help reinforce the illusion of the necessity of acquiring money and power to survive. In addition, the heroes and heroines of the culture become those who succeed most dramatically in living this illusion. 'Rags to riches' is even called the 'American Dream.' The problem of too-muchness in America is dramatically illustrated in the issue of obesity. It is as if Mother Nature, the material world, is saying 'I will show you how your too-muchness can destroy you.'

"The second great illusion harnesses the powerful energy of the sex drive. We need to reproduce for humankind to survive. This illusion takes this powerful energy and trivializes sex by overly sexualizing everything, from how people dress to what kind of cereal people should buy for breakfast. As sex is packaged in white culture, it is one of two extremes, glossily over-sexualized or sexually anorexic. Because there is so much channeling of this powerful energy destructively, there exists much sexual abuse among both women and men. The result of this abuse is a person who becomes a sexual predator or a person who becomes asexual—someone who depresses their life force as a way to avoid anything that brings up the idea of sexual need. What a tragedy.

"The overemphasis on sex turns everything into some form of sexually nuanced entertainment. Sex becomes something separate from who a human being is—that is the illusion. Sex becomes an adventure into self-centeredness rather than serving as a gateway into the spiritual life. Physical intimacy that combines the sexual with the spiritual, that is soul alchemy."

Tree smiles. "You and Grandmother Blaine have taught me that. Katrina seems to know it naturally, so our sexual experiences have never just been about sex, and they have always been wonderful."

Manuelito nods. He knows when something is sitting in its proper place and picking it up further in a conversation is not helpful.

"The third illusion is that religion is a vehicle for spiritual growth. Spiritual growth is about learning how to be joyous, free and present in your life—aware of all your connections to others and the Great Spirit. Religion as it has evolved is mostly about a system to make yourself depend on someone else for how you feel about what is right and wrong. At its worst, it is a kind of blackmail system that threatens your life force and the quality of your life by a superego interject that has nothing to do with reality. The worst wars, the greatest inhumanity of man to humankind, come from religious conflict.

"Those who are a part of these illusions are the ones who write the history books. There is only one book that doesn't recount the story from the perspective of the winners, who support these illusions. That book is the Bible. The Bible always takes the perspective of the rejected son, the woman who is barren, the outcast Gentile, the leper, the prostitute. Conveniently, the Christian religion avoids this obviously preferred perspective and instead focuses on what is needed to keep a system of religious conformity and control in place.

"Why do you think the Bible has this radically different perspective?" asks Tree.

"The Bible is many things, and it is, in part, a tribal history of the Jewish people. I expect that there are many other tribal histories that are similar. They just didn't get written down like the Jewish one did.

"I don't want to lose the important point I wish to make, and that is that there are three very different kinds of deceptions. There are the deceptions by those on the margin, which allow them to survive and which allow for the emergence and preservation of beauty, truth and goodness. And, there are deceptions, that I think more accurately are called illusions, by which we deceive ourselves about reality. These kind of deceptions are often self-deceptions and where deception causes evil. This occurs most often when a power elite keeps itself intact by using people's instinctual energies in a deceptive way in order to reinforce their power structure."

Tree is wondering why his Grandfather is going into this extensive discussion of deception with him at this particular time. "Grandfather, I think I understand what you are telling me. Is there something specific you believe I will be encountering where I will need to know all of this?"

Manuelito pauses. Is it best to wait and let the knowledge he is giving Tree simply arise when it is needed, or is there a need to let Tree know what he foresees? He decides the latter route is best.

"Tree, I have been telling this to you for several reasons. First, what I have told you is basic to understanding how to be in both cultures, something I have had to contend with and do all my life—sometimes well, other times not so good. In order to help get Grandmother Blaine home you will have to be deceptive. You are in good hands following the lead of Rat. He is a maestro at deception for the benefit of the marginalized.

"Second, to preserve the truth, beauty and goodness of our native heritage you will probably have to be deceptive. These are good deceptions. They are, as Father O'Donnell taught me when I was about your age, a third force that helps manifest a different reality. In other words, if it is just white culture bad, native culture good, this is a static dualism. The deception is not to be pulled into either polarity so the third force, which engenders something new and original, can manifest. Father O'Donnell described this as the meaning of the Trinity, or what others sometime refer to as the Law of Three. All those 'poor of something' folks mentioned in the Sermon on the Mount were descriptions of Law of Three solutions, where the reconciling force arises from a new unseen energy, which Father O'Donnell called the Holy Spirit. Father O'Donnell would quote *Colossians* 3:3 '[Y]our true life is a hidden with Christ in God.' In the deception of hiddenness is where truth is found—when found we are, in that moment, all momentary mystics.

"You will be lured by the white consumer culture. As you know it is a whole lot different from living on the res. If you get deceived by its illusions, you will suffer. Even worse, if you get entreated to join into and join the deceptions of its power and control of others, you will become a part of something that is evil. You would become seriously spiritually imbalanced. As you know, for many of our tribe, when this happens, the only release from it, which most find, is the solace of alcohol. Over time addiction exacts its own fearful price."

Tree nods. "I think I understand, Grandfather. Deception is a powerful force. Use it wisely and don't be used by it."

Manuelito starts laughing so hard the tea is sloshing out of one side and then the other of his tea mug. "Hey, I am the one who is supposed to be full of pithy wisdom. But you are my grandson. Well said. Do you need some more tea? Looks like I do."

Tree basks in his Grandfather's praise. He also realizes his Grandfather is going to all this trouble to talk to him again about deception because his Grandfather is worried that Tree might not be adequately deceptive or that he might become deceived in some way. Will the trip to Sweden be that difficult? Does some danger await him there?

Following Rat's advice, Tree takes the old pickup and heads for Minnesota. He will go to the SOS Convent there and, with the help of the Sisters, slip across into Canada. Little does he know that this is the same route that his grandparents traveled many years before.

KING ARTHUR & THE CONSIOUSNESS GENE

PART III

KING ARTHUR & THE CONSCIOUSNESS GENE

Chapter 1

Plouarzel
Brittany
Spring 538

The sea is calm and the sun warm as King Arthur and his retinue set off for Brittany. There is a favorable light breeze. Their ship's design is a descendant of the traditional Roman oar-driven galley with a central mast and sail. This galley has a shallow draught from a flat keel, ideal for navigating coastal inlets. There are two banks of oars, one on each side, with ten oars in each bank.

For Gwenynen, who has never traveled on the sea, except for crossing to Ynys Enlli, the journey is idyllic. She curls up against Gaiwain beneath his cape on the open deck as a gleaming red disk of sun disappears into the sea.

They talk quietly as the night sky darkens. As the night wears on, the stars seem to descend closer and closer to them, until the brilliant blaze of the Milky Way appears to be only an arm's length above their heads. Gwenynen feels thrillingly alive, in awe of the sky and embraced in her true knight's arms.

Gwenynen does not remember falling asleep. Later, she simply realizes at some point she had. When she awakes it is with a fright. She looks about. She is still within Sir Gaiwain's arms, but the sea is rough and clouds obscure the starry majesty of what had been a moonless night sky. She cannot shake thoughts of the dream that has awakened her.

In her dream she meets the four apostles: Matthew, Mark, Luke, and John. She knows who they are immediately by the quiet warmth of their energy, and the golden glow of the halos around their heads. In her mind she hears the words they are speaking to her. She is being asked to serve. They are affirming the progress she has made in her spiritual practices and saying that now she is ready. Her task is to help the King complete his transformation. She will be a guide to assist him access the energy field of the Goddess's and Christ's truth. How, she asks the four disciples in her dream, is she to know that this dream is a true message from the Goddess?

The four disciples look at each other, nod and smile. In her mind, in response to her question, she is told that the four of them will meet her when their ship arrives in Brittany. Then she awakes. Her spirit is charged. She feels excitement and anxiety. She is being asked to serve the Goddess in a manner she could never have imagined. She is far enough along on her spiritual journey that she knows her love for life, for nature, for Sir Gaiwain—all of what is good and true and beautiful—is asking her to humbly and joyfully accept.

By morning, it's as if the sea has turned from peaceful slumber to a demonic creature. Their small sailing vessel with its nearly flat bottom is lifted and pushed about by huge swells as if it were a toy. The ship's captain has taken down the single center-mast sail. Tired seamen are straining at the long oars as they repeatedly respond to the captain's commands to row hard to avoid the crashing break of a wave that is suddenly towering over the ship.

Gwenynen and Sir Gaiwain both love the adventure of nature, but Gwenynen is becoming steadily more anxious. She clings tightly to Sir Gaiwain beneath his cape, which is increasingly soaked by the frequent lashes of spray over the ship. She watches as Arthur rises and goes as far forward as he can into the bow. She turns to Sir Gaiwain and puts her lips as close to his ear as she can so he can hear her above the roar of the sea. "Gaiwain, my dear, I have had this dream. I must speak to King Arthur about it. Can you help me go forward to where he is? I am afraid if I try to move about alone, I will get thrown overboard."

"Whatever you desire, my dear," says Sir Gaiwain. The two creep forward, hanging on to anything they can grasp as they sway wildly about.

King Arthur feels their presence behind him and turns. "Sire, I beg a brief audience with you," says Gwenynen.

Arthur smiles. "You have me cornered, so to speak," he says with a twinkle in his eye. Fear seems to be something the King does not experience.

Gwenynen relaxes a bit. She feels the steady arm of Sir Gaiwain around her waist holding her.

"During the night, while the storm was rising, I had a dream. In the dream I met the four apostles: Matthew, Mark, Luke and John. They told me that I was to be of service to you in this next phase of your life. I know it is presumptuous of me to say this, but they were so persistent. I asked them if there was a way that their message to me could be confirmed. They said they would meet us when our ship comes ashore in Brittany."

"Gwenynen, my dear, that is indeed a bold dream. Let us not worry about it now, for the sea is asking us to be about our wits. Once we get to Brittany, we can talk more about the meaning of your dream."

Gwenynen nods. "Thank you, Sire, it has been helpful to me to tell you what is on my mind." She curtsies as best she can and still keep her balance.

King Arthur nods to her and to Sir Gaiwain and turns back to face into the storm looming before them.

Arthur also has enjoyed the ocean's calm when they were first out to sea. He has even enjoyed the rising of the swells as the ocean seemingly awakes from a deep sleep. Now Arthur is worried. It appears they are being drawn deeper and deeper into a violent storm. He has lived most of his life near the ocean. He has witnessed many raging storms along the coast. He knows something of the mystery of the Severn bore, though not why and how it occurs. All of these expressions of nature's power and mystery he believes are manifestations of the Goddess's authority.

As a king at court, deciding what is just, he always rules by patiently trying to ascertain the will of the Goddess. As a warrior-king, he has learned to always act quickly in response to a threat to his Kingdom. Arthur edges a bit further forward, as far as he can into the ship's bow.

He wonders, is the Goddesses's ever-increasing display of power for the purpose of destruction or creation? He knows the two are irrevocably linked. Does something in him needs to die before something new can emerge? He suspects there is something. What it is he does not know. Certainly, he does not want his need for transformation to bring destruction to everyone on the ship. As a king, he knows his first duty is always service to his people, not to himself. He prays for the Goddess in her mercy to let them be brought safely ashore. He promises that, when they are safe in Brittany, he will follow the true way on whatever path the Goddess leads him.

The captain requires each person to be tied to the boat, and he calls for everyone to hold on to the ship and each other. The rowers again and again throw themselves into their work at his urgent command. Maybe the rowers are too tired. Maybe it is impossible to escape this time. A wall of water crests over the ship and breaks above the bow.

The ship shudders. Buckets are passed about. Everyone who can quickly falls to bailing. The ship seems to be sinking. Then, slowly, ever so slowly, the ship shudders back to the surface.

Gradually, a way opens through the storm. After a few hours the ship's human cargo, wet and cold, point in animation as each first glimpses the coast of Brittany. The captain is busy about the boat. He needs all the boat's steering maneuverability he can muster. They are still a few miles from shore and it is apparent there are many rocky shoals to be navigated around. The sail is raised part way. The Captain begins to tack back and forth.

"How are we doing?" asks Arthur.

"We are lucky to have gotten through that storm," says the Captain. "The spring storms are the worst. The Goddess must be with you. I am tacking about until the tide settles. Our best chance to steer between those rocks yonder is on a neutral tide. We are coming to a lovely harbor. I have been here before, although I don't know that this harbor has a name. We should be safe in the harbor and anchored by midday."

Arthur smiles broadly. "Thank you, Captain, you have done a skillful job bringing us to Brittany."

"The tide is going slack now, King Arthur. We will give it a try." The Captain leans hard on the tiller and the boat moves toward the shoreline.

Gwenynen and Sir Gaiwain are as happy as everyone else to see their small ship begin to move toward shore. They step again into the bow next to King Arthur. The water of the inlet is a lovely clear, deep blue.

As their vessel gets closer to the mouth of a small inlet, Gwenynen suddenly exclaims: "Great Mother Goddess, there they are!"

Sir Gaiwain and King Arthur both look searchingly toward the shore unsure of what has caused Gwenynen to cry out.

"Holy Mother Mary," cries the King. "Your dream was right. Indeed, there they are." He points to four large house-sized boulders sitting on the left of the entrance to the harbor. Each of the large boulders has a fringe of golden lichen encircling the top of the boulder's crown.

"My King," says Gwenynen. "I think the Goddess is telling me that my dream is true.

"Quite remarkable," says King Arthur. "There is no doubt about it. We enter this harbor by passing Matthew, Mark and Luke and John, as if they are our welcoming party. Perhaps they are."

As they glide past the four disciple rocks into a beautiful, secure harbor, King Arthur speaks again. "I will name this harbor in honor of the holy man who was my first teacher, St Illtud. From henceforth this place will be known as Aber-Illdut, the port of St Illtud."

All the passengers shout their approval of the King's proclamation, as the ship slides gently into its anchorage. Sir Gaiwain and another knight are sent ashore to announce the arrival of King Arthur to the local population.

Once they discover that it is King Arthur arriving, the local farmers greet them warmly. The King and his entourage receive much assistance in off-loading their possessions from the ship. There is a small mill at the end of the harbor and the Welsh settlers are given freshly ground grain to make bread.

Sir Gaiwain is asked to go out and reconnoiter the area. He comes back to report to Arthur that it appears to be a safe place to settle without any signs of threatening enemies. He also reports that he has found something unusual.

"Sire, I think you should come with me. I have found an unusual stone raised by the 'old people.' I am not sure what it means. Or, what it is saying about where we should place our camp."

"Gaiwain, you know there are many standing stones placed by the 'old people' in Wales. What is unusual to you about this one?"

"My King, this is a huge stone, standing on a prominence by itself. It would appear impossible for human beings to have erected it there. However, the stone has been faced and is not a type of stone that would naturally be in such a location."

"Hmmm," says King Arthur. "Let us arise early in the morning and go out to the stone and see what it says to us. I have found that the time of first daylight is the best time to hear stone wisdom. Oh, and bring your bride, Gwenynen, with you. It appears from her dream that I will need to be listening to her more anyway. Which is as it should be, since here in Brittany I am without the counsel of Lady Geirwir, and the Goddess knows that I need and value the advice of the feminine in all my affairs."

*   *   *

It was pre-dawn when King Arthur, Sir Gaiwain and Gwenynen set out to encounter the Menhir de Kerloas. When they arrive at the menhir, dawn is just breaking. In the early morning light the thirty-foot-high, shaped stone casts a precise shadow on the ground.

"I expect the 'old people' were using this as a seasonal timepiece," says King Arthur. "The 'old people' placed their celestial clocks in places where the Earth's energy thinned the veil between the two worlds. These large stones work sort of like magnets to part the veil a bit more. Just as important as what this stone said to them—because it is probably on a thin place—is what it says to us today."

"Yes," says Gwenynen, surprising herself in speaking up so quickly. "Lady Geirwir always instructed me that it is a mistake to wonder why a place is sacred. It puts the mind in a dualistic logic. To avoid this confusion, the question is always 'what is the meaning of a special place in the moment for you. Or as she would've said, how is the Goddess speaking to you through this part of her body?'"

"Quite rightly put," says King Arthur. "What is being said to you, Gwenynen?"

Gwenynen closes her eyes partially. She can hear the distinct sound of birds singing their spring songs as they are building their nests. She is aware of the golden hue of the sun and the solemnity of the standing stone and its long shadow. Slowly, but surely, she can feel herself gaining access to the great field. To those around her, when she speaks again, she sounds as if she is in a trance.

"The Goddess says that in the direction the shadow points you are to build an abbey and a church, King Arthur. You are being called to give up the ways of the warrior-king and become a spiritual warrior. The people of Brittany welcome you here. The Goddess says you are in the right place for your new life to begin."

"Thank you, Gwenynen. Thanks be to the great Goddess." He weighs what Gwenynen reports to him in his mind. Finally he speaks. "We will follow her prescription. Let us go in the direction pointed by the sun's shadow and find a suitable place for us to settle and build a church for the Goddess and her son Christ Jesus."

"Oh, there is one thing more," says Gwenynen. "The Mother Goddess is telling Gaiwain and me to receive a blessing here before our marriage. Do you see those two notches about waist-high carved on each side of the menhir?"

"Yes," says King Arthur. Sir Gaiwain nods in agreement.

Gwenynen smiles at Gaiwain. "Gaiwain, you are to rub your parts on that notch and we will be blessed with fine, healthy children. I am being instructed to rub mine on the other notch and this will ensure that the Goddess rules our household."

King Arthur starts laughing. "Well, what are you two waiting for?"

Together Gwenynen and Gaiwain approach the giant menhir and touch themselves to the powerful megalith. Each feels a tingle as the huge rock brings up and focuses low level electromagnetic energy from deep within the earth.

"That was kind of fun," says Gwenynen, smiling coyly at Gaiwain.

"Don't get too carried away yet," says King Arthur. "Let's get this new abbey located first and then you too can be off on the Goddess's business."

They travel to a well-drained place of prominence in the direction the menhir's shadow points. To a place that later will be called Plouarzel. Plou is the Breton word for parish and Arzel a Breton spelling for Arthur. Here Arthur announces that they will build their shelter and eventually an abbey church. There are pink and blue hydrangeas scattered all about, auspiciously suggesting the suitability of the location.

Once the place of their settlement is located, Gaiwain asks Arthur how long the King thinks they will be here.

"Sir Gaiwain, my faithful knight, I must tell you I don't know. We will probably be here for some time, so there is no reason for you to put off your marriage to Gwenynen." Arthur chuckles and smiles at Gwenynen. "A king's job is to know things and this learning to admit not knowing is hard for me. A spiritual warrior's job is to know that he does not know things. Isn't that right?" asks King Arthur to Merlin, who comes walking up to them.

"Sire, not knowing is hard for all of us," replies Merlin. "Despite my ability to often see into the future, when we were in the midst of that storm, all I could see was walls of water coming over our ship. Not an auspicious sight."

"That is for sure," says King Arthur. "Let me tell you more. In the midst of the storm, I prayed to the Goddess for our safe passage. When I pray to her deeply, she often takes me into an awake dream. I am awake, and deeply in what seems like a dream at the same time. Do you know what I mean?"

"Yes, of course," Merlin says.

Sir Gaiwain looks nonplussed. Gwenynen nods knowingly

Arthur continues, "In the dream she is angry. She seems to say, *If I help you now, a successor of yours will come into this same energy field and want the same help years from now.* I asked her in the dream who that would be and whether something way in the future would prevent her from assisting me now. She laughs and says, *Henry VII, and certainly it wouldn't.*

"She assented, as you see. We are here. She told me that the time has come for me to give up this process of planning everything. She says the process of over-analysis is blocking me from hearing Her. I am to be like Christ in the wilderness for forty days, or four hundred, or whatever it may take, to find out what is in store for me next. I have at her request laid aside my crown for now. I do not know what she wants me to do next. I am to experience solitude and silence sufficiently so that what is hidden from me shall be revealed. She is asking me to serve in some new way. I do not know what it will mean."

Merlin nods as if he understands perfectly.

Sir Gaiwain, who is astounded the King speaks so directly before him and Gwenynen, finds his tongue at last. "Sire, whatever shall be, I am here to follow."

"I know you are. One of our first tasks here will be to build a church, for we have a wedding to perform, do we not?

"Yes, we sure do," says Gaiwain, with a huge smile.

"Good! Tell the bards to bring out their instruments tonight. Let us feast and celebrate our safe arrival. It feels good to have returned to the land where my sisters, and so many of my relatives and ancestors are," says King Arthur.

It is all Merlin can do to remain silent. The pain in his heart is for Britain, which no longer has a worthy king to follow.

"My King, there is even more to celebrate. Gwenynen tells me that she believes she may be with child," says Sir Gaiwain.

The King smiles broadly. "That, a safe arrival and being led by the 'old people's' standing stone to this place of settlement are indeed a triple blessing. The Celtic people know that the triple blessing is always a sign the Goddess is at work on our behalf. Tonight, we will celebrate."

*   *   *

Later that evening, King Arthur is making the rounds among his followers, bringing his warm presence to connect with each person, as they all struggle to move to the appointed site and begin to set up temporary shelter.

When he comes to Gwenynen, she is resting on a log looking as if she is still suffering from a bit of seasickness.

"Lady Gwenynen," he says, addressing her above her station as he often does out of his affection for her. "Sir Gaiwain spoke excitedly about your good news. Congratulations on your expected child."

Gwenynen stands and curtsies as she has been taught to do at Court. "Thank you, Sire. You are most kind to be concerned about me with all the goings-on of trying to get everyone settled. Yes, I am very excited about Gaiwain and me becoming parents, and I am feeling a bit sick."

"Yes, the last part of our sea voyage was treacherous. You should recover soon."

Gwenynen smiles, "I think it might be mostly the pregnancy. I am not used to carrying another."

Arthur ponders. "I am not used to not carrying a whole kingdom. In some ways it is a kind of sickness also. A melancholia."

Just then Merlin comes up to the King and Gwenynen. He, too, congratulates Gwenynen on being with child.

"Merlin, as I told you, I vowed to the Goddess if she would give us safe passage that I would try to discover more deeply how I might serve her. The Goddess has already blessed Gwenynen. It is propitious that we arrive on this shore with new life kicking, stirring in your womb, Lady Gwneynen."

"This is a beautiful land we are in," says Merlin. "We must all find a way to connect with this place. If we connect with the land, we have begun our journey to the Goddess."

"Gwenynen, I know now that I can talk about all things with you and Merlin. You learned to read at Court and were an avid reader of the volumes we had in the Court library. I have no question in my heart now that I am supposed to have returned to Brittany. However, I have for years been a warrior-king and an administrator of justice whose Court settles all disputes among my people. I fear I have lost my ability to keep a foot in both worlds—in the unseen world of the Goddess and the seen world of war, practicality and administration. My first chore is going to be to get my bearings. How am I supposed to serve my people and the Goddess and Christ? Gwenynen, I know the Goddess has asked you to help guide me in this."

Arthur turns toward Merlin. "Now that we are here in Brittany, the change that is needed in me feels a bit overwhelming, Merlin."

"Sire," says Merlin. "Any time a person goes from being on call all the time, as you have been for years, defending Britain at every turn, to a new way of life, it takes some time to allow the spirit to slow life's rhythm so that the soul can be in a place of emptiness to discover what is next."

Gwenynen is in part surprised and in part not that the King speaks so openly in her presence about matters so private and significant to him. Yet, she knows that he values above all, except for Merlin, the advice of his female counselors. And, after all, the Goddess appears to have given her this new role.

"Merlin," the King begins. "I have read much of ancient history and talked often with you about what has happened in human history. You have taught me that about a thousand years ago, five hundred or so years before the birth of Christ, there was a great burst of enlightenment among the peoples of the world. Before that time the Goddess reigned supreme and the spirits of all animals and plants and humans were held in her mythic reality. When the great Plato and Pythagoras lived, human reason emerged to stand equally alongside of human mythic consciousness. Art and literature burst forth in a dramatic new way in the Greek culture. Mathematics flourished. So did the religions that worshiped the Goddess. The Celtic people, with their fiery imaginations and love of music and art, spread throughout Europe at this time. They were the greatest warriors, poets and artists of all time. The Celtic tribes sowed seeds of cultural inspiration, which to them were more important than any kind of political unity. Then humanity belonged to both worlds without distress—the world of reason and the world of mythic participation in the Goddess.

"Since then, there has been a growing tension between being a part of the great mythic reality of the Goddess and the Roman penchant for orderly administration and rationality. The Romans would say they made us all more civilized. I would say that in the process we have become more fearful. This tension increased even more when Constantine made Christianity the state religion of the Roman Empire and a hierarchy of priests quickly emerged to hold sway over the souls of humankind. People are no longer encouraged to learn their genius gift from the Goddess but urged to follow rules, which fuel subservience to church leaders and marginalize the Goddess herself.

"I have tried to be true to both traditions. I know I was crowned and accepted as King of Britain because the people knew I revered the Goddess. At the same time, I am proud of my lineage of British Roman governors. Because of Roman peace and rule, trade with other nations has grown from nothing in Britain to commerce and exchange of ideas with the whole known world.

Merlin nods. "Yes, this growing tension between reason and intuition is causing fear and distrust, when for years the two together seemed to lend wholeness to a human's way of being. I think, if it were not for this growing malaise, you would have been able to reach some accommodation with the Saxons, rather than having to lead Britain in years of almost perpetual war. When people do not experience themselves held in the care of the Goddess, they turn angry and afraid. Their use of reason makes them excessively proud; they think they are masters of their own destinies. War quickly follows."

"Merlin, I do have some hope," says King Arthur. "As you know the Celtic people of Britain who live in Wales and also those in Ireland and the far north have stayed strong in their belief in the ways of the Goddess. This is not true of the Saxons and the Angles, who have increasingly invaded and populated southeastern Britain. Unfortunately, the Church becomes the ready handmaiden of which ever princeling comes to power. You know I believe in the message that Jesus taught. His message of love of others is the same core message as the Goddess has always taught of the abundance and goodness of creation. His message only refines and strengthens the experience of being in the glory of Her creation. The message is not the same thing as the container for the message. The container of the church that has been created, of asserting people are born sinful and must be under the authority of a church hierarchy, is a huge step backward. The priests and prelates have created this idea of sin and use it as a tool to manage people that makes the arbitrary power of the most cruel king seem mild.

"The Goddess has always taught us that people are all basically good, that we, like all the rest of nature, are to live abundantly. Our focus is to be on the many gifts of life She has given us, not on what to fear next. To be in sync with Her rhythms, not our own little whims." King Arthur shakes his head as if in disbelief that the church could have gotten it so wrong.

"The Celtic people have remained close to the Goddess because we have usually lived near the ocean and ventured upon the sea. Those who are seafarers retain a bodily knowing of the ways of the Goddess. She is the source of all creation and all destruction, but never has she abandoned those who remain faithful to her.

"We have come now to a land that is a cradle of the ways of the Goddess. I must find a means to rediscover the power of the mythic connection to Her and, thus, to all of life. When I find that, then I will know how I must serve her.

"Gwenynen, you have been kind to listen to an old man ramble. I have the grave good fortune, or mischief—however you would have it—of being one of those people who thinks out loud. Thank you for letting me ramble and, again, congratulations on your pregnancy. May all Grace and Blessings be yours in your journey to motherhood as you bring a new child into our realm."

With that King Arthur and Merlin turn and walk back across the field to the burgeoning activity centered in the hub of the new settlement.

*   *   *

Rat, tell Mother Mary to get over it. I am not coming back yet. It is not because I want to have another baby. Somehow my character has been promoted to a key advisor to one of the most important kings who ever lived. I can't abandon my character now, which would be to abandon King Arthur in this crucial moment. If a warrior-king can be transformed into a humble, spiritual presence, there really might be hope for humankind. We are talking about how to take NFL linebackers and turn them into hospice workers for Mother Teresa. I mean the stakes are that high. I do not want Manuelito to suffer by my absence any more than necessary. However, you well know he has been traveling with me as best he can. I have figured out a compromise. I can do more fast forwarding with Gwenynen to be there with her in the important events, when she is with King Arthur. Tell Mother Mary that. Tell her that I am really trying to complete this journey as soon as possible. Tell her also I have not yet discovered a place, which is a good spot to stow the shirt. I can't take it to the laundry and she can come back and pick it up 1500 years later. What do you mean she is losing her sense of humor with me? Yes, be sure you tell her that, about the laundry.

Chapter 2

Britain and Brittany
538-542

Manuelito awakes early. The high mesa is glorious at dawn. He puts on the tea kettle and prepares a cup of black, Irish tea to take with him as he watches the world awake. Once outside the hermitage cabin with his steaming cup of tea, he sits at his improvised writing table. After coming back from being with Blaine in the field for a lengthy period. Manuelito is eager to update his journal. He wants to preserve for Blaine a record of what he observes happening while she is in the field with King Arthur. He begins to write.

After Arthur leaves Wales, many follow him. This immigration is generated in part by fear that without Arthur to defend Britain, the Saxons will over-run it. The sea between Wales and Brittany does not separate the two areas, as much as it is what unites them. It is much easier to travel from Wales to Brittany than from Wales to London.

The Welsh immigrants to Brittany are so numerous that one part of Armorica where they settle is named Leon, after the principal city in Wales, Caerleon, which they leave behind. Ultimately the area the Welsh settle most heavily becomes known as Little Britain and then later simply Brittany.

Wales and Brittany hold in common extensive settlements of the 'old people' and their megalithic monuments. In Brittany there are more erected megalithic stones and Neolithic stone structures than anywhere in the world. Arthur's return to Brittany is a return to a more ancient sense of home. His homeward pull is a reflection of the nature of a spiritual journey.

A pilgrim is filled with a sense of outward pull in order to come home inwardly to his own soul. Merlin recognizes this and calls it the soul's deception; however, his pointing it out to Arthur is not an argument that causes Arthur to decide to return to Britain as Merlin hoped it might.

Unlike Arthur, Merlin is not a Romanized Celtic. He is a Druid. A Celt totally committed to the preservation of Britain, and to him that unity means preservation of a Celtic way of life. Merlin is distressed not only by the loss of courageous and solid political leadership symbolized by Arthur and the knights who follow him, but immigration to Brittany also reflects a British brain drain, as educated Welshmen who are peers of Arthur's, like St Gildas and St Samson, also move to Brittany.

This immigration reaches a crescendo in 542 when there is an outbreak of Bubonic plague. This outbreak begins in the Middle East but, because of flourishing trade, soon reaches Britain. The plague is so destructive that it stops the expansion of the Byzantine Empire dead in its tracks. The plague reaches its height in Britain just after 542 and in a short period destroys over half the population.

Arthur, as he settles increasingly into life in Brittany, free of the day-to-day duties of ruling a large kingdom, allows himself to be drawn to the life of a spiritual seeker. He founds an abbey and builds an abbey church at Plouarzel, a church that will one day hold large stained glass windows illustrating important events in Arthur's life as a spiritual pilgrim in Brittany.

Gaiwain and Gwenynen marry, and a few months later see a celebration of the birth of their daughter presided over by Arthur. Gaiwain and Gwenynen name their daughter Derwen in honor of Gwenynen's friendship with the young woman she first met on the isle of Ynys Enlli and who saved their lives when King Arthur was taken from the battlefield at Camlan to Ynys Enlli.

Merlin returns to England to try to assist Arthur's Regent, and Gwenynen becomes the King's closest advisor.

After a few years, Arthur's settlement at Plouarzel is flourishing. The King is not. He is mentally, emotionally and spiritually stuck. He is committed to not returning to Britain but has not yet abdicated his throne. His life's compass is directed by what he does not want to do, not what he desires. He is being asked by the Frankish King Childebert to come to his Court in Paris and be an advisor. His pride cannot swallow this. He correctly sees himself as a much greater monarch than King Childebert, and it appears to him an absurd step backwards to become an advisor to a lesser monarch. Arthur sees that his pride is an obstacle to his spiritual progress, but he cannot wish or work it away.

Gwenynen sees how deeply depressed Arthur is. At first, she sees that his stuckness is providing him much needed rest. Then it becomes apparent to her that his lethargy and despondency are slowly depleting his life force. She prays fervently to the Goddess every day for an intuition of how to help Arthur.

To those who are open to creation with love, the Goddess never withholds and Gwenynen can sense that She will lead Gwenynen to help Arthur when the time is ripe.

Chapter 3

One day a messenger comes to King Arthur from St Gildas. Gildas migrated to Brittany from Wales a few years earlier. He established a monastery known as St-Gildas-de-Rhuys in Brittany south of Plouarzel right on the coast.

When the messenger arrives, with an invitation for Arthur to visit his old friend Gildas, Gwenynen sees Arthur's eyes light up. She is sitting in her usual counselor's chair, just beside the King, and she notices how his voice strengthens. He becomes the most animated she has seen him since Derwen was born.

Then Arthur appears to list, like a ship taking on water and beginning to sink. He starts to dictate a response to Gildas expressing his regrets at being unable to accept Gildas' invitation. Gwenynen from her connection to the field immediately feels the force of the Goddess move her to speak to the King.

"Sire," Gwenynen says. "Why do you automatically turn down this invitation from your old school friend?"

"It is a good question, Gwenynen," replies Arthur. "I don't really know. I feel like I should stay here and work on my spiritual practices. I am making no progress. Merlin wants me to go back to England. I have promised the Goddess, for giving us safe passage, to stay here. The truth is I don't know what I should do."

Gwenynen nods. "I understand. We all go through places where life presses us down and forces us to go inward to discover what is next. You have been in that place, my King, for some time—you the king of the greatest action by a king the world has ever known. My leading from the Goddess is perhaps it is time for you to find a middle path—not all inaction, staying stuck here, and not all action, moving forward without any introspection."

"Say a little more. There is the ring of a truth I need to hear."

"I believe that the Goddess wants you to accept this invitation from Gildas. Go and visit your friend. He has found his life's work in the second part of his life in writing a history of the British kings. Maybe being with him and talking with him will get you out of your depression and connect you back to the Goddess's life force. Besides, spring is just arriving. It should be a beautiful time to make a trip."

"Thank you, Gwenynen. Your words are true. I shall make plans to go immediately."

Arthur turns to the messenger. "Tell St Gildas I will visit within the next fortnight. Thank him heartily for his invitation."

The messenger bows to the King, turns and leaves.

"You are making the right decision for two reasons," says Gwenynen. "The message I get from the Goddess is that you should visit St Gildas, and you should also visit the place of the 'old people' near him on the way. The Goddess believes there is much there for you to learn. She suggests that, when you get to the alignments of standing stones, walk among them silently at dawn."

Arthur nods his understanding. "Great idea. I have heard of the rows and rows of stones that the 'old ones' placed in the earth near Carnac and that just by walking among them a person can be healed. Perhaps this is where I will find the healing that my soul needs.

"Are you to go with me, Gwenynen, on this pilgrimage?"

"Sire, I will follow you in the energy field of the Goddess, but I shall stay physically here. For now the Goddess would that I spend my time here with my small daughter."

"Yes, absolutely, that is what should be. However, I would take your knight with me if that is not too much to your displeasure."

"I am sure it will be to Gaiwain's great pleasure to accompany you. What serves each of you, also serves me."

Arthur gets up from his chair. "I have much preparation to do. Thank you for your help, Gwenynen. For now I bid you adieu."

*   *   *

The most expeditious way to make the journey to visit St Gildas is by ship down the coast of Brittany. After a week of preparation, King Arthur sets sail for Carnac. For the most part the ship stays within sight of the coastline and with fair weather King Arthur and Sir Gaiwain are soon at a small port near Carnac. There they disembark at dusk and spend their first night ashore.

At first light, Sir Gaiwain awakens King Arthur. "Sire, it will be dawn soon. We just have time to walk to the alignments of stones, to be there as the day begins."

"Thank you, Sir Gaiwain," says King Arthur. "I am right behind you."

Soon the two are walking among a broad field of menhirs. The stones, in up to as many as ten parallel rows, extend for nearly four kilometers in a band just a couple of miles inland from the coast. The stones vary in size. All are larger than a good-sized man and the smallest easily weighs at least a couple of tons. It is, Arthur muses, as if the Goddess's body has been adorned with a grand, many-stranded bracelet. Maybe it has.

For hours the two men walk silently, as Gwenynen instructed them, among the menhirs. Around noon Arthur motions a halt.

The two men sit under the shade of a chestnut tree. Sir Gaiwain pulls out rations that he brought along. For a few minutes they silently eat their lunch.

"What incredible planning and massive employment of men it must have taken to accomplish this. And I thought the Romans had great organizational skills to get things done. Sir Gaiwain, what has been your experience of these rolling fields of stones?"

"Sire, I have not thought of the huge process of construction that must have been involved. My focus has been on the energy of this place. Do you feel what I mean?

"Yes, I do," says King Arthur. "I have not felt this light in years, surely not since I first came to Brittany. Somehow these rows of stones take the energy of the earth and concentrate it for those who walk among them. Even the soreness from my wound at Camlan, which has never before left me, feels today entirely gone."

"Yes, Sire, the 'old people' must have known something of the Earth's healing and how to use it that we have forgotten."

"Maybe that is why they left these stones; to tell us what we seek to know. Sir Gaiwain, I am just now having a revelation looking out at this seemingly unending, rolling hill after rolling hill, of stones. I am remembering what else Gwenynen instructed us: *Don't try to figure out what the 'old people' were thinking or doing thousands of years earlier when they made the field; rather, experience what the stones mean to you right now, what is their message to you in the moment you are experiencing them."*

"What I am experiencing is that the stones look like giant axe heads that have been buried in Mother Earth. My experience is telling me I have not gone to the lengths that I must go to bury my warrior approach to life. I thought building a monastery would be enough. This field is telling me I have only scratched the surface. I must find some greater way to sacrifice my warrior nature to the Goddess and her body, Mother Earth, to be restored to her life force."

"I see what you mean, Sire. It surely does look like this place is a gigantic celebration of the war axe being buried. I can palpably feel the good energy that flows out of the release of that angry axe energy into the earth. Let us take our experience of this energy to your friend St Gildas and see what thoughts he might have."

"Quite right. We shall do it. Let us walk leisurely back through the stones to be fully bathed in their energy, and then we will be on our way to visit St Gildas. We are not far from his abbey now."

*　　　　　　*　　　　　　*

St Gildas is delighted to see his old friend and fellow Welshman. News of Arthur's arrival proceeded him and the monastery is astir with great activity, as a feast is being prepared for the honored guest. The monastery is newly constructed and simple in design—with interconnected places for work, worship, meals and sleeping.

"Gildas, I am so appreciative of the opportunity to come visit you," says Arthur. "We have been long apart. When that occurs there is the tendency for men to stand apart somewhat formally.

My closest advisor has told me that I must speak candidly with you and I will."

"Of course you shall," says Gildas. "I am delighted to see you my old friend. You are not quite as ragged around the edges as I would have imagined for a warrior-king who has been in as many battles as you. Rest assured you may be totally candid with me and your words will be kept in confidence."

"You mean you will keep me out of the history book you are writing on British kings?"

"Certainly I will, if that is your desire," says Gildas.

"Thank you for holding my words in confidence, Gildas, for I am afraid I started my journey to you heavy of heart, though it has been lightened by my experience at Carnac."

"It is a strange place the 'old people' created with those lines of stone that seem to go on forever. What was your experience there?"

"My experience was that my spirit felt lighter than I have felt for years. My worst battle wound seemed more healed. And I had an awake vision of what the stones mean in my life right now—and that is what I urgently want to discuss with you."

"Let us go sit down at the feast that has been prepared by my fellow monks in celebration of your visit. We will not hold up their celebration and you can tell me everything."

The two men go into the refectory. It is decorated with large bouquets of pink and purple hydrangeas interspersed with wreaths of wild roses. The hydrangeas have no discernible scent, but the fragrance of the roses is sublime. The food is blessed by Gildas, and the monks, being released for the celebratory meal from their traditional vow of silence, begin chattering like spring birds as they fall to their dinner of steamed mussels and scallops piled high in the center of each table.

Gildas and Arthur eat slowly, their attention is focused on their conversation.

"As I was saying," says Arthur. "My experience in the field of stones is that these are thousands of war axes buried in the ground. You know how it has long been a Celtic tradition going back centuries to sacrifice to the Goddess your most precious possession in order to stay in spiritual balance. The sacrifice is usually made into water, because water is the medium between land and air, between this world and the next."

"Yes," says St Gildas. "I know many holy springs in Britain where hundreds of war axes and swords have been cast. And I recently myself found two beautiful jadeite axe heads on the beach that must have been thrown into the sea during the time of the 'old people' thousands of years ago."

"I have not parted with my great sword, Caliburn. Nor have I parted with the fruit of that sword, the Kingdom of Britain. After Merlin finally gave up on me returning to Britain, he has been after me to completely abdicate and turn the throne over to my cousin Constantine, whom I made Regent when I came to Brittany. He says Constantine needs all the authority he can get. Yet I have dallied and done nothing about his wise request."

Gildas laughs. "Oh, you have the green dragon problem. All the young novitiates have the same issue. It is more complicated when you enter Holy Orders at middle age and as a king at that. Sort of like starting a race two lengths back."

"What is the green dragon problem?" interjects Arthur.

"The green dragon is the ego's hold on our life force. The sign of your authority as a Celtic king is the red dragon. It symbolizes your putting service to your Kingdom ahead of your own self interest and you have done that courageously, Arthur. If you had not foreclosed me from writing about your kingship, I would have sung your praises for the halls of history to hear. Be that as it may. The problem is basically that having given up your kingship, you have given up the greater good that allowed you to overcome your ego. You have regressed, my friend, back into the clutches of the green dragon."

"Well, maybe I should go back to being King?"

"You could, my friend, and it would create even greater difficulties if you have promised the Goddess that you would give up your kingship for her."

"You are astute, Gildas. Certainly, I made that promise to her and she brought me through a storm that would otherwise have meant my death and that of my most loyal followers. So what am I to do now?"

"Slay the green dragon! It may not be easy, but at least you are engaging the green dragon on familiar terrain. By that I mean the battlefield, though this battlefield is an interior one."

"That is what I was afraid of," says Arthur. He pops open a scallop shell and puts the succulent white meat in his mouth. "Gosh, these scallops are magnificent."

"Yes, we are very lucky. They are plentiful everywhere along the sea. We walk out at low tide and collect them easily by the basket. We bring them back and steam them in a broth of butter and herbs. I could eat them every meal."

"Gildas, the Goddess has indeed blessed you. Are you thoroughly happy here, no longer being in Wales?"

"I believe the Goddess wants me to set down a record about the kings of Britain that have preceded you. Doubtless I will ruffle a few feathers. If I was to do this in Britain where word would get about of the truths I have to tell, then I might face difficulties. So it is better for me to be here, and I like being near the stones of the 'old people.' As you experienced, there is a soothing energy in this place. In addition, you can't beat the bounty from the sea."

"Gildas, you are a wise man to have found this calling now in your life. The Goddess appears to support you in your decision completely. Tell me, where can I meet the green dragon to do battle? It seems he hides always in my shadow."

"You are precisely correct. Because the green dragon is a part of you, it is next to impossible to battle it head on. I would suggest you go and sit among the stones for forty days and nights. Their energy works like leeches pulling poison out of the body, pulling green ego-slime out of the soul. Once it is pulled out of the shadow, you can lead it by the stole you wear over your monk's robe into whatever chasm you want. To get the green dragon out of the shadows, you must see clearly what fear this ego pattern, which wants to keep you as king and wants to keep your terrible sword at hand, is seeking to protect."

"Gildas, yours is not a prescription that I guess anyone wants to hear, much less a warrior-king. However, I believe it is true and I will do as you instruct. Tonight I join the celebration you have set for me." With that he raises his wine glass. "To the Goddess, her son Jesus Christ and to those who keep true faith."

Chairs begin scraping back. Arthur becomes aware that the monks sitting near him have heard the toast and begin standing holding their glasses high. Soon the whole room is standing and Arthur and Gildas push back their chairs and raise their glasses.

"To the Goddess and her son Jesus Christ," the room thunders. Every glass is raised high and every drop that has been poured is downed, till every glass is dry and every face is beaming.

*   *   *

"That was certainly a joyous celebration Gildas put on for us last night, Sir Gaiwain," says Arthur. The two men have slept late in the guest quarters at St Gildas' monastery. Birds are chattering away noisily outside their window.

"That it was, my Lord. I have not seen you enjoy yourself so well in a long time."

"Hmm, I guess you are right. However, now I begin earnestly the true purpose which was revealed to me for my visit. I will go and stay among the standing stones and fast for forty days and see if I might slay the green dragon. This is work that I must do alone. So I request that you go back to Plouarzel and let those at the settlement and abbey know where I am and the task that lies before me. Ask a trusted courtier to go to Britain and request Merlin to return to Brittany to counsel with me when I return."

"It shall be done, Sire," says Sir Gaiwain.

"You always are my true and trusted knight, Sir Gaiwain. You have my deepest thanks and prayers. Blessings for your safe return."

"I shall be back in forty days to attend you for the return trip home."

"That would be a gift to me. Thank you, again, Sir Gaiwain. Now I must speak again to Gildas before I begin my fast."

Sir Gaiwain turns and leaves his King.

Arthur goes in search of Gildas. He finds him in his scriptorium writing away.

"Gildas, I am about to be off to begin my retreat, to see if I can subdue the green dragon. I have one question."

Gildas nods for Arthur to continue, slightly irritated at having his work interrupted.

"Last night at the wonderful celebration dinner, all your monks seem to not only understand but to be filled with joy from the knowledge that Jesus Christ is the son of the great Celtic Mother Goddess. How do you instruct them to have an experience of this mystery and not run into problems with the Roman Church?"

Gildas appears to ponder what he is writing. Then he speaks. "Arthur, you have lived too long in the warrior world of black and white. Here we know that it is impossible to experience the full energy of the Goddess and remain in this material world. We serve her by seeing her reflection in all things. You could say this is the deception she asks us to participate in. She is only accessible through the mirror of reflection in the created world, as well as by our participation with her in a state of lucid observation when we are in enlightened consciousness."

Gildas picks up his writing quill and then sets it down again. "The Roman Church has lost touch with inner knowing and is mired in fear of loss of its power. From that position it is impossible for it to understand much less appreciate that we come to the Goddess through her deception. So we don't talk about it with Rome. Why should we? It is after all an experience, and to talk about what can only be understood by experience is to fish for fish in the air. You could say that Rome has its own green dragon that gets larger and more unseen by it each year, if you follow what I am saying."

"Gildas, I am afraid I follow you all too well. Though I might not have at all just a few days ago. This is a sharp learning curve for an old king."

Gildas smiles. "You are the best king that Britain has ever had and the best she will have for a long time, I expect. However, kingship is for the most part a dualistic task. The one you have embarked on of spiritual transformation is completely non-dual. This new way of thinking comes as a bit of a shock at first. You will learn it quickly, and as you do, the green dragon will be slain."

"Thank you for the hope you inspire and for the lovely feast last night. Now I am off to encounter the green dragon. Keep me in your prayers to the Goddess. If I succeed in this interior journey, I shall return in forty days."

"We can do better than that," says Gildas to his friend. "A trip as you are undertaking should always be done with some spiritual guidance. I will journey up to where you are in silent retreat among the megaliths on the tenth, the twentieth and thirtieth day of your retreat. It is permitted at such times for a retreatant to speak with a spiritual director and seek whatever guidance may be needed at that stage of the interior journey."

"Gildas, my countryman, you are a true friend, indeed. Thank you, for your willingness to help me walk deeper on my path. I am buoyed by the good fortunate of knowing I will have the opportunity to have your guidance."

"It will be my pleasure to be of any assistance I can," says Gildas. He looks steadily at Arthur and as he does his face gradually becomes more lined. "Be forewarned, the nature of such a lengthy, silent retreat is that you make it alone. My brief visits will not be much comfort to what you may encounter."

Arthur nods his head. *Yes*, he thinks, *I really have no idea what an encounter in the wilderness with a green dragon is all about.*

Chapter 4

By day three of his retreat, Arthur is bored. As much as he tries in his prayer time to still his mind, he cannot stop its constant racing. He comes to his first awareness—the more restless his mind is, the more bored he feels. The only thing that keeps Arthur from quitting his retreat at this early stage is the strange grounding presence of the standing stones all around him. He wanders in and through the giant megaliths all day each day. The stones are like a charm bracelet that the 'old people' put on the earth, and the effect of the charms is to ground his restless energy, to over and over again pull him out of a stream of thoughts into a simple awareness of his breath and how it flows rhythmically with the earth's breath—the gentle breeze from the sea that is constantly around him.

After the first five days Arthur becomes aware that his fasting is helping. He is no longer hungry, though the air is full of the scent of wild roses and blooming crab apple trees. The experience of physical emptiness from the absence of food brings his focus to a more interior perspective. Each night his dreams are more vivid.

When St Gildas comes to visit Arthur on the tenth day, Arthur has just awoken from a very vivid dream. He is eager to tell Gildas about it.

Gildas arrives by horse. A Brother who comes with him immediately sets about starting a small fire and boiling water for rose hip tea for Gildas and Arthur.

"Gildas, it is good to see you. I know you value dreams, as the Old Testament is full of them. You must help me with this one."

"Arthur, you are looking well for a man who has been ten days without food. It is good to see you. Tell me about your dream."

"I am confused by it, but in a way maybe it's not so strange. In my dream Merlin comes back to Brittany. He seeks to convince me that both my knights and my people need me, that they suffer without my presence both for lack of their king, and because of the incursions of the Angles. Merlin finally persuades me to go with him back to Britain to regain the throne. On the return passage from Brittany to Wales a storm occurs, very similar to the storm we were in on our trip coming to Brittany. The storm drives the ship below the water and the ship descends to the bottom of the sea."

Gildas nods his head in a knowing way. "Quite wonderful, how we survive things in dreams. Keep going."

"At the bottom of the ocean, Merlin changes into a fish. Just like that, the old rascal swims away. I am left alone with no guidance from my trusted Druid. I am restless and bored like the fish with glazed eyes swimming back and forth around me. I discover a star fish on the ocean floor. I pick it up, and suddenly I am back on land here in Brittany sitting by the ocean leaning against a tree where I awake."

Arthur looks at St Gildas inquisitively.

"Arthur, it is an interesting dream. I am not sure what it means, and what it means for sure is something only you the dreamer can know in your heart. However, if you want them, I will give you my thoughts.

"Please do. I would like that very much," says Arthur.

"The dream suggests that you are stuck in your life, right now Arthur, in a sense literally and figuratively between Brittany and Britain because you have not gone deep enough in your soul to discover your source of guidance from God.

"We all start off needing guidance from others; it is an essential early life lesson to learn the importance of learning from those who have gone before us. You have been gifted with the guidance of the Arch-Druid of all of Britain. It has been a gift in your life and the reason you have been so successful in defending your kingdom of Britain and its people. Still, at this stage of your life in order to have a deeper experience of God, you must let go of your dependency on even your most trusted outside counselor so that you can be guided by your own inner knowing to a deeper connection with God.

"Yes, you could return to Britain, and probably regain the throne, but it would only give you external power, a power which is always illusory. Your dream, I believe, is telling you that even though you have given up your crown, you have not yet completely let go of your need to rule others because you have not yet learned to surrender your own rule of yourself to God."

Gildas stops speaking. Arthur makes no response for a long time. Finally he speaks. "Your interpretation is helpful and sounds accurate. If I am honest, I have been stuck in wanting both to rule my Kingdom of Britain with my counselor Merlin at my side, and also to be here in Brittany with my extended family safe from the ravages of the plague. I want it both ways."

Gildas replies. "We desire power for one of two reasons: either to provide a way to protect our ego or to engage the life force to do God's will, to live our destiny. The dream is saying, I believe, that in some way you have not completely surrendered your will to God."

"What should I do?" asks Arthur.

Gildas gives a hearty laugh. "Well, this is the beauty of your being on this retreat. Surrender is a practice more than a onetime event. You must practice surrendering to God your ego's need for power and control by asking the standing stones you walk among every day to draw off that ego energy from you, to make you again pure and innocent."

Arthur looks perplexed.

Gildas continues. "Yes, I admit, it is harder than I am making it sound. You do, in fact, have to drown, to let the ego die. So the dream is a good start. Remember you have a talisman, a star fish. Perhaps there is some answer for you in the stars.

"Arthur, I would stay with you longer, but a retreat as you are on is not to be interrupted for long. I hope what I have said is helpful. I will be back to see you again in ten days. Until then, peace and grace in God's hands."

*   *   *

The second ten days of Arthur's retreat go much quicker than the first. He spends part of each day wandering among the megaliths, sensing the nature of each stone's energy connection, and the other part of the day in silent meditation, allowing his mind and emotions to become ever quieter.

When Gildas arrives for his second visit, Arthur is much calmer and not nearly as agitated as he was during Gildas' first visit, when Arthur was full of questions about his dream.

As before the monk accompanying St Gildas prepares tea over an open fire for the two men. The spring nights have been cold. It is still early in the morning and the morning rays of warming sunshine are just beginning to reach where they sit under a large oak tree to take their tea. The conversation is not rushed. Finally, Gildas speaks. "How has it been with the temptation of power and control?"

Arthur looks at Gildas. "Gildas, it is good to see you." Slowly a wry grin emerges on Arthur's face. His friend is here to assist him, not to comfort him. "You get right to the point, don't you?"

Gildas nods his head gently. "This is the nature of my role, to help hold you in your process."

"I have prayed deeply every day to be free of the need for power and control, and I do have the sense that this has been lifted from me," says Arthur.

Gildas waits a few moments, then speaks. "And...?"

"I have not had another dream of such lucidity, but my mind, even though it is much stiller, has been constantly barraged with thoughts of what I should do for my people here in Brittany. On the one hand, I hear this loud voice in my head telling me I need to be of greater service to my people. On the other hand, I hear an equally loud voice telling me it is time for me to rest and look after myself. I wake up every morning of every day still in pain from my wound at Camlan."

Gildas smiles. "This is good progress, Arthur. You have moved from the ego's need for power and control to the ego's need to be needed."

"Wait just a moment, Gildas. Surely there is nothing wrong with me wanting to be of service to my people. That is the true mission of a king, is it not?"

"There are two possibilities, Arthur. The first is the ego possibility that you need to do for others in order to feel okay yourself. Quite frankly, you can appreciate that this is a gross expression of disrespect for the competency of others. It leads to the sin of pride, of an over-inflated ego doing for others out of some false sense of superiority over them. You may be their king, but we are all equal as humans under God."

Arthur looks chagrined. "I was afraid you were going to say something like that. What about the other possibility?"

"The other possibility is that your service to others as their king, or leader, or priest comes, not from you, but from God."

"Gildas, that sounds facile enough, but seems to me to be a quite useless distinction unless I know how to discern the source of my energy to serve. I think my desire to be of service springs from an honorable source."

"Don't distract yourself, Arthur. It is not a question of honor. Just putting it in language of that construct suggests the ego is running the show. No, the discernment is really not that difficult. Do you feel this compulsive energy to do, to be of service for your people?

"Absolutely," says Arthur. "It is one of the things that has made this retreat the hardest—the feeling that I should be back at my monastery performing my duties as abbott, looking after these people who came with me to Brittany."

"You are in the right place among these stones," says Gildas. "Try in the next ten days to see if you can surrender to God your ego need to take care of others.

Arthur looks puzzled. "How?"

"Whenever the feeling comes, let go of the story about the feeling—why you think you should do whatever for whomever. Just hold the energy of the feeling until it moves through you. In our monastery novitiate program, we call this 'passing the kidney stone of pride.'"

Gildas stands and prepares to depart. Arthur looks alarmed.

"Gildas, it is so helpful for you to come visit. Must you rush off so quickly?"

"I know it's abrupt, Arthur, but that is the nature of retreat guidance. My visit is to be a quick stroke, not a long conversation. Sometimes our psyche needs an abrupt tap on the forehead for us to wake up. At least that is how it's supposed to work and my experience of how it does. See you in ten days." With that Gildas and his companion mount up on their horses and gradually disappear into the still lingering morning mist.

*   *   *

When Gildas arrives at the thirty day mark of the retreat, Arthur is looking haggard. His eyes are sunk back in their sockets. The light which usually glows in them is gone. His clothing is soiled and he moves slowly.

Gildas puts his hands on both of Arthur's shoulders and peers into his eyes. "How is it going, my friend?" he asks.

Arthur shakes his head in both a *yes* and *no* motion. "The kidney stone has been painful to experience. I am not sure I have passed it, but I have given my best effort to surrender to God my need for affection and adoration. I have hardly slept at all the past few days. I have felt so much self-hatred for the way I thought I was helping others when I was only massaging my own ego. I am cranky and need a bath and don't feel worthy of anyone's attention much less approval."

Gildas, completely unruffled by Arthur's distress, asks, "Have you had any dreams?"

"I have been hoping for a dream as a way to show me the way through the quagmire of the ego, but nothing has come. Memories, they have been vivid. Painfully so. Like sand being rubbed into a sore. I have had no comfort except for the calm assurance of the standing stones.

"Arthur, this is good. You are making progress in what is often called the tunnel of midnight. You have faced the temptation of the body for power and the temptation of the heart for affection. The final ego temptation is by the mind. It is the original temptation of Adam in the garden of Eden when they ate of the tree of knowledge. In this final battle for your soul you must face letting go of what you reason out through your own bright mind.

"You may find this temptation awaits you here in the next days, or you may find it can only be encountered when you are in the midst of the demands and challenges of the world and your mental intelligence seizes on something it must figure out in the moment."

For the first time that morning, Arthur's gaunt expression eases. He gives a slight smile. "I wouldn't mind putting off what I am now realizing is taking-off-your-clothes, down-and-dirty spiritual work and going back with you and having a good bed to sleep in and some of your first harvest wine."

"You are always welcome at our monastery, Arthur. As your spiritual director for your forty day retreat, I must counsel you by all means to finish your retreat. You are quite correct to recognize that spiritual work is hardly the lofty, airy fairy image that people outside of the walls of a monastery think. The way up starts by going down, and until we get to the deepest part of our ego protections our opportunities to ascend are all short-lived."

Arthur raises his hand. "I will stay. Don't worry, I may not be good at surrendering my ego, but I am a tough old warrior. I can stay in the fire of battle as long as I have an ounce of strength."

Gildas reaches and embraces the bedraggled Arthur. "I will see you in ten days to celebrate the breaking of your fast and the end of your retreat. Even though you are not eating it is imperative that you drink as much water as you can each day. The more fluids you have the more easily the toxins of your ego's protective emotions are released from your body. Several of my Brother monks will be here with a cart to help you back to the monastery. Until then, may God bless you with courage and may the Goddess' love for you sustain you.

*   *   *

After his retreat is concluded, Arthur stays another two weeks with Gildas at his monastery. It takes that long for him to recover his strength. However, immediately upon the completion of his forty days in the megaliths, Arthur feels a lightness of spirit he has not known for years.

St Gildas does not quiz Arthur about the last ten days of his retreat.

"Arthur, it is my belief that I have assisted you as much as I can on your spiritual journey. My heart is with the history of the British kings. I do not have spiritual training to take you the last part of your journey where, in surrendering the remainder of your ego, you will find an integration in yourself of the masculine and feminine. You will need the guidance of a Druid woman, someone who has given birth and understands the way of the Goddess. Maybe you already know who such a person might be?"

Arthur was always amazed when those, like Merlin and Gildas, gave him prescient spiritual succor. He could taste its realness. "Well, indeed, I do. Thank you again for all you have done to allow my spiritual journey to unfold here among the megaliths.

You are a true friend." He chuckles. "Just don't forget to leave me out of whatever you are writing. May the Goddess keep you in her Grace."

"And may She bring traveling mercies to you."

Chapter 5

Tree drives the old pickup north to Minnesota with his faithful dog, Two, sitting in the passenger seat, ever alert the entire drive. Upon arriving in Minneapolis, Tree is in contact with Rat.

It turns out that Rat has a hacking buddy who is a member of a First Peoples' tribe in northern Alberta. Rat has never met his buddy; however, they have become quite close through their Internet sleuthing activities. Rat's friend thinks in a very nonlinear manner and he is extremely skilled at the fine nuances of the art of hacking.

Rat advises Tree to use one of the many backwoods roads to cross into Canada. After Tree crosses into Canada, he drives up to northern Alberta to meet Rat's friend. He trades the old pickup to him in exchange for a tribal identity and a Canadian passport. Tree and Two then hitchhike back down to Winnipeg, where, after a brief quarantine for Two, they catch a flight to Reykjavík, and from there on to Copenhagen. From Copenhagen, Tree, with Two traveling as a service dog, goes by bus northward to the closest Swedish bus stop to the Convent, where his Grandmother Blaine is doing her time traveling.

The Sisters are all delighted to see Tree and Two. The Convent is stuck off in the backwoods and the young Sisters are particularly aware that they do not often have a tall, darkly handsome man visiting. Mother Mary is glad to see Tree for another reason. She hopes that having Blaine's grandson at her side will convince Blaine to complete her journey with Gwenynen and get back to the current time-frame. Shortly after he arrives, she invites Tree to her office.

"Tree, thank you so much for coming to welcome your Grandmother back from her time travels in the quantum field," says Mother Mary. "I hope the Sisters have all made you feel comfortable here?"

"They have been most kind to both me and Two," says Tree. "When do you expect my Grandmother to return?"

"Honestly, I do not know," says Mother Mary. "I have been pleading with her through Rat for some time to return. She has the goods. All she has to do is stow them somewhere safe, where we can go collect them. So far she has been unwilling to do that. I'm not sure why."

"Yes, my Grandmother can be quite stubborn, when she wants to," says Tree.

"I was hoping that you would be willing to sit beside her and if possible visit her in the field and urge her to come on back," says Mother Mary.

"As you probably know from talking to Rat, Two and I were with her in the field, through her friend Derwen, helping support her when her character Gwenynen assisted in rescuing King Arthur from the battlefield."

"Rat told us all about that," says Mother Mary, and she smiles hopefully at Tree. "So you have just the right expertise to visit with her now and urge her to return."

"Yes, I obviously want very much to visit her, but in linear reality, not in the field," says Tree. "I would never urge my Grandmother to do anything she did not want to do. From what you are saying, it sounds like she's made up her mind. My Grandfather Manuelito sent me here to be awake and ready to assist her when she returns from the field. It is very tiring being in the field and you lose much bodily energy. I do not want to be in that hampered state when my Grandmother returns and will need my help."

Mother Mary can tell that her argument is completely foreclosed before she has even made it solidly. Her desire for Blaine to return is not her own foolish wish. She knows that time is running out for the light of human consciousness to prevail. However, at this stage she knows nothing else she can do but try to learn greater patience. Mother Mary turns directly toward Tree.

"Tree, I am so glad that you are here. I would not ask you to do anything that would make you uncomfortable. I know you went immediately to look in on your Grandmother when you first got here. Even though she is all wired up, feel free to go sit with your Grandmother at any time. I have the hope that your just being around will make her decide to return more quickly. Please let me know if there is anything I can do to make your stay here more pleasant. And that includes the stay of your dog," she says, glancing down at Two.

"Thank you, Mother Mary. I think we are being well taken care of. Two and I will visit with Grandmother Blaine every day and also enjoy getting out for some long hikes. I hope to see some of the plentiful wildflowers that grow here in this beautiful summer weather. Rest assured I, like you, hope that my Grandmother returns soon."

Just then, the door to Mother Mary's office abruptly pushes open. "Oh, I did not mean to intrude," says a young Sister.

"No, that is quite all right," says Mother Mary. "Tree and I are just finishing our conversation. Please, Sister Julia, take Tree with you and give him a full tour of our Convent and maybe you can help him find some of our twin flowers."

Tree looks at Sister Julia. She is tall and willowy. Though she is long-waisted, her long blonde hair reaches well below her waist. Her eyes are a soft blue, like calm water. She looks directly at Tree. It is not a stare, nor is it coy. Tree recognizes the kind of look immediately. It is a look from a lucid inner observer. She is looking at him, not just with her own eyes, but also with vision connected to the field of humankind's soul. He returns the look in the same manner. A space of timelessness transpires between them. Mother Mary, distracted about getting back to her work, suddenly looks at them both.

"Sister Julia, please see to giving Tree a look around. I have work to do. Tree, thank you so much for our conversation. I am sure there will be much more for us to discuss later."

"Thank you, Mother Mary," says Tree as he, Two and Sister Julia leave Mother Mary's office.

The threesome walk outside. Sister Julia and Tree turn to meet each other's gaze again. Quickly they slip again into a timeless moment. Some time passes, and neither Julia nor Tree could have ventured a guess how much. The moment is finally broken by Two's low growl.

Tree speaks first. "I am sure Mother Mary is springing this tour job on you. I know you must have plenty to do. I am planning to take a little hike with Two. Perhaps you can give us the tour later on."

As he is speaking, Tree begins to take in Julia's earthly appearance. Hard to believe, he thinks, he had not immediately noticed that the young woman is only clad in a light blue leotard which seems to exactly match the color of her eyes. The leotard does not leave much to the imagination about Julia's winsome shape, and yet, at the same time, it offers everything to the imagination.

Julia smiles like a prayer at sunrise. "I am going to a class where I teach body prayer to the Sisters. I will gladly accept your invitation to lead you on a tour later. Of course you must have the pleasure of discovering our twin flower. This wildflower is called twin because it has two flowers on top of each very thin stem. Its foliage is in the form of creeping runners, which grow in deep moss. The flowers are pink, bell-like, very fragrant." She pauses and extends her hand to Tree and begins to open her mouth to speak as their eyes return to the soft mediation between the two worlds, to the place where words are of little use.

Two growls. Tree unconsciously puts his left hand in his pocket and his fingers, as they do so often, enclose the medallion his Grandfather gave him. The spell is broken. Wordlessly, Julia turns and heads off in the direction of her task.

Tree looks down at Two. As he continues to turn the medallion over and over between his fingers, he remembers not only the wisdom of Black Elk, but his Grandfather's lecture before he left him about illusion and deception. He looks at the retreating figure of Julia and squints. Yes, from a dualistic gender perspective, he can see her as a blonde bombshell or—and he lets his eyes widen and his gaze un-focus—just another human soul, with a heart craving love. As he often does when he and Two are out together alone, Tree starts talking to Two. "Let's go find a coffee, Two. My system is still askew from the airplane flight. A little caffeine wouldn't be a bad idea."

Two gives an approving whine and man and dog start off in the direction of the refectory. Tree finds coffee and a bowl, which he uses to give Two water. The two settle by one of the refectory's large floor-to-ceiling windows. As he drinks his coffee, Tree can see across the inner courtyard the room where Sister Julia stands before her class, moving her body in a graceful sinuous flow. Tree begins again to talk to Two.

"You know, Two, there would have been a time I could only have seen that Sister Julia as one hot chick. Now, thanks to all of Grandfather's training, I can see her just as one of God's kids, and a lonely one at that, and also one gorgeous hot chick. You know what I mean?"

Two growls in a way anyone would recognize as an affirmative growl.

"There is that point, right in the middle, where it is almost impossible to discern the source of the vibrancy of the life force's call—a sweet, beautiful sexual desire or desire for the Divine that just happens to be reflected in something sweet, sexual and beautiful. A longing summons. You know what I mean?"

Two growls again. Tree tries to discern the meaning of this growl; it is not one he has heard often.

"I have to confess I am so glad we have Katrina waiting for us back home. I can't tell which call Sister Julia might be," Tree says, nodding his head in the direction of Sister Julia. "However, I think we might take Mother Mary up on her request to tell Grandma Blaine to get on back. Might not be a good idea to hang around here too long. You know what I mean?"

Two lets out a long low howl like the kind he sometimes offers up on the rez in New Mexico under a full moon.

Chapter 6

Manuelito loves the dawn. The way the day breaks itself open slowly at first and then suddenly with its full vivid presence. He has settled himself at his outside writing table to catch up on his journaling. As much as he is enjoying his dreamtime way of eavesdropping on his dear wife's journey in the quantum field, he is ready for Blaine to return home. He didn't agree with Mother Mary at first about her insistence to Rat that Blaine should return, but he does now.

I want to be in Blaine's calm spirit and gentle laughter in linear time, he muses. In the meantime, let me get caught up on my journaling, maybe that will help bring her back. He picks up his pen and begins to write.

As Arthur's spiritual guide, Gwenynen anxiously awaits King Arthur's return from his retreat. When he returns he describes to Gwenynen the healing time he has spent among the stone alignments and how he wrestled with his fear of not knowing who he was if he was not a king. After their conversation in the days that follow, it seems to Gwenynen for a time as if Arthur's green dragon has been banished.

Shortly after King Arthur returns to his abbey, Merlin also arrives. Following Merlin's long standing suggestion, King Arthur abdicates his throne completely in 542 and hands the crown of Britain over to his cousin Constantine. Merlin leaves Arthur and returns to Britain for the crowning of the new king. The two men, who struggled together for years to keep the Kingdom of Britain aright, sense that they may never see each other again and their parting is grievously sad for both men.

Arthur and Merlin hope that by completely consolidating the rule of Britain in Constantine, the new king will be aided in his efforts to hold Britain together against the ravages of the plague and the menace of the Angles and the Saxons. History will recount that Constantine was not up to this daunting task.

With his crown put aside, Arthur responds positively to the request of King Childebert. He goes to King Childebert's Court, and when asked, seeks to render helpful advice to King Childebert. The advice sought is usually over petty matters. Or if the matter is more serious, King Childebert appears unable to act after receiving judicious advice, much to the consternation and frustration of Arthur.

To try to keep his spiritual focus, Arthur founds another abbey, this one at the town which becomes known later as Ploërmel, another Breton variant meaning Arthur's parish. Ploërmel is located centrally in Brittany. In founding his new abbey Arthur goes to visit with his childhood school chum and cousin St Samson, who is, at the same time, building an abbey at Dol-de-Bretagne. The two old friends enjoy their time together and Arthur is impressed with the huge scope of the plans that St Samson has for his abbey.

They are the kind of old friends who can joke with each other that it would be unseemly for the Bear King and a man named Samson, who has been sainted by the church, to be in competition over who will have the tallest spire.

Nonetheless, the result of Arthur's visit to Dol-de-Bretagne is that the church Arthur is building at his new abbey at Ploërmel is on a grander scale than the one at Plouarzel. The church will later be rebuilt several times and become a magnificent building housing the tombs of Dukes of Brittany and containing stained glass windows portraying the life of Arthur.

Beside building monasteries and churches, Arthur's spiritual growth is evidenced in other ways. He finds that by spending even more time among the megaliths that he receives Christ's power from the Goddess to help heal others. In his first encounter with the stones, he saw them as axes that needed to be buried. Now he sees them like teeth in the earth whose purpose is to consume him so he can become a part of the land, a part of the Goddess herself. From this connection with the Goddess his power to heal flows. His hope is that from this connection a new understanding of his life will grow.

Arthur continues to struggle with the extraordinary psychological and spiritual task of going from a warrior-king, who has spend most of his adult life in leading soldiers into battle and ruling an extensive kingdom, to some new way to understand the meaning of his life.

Manuelito puts down his pen and muses upon thoughts that come un-summoned. He picks up his pen again.

History is littered with warrior-kings and generals whose early heroic episodes are followed by second-half lives that are filled with retreats into bitterness or, at best, years of nostalgia. The forgotten hero can succumb to making a fervently worshiped idol out of the heroic intensity which he once lived.

Arthur is seeking to walk a different path. One that has never been walked before by a warrior-king and one that has rarely been followed since. He faces the most difficult adversary anyone can ever face.

Over and over again, Gwenynen helps him journey onto this internal battlefield where he faces himself. At the heart of his struggle is the very process of transformation which he is seeking. Increasingly he begins to experience that the Goddess is speaking to him through the land.

The more time Arthur spends among the megaliths of Brittany, the more his ability to channel the healing power of the Goddess increases. Indeed, as his spiritual connection to the Goddess grows, he heals a man of the dreaded disease of leprosy.

Still, most of his time is spent in King Childebert's Court and this is a constant source of spiritual tension and discomfort. Gwenynen remains Arthur's principal spiritual counselor and she senses that despite having abdicated his crown and building a second new abbey things are not right spiritually.

Gwenynen finds, as Sister Bendithion had suggested she might, that being a mother and a wife is the perfect spiritual Convent for her continued spiritual growth. She has gone through her own process of green dragon slaying in becoming a new mother, wife and counselor to the King. She finds that she needed all the experiences of her personal spiritual journey to be ready to help the King.

One day, on a visit with Gaiwain to Ploërmel, she finds Arthur brooding again. He recently received word that St Dyfrig died at his hermitage on Ynys Enlli and that has Arthur depressed. Gwenynen understands that grief is one thing, dark ruminating is quite different. Arthur's brooding is not a good sign. Those in touch with the creative life force of the Goddess do not spend time brooding. She knows that the role she has been given by the Goddess is to try to help Arthur find his way. He has surrendered his crown to the Goddess; however, Gwenynen is well aware that he still has his famous sword. As a spiritual guide she does not know the answer for him, but she has the ancient tool that all spiritual guides offer, the embodied question.

Chapter 7

"Tell me, Arthur, what has you looking so world weary?" asks Gwenynen. The two are sitting under a tree beside the site of the new abbey's construction. It is spring, birds are chattering gaily and apple trees are blooming. Derwen, who is now a cherry-cheeked teenager, is sitting at Gwenynen's feet working a small handloom weaving a bright cloth. *To brood in this season one's spirit has to be deeply out of touch with the Goddess,* realizes Gwenynen.

"My heart is heavy, Gwenynen, and I am not sure why. I think the problem has to do with what is going on at Childebert's Court. Let me give you some history."

"Sure," says Gwenynen. She looks down at Derwen skillfully working her handloom. "We have plenty of time."

"This all goes back to my nephew Riwal Mawr, who left Wales years ago and established a wonderful kingdom here in Brittany. He is the son of Emyr Llydaw to whom both I and my predecessor, as kings of Britain, are deeply indebted. Many years ago, in the beginning of this century, when I was in my early twenties, the Visigoths invaded Riwal's kingdom. I gathered a force of knights and came to Brittany and helped drive them out."

"So not only are you kin, you have the kind of deep friendship that often can only arise between men fighting side by side each other on the battlefield," says Gwenynen.

"You always surprise me with your quick grasp of things, Gwenynen."

"Please, go on Arthur," says Gwenynen.

"At one point I even left part of my army with Riwal and we were able to effectively rule a large swath of Brittany together, while I continued leading the fight against the Saxons in Britain.

"When Riwal died, he was succeeded by his son Deroch. Deroch died as a young man and left the kingdom to his son Jonas. Now here is where the plot thickens. Jonas, who had just gained his majority, died suddenly and mysteriously. He left a very young heir, a young son named Judwal.

"Almost immediately after the mysterious death of Jonas, his widow married Count Conomorus, who then became Regent to rule, during Judwal's minority, over the kingdom Riwal and I built."

"This is indeed a twisting tale," says Gwenynen.

"Well, it gets worse," says Arthur. "Conomorus was an exiled prince from Wales who was forced to leave Wales, and I said at the time 'good riddance.' He always had some self-serving excuse to avoid assisting in the wars against the Saxons. His only allegiance was to his own selfish interests. After he came to Brittany from Wales, he sought to establish himself here. His marriage to Jonas' widow gave him the leverage he sought and he now seeks to claim much of Leon as his kingdom, including the lands that I helped win for my kinsman. To add insult to injury, Conomorus has taken the title of Count of Leon.

"His next step was to plot the death of Judwal, for whom he served as Regent. His ends would have probably been gained in the same manner as he caused Judwal's father to be killed; however, young Judwal escaped the plot. Judwal fled to King Childebert's Court and has been seeking assistance from the French King to regain his kingdom. My old friend St Samson has taken up Judwal's cause and came to Childebert's Court to persuade King Childebert to back Judwal in a bid to regain his throne from the scheming Conomorus."

"Well, there you have it, Gwenynen. I am weary with all the back and forth at Childebert's Court about whether to help Judwal or not."

"Arthur, I take it that this debate has resulted in a lot of pressure on you?"

"Yes, both internally and externally. Externally, my friend St Samson is pleading with me to get into the fray to help Judwal. Internally, Judwal is the direct heir of my dear kinsman Riwal with whom I established the very kingdom that Conomorus is seeking to steal away. What can I do?

"I have given up my crown for the Goddess. I am trying to live a peaceful life in service to God and yet I am an old warhorse. I cannot stand aside while wrong is perpetrated against my kin, can I? What, Gwenynen, does the Goddess want me to do? I do not know how to serve her and fulfill the destiny she has for me."

Arthur looks down at the teenage Derwen working her small hand-loom beside her mother. Arthur realizes that Gwenynen's daughter is rapidly becoming a young woman. He smiles. "I am much more lost than your young daughter."

Gwenynen looks directly at King Arthur. "Perhaps you are, and perhaps you are not. You have done much work in surrendering to the Goddess's will for you. Maybe the answer to this conundrum is nearer at hand than you think. Tell me the reasons you think you should take up arms to aid your kinsman."

Arthur hesitates. He knows the process that is about to unfold. Gwenynen is not going to tell him what she thinks he ought to do. Instead she will try to ask the questions that lead him to his own inner knowing. He takes a deep breath. Slowly he feels that part of himself, which is resisting this process, beginning to melt.

"Okay, Gwenynen, there are many reasons. Here is what pops in my head. First and foremost, there is my kinsman's need for help. Second, there is the need to correct unfairness and injustice, to see that the rapacious seeking after wealth of the evil Conomorus is stopped. Third, this task of warfare is what I am gifted to do. I know how to keep fighting men's spirits strong and guide them in battle."

"Now tell me," says Gwenynen, "why you should not pick up your battle sword and go to war on behalf of your kin?"

Arthur nods his head. He knew this question was coming. "First, I have sworn to the Goddess to put down my sword, to leave behind my warrior-king ways and lead a life of peaceful devotion to her. Second, I'm getting old. My hair is almost all gray. War is a young man's game. Third, if my kinsman is to rule this area of Brittany successfully, he will need to show that he has the warrior-king's ability to gain and keep this land. In the long run, I do not help him, or his subjects, by trying to prop him up if he would be a weak ruler."

"Is that all?" asks Gwenynen.

Arthur glances down at his feet and shakes his head. "No, that is not all. If I were to engage in this war, it would be a battle of Welshmen against Welshmen. Among the ordinary warriors on both sides, there would be relatives and many former subjects of mine. I would be a killer of kinsman. What would be worse, to win the war or to lose it? How could I enjoy victory, if I knew that my sword was cursed with blood guilt? If I must kill my own people again I do not wish to live. I would rather spare my sword the blood of Welshman and become a beggar. My heart grieves."

Gwenynen feels herself link-up with the great field of the Goddess. Gwenynen's response comes from the Goddess. "Your words sound wise, but they and your sorrow are for nothing. Is the Goddess not the great force equally of destruction as she is of creation? The truly wise mourn neither for the living nor for the dead. The wise are not led astray by the deception of death. You have been doing your spiritual work, Arthur. By now, from your meditation practice you should experience that the dweller in the body passes to childhood, adolescence, middle-age and old age and then merely passes to another place. The energy of life does not cease. It is impossible for our essence to become some empty vacuum. Have you not experienced the truth of this?"

Arthur nods *yes*.

"If you know in your inmost being the true nature of Reality, you know that our true nature is indestructible. You are seeking to make this decision to fight, or not to fight, with your mind and your feelings. Those are not the part of you that knows the great Reality. Yes, the body dies, but that which possesses the body is eternal. Before birth we are not manifest to our human senses. Between birth and death we are manifested to our human senses. At death we return to the un-manifest again. What in all of this is there for you to grieve over? Die and you win eternity, conquer and you bring greater justice to the earth. Therefore, if the Goddess says fight you must fight."

Arthur looks directly at Gwenynen. He is taken by the authority in her voice. "Dear Gwenynen, my wise and true counselor, I do not really know that the Goddess wants me to fight. I have spent years letting go of my warrior-king image of myself. How could she possibly want me to pick up the sword again?"

"In order to know, you must be free of the dualistic way you are looking at this decision. Here is the rub. Yes, you have surrendered the warrior-king image you had of yourself. Now you must give up the idealized view you have of yourself as a deeply peaceful, spiritual man who builds new abbeys. You must surrender all the good mental stuff that your ego has become attached to about who you think you are—an abbott, a healer, a wise leader of people and so forth.

"As you know freedom is achieved by surrender to the Goddess so that your actions come from her. Unless this occurs your response to this situation is simply an illusive feint by the false self.

"We have talked much in our spiritual guidance time about overcoming duality. The abstinent run away from their desires but carry their desires hidden in their cloaks. Understandably, Arthur, you wish to be free of war. However, the world has brought the question of war to you, and you must answer it from the place of inner freedom, where your decision will be made free of anxiety, because the Goddess is deciding through you, not from a place of your ego's image of who it thinks you should be.

"If the Goddess wants you to go to war, you must perform your actions in war-making as you would perform all actions, sacramentally. It is through observing the sacred in everything that we are kept free from attachment to the results. You must let the Goddess's genius of who you are speak through you to each situation you encounter. The results will always be right action. Otherwise, your action or inaction will spring from the illusion of the false self.

"This is why the Celtic way of being has been so successful, despite the lack of political unity among Celtic peoples throughout most of our history. The Celtic people see all of life as sacramental. It is through this basic way of seeing life as a sacred ritual connected to the Goddess that has allowed the creative spirit of the Celtic people to flow. It is what has kept them open to the wisdom and life force of the Goddess.

"So what would you decide, my King? Action rightly renounced brings freedom. Action rightly performed brings freedom. Will you decide for freedom?"

"Gwenynen, you have spoken strongly and bravely to me. I needed it. I know that when I am seeing the world from the place of lucid observation that my mind is not restless and unquiet and does not wander. It is from that place that my soul is in contact with the Goddess. I believe what you are telling me is that it is from that place that I must decide."

"You have learned well on your spiritual path, Arthur. You have always been a fearless leader. You will be fearless in whatever decision you make from the sacred place of the Goddess's knowing. When a man who seeks to live a spiritual life goes astray from the spiritual path, which the Goddess and her son Jesus Christ offer us, he misses both lives, the worldly and the spiritual. He is as lost as a broken cloud drifting aimlessly across the sky."

At that moment something in Arthur shifts. He looks at Gwenynen and she can see that he is looking from that place of connection to the quiet place of inner knowing where access to the Goddess is possible.

"Gwenynen, I have troubled you long enough. Thank you for our conversation. It has probably saved my soul. I now see my way clear to do the Goddess's will. I have this image of myself as retiring and being peaceful and spiritual—and that is all it is—an image that my ego wants me to have of myself. I shall go and let my hand become at one again with the hilt of the sword the Goddess first gave me years ago. Caliburn and I will go to war for my kinsman and the Goddess's will shall be done."

Arthur stands, straightens his shoulders and heads to the center of his still unfinished abbey church at Ploërmel. He kneels in prayer and thanks the Goddess.

*   *   *

Yes, Rat, tell Mother Mary I will be back soon. I am on fast-forward for her. Here is what happens. Assisted by reinforcements provided by King Childebert, a formidable army is gathered to assist Judwal in regaining his kingdom from Conomorus. The army is led by two men who will be known as two of the greatest soldier saints who ever lived, Arthur and Samson. They meet the army of Conomorus at a place known as Brank Aleg along the edge of the Montagnes d' Aree. The warriors and their leaders engage in three fiercely fought battles over three long days. Toward the end of the third day, Judwal runs Conomorus through with a javelin, so that he is knocked from his horse and trampled to death in the press of charging horses and warriors.

Judwal then becomes King of a large swath of Brittany. As a reward to Arthur for his services in battle, Judwal grants Arthur a large tract of land beside the Seiche River, in an area now known as Ille et Vilaine.

At first, Arthur protests the bequest, but then remembering again the words of Gwenynen to him before he decided to go into battle, he accepts the bequest and moves there to establish another monastery. The village and the church are today known as St Armel-des-Boschaux.

My character, Gwenynen, is on her way there now. I feel that my time with Gwenynen has about been fulfilled. I will help her find a place in the new church for the shirt, stained with Arthur's blood at the battle of Camlan, to be hidden.

You can send Rat to the church now. In your time, of all three churches Arthur founded, this one will have the most beautiful stained glass windows illustrating Arthur's life. In addition, it will have his empty sarcophagus. I guess, like Jesus, he decides not to hang around in a corporeal kind of way. However, his jawbone is a relic that will still be kept there in that church. If

Rat can't find the bloodied shirt, he can always fall back on using the jawbone for DNA testing.

KING ARTHUR & THE CONSCIOUSNESS GENE

Chapter 8

Armel-de-Boschaux
Brittany
Summer 556

"Gwenynen, how old is your daughter now?" asks King Arthur. He is out for his morning walk at the abbey of St Armel-des-Boschaux and happens on Gwenynen along the same lane. Beside Gwenynen, munching on a golden red apple, is a slim young woman with flaming cheeks and flashing green eyes.

"Good morning, St Arthur," says Gwenynen, unconsciously letting her knees bend in the bob of a curtsey.

"I am almost eighteen, Sire," interrupts Derwen, eager to show she is quite capable of answering questions about herself directly.

"Her birthday is soon," explains Gwenynen. "It is the same day as the celebration of the founding of your monastery here at Armel-des-Boschaux and the completion of the abbey church. Gaiwain and I are looking forward to the celebration of the dedication of the new church. We get to celebrate the Goddess, you being honored by the church and our daughter coming of age all at the same time. A true triple blessing." Her hand unconsciously goes up to the finely wrought silver clasp that holds a scarf in place around her neck. She feels the familiar three-sided Celtic knot design and smiles to herself.

Arthur ponders thoughtfully. He is in amazement about the new world he is in. After leading warriors into battle again and helping bring victory to his kinsman, Judwal, he has once again followed his pledge to Christ and the Goddess and built another monastery. His workers have been engaged in building the monastery church in which the monks and the community will worship. King Childebert has made him head of the monastery, not only with the title of Abbot, but with the assent of the church at Rome, also with the title of Saint.

Arthur protested. The King insisted. Arthur defended King Childebert's kinsmen in his early years as the warrior-king of Britain and now King Childebert will not have it any other way. The church is almost complete and about to be dedicated with a visit by the King.

"Your being made St Arthur by the church is truly an honor," Gwenynen says.

Arthur laughs. "I am trying to come to terms with being sainted. I can tell you, Gwenynen, frankly I don't like it one bit. My ego will soon be like a dog spoiled from being fed from the king's table. I fear I will become as stiff as these Roman churchmen, and it will be a pain for me to be around my own self."

Gwenynen looks intently at King Arthur. He is wearing a coarse woolen robe, which seems a bit heavy for this time of year. His feet are in sandals. Instead of a belt he has a rope around his waist. Where his Pendragon sword used to hang, the loose end of the rope dangles.

"Being sainted must be a strange experience for you. Because your Celtic blood runs so deep, I know that you do not care much for the inflated hierarchy of the Roman Church. However, you have been sainted by it. Maybe the Goddess needs a hard-nosed, materialistic, patriarchal church to preserve her message through hard times that will be encountered in the next thousand years. I don't know, Arthur, and you do not either. So maybe you should embrace your sainthood for the glory of Christ and the Goddess."

Arthur's expression in response to her words tells Gwenynen he is already on his way to a place of non-dual acceptance of his new title.

"Your daughter is flourishing and looks for all the world as fair as her mother," says Arthur. "She makes me recall the day so long ago when you first came before me at Court and Merlin prophesied that you would one day be a wise counselor to me. You, at the time, were even younger than your daughter is now. How right he was and how faithful in your wisdom you have been. I am deeply honored by the kindness, and, often times needed toughness, of your counsel.

"Your words about this saint business ring true. For a gentle and kind woman, you are right more than any man could ever be and keep the humility needed for true wisdom," says Arthur. "I came to Brittany wanting to live a quiet peaceful, spiritual life among my kin. Or at least my ego self thought it did. Only when I heeded your counsel and surrendered that goal, has it been effortlessly achieved."

Arthur gazes into the trees above her head. She knows that he is practicing what she has taught him—disconnecting from the blurred vision of his false self and connecting again with the lucid observer that sees with the eyes of the Goddess and Christ.

"The Goddess has taught me that when I give up my self-centered control of my own life, I receive abundantly. Interestingly, for some greater purpose this truth in my life will be veiled from those who follow. Of course, you know this truth better than anyone because you helped me learn it. But the Goddess has told me this truth will be hidden for those who come after us, for hundreds of years, until revelation of this truth serves, like everything of the Goddess, a larger purpose—to help others far in the future wake up to her divine reality." Arthur chuckles to himself. He looks the picture of perfect contentment.

"Good day to you, my ladies." The King nods to Gwenynen and her daughter.

He re-made his connection, Gwenynen thinks—his ego's self critical judgment about being sainted has gone the way of all dualistic thought. "Good day to you, my King."

Gwenynen looks after Arthur as he walks away down the lane. For a moment she feels she is at a loss for what to call him now—King or Saint. She notices a beautiful hydrangea along the path. There are exquisite pink blossoms and a sole purple one on the same plant. She sighs, *God speaks through everything.*

What he is called doesn't matter to Arthur; and she knows, for her, he is and has always been both King and Saint. More than anything he has been a human being who has struggled to greater consciousness. She smiles to herself. His consciousness has bloomed.

Derwen turns to her Mother. "You know, sometimes I can't imagine he was ever a king. He looks so unassuming in that brown robe, which looks like it needs a good wash."

"You are right, Derwen," says Gwneynen. "Arthur has reached a place of spiritual growth we would all do well to attain, and the truth is his clothing is so ordinary it is a bit deceptive. Its humbleness conceals the depths of the man inside."

"But there is a give away, isn't there?" says Derwen, "A way to know he is not ordinary."

Gwneynen focuses her attention sharply on her daughter. "What do you see?"

Derwen replies, "I see it in his eyes."

"You are very perceptive, my daughter. No one I have ever seen has eyes that sparkle like Arthur's. He has always been a handsome man, but in these last few years all the spiritual changes he has gone through are reflected in his eyes. When you are near him you can feel the energy of his love flowing toward you from his eyes' flashing sparkle."

"But don't you like my eyes, too?" says Derwen, giggling and turning her bright green eyes on her Mother.

"I certainly do. Your eyes are beautiful. They reflect your beauty in search of your truth. Arthur's eyes reflect love overflowing from the Goddess by a man who lives his truth. Since I was first at Arthur's Court, whenever there were tough times, the brightness in Arthur's eyes is what gave hope to me and so many. Everyone should lay claim to such a king and saint. We are most extraordinarily blessed."

Gwenynen grabs the hand of her daughter and starts on her way down the path. She thinks again, as she has so often recently, about the efforts she and Gaiwain have made for this occasion that will honor Arthur. A special plaque, with an image of the cross and the Greek letters alpha and omega, is being installed under an arch behind the main altar in the church to commemorate the founding of the church by Arthur and its upcoming dedication by King Childebert. Almost any memorial that could have been created seems inadequate to express the meaning of Arthur to the lives of all the people who have seen the flame in his eyes when he waged war to protect those treated unjustly and the light of love in his eyes always burning for the peoples of Britain and Brittany.

*   *   *

Gwenynen has been consumed with an overpowering urge to bring the bloodied shirt of the King, which she took from him when he was wounded at the battle of Camlan in Britain, and place it in the church. She kept the shirt with her on Ynys Enlli, then brought it with her to Brittany, and it has remained in an old saddlebag at the bottom of a chest.

She talks with Gaiwain about her intuition that she should bury the shirt in the chapel wall of the church behind the plaque that is to honor Arthur. Gaiwain is not as taken with the idea as she is but gladly lends a hand to help with what is very important to Gwenynen.

They wrap the bloodstained shirt in soft deerskin leather which is then placed in a small wooden box. On impulse Gwenynen also encloses a small packet of seeds from the Ynys Enlli apple tree that she has grown in Brittany from the golden red apple Sister Bendithion gave her, when she left the isle so many years ago. The box has been deftly made and its lid slides down inside the box giving an almost airtight seal. It is easy for her to slip the box down inside the wall, when the wall is being prepared for the commemorative plaque. She even goes to the trouble to put some leftover mortar all around the box in the wall, after the masons leave for the day.

When she finishes her task, she returns home to find Gaiwain working outside their house with their daughter. She announces to her husband: "Gaiwain, I feel a huge sense of relief."

Gaiwain looks at his wife Gwenynen. Often times he is not sure he understands his wife. "That is wonderful. I am glad you feel you have done what you needed to do."

"Yes, somehow a great burden, which I didn't even know I was carrying, is lifted. I feel so much better."

Gaiwain looks at Gwenynen closely. "Maybe it is not good to carry around things with the harsh memories of war for too long?"

"Gaiwain, I am not sure what it is. Somehow I have completed a task that the Goddess set for me. She can be demanding in a way, you know."

"What way?" asks Gaiwain.

"Oh, you know, have things for you to do, and you don't even know why you are doing them." Gwenynen comes over to her husband and puts her arm around his waist. "Like what happened to you, when you risked displeasing your King and finally asked me to be your wife."

Gaiwain looks down at his wife and smiles. He has never lost his fascination with this woman he has married. "Yes, you are exactly right. I didn't know what happened then and I still don't. Something just came over me."

After looking to be sure their daughter is occupied with her outside chores, he picks Gwenynen up and takes her inside. She has both arms tight around his neck.

*   *   *

Early the next morning, Gwenynen awakes with a startle from a lucid dream. Gaiwain turns toward her to see what is happening.

"You won't believe this, Gaiwain, but I had this crazy dream; and, well, it all seemed so real. The dream occurred in a far distant future. I was this woman named Blaine, who had been away, and I was brought back home by my grandson after being gone on a long trip. It was a wonderful reunion with my husband. He was so glad to see me and I him.

"Somehow I was away much longer than I thought I would be and our reunion was so sweet. We both cried from the tender joy of being reunited. He was just like you—quiet and reserved— and so full of love for me. We held each other all night, just as we did last night.

"In the dream I experienced this excitement upon returning home because my grandson was soon to marry his fiancee, Katrina, who also met us when I returned. My grandson was named for sentient beings that are sacred to the Druids. Seemingly, because of that, and this is the wild and crazy part, all the true Druids that I have ever known—Merlin; Derwen, my dear friend when I was on Ynys Enlli; Sister Bendithion; even Lady Bridgette; and best of all, Arthur—they were all coming to the wedding."

"I hate to interrupt but I have a question," says Gaiwain.

Gwenynen nods for him to ask. "What did you learn from this long time that you were away from home? I mean, this is what you have always told me as why dreams are important. What do we learn in them that will help us with our waking life?"

Gwenynen's smile acknowledges the importance of Gaiwain's question. "Oh, what a good question. What I got from the dream was this feeling that my life is not really mine. You know all the things that can and do go wrong in life. We are not to take them personally. I had the sense from the dream that I could just blink and I might be in another life. Sounds weird, but it feels so true."

Gaiwain returns Gwenynen's smile. *Yes,* he thinks, *I don't always understand her, but I could love this woman down through all the ages.* "Gwenynen, what a wonderful dream. Maybe tonight you will be in the dream of the grandson's wedding presided over by Saint Arthur. Then we can celebrate their wedding."

Gwenynen puts her arm around Gaiwain and pulls him back under the down comforter that covers their bed. "Why, my dear, you know when it comes to celebrating life the Goddess would never want a celebration to wait!"

*   *   *

For such a long time Blaine has been hearing Rat in her mind telling her it is time to come back, that she has completed her mission more successfully than anyone could have ever imagined.

She has kept telling him that she feels she needs to stay just a bit longer. He is now laughing and saying that Mother Mary is telling him to tell Blaine not to hang around just to be sure her character's life turns out the way Blaine thinks it should.

Blaine can also hear, further away in the distance, Manuelito telling her what a good job she has done and how eagerly he is awaiting her return. He tells her he knows no one who has given so willing such a portion of their life for humankind, and the thought of how much she has given makes his heart ache with love for her.

Blaine knows deep in herself she could never have made this journey without Manuelito's love so freely given to her every step of the way. She is not sure what the reason is that she kept being told by her own inner direction to stay a bit longer. After all, she, more than anyone, is eager to get back. She is worried about time also. In a sense she feels like she has only been gone a few days, though in that time her character Gwenynen has experienced most of her life and provided spiritual guidance to King Arthur for the second part of his life. Her worry is about the amount of linear time that she will find has actually elapsed on earth.

An inkling she has is that the reason she has been asked to stay a bit longer has nothing to do with uncovering the mystery of the expression of the consciousness gene, but is about letting the lesson of Arthur's life history be completed so that she can take its whole meaning back to the twenty-first century. Being with King/Saint Arthur in the field has taught her many things, but most of all the message of Arthur's life for the twenty-first century is that his life was never really about Arthur—it was always about connecting with the Goddess so he could serve all of humankind, especially the people of Britain and Brittany, and marginalized people like the outcast leper.

She is sure that when Rat finds the blood-stained shirt (and hopefully the apple seeds she promised Katrina and Tree for planting beside their boulder book-ended hogan on the rez) and has the DNA tested, it will show the same expressed gene of consciousness that Rat found in Jesus' blood on the shroud of Turin. Jesus came to build on the Buddha's lesson of non-attachment, to teach that only the illusion of our false self blocks our connection to the Divine and all things, and that surrendering the illusion and being in the experience of this connection is love. Jesus adds a course correction to those ascetics who changed the Buddha's message. Yes, non-attachment is needed, but not just as a way to store energy for one's own transformation; rather it is so that we can give all our energy away as love for the transformation of all humankind. We don't have to work to love. If we are working to love, it is the ego's manipulation to try to get love returned. If we see the world through the eyes of reflective consciousness, love flows through us effortlessly. We become disengaged from the ego self, and deeply engaged with the world around us. We see the Goddess in everything.

Blaine also sees that when the consciousness gene got expressed in St Arthur, he added the next block of understanding to humankind's journey of transformation by teaching the Celtic wisdom that the Divine is not out there, up there, somewhere, but is down here in the earth, literally in the solidity of matter, maybe especially among rocks, and that the love the Goddess and Christ bring is discoverable in all things, even in something as un-loving as war. The deception of truth, love and beauty is that they cannot be cornered. They always emerge freely from some hidden place and shatter the illusions of those who believe they have captured them in their ideologies and the institutions they build to hold what cannot be contained.

Afterword

King and Saint, Arthur died in 562 at his monastery at St Armel-des-Boschaux at the age of eighty. His kinsman, St Samson, died in 565 at his monastery at Dol-de-Bretagne. St Gildas, the first historian of Britain's kings, died in 570 at his monastery at St Gildas du Rhuys at the age of 94.